AVENGED BY AN ANGEL
ETERNAL MATES BOOK 16

∞

FELICITY HEATON

Copyright © 2019 Felicity Heaton

All rights reserved. No part of this publication may be reproduced, stored in a retrieval system, or transmitted, in any form or by any means mechanical, electronic, photocopying, recording or otherwise without the prior written consent of the publisher, nor be otherwise circulated in any form of binding or cover other than that in which it is published and without a similar condition being imposed on the subsequent purchaser.

The right of Felicity Heaton to be identified as the Author of the Work has been asserted by her in accordance with the Copyright, Designs and Patents Act 1988.

First printed August 2019

First Edition

Layout and design by Felicity Heaton

All characters in this publication are purely fictitious and any resemblance to real persons, living or dead, is purely coincidental.

THE ETERNAL MATES SERIES

Book 1: Kissed by a Dark Prince
Book 2: Claimed by a Demon King
Book 3: Tempted by a Rogue Prince
Book 4: Hunted by a Jaguar
Book 5: Craved by an Alpha
Book 6: Bitten by a Hellcat
Book 7: Taken by a Dragon
Book 8: Marked by an Assassin
Book 9: Possessed by a Dark Warrior
Book 10: Awakened by a Demoness
Book 11: Haunted by the King of Death
Book 12: Turned by a Tiger
Book 13: Tamed by a Tiger
Book 14: Treasured by a Tiger
Book 15: Unchained by a Forbidden Love
Book 16: Avenged by an Angel
Book 17: Seduced by a Demon King
Book 18: Scorched by Darkness
Book 19: Inflamed by an Incubus (2022)

CHAPTER 1

He had a mission. One different from the others he had completed before. This time, he wasn't charging through the bridge he had created between Heaven and Earth in order to eradicate a demon.

He was heading to the mortal plane to retrieve a half-breed, one who would soon take her sire's place in the Echelon. A female.

He couldn't recall the last time a female had served as a member of the Echelon, the revered small squadron of angels gifted with the power to hunt and destroy demons. It had certainly never happened in his lifetime.

Lightning crackled and snapped around him, causing the hairs on his nape to stand on end as he breached the mortal realm. He shot through the layers of the elegant sandstone building in central London where he had spotted his target, passing through them as if he was made of air, and materialised as he hit the room where she stood.

He landed hard, shaking the building to its foundations, and rose to his feet as the electricity that charged the air around him dissipated, the light each tiny bolt of lightning caused gradually fading to allow him to see the one he had come to retrieve.

Sable stared at him, her golden eyes wide and bright, reflecting the lingering flickers of white-blue lightning that sparked from him. Her lips slowly parted, her surprise written plainly across her face.

Beside her, a blonde female gawped, her deep blue eyes large with shock.

He revelled in it.

Savoured it.

His silver gaze flickered to beyond the two females and he curled a lip at the white-walled room on the other side of a sheet of glass. He had witnessed what the organisation the half-breed worked for was capable of and it did not sit well with him, or any of the broader immortal community if the rumours were to be believed. Not only demons despised this place, innocent species did too. Shifters who wanted only to live their lives in peace within their packs. Witches who were more human than many of the people who worked for this organisation.

Archangel.

His lips compressed as he clenched his jaw, his black eyebrows drawing down as a spark of anger ignited in him.

Insolent humans.

Using the name of an elite of his kind for their nefarious ventures.

He flinched as a piercing, shrieking noise filled the pleasant, stunned silence, grating on his nerves and fraying the weak threads holding his temper in check.

Upon opening his eyes, he realised it was the female he had come to detain who had dared to raise the alarm. She stood farther away from him now, the blonde held behind her and her other hand still on the red button on the black wall.

The hard, sharp edge to her golden eyes challenged him to make a move against her.

Movement in the adjoining room gained his attention for barely a second, long enough to see they were removing the semi-nude shifter male from it and the mortal males who had accompanied him were fleeing in fear.

Pathetic creatures.

He calmly returned his gaze to the reason he had been sent to this wretched realm.

Two more females rushed into the room and flanked her, their silver swords drawn and aimed at him. As if such paltry weapons could pierce his flesh.

"What do you want?" the one called Sable spat at him, her icy glare declaring her intent to fight him.

Brave. Courageous. He gave her that. But also foolish. She knew she was no match for him, and yet she sought to intimidate him. Many had attempted to cover their fears with such a poor façade when faced with him, and all had eventually cracked and crumbled, falling to their knees to cower before him.

He furled his white wings against his back. Their longest feathers grazed his bare feet, and he decided that he should have gone with wearing his armour rather than a simple white-and-gold tunic over his trousers. It would have made a stronger impression on the puny mortal females huddled before him and might have sped things along.

It certainly would have stopped the bastard offspring of an angel from being so mouthy.

"I came as soon as I learned of your existence. I am come for you." He pointed to the silver cuff around her wrist and she looked down at it, the colour slowly draining from her face, adding a satisfyingly fearful pallor to it.

Now he was getting somewhere. Perhaps she would be more compliant now.

"What's he talking about?" the blonde female whispered with a curious edge to her frown as she looked at Sable.

"It's not important. I'll tell you later." Sable turned from her comrade to face him again. "Listen, buddy, I'm not going anywhere and definitely not with you. I don't even know who you are."

Perhaps she wouldn't be more compliant after all.

They had warned him that she was a difficult thing, but he hadn't listened to them. Mostly because his superiors had said she had a difficulty rating the same as his and he tired of their taunts about his temper. He had stated he would easily take her into custody and he meant to do that. Swiftly. He had no desire to linger in this realm, around such lowly beings.

"You got a name? Other than Tall, Dark and Pompous?"

Pompous?

He glared at her and unleashed a fraction of his power. She straightened her spine in response, resisting the pressing weight of his power as it buffeted her. Her three comrades didn't fare so well. They all staggered back a few steps towards the door, and beads of sweat broke out on the brow of the weakest.

"Give me your sword, Anais." Sable held her hand out to the blonde female, who did as she instructed, drawing her weapon and placing it into Sable's palm. Her fingers closed around the hilt and she held it out in front of her, pointing it at him. "I'm giving you to the count of three. Tell me your name or bugger off. Fail to do one of those things and I'll kick your arse. Choice is yours."

Amusing, but boring. He had heard better threats, from more dangerous foes. She was part angel, but no match for him in a fight. Still, he had strict orders to bring her back with him, unharmed, and that meant he had to lower himself to select the first ridiculous choice she had given him.

In a manner of speaking, anyway.

"I have no name. No angels do. All I can give to you is that I am of the Echelon."

He held his right arm out to her, revealing the cross marked on the inside of his wrist.

A cross she also bore on her skin in the exact same spot.

The irritation that had been building in her eyes gave way to a flicker of curiosity and something akin to hope, but she didn't move from her spot near the other females. He needed her away from them. While their weapons couldn't kill him, they might land blows while he was attempting to detain Sable, and he would lose his temper.

He didn't think the council would forgive him if he killed three mortals.

They hadn't mentioned any restrictions when it came to humans, but the council rarely took a favourable view on killing them.

"I met an angel with a name. Aurora. Heard of her?" Sable said.

He barely held back his irritated sigh. "The one you speak of is no longer an angel... and you will come with me."

She pinned him with a glare when he considered just crossing the distance between them and grabbing her, putting an end to this farce. It seemed she was better attuned to the feelings of others than the council had suspected. She could read him. A rare gift.

The huntress who had sweated when he had unleashed a fraction of his power edged backwards towards the door. He shifted his focus to her and used another gift of his to change her mind about sneaking away and going for reinforcements. She stilled and stared blankly at him. A weak mind was always a glorious thing. So easy to influence. He wished the other two were weak too, but he had tested their minds and found them strong. As strong as Sable's was.

Influencing them would hurt them.

"What's it like having no name?" Sable casually waved the sword at him, the curiosity back in her eyes. "How does that work? How do other angels get your attention?"

Her constant questions perplexed him. He couldn't remember ever appearing before anyone who had been so irritatingly unaffected and able to string words into sentences in his presence rather than just staring at him in a dumbfounded manner.

"They address me as Fourth Commander of the Echelon if they desire my attention." He wasn't sure why she needed to know or why she had such a problem with angels having no name.

He had a rank, and that was all he required.

"That seems like a pretty crappy way of getting someone's attention... and you're only the fourth commander?" She frowned and shook her head, a teasing note to her tone and expression that he found annoying. None of the people he had graced with his presence had ever dared to tease him before either. She smiled and he knew she had read him again, had felt his irritation and dislike of her conversation, and she was going to use that knowledge against him. "That must grate a little. Who's the first? Oh, wait! He doesn't have a name, so I guess he's just First Commander of the Echelon."

He frowned at her now, his pride a little chafed by her taunting and his patience wearing thin.

"How many are there?" She swung the sword up to rest on her shoulder.

So casual.

Would she be so casual if he exerted a little power and popped one of her comrades' heads with nothing more than a thought?

"How many what?" He played along with her, lost in the pleasing thought of terrifying her by killing her little friends in front of her.

"Commanders."

"Six." He could see where this was heading and he folded his arms across his chest, warning her not to go there.

She did. With a huge grin. "Six, and you're only number four. *Ouch*. How long did it take you to reach number four?"

"Silence," he barked and even the alarms stopped shrieking. "I am not here to speak of my rank. You will come with me. Echelon are rare now, and all must serve Heaven."

Sable shook her head. "If you haven't got the memo, maybe I should tell you... I'm a queen of demons."

That surprised him, moderately, but didn't sway him. "You will come with me. The demons are of little consequence. They may find another queen."

Her expression turned horrified and she had the sword pointing at him again before he could blink, the darkness in her eyes warning him he wasn't the only one close to losing his temper now. "That's my husband you're talking about so callously. My people! I'm not going to Heaven. I'm going back to Hell."

His temper snapped and the room darkened in response, the light forced out of it as he stepped towards her, glaring down at her as he spread his wings. They spanned the room and drew fearful glances from the three mortal females. Sable stood firm in front of him, her blade never wavering, not even when his power began to slip beyond his grasp. He held his hand out in front of him, filled with a dark need to call his blade to him and teach her a lesson in humility and respect.

The steely determination in her steady gaze challenged him to try.

A sensation shot down his spine and fire arced through his blood, a warning from those on high that he was close to overstepping the line.

Again.

He drew a deep calming breath, reined in his temper enough to regain control of his powers, and tried again. "I am not known for my patience. I would not test it. You will come with me. By force, if necessary."

The blonde female called Anais and a second female jumped in front of Sable, blocking his path to her.

His gaze caught on the second female, a slender brunette with fierce green eyes. Strange warmth flooded him at the sight of her, but it was swiftly followed by fury so dark and deep that it threatened to shatter his carefully controlled calm and send him into a killing rage.

She bore wounds on her fair skin, visible above the collar and below the sleeves of her black top.

She had been beaten.

"What did this to you?" The words seemed to leave his lips of their own volition, coming from an unfamiliar part of him, one that felt alien and rocked him with the strength of its will and the depth of its feelings.

She shook her head and backed away from him, her eyes gradually widening and filling with fear.

Her lips wouldn't answer him, so he sought it from her eyes.

He stared deep into them and saw it all for himself.

He witnessed her suffering at the hands of a dragon.

His blade was in his hand before he knew what he was doing. Blue flames flickered along the length of it, darkest near the hilt. Almost black. A need filled him, a terrible hunger that he couldn't hold back or deny.

"A dragon resides in this place. I will slay him for you." He swept the blade down at his side and focused his senses to find the dragon shifter who had been in the other room when he had arrived.

Sable shoved the two huntresses behind her. "Don't you bloody dare! That dragon had nothing to do with what happened to Emelia."

Emelia?

His gaze drifted back to the slender female. She had bowed her head, her dark hair falling down to obscure her face and steal the pleasure of seeing it from him, and had wrapped her arms around herself, holding herself so tightly, he felt she feared she might fall apart.

"Where does the dragon who did this to you reside?" He spoke to her, but it was Sable who answered.

"In Hell."

His mood darkened again on hearing that, but he recalled that all dragons had been banished from the mortal realm millennia ago by a powerful witch.

He flexed his fingers around the hilt of his blade, his mind working to find a solution to his problem so he could hunt and slay the dragon, but none presented itself.

Irritated by a seemingly irremovable object in his path, he muttered, "I cannot enter Hell."

And regretted it when Sable's eyes lit up.

"What a shame," she said with a victorious smile.

She believed she would be safe from him there, but he wasn't going to give her a chance to escape him.

He lunged for her.

A huge bare-chested demon male appeared between them, his eyes blazing red and dusky ridged horns curling from above his pointed ears, twisting around themselves to flare forwards like daggers on either side of his temples. The male bared sharp fangs and grew even larger, his burgundy leathers creaking as his muscles expanded and bones lengthened, and he came to tower over him. His dark leathery wings brushed the walls and ceiling as the male hunched over in the room.

He readied his sword.

The demon didn't give him a chance to use it.

The enormous male spoke in the demon tongue, each word piercing his ears like white-hot needles and slithering through him like oily darkness, warning him away from the female.

She had not lied.

She was a queen of demons.

But she was Echelon too.

"This is not over." He spat the words at the demon and teleported just as the male swung at him.

He reappeared on the balcony of his apartment in Echelon headquarters, surrounded by the vast white city known as Heaven in the mortal tongue. He looked down on the human world, seeing back through the layers of the building to the room where he had been just a second before.

It wasn't Sable or the demon who was the focus of his gaze, though.

It was Emelia.

He watched her as she shrank away from the group, still holding herself, entranced by her beauty and angered by her suffering.

He would find a way to slay her dragon for her.

He would bring the wrath of Heaven down upon all of Hell.

CHAPTER 2

Electricity still charged the air, causing prickles across Emelia's skin. She shivered and rubbed at her left arm, the one Linda clutched as she marched her down the pale corridors of Archangel HQ, leading her away from the room where the angel had appeared.

An angel.

The imposing black-haired male hadn't seemed much like an angel when his mood had turned, when he had demanded she tell him what had happened to her. Her throat closed, stomach twisting and heart beginning to pound faster as memories crowded her mind. She tried to shake them loose, bit back the cry that wanted to burst from her lips as they pressed harder, starting to take shape despite her best efforts to deny them.

As a hazy figure formed, the silhouette of a male whose hunger for violence had exceeded that which the angel had shown to her, she breathed harder, fought to shove him out before he could rise to torment her once again.

Linda flicked her a glance, a well-practiced worry shining in her deep brown eyes, one that made Emelia want to lash out at the psychiatrist. A hunger of her own rose inside her, a powerful and consuming urge to tell Linda exactly where to stick that look and to push her away, to shove and hit her until she left her alone.

She just wanted to be alone.

She didn't want to talk.

Talking did nothing. She had spent hours on that couch in Linda's office. Talking. It hadn't changed a single thing. It wasn't fixing anything. She was still broken, weakened by what had happened. Talking to the shrink only reminded her that she was weak, that she hadn't been strong enough to protect herself.

So she didn't want to pore over every damned thing that had happened to her.

Things the angel must have seen somehow.

The shivers wracking her deepened, causing her limbs to tremble and her feet to stumble. She wrenched away from Linda on a frustrated growl as the woman threw her another concerned look, one that veiled what she was really thinking behind that placid, oh-so-professional exterior.

She was the same as everyone else at Archangel.

Emelia knew it.

They talked about her behind her back, cast her glances when they thought she wasn't watching, ones that questioned her sanity and held a hefty dose of pity. A dose Emelia found impossible to swallow.

"Emelia." Linda's soft voice, so calm and gentle, only increased the need to turn and smack her away, to rail at her until she left her alone.

It never worked.

If she lashed out, it only gave Linda more cause to push her into another session.

So Emelia drew down a secret breath to steady herself, to still her turbulent mind and whirling emotions, and even out her pulse.

Because Linda wasn't the only one who could construct a veil to conceal what she was really feeling.

It hadn't taken Emelia long after returning, after being subjected daily to hours of probing and poking from Linda on that wretched brown leather recliner in that infernal magnolia room, with its perfectly positioned flowers and scents meant to soothe, to realise that she needed to construct walls.

Ones that no one could penetrate.

Her mind flashed back to the angel.

The way his silver eyes had held hers, how that golden fire had flashed in them, and his fierce reaction still shook her. The room had visibly darkened, as if his anger had been sucking all the light from it, and despite how desperately she had wanted to look away, she hadn't been able to wrench her eyes from his.

She hadn't been able to move when he had demanded to know what had happened to her.

When he had vowed to slay the dragon who had harmed her.

A chill rushed through her.

Not fear.

Not this time.

This was something else.

It shook her harder than how fierce he had appeared, more like a dark warrior than the image she'd had in her head of angels.

He had wanted to go to war for her.

Everyone at Archangel wanted to smother her and the other women who had returned from Hell, where they had been snatched from the battlefield in the war between the Third Realm of the demons and the Fifth Realm and taken to the dragon lands. Handed out by the dragon chief like a commodity, given to his warriors to use as they saw fit.

A colder shiver skated down her spine and she clenched her fists against it. The heat of her anger soon burned it away as it blazed like an eternal flame inside her, one she knew would never die. It would only ever fade to a flicker under the onslaught of her memories, was quick to rage back to a roar whenever those vile images released her from their hold.

Whenever that happened, did she look as fierce as the angel had?

Archangel wanted to lock her away, to cage her in a new prison, treating her as a fragile thing that might break at any moment.

Making her fragile.

Weak.

The angel?

His fury had been real, explosive, and *thrilling* in a way. She believed him when he had growled that he wanted to slay the dragon who had abused her. She ached for that to happen.

She had been close to shattering the hold her fear had had on her, to find her courage and her voice with it to tell him that she craved vengeance, needed closure, wasn't sure she could last another day without knowing that dragon was dead.

But then Sable's demon king, Thorne, had appeared and had driven the angel away, and all the hope that had been building within Emelia had instantly flooded out of her, leaving her cold and empty, and her legs weak beneath her.

She had wanted to curse the towering demon male, had wanted to pound her clenched fists against his broad, thickly muscled bare chest, to claw and hit him and scream at him for making the angel leave.

Sable, her commander and a woman Emelia had been close to from the moment she had moved south to the London headquarters of Archangel half a decade ago, had mistaken Emelia's shaking for fear and had summoned Linda.

Her friend meant well, but Emelia cursed her in her mind.

She didn't need another round with the shrink, didn't need someone fussing over her right now. She needed to fight. She needed to punish the man who had hurt her, had been cruel and vicious to her.

Had stolen a piece of her, stripping away her strength and confidence to leave her a shadow of herself.

She glanced at a window they passed as Linda calmly talked to her, leading her towards her office on a lower floor of the sprawling building.

She didn't recognise her reflection.

That wasn't the face of the Emelia who had bravely ventured into Hell to fight in a war between demons. It wasn't the face of the Emelia who had been bold and courageous, had taken down countless foes to protect her teammates and the immortals who had been on her side. It wasn't the face of the woman who had been on track to secure a position commanding her own squadron.

When she looked into those dull green eyes staring back at her, she saw a weak, timid, frightened thing, and she hated it.

Alarm bells tore through the silence, ripping her back to the world, and she glanced around as everyone sprang back into action, her fellow hunters racing from the rooms lining the corridors to seek out the source of the threat.

Emelia saw her chance and took it.

"I should go help." She twisted away from Linda.

The woman regarded her with a cold and critical once-over. "Are you sure? You need to talk."

She didn't need to talk. She needed to get the hell out of there. She needed to go to her quarters and surround herself with quiet. Although, that would be difficult with the alarms blaring.

Was it the angel?

Had he returned?

She shoved him out of her head and did her best to ignore the strange thrill that swept through her at the thought he might have come back.

It was more likely that Thorne had caused the alert to sound.

Either that or Anais was finally going to set her dragon free.

Emelia had noticed the way her friend had looked at the blue-haired shifter. It didn't take a genius to figure out that she hadn't been the man's prisoner, not as Emelia and the others had been the captives of the dragons who had taken them. There was a connection there, and it blazed as brightly as the one Sable shared with her demon king, Thorne, and Olivia shared with her elf prince, Loren.

Anais had fallen for an immortal.

Emelia suppressed another shudder as a memory popped into her mind before she could block it, one where the green-haired dragon who had held her captive had returned to her, badly injured and growling about how she would love him as Loke's female did.

She squeezed her eyes shut.

Remembered the single word she had spat at him, filled with defiance despite how crazed he had appeared.

Never.

"Emelia?" Linda shuffled closer, and Emelia backed off a step.

A group of hunters rushed towards her and she allowed herself to get swept up in them, jogged shoulder to shoulder with them a short distance, until they rounded a corner, heading towards the cafeteria, Thorne's usual landing place when he was causing a ruckus.

She tossed a glance back over her shoulder, assuring herself that Linda hadn't followed, and broke away from the group to duck down another corridor, one that would take her to the stairs leading up into the wing where her quarters were.

Emelia sprinted down the corridor, picking up speed as the weight of her memories began to grow heavier, pressing down on her. She refused to crumble, pushed back just as hard, determined to make it to her rooms before they hit. She wouldn't let everyone see her weak.

Not anymore.

The corridors passed in a blur, and her breath was sawing from her when she finally reached her door. Her hand shook as she fumbled with the knob, twisted it, and pushed the door open. She staggered inside, her pulse pounding, throbbing in her temples. The door slammed behind her, and she stumbled a few steps until she bumped into the dark brown leather couch that occupied the centre of her studio apartment, facing her small TV.

She clutched the back, the leather creaking beneath the pressure of her grip, and breathed. Just breathed. She focused on each breath, until they fell into a steady rhythm and she felt her control returning, her strength welling up with it. She stared at the dark screen of the television, slowly piecing herself back together and pushing out the memories that threatened to send her to her knees.

She was done with being weak.

She was strong, had fought immortals, slain them in double digits. She was powerful, courageous. She was still the woman she had been before entering Hell. Before that vile dragon had laid his filthy paws on her.

She was strong.

Her knees buckled and she grunted as they slammed into the wooden floor of her apartment, her chin striking the back of the couch. She slumped towards it, pressing her cheek to the cool leather, and closed her eyes.

The alarms ceased.

Had it been the angel?

She found herself hoping that it had been, found herself using her grip on the back of her couch to pull herself back onto her feet, and found herself twisting to face the door. A door she wanted to walk towards, to open and venture out again.

In search of him.

Why?

He was dangerous. Too powerful. A warrior. An immortal she knew just by looking at him that she could never best in a fight. It would be over in mere seconds. Her life obliterated without any effort on his part.

He was everything the dragon had been.

But the rage that had been in his silver eyes had been immeasurable. Real. Intoxicating. And his vow? It had shaken her, but not in a bad way. For the first time since returning from Hell, she had felt a glimmer of hope.

Hope that the dragon might pay.

If he got the punishment he deserved, if she knew he was dead, would the nightmares end?

She closed her eyes and swayed forwards as a wave of fatigue hit her. She didn't want to sleep. Whenever she slept, she saw things. She remembered things. It all played out in her mind like a horror movie and she was powerless to stop it.

Now, she couldn't remember the last time she had slept for more than a few minutes. She glanced to her left at the double bed, at the smooth burgundy sheets that had been left undisturbed since she had returned. She lowered her eyes to the spot on the light wooden floor beside the bed, where a quilt lay rumpled and twisted.

Her nest.

If Linda saw it, she would probably throw Emelia into a padded room.

Emelia had tried to sleep in her bed the first night back in her home, and had woken curled up on the floor, hurled from a nightmare and covered in cold sweat.

She had ended up in the bath, shivering despite the hot water that scalded her.

She drifted to the door of her apartment, lifted her hand, and slowly pressed it to the wood.

If he could, would the angel really slay the dragon for her?

She wanted Zephyr to suffer for what he had done to her, and for the terrible things he had probably done to other women in the past. She needed closure, and Archangel refused to give it to her. The few times she had pressed him to let her lead a team back into Hell to hunt the dragons down, her superior, Mark, had flatly stated that Archangel wouldn't risk another war and they were focusing resources elsewhere right now.

They wouldn't help her.

They wouldn't give her and the other huntresses who had been held by the dragons the closure they needed.

She shifted her hand to the knob, lowered her eyes, and stared at it. The angel was dangerous, possibly even more so than the dragons. She couldn't trust him.

She raised her hand to the locks and twisted them into place, then pushed away from the door, taking steps backwards towards the couch.

She couldn't.

Emelia turned away and strode through her apartment, heading towards the door to the left of her untouched bed. She stripped off as she went, not caring where her T-shirt and trousers fell. Her bra and panties followed. By the time she entered the bathroom, she was naked.

She kept her eyes away from the mirror above the sink, not wanting to see the scars that marked her pale skin, wounds that would forever remind her of what had happened.

Her fingers drifted over the small docking station on the shelf beside the mirror, dipping in at the power button, and the soft sound of music filled the small space.

She sank to her backside on the edge of the bath and ran the water. The sound of it thundering into the white tub soothed her, instantly smoothing the ragged edges of her nerves. While the bath was filling, she idly swept her fingers back and forth beneath the flow of water, her eyes shifting out of focus as she stared at it.

She didn't need to talk.

This was what she needed.

This ritual.

It settled her like nothing else could.

She poured some bubble bath into the water and swished it around, creating a frothy white blanket, savouring how the heat seeped into her skin and the smell of lavender rose to permeate the humid air.

When the bath was full, she twisted the taps and stepped into the tub. She sighed as she sank into the water, deep enough that it lapped up to her chin. Her eyes slipped shut. Bliss. The quiet, the warmth, the music, and the scents that swirled around her. This was the therapy she really needed.

Her mind drifted, and she let it, safe in the knowledge it would remain away from the dragon as it always did whenever she soaked.

She went over the new rosters, the recruits Mark had assigned to the team she was in and the changes to the patrol schedule. She was going to need to speak with Sable about that.

Sable.

Emelia frowned. Wife of a demon king and queen to his people. She doubted Sable was going to be working for Archangel much longer after declaring that in front of everyone. Even Olivia had cut her hours back to practically nothing, was spending most of her time with her elf prince in Hell. Would Anais follow suit?

Was she going to lose all her closest friends to that place?

She wrapped her arms over her chest beneath the water and sank lower so it swept across her lips.

She hoped not.

Even as she knew it was going to happen.

Because apparently, Sable wasn't just a queen of demons now.

She was half-angel.

What had the man called it? *Echelon*. He had said that Echelon were rare now and all were meant to serve his realm. He had announced himself as the fourth commander of that legion, or group, or whatever it was. What were Echelon?

Were they different to other angels?

She tried to push him out of her mind, but he refused to go. He had been imposing. Not just because of his towering seven-foot height, but because of the way he had held himself, how he had turned dark in the blink of an eye, transforming into a savage warrior ready to do battle. Terrifying. He had seen things she hadn't wanted anyone to see, and now that she was calming down, it left her feeling scraped out and hollow inside.

He had stolen memories from her without her permission and she felt a little violated by his actions, but also strangely relieved. That there was someone in this world who could simply look at her and see what had happened to her was a blessing in a way. She had been forced to talk so much about the things she had experienced in Hell that not having to speak about it was a relief.

Had he seen the things she hadn't been able to bring herself to tell anyone?

Her focus shifted to behind her, to the door of her apartment and the corridor beyond it, and surprise rippled through her when she realised she wanted to see him again, wanted to know if he had witnessed *everything* that had happened in that dark realm.

Had he witnessed the source of her deepest fear?

She sank deeper still into the water, desperately trying to ease the tight feeling that built inside her, squirmed in her chest like a living thing, making her restless with a need to run.

It whispered that she wasn't safe here.

Zephyr *would* come for her.

She shoved that out of her head. She was safe here. The dragon couldn't enter the mortal world without losing his powers and slowly dying thanks to some sort of curse on his kind. She was safe here. She was safe.

An image of Zephyr flashed into her mind, his green eyes crazed with a need that had terrified her, flooded with determination that left a cold feeling inside her, a chill she just couldn't shake no matter how hot she ran her bath.

He wanted her to choose him. He wanted her to *love* him.

Did he want that enough to risk leaving Hell? Was his need of her powerful enough to drive him to breach the barrier the curse created between them?

When that happened, would she be strong enough to fight him, or would he take her back to Hell?

She swallowed hard.

When?

She struggled to breathe, to convince herself it wasn't a case of when. It was a case of *if*. She was safe at Archangel. Even if he did come, he wouldn't dare try to reach her in this place. He couldn't shift in this world. He was weak here. If he tried to get to her, they could easily defeat him.

That thought had another desire rising, born of the rage that constantly burned in her blood. She sat up and clutched the edges of the bath as it blazed hotter, fuelled by her thoughts and a single one that stood out among them.

A thought that had fear shifting towards hope again and had strength and courage coursing through her once more.

If he was weak in this world, then let the bastard come.

Because she would kill him.

CHAPTER 3

Blood dripped into his left eye. A lucky shot by the male demon now fleeing across the moonlit park, his black jeans and long-sleeved top making him blend into the darkness. He swiped it away with the back of his hand and narrowed his gaze on the fiend's back.

The cross emblazoned on the inside of his right wrist burned beneath the sleeve of his white tunic, shone fiercely in the night, pushing him to pursue the male and cut him down.

He kicked off, chasing the demon and determined to stop him before he entered the trees that lined the edges of the broad swath of grass in the southern end of the park in a busy district of Shanghai. Ahead of him, futuristic towers speared the sky, a multitude of colours that shifted and danced, attempting to distract him.

He was distracted enough without their help.

The demon made it into the trees, cutting through them with little finesse. The sound of branches breaking and leaves swaying filled the air as thickly as the distant honking of car horns and rumbling trucks and buses.

Determined not to lack refinement like a demon, he spread his white wings and beat them. It took a single flap to lift him above the height of the trees and another to have him gracefully gliding over the dense canopy. He easily tracked the demon, his acute senses pinpointing him in the darkness below. The male broke out onto the path on the other side of the small woods and banked left, following it back towards the busy road.

He swept down, calling his blade to his hand at the same time. It had been a mistake to believe he could defeat the wretch without a weapon or his armour. He swiped the back of his free hand across the cut above his eye again, brushing the blood away before it could impede his vision.

His boots touched the earthen path, and he spread his wings to block the demon's path. The fiend ground to a halt, his lips curling back off bloodstained fangs, a reminder that the male had been gorging himself on humans before the Echelon had received orders to eliminate him.

He curled his fingers around the hilt of his blade and grimaced as a wound on his arm burned in response.

It had been a mistake to leave Heaven immediately to hunt the demon down. It had been another mistake to believe this demon would prove an easy kill. He should have taken the time to swap his white tunic and trousers for his armour.

His superiors' words rang in his mind, a thousand replays of them teasing him for being rash, for letting his temper control him and cloud his judgement.

He curled his own lip at that, flashing blunt teeth at the demon as anger coursed through him. Blue flames erupted along the length of his white blade and darkened near the guard, a sign his mood was degenerating again. He tried to rein it in, aware that at any moment, his superiors could turn their gazes to him to check on his progress and would see he had allowed anger to take control again.

"Let us not dance around this. Kneel and we shall get this over with." He gestured to the ground between him and the demon.

The male spat blood on it, his glowing gold eyes hurling a challenge at him.

He gladly accepted it.

He had been born to cleanse this world of demons, relished the duty that was everything to him, and carried it out without hesitation.

The demon eased back a step, and for a moment, he thought the male intended to make another attempt to flee.

But then the dark-haired male's lips quirked and his pupils began to thin in the centre of his irises. The colour bled from his irises into those elliptical pupils, so they burned gold instead, leaving his irises as black as the pit he had crawled out of tonight.

The male rose to his full height, coming to match his seven feet, and rolled his shoulders back as he held his left hand out palm down in front of him. A sword formed, rising from the dirt towards the demon's palm. The muscles of his arm tensed beneath his long-sleeved top as he slowly twisted his hand. The glowing amber pommel reached it, and he slid his palm down the black-leather-wrapped grip.

Perhaps he had underestimated this demon more than he had first believed.

"Satan spawn," he spat at the wretch, putting every ounce of the venom he felt into the words as he narrowed his silver eyes on the vile creature standing before him.

That he was breathing the same air as one born of the Devil had disgust rolling down his spine and a need to back away flowing through him. He denied it and stood his ground, aware that the demon would view any movement to distance himself now as a sign of weakness and would attack.

The flames rolling along his white blade blazed brighter, beginning to turn gold as the mark on his wrist burned like an inferno, searing his skin.

He hadn't anticipated this, but he wouldn't back down from this battle. Tonight, the Devil would lose one of his men, and the world would be better off for it.

It was his eternal duty.

He launched forwards on a battle cry that shattered the night.

Brought his blade up at the same time as the demon and grinned as they clashed hard, forming an X between them. The male growled, flashing daggers at him, and the horns that curled from behind his pointed ears flared, a sign of aggression that didn't stop him. He shoved with all his strength, driving the male back.

The demon might be powerful in Hell, feeding off his master's power, but here in this world, he was weak. Vulnerable. And he knew it.

It was there in his eyes when he staggered back a step, gaining space. A flicker of fear.

He relished that too.

It wasn't every day he got to fight a demon this powerful.

Normally, he hunted demons from the numbered realms, those who had mutinied against the Devil. They were as strong in this world as they were in Hell, but their strength couldn't match this male's. His surpassed theirs even when he was limited, some of his power drained from him by the mortal world.

The male rallied. Leathery black wings burst from his back and he beat them, propelling himself backwards.

"Running?" he sneered and readied his own white-feathered wings, aware of what came next.

His superiors would tease him about taunting his prey too. It was *unbecoming*, apparently. Taunting was not only a source of pleasure for him, but it produced consistent results too. He wasn't the only one with a temper. Demons had one too, and it often only took a little poking, a derogatory remark here and there, a little questioning of their strength or spine, and they flew into a rage.

When they were enraged, they were predictable.

Easy to defeat.

Any moment now, this demon would snap and rush him, and he would skewer the male on his sword, clamp his right hand down on the male, and be done with it. The demon would be ashes in seconds, burned from the inside out by his Echelon gift.

The demon disappeared on a snarl.

Not what he had anticipated.

He turned, sure the demon would appear behind him and berating himself for another lapse in judgement.

His senses blared a warning.

He dodged right.

Fire blazed in his left side and he grunted as it rapidly swept through him, spreading outwards from a point just above his hip.

A low chuckle sounded behind him. "Kneel, Angel, and we shall get this over with."

Cold sweat broke out across his brow as he edged his eyes downwards and he swallowed hard, his stomach roiling at the sight that greeted him. Blood covered his left side, spilling like a crimson waterfall down his white tunic and trousers. He watched as it spread beyond his knee to soak into the leather of his white boots.

His lips tugged into a tight smile.

Another lapse in judgement.

He seemed to be having them a lot lately.

He gritted his teeth and grimaced as he gripped the point of the blade protruding from his side and pushed it towards his stomach.

The demon clucked his tongue and drove the sword deeper, ripping a cry from him that echoed in the night.

Damn.

"My dark lord will have your wings mounted on his wall by daybreak," the demon snarled close to his ear.

The first and last mistake he would make.

No one in this world was going to cut his wings from him.

On a defiant roar, he dropped his sword and twisted right, fiery agony sweeping through him as the blade cut through his flesh to drown out the scents of the human world with that of his own blood. He gritted his teeth against the pain as his vision swam and kept turning, desperately pushing himself onwards through the agony of the sword tearing a larger hole in his left side as he reached a trembling hand over his right shoulder, blindly groping for the demon.

A laugh broke from his lips as he made contact with the male's shoulder.

He sensed it the moment the sleeve of his tunic fell back to reveal the stylised cross on the inside of his right wrist and the demon grew aware of what he was. The male tried to rear back as his panic flooded the air, the sharp scent of it mingling with the coppery odour of blood. He gripped the male, refusing to release him, and heat rolled through him as his Echelon gift triggered.

He sank into that heat and the pleasure it offered as fire burned beneath his palm and the demon roared, deafening him. The male made one last attempt to wrench free, managing it this time. The demon's sword slid free of his flesh with a wet sucking noise, and he staggered a step, struggling to keep his balance as the fiend wheeled away from him.

Too late.

A single touch was all it took.

He turned slowly, breathing hard, both hands clamped over the wound in his left side as he came to face the demon.

The male looked himself over, panic flaring in his wide eyes as he desperately tried to stem the flow of black devouring his flesh. It spread rapidly, consuming the demon, and as it crept up his neck to his face, the male lifted his head and locked gazes with him, fury burning in his eyes.

His lips parted.

He would never know what the male had wanted to say to him with his last breath.

The flow of his Echelon gift devoured those words. The demon's charred black skin fractured in places, fissures appearing that glowed gold in the darkness, and then he shattered, falling in pieces to the ground and turning to ash on impact.

He watched as the breeze caught those ashes and they swirled across the earth.

The burning in his side grew hotter and he pressed harder, grimacing as his hands slipped in the blood.

He had been lucky tonight.

But luck never lasted, and he had never relied on it before now.

He focused on his body, seeking the power he needed, closing his eyes as he formed the bridge between the human world and his. His head turned as he teleported, and he kept his eyes closed as he landed in his apartment in Echelon headquarters, waiting for the dizziness to pass.

He cursed himself.

This demon wasn't the first one he had underestimated, but it would be the last. He would sharpen his mind and his blade, would hone them both again until he was back to his normal self. No more distractions. His duty was all he needed.

He slowly opened his eyes and frowned at the pool of blood slowly spreading outwards from beneath his left boot, creeping across the white marble.

The room swayed and rocked.

The double doors set into the white wall behind him creaked open and he sensed the female enter.

"I have been sent to you," she said softly, her voice low. Respectful.

Unlike the half-angel he had been sent to collect.

She had shown no respect. None of them had.

He didn't spare a glance at the petite female who stopped beside him, the same one they always sent to heal him. She would appear as she always did, her blonde tresses tamed in twined braids at the back of her head and her long white dress cinched with a gold belt around her waist.

A white dress that was always stained crimson when she left him.

He didn't stop her as she removed his tunic and then his boots, felt nothing as she stripped him of his trousers. He stood there in the middle of his rooms, his focus slipping again just moments after he had vowed he would sharpen it and would banish all distractions, resuming command of himself.

He stared down at the floor as the female bathed his wounds with water steeped in herbs that had a faint antiseptic scent to them beneath the lavender and soothed his aching body. A gentle heat followed the sponge, soaked into his skin, and relaxed him.

His focus shattered.

His gaze penetrated the layers of the building beneath him, each of them sweeping past him in a blur that picked up speed as his eyes unerringly locked on to a location in the mortal plane.

The sprawling flat roof of an elegant sandstone building in the centre of London came into view and he slowed, needing to take his time now in order to stop his heart from racing as it did whenever he turned his gaze to her.

He braced himself as he focused. It took only the smallest shift, the tiniest effort, and she was before him.

Emelia.

He swallowed hard.

Faintly, he heard the female angel ask, "Am I hurting you?"

He shook his head, too mesmerised by the petite brunette at the centre of his focus to notice whether the healer was hurting him or not.

Emelia looked brighter today, filled with vibrant energy as she rained hell down on a cylindrical bag that was taller than she was, hung from the ceiling of what appeared to be some sort of exercise area within the compound. Her small fists were wrapped in red bandages, and sweat glistened on her back and arms, soaking into the form-fitting black sleeveless top she wore. The strands of hair that had escaped the twisted knot at the back of her head were damp, sticking to her pale skin.

He frowned as he peered closer, focusing harder on her.

A scar ran over her right deltoid to dart beneath the section of her top that followed the line of her spine to expose her shoulder blades.

He gritted his teeth as an image of a green-haired male flashed into his mind. He lowered his eyes to his dirty bare knees, fear and shame sweeping through him as fiercely as the pain did. No. Not his knees. Hers. Emelia's.

He lifted his hand and touched that claw mark, felt the blood on his fingertips, and wanted to retch.

"I am hurting you." The female angel's voice penetrated the memories, shattering them and almost shaking his hold on the human where she continued to hurl punches at the weighted sack.

"You are not," he snapped, then heard her gasp and gentled his tone. "Please, continue."

He drifted away from her again as his focus resettled on Emelia.

In the weeks since he had met her, the burning need to see her in the flesh again had only grown fiercer. He had been sure it would abate, that he would forget what he had seen in her eyes and the need he felt to punish the male who had harmed her.

He had lasted mere days after meeting her before the need to see her again had gripped him and refused to release him. He had turned his gaze to her then, had only meant it to be a brief look to ensure she was safe.

He had ended up watching her for four hours, studying how she reacted to others, how she behaved when alone, and the tasks she carried out within the hunter organisation.

Since then, the intervals between turning his gaze towards her had steadily grown shorter. Now, he couldn't go a day without looking in on her.

She seemed brighter each time he took a moment to watch over her, and at first, he had believed she was making progress, overcoming what had happened to her.

Two weeks ago, he had realised it was a lie.

He had felt it in the pit of his stomach when she had been smiling at an older male seated on the other side of a large wooden desk. A rather prim female had sat rod straight beside her through the entire meeting, and Emelia had tensed whenever the female had leaned over to touch her arm and speak with her. After that meeting, Emelia had appeared drained. She had returned to her quarters and indulged in a large quantity of wine whilst curled up on her couch.

Since then, he had studied her more closely, and now he was able to see the truth behind the false smiles she used to keep everyone else at bay, ones designed to make them leave her alone.

Strangely, the thought that she wanted to be alone made the need to go to her burn fiercer within him.

The familiar ache to speak with her built inside him. He wanted to hear her voice and know it at last. The distance between them was too vast for him to hear it, clawed at him in a way he didn't understand. It left him hollow inside, as if a piece of him was suddenly absent.

Missing.

As he watched her, that unsettling sensation faded. The more he fell into studying her, cataloguing her graceful movements as she fought her inanimate foe, the less aware of the world he grew. The less aware of himself.

Until he was only aware of her.

And then a new ache bloomed. It rapidly grew into a beast that devoured his restraint, one that pushed him to go to her so she wouldn't be alone. He fought it with the same ferocity he always did, although his reasons for resisting it had changed over the weeks.

At first, he had stayed away from her because he had been sure she wouldn't want to see him, that his presence would terrify her after her ordeal.

Then, he had stayed away because he was sure she would have forgotten him, and he didn't want to remind her of the things that had happened to her when she had been overcoming them.

Now, he stayed away because he had witnessed the truth—that she was concealing her true feelings and was scarred by what had happened—and he felt he had already failed her.

The dragon who had harmed her both physically and mentally was surely still alive in Hell, was very possibly inflicting pain upon another innocent female, and he had done nothing to stop the male.

He curled his fingers into fists and clenched them as rage burned through him, aimed at himself and his inaction, and at the dragon.

A dragon he wanted to destroy.

But he couldn't.

He knew what would happen if he ventured into Hell. To set foot in that realm was to weaken himself dramatically. He had read the reports, had scoured every damned scroll and book in the Echelon library, each record of an Echelon angel entering Hell.

The fallen angel, Satan, had invoked barriers around that realm, ones designed to strip angels of their powers, rendering them weak and unable to challenge him.

The things that could happen to him, the pain he would suffer if he entered Hell, didn't bear thinking about. He couldn't do it.

He wasn't sure how much longer he could deny the hunger that blazed inside him, though. It constantly pushed him, had him on edge at all times, restless with a need to do something. He had to do something.

"I am done."

He barely heard those words, didn't acknowledge the female or notice her leave.

He kept his focus locked on Emelia.

Because she alone grounded him.

She alone gave him the strength to remain where he was, away from the danger of Hell.

But the effect she had on him was wearing thin now, in danger of breaking, and he was sure he would do something rash and dangerous, potentially deadly to himself, if the power she had over him shattered.

There was only one thing he could do to stop that from happening.

He needed to see her again.

CHAPTER 4

Emelia ran her hand through the water, the soft music filling her ears as she let her thoughts drift. Every inch of her ached, her muscles tired from her workout and her knuckles sore. It felt good to push herself this hard, though. She had even managed to sleep a few times after a boxing session this vigorous, and one of those times, she had been nightmare-free.

At first, the ever-annoying Linda hadn't been impressed with her 'funnelling her anger and pain into fighting', but then Mark had called them both into his office and had sided with her for once, reassuring Linda that Emelia had always handled things this way.

Some people did their therapy with words. Emelia preferred to do it with her fists.

Boxing had been her go-to method of getting all her feelings out ever since her parents had passed away. It was how she dealt with frustration and anger, and hurt. It was how she built herself up and made herself stronger.

Linda had reluctantly accepted that, but still insisted on twice-weekly sessions.

Emelia begrudgingly admitted they were helping, but they felt invasive too, and sometimes she felt as if she was suffocating and had to make her excuses and leave early.

Like today.

She had gone straight from a failed session to the gym and had spent three hours working up a sweat and wearing herself out. She felt better for it.

Although she wasn't sure she would be able to sleep tonight.

She had woken from a nightmare this morning, had shot awake with her heart thundering and sweat crawling down her spine, drenching the covers. She had been shaking so violently, she had been afraid to try to move from the bed, had been sure her legs would give out if she had tried. Tears had burned the backs of her eyes when anger had swept through her, not anger directed at Zephyr for the things he had done, but fury directed at herself for letting him strip all the strength she had clawed back together from her.

"Shit," she muttered as the water sloshed into the overflow.

She reached into the water and pulled the plug to let some out. She stared at the water level as it dropped, thoughts crowding her mind. She let them come, but refused to let fear take hold of her. This was her space, and she was in control here, not the dragon.

She pushed the plug back into the hole and shirked her damp workout clothes. The water was cooler than usual, but it was still bliss as it warmed tired muscles. She sank into it, stopping at her breasts, and rested her arms along the sides of the tub.

Therapy and intense boxing sessions weren't the only things that had been helping her recover.

Whenever thoughts of Zephyr flooded her mind, she let them come now, twisted the memories so he was in her place. She pictured the things she would do to him if he ever came for her. Over the last few weeks, the swift death she had imagined had evolved into something darker.

She wanted him to suffer as she had. She wanted him to know the fear she had, the terror and pain she and every other female who had been taken by his kin had experienced. She wanted him to taste what it was like to be weaker, the victim, unable to fight and free himself.

She curled her fingers over the edge of the tub and gripped it as her mind traversed dark paths. He deserved to know what it was like to be tormented, physically hurt whenever he attempted to escape, and mentally wounded whenever he was caught. She wanted to tease him by making him believe the attempt to escape would work and then take pleasure in stopping him.

She wanted to lash out at him, wanted to grin down at him as he had at her whenever his strength failed, wanted to torture him with the thought she might do things to him against his will and he was powerless to stop it from happening.

Every cruel act he had committed against her, she would commit against him. She wouldn't threaten him with the thought he might be used against his will, though, because he wanted her, would welcome it. She would give him pain instead, would threaten him with the thought he might die.

No.

She closed her eyes, tipped her head back and slid lower in the water. She wouldn't. Couldn't. She wasn't like him.

He was sick. He had taken pleasure from hurting her, from making her believe he was going to do things to her against her will. She was sure he would have taken pleasure from committing those acts on her, but she had fought him every time, clawing him and hitting him, desperately driving him away. He had looked satisfied whenever he had released her, tossing her to the ground like garbage, and she had dragged herself away from him and cried.

He had told her he wanted to break her.

And then he had changed.

She scooped up water and swept it over her face, let it roll over her skin and drip from her jaw as she pondered that for the thousandth time. Why had he changed?

What had happened when he had gone to the dragon clan village and come back injured? What had made him wild with a need to make her belong to him?

She took a deep breath and sank beneath the water.

She didn't care what had happened.

It wouldn't change anything.

He might not have abused her as the other dragons had abused the huntresses they had been given by the clan chief, but he had taken everything from her.

She had fought so hard for her position within Archangel, had risen through the mostly male ranks to gain the respect of her peers, and now everyone was treating her as if she was weak, a feeble female more fragile than glass, who needed protecting.

She hated the way they looked at her. Sometimes with pity. Sometimes as if she no longer belonged at Archangel. She felt singled out by everyone, because no one knew how to treat her.

They knew how to handle the other huntresses who had been rescued after her, the ones who were in daily therapy sessions and on serious medication, and the ones who had quit Archangel.

They just didn't know how to handle her.

Sometimes, she wasn't sure how to handle herself either.

Part of her wanted out of Archangel, but she didn't want to give up everything she had worked for. This was the only home she had now. It had become her family.

She felt guilty whenever she saw any of the women who had been taken together with her though. Zephyr had been cruel, sadistic, and twisted, but he had grown to want her to want him, and in the end, she had used it against him. She had manipulated him, and she had gained her freedom.

She didn't want to think about what might have happened to her if he hadn't gone away and come back different.

Would she have ended up like the huntresses she saw wandering the halls with Linda, heavily medicated, or worse, like the huntresses who hadn't survived their ordeal?

Emelia pushed away from those sombre thoughts as she broke the surface of the water. The soft melody of a ballad surrounded her, and she focused on it, on sweetly murmured words about love and revenge.

Revenge was all she cared about.

Mark had ordered her not to even consider it, had made it painfully clear that it wasn't going to happen by denying her a team she could take to Hell. She was no longer sure she would have been strong enough to head into that realm even if he had given her an entire army to lead.

She was sure she wouldn't come back, though. None of them would. The dragons were too strong in their own realm. The only way for her to defeat Zephyr was to fight him in her realm, where he would be weak just as Loke had been when Sable had brought him to Archangel HQ.

Loke had escaped, though, with the help of the elf prince and King Thorne, and Sable and Anais, if Emelia had to guess. Her mind drifted back to that night when she had met the angel. The second alarm had signalled a break-in, but it hadn't been him. Two immortals had teleported into the building, leaving a path of destruction and bodies in their wake, and snatched someone from the cell block. During the chaos, Anais's dragon shifter Loke had also escaped.

It had been quiet since then.

Too quiet for Emelia.

Her thoughts kept drifting to the angel she had met.

He had been the first and only person to offer her vengeance, and she would be lying if she said she wasn't disappointed he hadn't returned to make good on his vow.

Sable didn't like him and had gone to ground because of him, but had popped back up on the radar a couple of weeks ago. Emelia had bumped into her in Underworld, a local nightclub run by immortals, and had found the courage to ask about the angel and what an Echelon was.

Apparently, they were demon hunters and very important angels, or VIAs as Sable had called them. It explained why Thorne hadn't liked him, although his hatred probably had more to do with the fact the angel wanted to steal Sable away from him and take her to a place Emelia felt certain the demon wouldn't be able to reach.

Of course, Sable had also called the angel numerous, less complimentary things during the couple of beers they had shared at the bar with Thorne watching over her like a hawk.

He hadn't liked Sable talking to her about the angel, or anything related to that breed of immortal, but Emelia hadn't been able to stop the questions once they had started to flow.

Sable had only been able to answer one since she was only just learning about all things angel herself.

Had the angel really seen her memories?

According to Sable's angelic source, the woman her friend was learning from, some angels could see into people's minds and even manipulate them if they were weak enough.

Was she weak-minded?

She had pondered that question a lot.

She didn't think she was. When the angel had been present, she had felt a pressing sensation in her head, like a headache.

Or him prodding her mind?

Had it really been him testing it?

She had talked to one of the other women who had been in the room, and what she had felt was different. She had told Emelia that she had experienced a sensation that she wanted to stay just seconds after she had been drawn to going for reinforcements.

Emelia didn't doubt he had manipulated her.

She also didn't doubt that he hadn't felt a single shred of guilt over what he had done, bending someone to his will, forcing them to do something against their own.

Anger flared but swiftly faded, washed away by the question that always rang in her head whenever she thought about him, a question she felt sure only he could answer.

Was she weak-minded?

She didn't feel strong now, but perhaps she was, because she had survived everything that had happened to her. Maybe she was stronger than she realised.

She would never know the answer, though, because she was never going to see him again.

The hair on her arms rose, and a prickling sensation swept over her nape.

Static electricity flooded the air, setting her on edge.

She sat up, her heart starting to pound as the unnatural charge built and tingles rushed down her spine.

There was a breath of silence, filled with anticipation.
And then the alarms blared.

CHAPTER 5

The alarms were still blaring ten minutes later as Emelia ran beside a group of black-clad hunters down a corridor on the second level of the building. The flashing red lights hurt her tired eyes, and her muscles protested, threatening to cramp as she pushed herself to keep moving.

"Might be a breach in the cell block," a hunter said to his companion as they broke off, turning down a hallway to her left.

She doubted that. Any breach in the cell block would have been dealt with by now by one of the teams that had been dispatched there.

It was him.

She knew it.

She would never forget the way electricity had charged the air when he had appeared in the building the first time they had met. The strange sensation had faded now, but she hadn't imagined it.

It was the angel.

He had come back.

She just wasn't sure where he was.

She had checked the place where they had met, a small observation room next to one of the grim white medical cells where the scientists and doctors at Archangel often studied the non-humans the hunters captured and brought in for them. The angel hadn't been there.

Where would he go?

She ground to a halt as she realised something.

She wanted to find him. She wanted to see him again.

Her pulse pounded for a different reason as that hit her, and she moved to the cream wall and pressed her palm to it for support as she stared at the wooden floor. Awareness rushed through her, the past few weeks rolling up on her and leaving her stunned. She had been drawing further and further away from everyone else, even her friends.

But not from him.

What was it about the angel that had her moving towards him, seeking him?

He was a stranger to her, and a dangerous man. Very dangerous. She had witnessed that for herself.

So why was she experiencing a rush of adrenaline, a quiet thrill at the thought he had returned?

Why was she *happy* that he was here?

Because he was an angel, so she felt he could help her by using his power to free her from the pain of her memories by healing her battered mind somehow?

Or because she had seen the darkness in him, the savage side that had startled her at the time because he was an angel, and had felt the power he commanded, strength that matched, if not surpassed, what Zephyr possessed?

Her fingers tensed against the cream wall.

Did she want the angel to heal her... or destroy the dragon?

She lifted her other hand and pressed it to her chest. Her heart thundered against her palm as she dug her fingertips in, clawing her black T-shirt into her fist.

She wasn't sure.

A prickling sensation ran up her arms. She dropped her gaze to her left forearm, frowning as the hairs stood on end. A moment later, the familiar charge began to build, barely noticeable at first, but as she focused on it, she could feel it growing.

Was he planning to leave?

Panic propelled her feet into action, and she sprinted down the corridor only to stop at the next cross junction. She slowly turned back the way she had come. The charge was weaker here, away from the spot she had just occupied. Was she moving away from him?

She ran back the way she had come and focused as best she could on the strange feeling. Her breaths came faster as it built inside her, and she was sure she was moving closer to him now. She followed it up through the building, letting her instincts and that electrical charge guide her.

She ground to a halt in front of the fire exit that would take her to the roof.

The charge was strongest here, a rush of tingles constantly running up and down her spine, tripping over her skin beneath her black combat gear. She took a moment, trying to settle her heart and level out her breathing. Her hands shook as she smoothed them over her damp hair, using the action of drawing the dark ribbons of it into a rough knot at the back of her head to calm herself.

Emelia blew out her breath, gripped the handle, and pushed. The heavy door creaked open, and she stepped out onto the flat roof. The cool night air chilled her, brushing across her damp nape and raising the hairs on her bare arms as surely as the angel had.

Was he here?

She shuffled out onto the roof, her eyes adjusting to the dim light that rose from below her, allowing her to see through it. Objects gradually appeared, gaining form and depth as she moved deeper into the darkness, leaving the safety of the door behind. Nerves threatened to send her running back that way, a whispered taunt in her mind reminding her that she hadn't left the building in more than a week.

That she was in danger out here in the open.

She instinctively glanced up and then shook her head. The dragon wasn't here, and he couldn't shift in her world. There was nothing to fear from that inky sky.

She moved around one of the air-conditioning outlets and paused.

Her breath hitched.

Heart lodged in her throat.

She clenched her fists to stop them from trembling and lingered in the shadows, away from the sphere of slender light that emanated from the pitched glass windows that formed a skylight for fifteen feet down the middle of the roof.

Slender light that washed over the man lazing on the gritty dark ground before her, his hands tucked behind his head, supporting it as he stared at the sky.

Looking nothing like she had expected.

The thick onyx hair and silver eyes had remained the same, the chiselled contours of his face and strong line of his jaw exactly as she had remembered them, but everything else was wrong.

He looked more human than angel.

No huge white wings.

No pristine white tunic suited to one of his breed.

A dark turtleneck and black slacks hugged his powerful physique, emphasising muscles that roused a wariness in her and had her wanting to take a step back from him. She knew he was strong, he didn't need to drive the point home by showing off honed muscles that screamed he could easily overpower her.

Emelia fought the wave of panic that rose inside her.

If he wanted to hurt her, he probably would have done it by now. He was aware of her. She wasn't an idiot. He was pretending to be oblivious to her standing in the shadows, looking at him, on the verge of a panic attack. To give her time to calm herself and adjust to his presence?

It certainly seemed like an angelic thing to do so she rolled with it as his reason for not even glancing at her.

She swallowed to wet her dry mouth and throat and risked a step towards him. "What are you doing?"

The black slashes of his eyebrows rose but he still didn't look at her. "Trying to relax."

Funny that. She had been trying to relax too, before the alarms had sounded. Now she was trying to relax all over again, repeatedly telling herself that he wasn't going to hurt her.

She braved another step closer so she could see him more clearly in what little light shone on him. He did seem tense.

Lines bracketed the corners of his full mouth as he moved his right arm, lowering it to his stomach, and she didn't miss the way he shifted that hand to his left side.

"Any reason you've chosen to relax on the roof of Archangel?" She canted her head to her right, peering at his face.

He didn't answer.

She glanced over her shoulder towards the fire exit as the alarms continued to ring. It was only a matter of time before one or more of the hunters scouring the building below her for the intruder ended up checking the roof. What would he do then?

What would she do?

"The alarms are ringing because of you," she murmured, her eyes still on the door.

It beckoned her, luring her with a promise of safety. She was safe in there, shut away from the world.

"My apologies." His deep baritone rolled over her, chasing that desire away, together with her panic. It slowly faded as she shifted her focus to him, coming to face him. The alarms ceased, but he still didn't look at her as he said, "Is that better?"

He had silenced them the last time they had met too. What other powers did he possess?

She nodded, relieved the world had fallen silent again. Hopefully the hunters would believe the intruder was gone or was never there to begin with, and would go back to their duties. It might buy her time to find out why there was an angel lazing on the roof, his eyes on the night sky.

Those eyes shifted like mercury in the weak moonlight, eerily bright despite the darkness.

"Are you here about Sable again?" She inched closer, narrowing the distance between them down to under ten feet.

He finally looked at her.

It was nothing more than a brief glance, a bare brush of those dazzling silver eyes over her from head to toe before they fixed back on the stars. Nerves instantly rushed through her, thoughts filling her mind that had butterflies whirling in her stomach like a damned hurricane.

Emelia edged another step closer as her memories pushed harder.

And hell, that was just as bizarre as finding him dressed like a regular guy on her rooftop.

Normally when the crush of memories happened, she wanted to get away from everyone.

Not get *closer* to someone.

She reminded herself that she couldn't trust anyone now. Whatever trust she'd once had, it lay broken now, fragmented like her strength.

Fractured like her soul.

"I will not hurt you," he murmured softly without looking at her, his voice a balm to her ragged nerves, soothing the torn edges of them. "I did not come to upset you."

Had he sensed her mounting panic?

Immortals had acute senses, but she hadn't expected his to be that sharp. The panic hadn't even gripped her yet, had only been on the verge of seizing her, but he had felt it, and he had sought to reassure her.

She breathed a little easier, managed another step closer to him, and was rewarded for her courage by the memories that had been surfacing fading away instead. She tried to relax, but it was difficult. No matter how many times she told herself that he was an angel, that he wouldn't hurt her, the tension in her body remained.

A different memory surfaced as she looked down at him, a flash of him in that observation room, his face a mask of darkness and eyes as hard as diamonds as he had growled that he would kill the dragon for her.

"I like the view of the stars from here." His deep voice wrapped around her again, pulling her back to the present, and she had the feeling he had known she was slipping away again and had wanted to bring her back to him.

She tipped her head back and charted the faint pinpricks that struggled to pierce the lights of the city. Calm washed over her as she gazed at them, carrying away her fears and leaving her feeling lighter, freer than she had in a long time.

"The city lights drown them out, but... I like to look at the stars too now." She lost herself in them and everything fell away, all the weight lifting from her with it.

"Why?"

She couldn't tear her eyes away from them as she let the words slip out rather than holding them back. "They help me remember I'm not in Hell anymore."

The briefest trace of cold washed over her exposed skin and the stars seemed to dim for a heartbeat before they returned.

"The stars are always more beautiful from your world." His voice was tight now, held an edge that was sharp as a blade and at odds to his words.

Was he trying to control his mood? The world had darkened as it had before when his temper had snapped, but it had only lasted a split second this time. Because he didn't want to scare her?

He sounded like she did at times when she was close to snapping, trying to be polite to stop herself from lashing out at those who were trying to smother her.

"The lights drown the stars out." She squeezed the words past her tight throat and told herself to breathe, because she was safe here.

"I can see them," he murmured. "I see things a little differently to you."

She could imagine.

She tried to find her favourite constellations, wishing she could see the stars as clearly as he could. She had seen pictures of the Milky Way viewed in complete darkness, and she would love to see it with her own eyes. She wanted to immerse herself in nature, in everything that Hell lacked. Stars. Trees. The sun. She had basked in it more than once in the doorway behind her, not quite brave enough to laze on the roof as he was and bathe in it.

"Why are you here?" She lowered her eyes to him.

He looked at her at last.

"I am sorry. I could not stay away any longer." His voice was low as he spoke, an honesty in his silver eyes that drew a frown from her.

She hadn't seen honesty in anyone's eyes in a long time. She had seen pity, disgust, guilt, and everything in between, but not honesty.

He was truly sorry, but she wasn't sure why.

"Couldn't stay away?" The answer struck her. "You mean from Sable."

He had come for her friend again, sent here to make another attempt to take her to his realm. He was going to be sorely disappointed.

"She isn't here. As far as I know, she's in Hell with Thorne."

His gaze locked with hers. "From you."

Emelia stared into those honest eyes, saw the truth in them as they brightened, turning gold at the edges, and panicked.

She backed off a step as the fear he had chased away surged through her, memories fighting to the surface to twist her thoughts. She had to get away. She had to go. It wasn't safe here. She swallowed her racing heart and tried to calm her mind, but fear sank icy claws into both of them, and she couldn't breathe.

He sat up, grimacing as he clutched his left side. "I am sorry. Do not fear me. I would never hurt you, Emelia."

She couldn't convince herself to believe that.

Zephyr had told her he would never hurt her again, and then he had struck her so hard when she had refused his advances that he had broken one of her ribs. She lowered her hand to her right side, mirroring the angel as he struggled to his feet, pain tightening his features.

"Emelia," he murmured, his soft voice doing nothing to calm her this time. "I need to know more about you... about that diabolical bastard who hurt you."

She shook her head. She didn't want to speak about such things. She just wanted to leave. She needed to leave. So why couldn't she convince her feet to move?

Why did part of her want to stay?

"I tried to forget you," he grated, the gold that ringed his irises beginning to invade them now as the air around him darkened. "I tried to forget what I saw... but I cannot... and I cannot focus on my duty anymore. The dragon *must* pay."

All her fear and panic flooded out of her just like that, as if he had uttered magical words not a simple vow to avenge her. Calm flowed in, cold and clinical, erasing all feeling in its path, leaving her feeling empty inside.

She stared into his shifting eyes, ones that were still honest and open, hiding none of his feelings. His anger. His fury. It was all there for her to see.

"The dragon lives in Hell," she uttered.

A place he apparently couldn't go without experiencing great pain.

"I do not care." He ground the words out as the air around him continued to darken and his eyes brightened further, pulling her under their spell. "I will slay this dragon for you."

She wanted that.

She wanted Zephyr dead.

But if the angel ventured into Hell, he would be weakened, in danger of being killed by Zephyr. Sending him to hunt the dragon might be sending him to his death.

Was that a price she could bring herself to pay for a shot at revenge?

CHAPTER 6

To say he was buzzing as he waited for the petite mortal to speak would be the understatement of his long life.

Emelia was here, in his presence, more beautiful than he recalled. Fire had sparked in her emerald eyes from time to time when they had been talking. *Talking.* He knew the soft tones of her voice, the rolling way her words flowed, gaining strength at times and gentleness at others. He knew how emotions moved like tides within her, panic and fear at the helm one moment, and calm and resolve in command the next.

Her mood was as mercurial as his.

He hadn't meant to scare her, and he definitely hadn't handled her well so far. He had only meant to see her, to perhaps speak with her a little about everyday things, and now he was in danger of driving her away.

Fear still coloured those entrancing green eyes that were locked on him, and he would be a fool if he believed she had forgotten her desire to leave. She stood unmoving, a quiet strength to her as she assessed him, mulling over his offer, but he could read her. Part of her still wanted to flee back into the building where he couldn't follow, not without stirring up the humans who lived in it again.

He didn't want her to go, though.

There had to be something he could do to convince her to stay, to make her believe he had no intention of harming her.

He wasn't sure what that was, though.

He had thought offering to track and slay the dragon for her would work, but now she looked even more as if she was considering walking away from him.

It had been a mistake to rush here to her, without taking a moment to plan. He had seen many people involved in relationships of every type, not just friendships or short-term partnerships. Angels indulged in more pleasurable forms of relationships, and some paired for life, as humans did. He had seen every kind of relationship in his years, but it hadn't prepared him for handling Emelia.

He wasn't sure what he was meant to do in this situation.

And damn, it was daunting.

He had expected to feel the same pressing need to fight when he had come to her, that same surge of rage and a hunger to hunt.

The moment he had heard her voice, a different sort of pressing need had filled him, and a wholly unexpected hunger had surged through him.

He should have left then.

But he had made his second mistake.

He had looked at her.

Her beauty hit him hard whenever he dared to glance at her, and it was difficult to take his eyes off her. The flawless cream of her skin against the rich brown of her hair. The elegant arch of her neck. The soft curve of her jaw. The delicate slope of her nose. The entrancing emerald of her large eyes.

The tempting soft pink of her full lips.

She fidgeted with the hem of her black T-shirt, her nerves clear.

His staring was unsettling her, but he couldn't help himself.

His eyes didn't want to leave her.

He wanted to drink his fill of her soft features, ached to drown in her eyes as she steadily held his gaze. His fingers twitched with a need to brush her damp hair back, to capture the band she had hastily tied it with and tug it free so he could tangle his fingers in her fall of dark hair.

He wasn't sure what to do now, but he knew *that* wasn't a wise move.

What was?

The bond that linked him to Emelia was fragile, and he could easily, accidentally, break it if he wasn't careful. Just one misstep might be enough to end things before they ever really began, and part of him feared he had already made that wrong move.

He reined in his temper, clawing back calm, aware that the fear that gripped her now was his doing.

The air around them lightened, and as it did, he saw the fear in her eyes fading. A right move, then?

One that might bring him back to where he had been before he had let his anger get the better of him and pressed her too hard?

He hoped so.

He still wasn't sure how to proceed, even if he was back to square one.

He was a warrior, a hunter. He didn't know how to be gentle. He was governed by a darker set of instincts, and his temperament was hard to deal with at the best of times. At his worst, he was aware that he was a formidable male, one who might appear as a monster to the gentler sex.

Especially to a female like Emelia.

"What did you see?" She had barely spoken that question before she shook her head. "Don't answer that. Maybe it's better I don't know. I don't want to know."

Mercurial female.

"Do you know where the dragon resides?" He wanted to move closer to her, but he didn't dare risk it.

She tensed, her slender body going rigid, and looked away from him. "I don't want to talk about it. I always have to talk about it, and I hate it."

Understood. No talking about the dragon. Not yet anyway, not until she was more comfortable around him again.

"You saw it, though… didn't you?" she whispered without looking at him.

"I did." But he hadn't seen it all.

Rage had been swift to claim him, and he had only seen part of what had happened to her. He wanted to know the rest. It plagued him as fiercely as the need to hunt the dragon.

"Is that a power all angels have?" She lowered her hands to her sides and he marvelled at how she visibly altered before his eyes, her nerves fading as she straightened and brought her gaze up to meet his.

"No. It is one of my gifts." He had a few, not the most sought-after ones, but they had helped him in some tricky situations. Would they help him through this one?

He studied Emelia, charting the subtle changes in her body language and her emotions as she mulled over his answer. She seemed to grow stronger with each passing second, and he suspected it had to do with the fact she was shutting down her emotions. Fear. Nerves. Panic. It was all subsiding at a rapid rate as something else clicked into place.

He wanted to smile when it dawned on him.

The hunter in her.

Perhaps they weren't so different after all.

The question was, was she using her duty as a hunter to merely learn more about him, or was learning about him an excuse to linger on the roof with him?

He wouldn't deny her information either way. Her legion of mortals weren't strong enough to detain him if he wanted to leave, and he wanted her to be more comfortable around him. If learning about him would grant her that comfort, would bring her closer to him, then he would answer any question she posed.

"One of the huntresses mentioned she had wanted to leave to find reinforcements… and then she had wanted to stay." Emelia held his gaze, hers impassive as she studied him, but he could see beyond the veil to her rising nerves. Whatever she wanted to ask, it unsettled her for some reason. "Sable told me you can control weak-minded people—"

She cut herself off when he frowned at her.

Sable was more trouble than he had realised. She had been poisoning Emelia's mind.

"I cannot manipulate you." He barely dulled the sharp edge to his tone. "You are too strong."

That seemed to relieve her.

A sharp sensation shot down his spine. Not now. He gritted his teeth and ignored the summons from his superiors. They could wait. He didn't want to leave her.

"What's wrong?" Her dark eyebrows knitted and he realised he wasn't the only one who could see through someone to the real them.

She could read him too.

"A summons," he muttered. "It can wait."

She tilted her head back and her eyes traced across the night sky. "Won't you get into trouble?"

Was she looking for Heaven? She wouldn't find it there. As Hell was linked to this plane, so was his. It was above her world, but not. She had been to Hell, so he presumed she knew it was a different plane, another dimension in simple terms.

She lowered her gaze back to him. "You should go."

He shrugged. "I do not want to."

The corners of her lips curled, but the smile died before it could manifest. "You'll get in trouble."

He had the feeling he had been in trouble from the moment he had met her. "No worse than usual."

He ignored so many summons that his superiors had once joked about fitting him with a GPS anklet because it appeared he kept getting lost and someone had to keep finding him.

"Go." She looked ready to shove him.

He didn't like that at all. Now she wanted him to leave? Had he outstayed his welcome or done something wrong? He really needed to read up on relationships, or at least on females. He was finding it hard to fathom what she wanted when she kept changing her mind.

"You were asking me questions, though." And he had been enjoying it. "If I leave, will you permit me to return another day? I would speak with you again if you would allow it."

She stifled a smile that was at odds with the nerves he felt rising inside her.

"You're so formal..." A frown wrinkled her button nose. "What am I meant to call you? It's weird I don't know what to call you."

Not really.

"You may call me Fourth Commander."

She pulled a face at that and it was his turn to frown at her.

"I can't call you a title. Is a title who you are?" She seemed to have forgotten the nerves he had stirred in her by asking to see her again, although he wasn't sure he was glad of it, as she now appeared determined to make him question himself.

Was a title who he was? A title was enough for him. It was more than many angels bore.

"Everything has a name," she said. "Hell, my childhood pets had names. I named the damned spiders in the garden too."

"It is all I require," he countered, his mood taking a dark turn as he considered what she had said.

She had given wild arachnids names and he didn't have one to offer her. Did that mean she would see him as something less than a common garden spider?

"You really should have a name. It's stupid... not having a name. Sable is right about that." Her eyes lit up. "I could call you what Sable did, although I imagine you wouldn't like it."

He glared at her now. He remembered what the half-breed had called him.

Tall, Dark and Pompous.

"I would rather you did not." He folded his arms across his chest and grimaced as the wound on his side pulled. She glanced down at the spot above his hip and looked as if she might ask about it, so he continued. "Do I really require a name? Is it not something you can overcome?"

She shook her head, his wound forgotten. "It's just strange. Maybe I could grow used to it, if you insisted on having no name."

Was she planning to see him enough to grow used to things about him?

Heat spread through him at the thought and he took it as a sign she did want to see him again, would allow him to visit her another time, and perhaps more than once. If he visited her enough, he might come to understand her, and she might open up enough to tell him more about the dragon.

Then he could hunt the bastard down and slay him.

"Your eyes are shifting again and it's cold. I'd rather you kept your temper in check." Her soft words tugged him back from his pleasant thoughts and he reined his mood in before it slipped beyond his control. Another frown put a furrow in her brow. "I don't like it when you lose your temper. It's cold and dark…"

He didn't like the way she trailed off, or how she wrapped her arms around her waist to tightly hug herself as if she feared she was falling apart.

"I apologise." He bowed his head.

"No problem, TeeDeePee."

He arched an eyebrow at her. "TeeDeePee?"

"Short for Tall, Dark and Pompous."

If she wanted him to keep his mood in check, she was going about it the wrong way.

"Fourth Commander," he said.

"EffSee." She pulled a face. "Echelon?"

She was determined to give him a name. It wasn't going to happen.

He huffed. "Do you like your name? Do you feel it suits you?"

A little shrug. "I like it. Sometimes people can't spell it. I can't tell you how many Starbucks I've had where they've called me Amelia. Sometimes people try to shorten it."

The flicker of disgust in her green eyes said that didn't go down well with her.

"Shorten it?" He tried to think of ways to shorten her name, none of which he would tell her, because he was enjoying this easy banter.

She was slowly relaxing again and had forgotten he was meant to be leaving, both of which were good things.

She nodded. "Mostly to Em."

"Em." He liked that. It had a cute ring to it, the sort of name a lover might whisper in her ear.

The look in her eyes said she hated it, though.

He looked himself over, from his black leather shoes, up his trousers, to his turtleneck sweater.

What name would suit him?

He lifted his eyes to lock with hers and that heat flooded him again, stirring hungers best denied, ones that were new and startlingly powerful.

"Your eyes are shifting again," she murmured, a little breathless, her voice softer than before, barely there as she stared deep into his eyes, as if he had cast a spell on her. "You look like a wolf."

"I am an angel," he countered, a little too deadpan judging by how the corners of her lips tilted in that teasing way he had never seen before tonight.

"I know that, but you keep looking at me like a predator." Her voice dropped lower, but he still heard her. "As if you want to devour me."

He did, but not in the way she meant it.

She took a step back and he barely stopped himself from moving one towards her. It was hard, but he let her distance herself and dragged his gaze away from her, fixing it back on the stars so he was no longer unsettling her. He needed to handle her carefully. Gently. How did one go about that?

"Why do you want to fight the dragon?" Her words drifted around him as he focused on the stars.

"I simply want justice served to him." A lie.

"Other huntresses were taken... hurt worse than me. Some were killed. Do you want to avenge them too?"

He picked out one star and fixated on it. It was brighter than the others, flashed blue and gold. "After I have dealt with your dragon."

"He isn't *my* dragon," she snapped and he had the feeling he had hit a raw nerve.

"My apologies," he murmured, distracted by the star. Was it a binary? Two stars snared in an orbit that had them crossing paths at intervals. He knew how that felt now. How long would it be before he could cross paths with Emelia again?

The fire arcing down his spine said it might be a while if he didn't return to his superiors soon to see what they wanted. He had been confined to Echelon headquarters for a lunar cycle once, his punishment for what they had termed his 'disobedience'. That time, they hadn't been joking.

A lunar cycle locked away from Emelia, only able to watch her from afar, would be torture now he knew the sound of her voice, the sweet scent of her perfume, and had been close to her.

"So you want to kill him just because he hurt a human?" Her voice gained strength and her mood shifted, darker emotions surfacing.

She didn't believe him.

"I am an *angel*." An excuse, and a good one as far as he could tell.

Mortals believed angels watched over them, protecting them from afar, and he was sure that by now, she knew that he was a demon hunter like her, tracked and killed any creature who was a danger to her kind.

It was possible she would believe him.

"I don't buy it," she bit out.

Perhaps not, then.

She moved a step closer and his senses lit up, that heat she caused inside him rising another ten degrees, until he was burning with a need to look at her again and see how near to him she was.

Until he was on fire with the hunger to reach out, slide his arm around her narrow waist, and draw her against him.

He forced his eyes to remain on the stars, because she could read him, and he didn't want her to know the real reason he needed to kill the dragon.

He was unequipped to deal with her, uneducated in the ways of relationships, but he was old enough and wise enough to know that telling her he desired to slay the dragon because it had harmed *her* and that he would kill anyone who had done such a thing to her, including another angel, would only end with her leaving and never wanting to see him again.

Which was hardly surprising, but also unfair.

He wasn't sure he had much control when it came to Emelia. The anger that had awoken in him when he had seen through her eyes the things the dragon had done to her, the torment she had suffered, was too powerful to wrestle into submission. He needed to do this for her, could only keep denying the deep and consuming hunger to hunt and destroy the dragon for so long before it devoured what little control he had and he found himself traversing the distance between this world and a place that was forbidden.

Hell.

He would go there, whether she wanted it or not. Whether he wanted it or not. He had to go. The dragon was there, and he wouldn't be able to settle until he knew the male was dead and would never harm Emelia again.

All he could do was prepare himself for that day as best he could, and that meant learning as much as possible about the dragon, which meant convincing Emelia to confide in him and trust him to carry out this task for her.

"What do you think will happen if you kill Zephyr?" she husked in a tight voice, one that cracked on that bastard's name.

Zephyr.

He had a lead at last, but at what cost?

Tears lined Emelia's dark lashes and she turned her face away from him. Her shoulders shook as she closed her eyes, and he ached to reach for her, to lay his hand gently on her cheek and reassure her that whatever nightmare she had survived, it would never happen to her again. A fool's move and one he wouldn't make.

He had seen other males attempt to touch her in order to comfort her, and she had lashed out at all of them, driving them away.

A male's touch terrified her now.

When her head lifted and her eyes opened, rising to lock with his, he realised he had made another mistake. It wasn't fear or pain that had her trembling. It was anger. It flashed in her green irises as she glared at him.

"Do you think I'll hug you, and pet you, and squeeze you and call you George?" She hurled the words at him and scoffed when he frowned, confused by them. "Of course you wouldn't know the reference. You're an angel. Go back to your world, *Fourth Commander*."

She meant to push him away. It wasn't going to happen.

Without missing a beat, he said, "George? I like that name."

Horror danced in her eyes as they shot wide. "No. You don't. It doesn't suit you."

Had she considered names that might suit him then?

He smiled. "What about Jorge?"

The horrified expression on her face only worsened, but a touch of colour stained her cheeks for some reason.

"No," she stuttered, recovering from whatever had caused that alluring hint of rose. "No George. Certainly no Jorge."

She pivoted on her heel and swept away from him.

He followed. "Why not?"

She glanced over her shoulder. "You don't need a name, remember? That's what you said, Fourth Commander."

He knew what he had said, but for some strange reason, he was beginning to desire one. It probably had something to do with how she said his title, with venom that drove each word like a spear through his chest and made him feel lacking.

"Go," she snapped when she reached the door and gripped the handle. She twisted it and yanked it open, then stepped over the threshold. As it swung closed behind her, she growled, "I don't need someone to fight my battles."

He let her go.

She needed space and he had pushed her too hard, had made her uncomfortable.

He had frightened her more than once too.

He ran over everything that had happened, every small detail, studying her words and behaviour, the shifts in her mood and her body language, cataloguing it all in an attempt to understand her and what she needed from him.

Apparently, she didn't need someone to fight her battles.

A lie, but one that revealed something vital about her.

She didn't like anyone belittling her strength. She had feared she had a weak mind, one he could manipulate, and she hated the way others treated her, as if she was fragile. She wanted to be viewed as strong, because she had lost sight of her strength. She believed it was gone, stolen from her by the dragon, but she was blinded by her pain and her memories. He had seen flashes of her strength tonight, revealed to him like lightning strikes, bright and blinding.

She was strong.

And he had foolishly thought to treat her as the others did, as if she was fragile and liable to break.

"Idiot," he huffed and turned away from the door.

She didn't need to be coddled, just as she certainly didn't need him unable to control his temper when he was around her.

No. What she needed from him wasn't violence. It was the opposite. She needed someone who made her feel safe, who was there for her without pressuring her, offering her a calm and unjudging place.

He needed to be careful with her, gentle, but not to the point where she felt as if he thought her fragile.

Damn, he wasn't sure he could manage it, but he was going to try.

He focused on his apartments and teleported there without his usual display of power, disappearing from the London rooftop to reappear in the main living space of his quarters in the blink of an eye.

He turned his gaze towards Emelia and stopped himself.

He had no right to watch her, not tonight. She needed space and time to master herself again, to conquer her emotions and bring them back under control. Watching her now would be prying, violating the sanctuary she needed in order to find calm again and the strength to keep moving forwards.

Plus, she was probably angry with him.

He would rather not see her angry with him.

He strode towards the doors of his apartment, his mind on Emelia as he exited it and headed down through the building and out into the bustling white city, his feet carrying him to his superiors' office on autopilot.

She was strong, incredibly so. Not only had she survived, but she was carrying on with her life, determined to pick up the pieces and put herself back together. He admired her for that. He had seen many mortals come apart, had witnessed despair and depression destroying them. He had seen angels go the same way.

She *was* a fighter, but she wasn't strong enough to fight this battle. The wounds she bore were too fresh and raw, and he knew she hated herself for that. He had seen her battling with herself whenever she woke from a nightmare, desperate to hold herself together. He had seen her guilt whenever she saw one of the other huntresses, born of both the fact she had fared better than them and that Archangel were carrying on as if nothing had happened.

He had witnessed her despair after several meetings with the older male, how she held herself together until she reached her small apartment and how anger consumed her when she was alone, had her hurling objects and yelling words he couldn't hear.

He didn't need to hear her screams to know what tore them from her.

No army was heading to Hell to cut the dragons down.

Her own people wouldn't do as she wanted, so he would.

He would be her sword and he would be her shield too.

He would protect her.

With his last breath if it came to it.

CHAPTER 7

Mundane didn't cover the last two weeks. His superiors had berated him for his tardiness and handed him three thick files to study, all of them strong demons associated with the one he had killed in Shanghai.

It had turned out they weren't as powerful as expected, though.

The three had died too easily, the fights not satisfying him in the slightest. Granted, the last one had got a lucky blow in and had reopened the wound in his side. Which meant he had that demon to thank for his current predicament.

A week off.

Things were looking up.

He was meant to be resting, but he wasn't going to squander the time he had been given.

His elbow ached as he leaned on it, his head propped up on his palm on the long white oak desk in the centre of the library in Echelon headquarters. He flicked the yellowing pages of the thick tome opened in front of him, one of twenty he had plucked from the shelves today, and scanned the scrawl that passed as the penmanship of the angel who had written the account, seeking any mention of dragons hidden among the fading ink.

So far, the knowledge of dragons he had gained from spending the past two days poring over scrolls, books, and parchments boiled down to nothing.

He had learned a lot about various species of demons, though, some of which could prove useful in completing his other mission to bring Sable in so she could serve the Echelon.

He flipped to the next page and sighed as he skimmed it. The prose was more flowery than a cottage garden in England. It offered little information about demons, let alone dragons.

The only information he had found on them had been in translated versions of older texts, ones ancient enough that dragons had still roamed the mortal world when they had been written in old angelic, a language no one had spoken in millennia. They were of little use to him. He needed to know how Hell had affected the dragons and where they had made their home in that dark realm.

He closed the book, shoved it aside, and dragged another in front of him.

He had to keep reading. He had to do something.

Because he felt as if he was going to go out of his mind as he struggled against the gnawing hunger to hunt that goaded him into setting foot in a realm where he would be stripped of his powers.

He couldn't go rushing in there without a clue about the location of the dragon lands, and certainly couldn't risk going there without knowing what effect it would have on him.

But the itch to go there was growing stronger every day.

White feathers obscured the corner of his vision.

He gritted his teeth and waited.

He didn't have to wait long.

"You are quieter and more distant than usual, Fourth Commander." The teasing note in the male's voice didn't stop his mood from darkening as it always did whenever he heard his title now.

It echoed in his mind in Emelia's voice, each word hurled at him like an insult.

Because he didn't have a name.

His vision swam out of focus as his mind leaped on the chance to conjure an image of her, with that pretty pink stain on her cheeks. What had caused it? He had wondered that often over the last few weeks. She had blushed. Why? Because of something he had done?

"Do you think he hears me?" A hand appeared in view now, palm pressing against the desk beside his book as the male leaned back and twisted towards him, evidently seeking the answer from the other angel in the room.

"Probably," the Second Commander grunted, clearly not interested in playing whatever game the Third Commander had in mind.

Tease the Fourth Commander never ended well.

"For a male two hundred years my senior, you act like a fledgling at times," he muttered and brushed the male's hand away when he went to turn the page for him.

"What are you reading? You are always in here reading… I had always thought you a bit of a dull angel, but I had never considered you bookish." The Third Commander made another attempt to turn the page.

He grabbed the male's wrist, locked it tight in his grip and barely bit back the growl as he pushed the Third Commander's hand away.

"You're lucky he didn't bite you." The Second Commander chortled as he moved to one of the windows that overlooked the sprawling white city.

This was the downside to having time off.

His comrades moved Heaven and Earth to irritate him whenever he was around. They were worse than their superiors, had teased him from the moment those angels had dared to make the first joke about his temperament when he had been but two hundred years old and had entered the service of the Echelon.

He took his eyes off the Third Commander's hand for only a second, but it was enough for the male to flip his book closed. The heavy cover slammed shut and he sighed, leaned back in the chair, and tipped his head up to stare at the ceiling, seeking the strength to stop himself from throttling the male.

The last time he had done that, the First Commander had been forced to haul him off the brunet.

"Come out with us." The Third Commander hopped up to sit on the table beside him. "Stop being so boring."

He slid his gaze down over the male, from the wild tips of his short chestnut hair to the form-fitting white and gold tunic he wore and his tight trousers, and riding boots. An outfit that was only meant to be worn during special occasions.

"I did not realise there was to be a celebration today." He looked across the desk to the Second Commander where he stood in front of one of the towering bookcases and found the raven-haired male wearing the same uniform.

The Second Commander's aqua eyes darted to the floor and then the window to his left.

"There is not." The First Commander didn't even spare them all a glance as he strode through the library with purpose, a book tucked against his broad chest as he shoved the fingers of his free hand through his neat white hair, preening it back in a way that screamed of frustration.

Which meant the Second and Third Commanders were at it again.

"I thought you were reprimanded last time you did this?" He looked from one to the other as the library door closed behind the First Commander.

He couldn't blame the male for leaving. It was either that or he had to report his subordinates, and the male preferred not to get his own men into trouble. His normal modus operandi was getting them out of trouble once they got themselves in it.

The Third Commander shrugged. "It was hardly a reprimand. More like a tap on the wrist."

As far as he knew, they had both been banned from the city for three weeks and told that if they were seen in the vicinity of females for the following three weeks that they would be locked away for six months.

"Wear your off-duty clothes if you intend to go into the city to seek females." He leaned his elbow on the desk again and pulled the book back to himself, flipped it open and flicked through the pages until he found the one where he had been.

"But the females love the dress uniforms."

He couldn't really argue with that. Many females in the city sought to breed with the Echelon, believing that bearing their offspring would elevate them within angel society and bring them power, especially if that child was born with a faint echo of the mark he bore on his right wrist. An Echelon in full regalia was an alluring prospect, always drawing gazes and often more than a few attempts to garner their attention.

The way the Third and Second Commanders abused it was making the Echelon appear as if they were seeking to bed a female whenever they wore it.

It was a disgrace to his noble order.

"Come with us." The Third Commander poked him in the shoulder.

The one that was still healing from one of the demons attempting to wrench it out of its socket.

He turned a glare on the male's finger and the Third Commander quickly removed it.

"We know you are off duty. You look tense. You need a little time down in the city." The male attempted to close the book again.

He slapped the Third Commander's hand away and glared up at him.

"Leave it," the Second Commander said, and he was a breath away from thanking him when the male added, "What is it you're so fascinated with researching anyway? I've never seen you reading battle reports before."

"I am not researching." He was researching. They just didn't need to know it.

Neither the Second nor Third Commander looked as if they believed him. He wanted them gone, which meant he needed to find a good excuse, one that they wouldn't be able to see through or poke holes in.

"I am trying to discover whether any Echelon have brought a half-breed Echelon in before. I am to make another attempt to bring the female, Sable, into the fold." Which was true, but he had no intention of rushing to carry out that mission.

Slaying the dragon took priority.

"Imagine that... A female Echelon."

He wasn't surprised when he looked up and found a wicked shimmer to the Third Commander's golden eyes.

"A female Echelon mated to a demon king. Imagine that instead." He pushed the book aside and grabbed a new one.

"He'd hang you by your entrails." The Second Commander chuckled.

"I could take him." The Third Commander looked as if he believed that.

He shook his head at that but didn't take his eyes from the page. "He is powerful, knows we are vulnerable to the demon language, and has taken her to Hell. The Second Commander is correct. The demon would hang you by your entrails."

"So how do you plan to get your hands on her?" The Third Commander slid off his perch and leaned over him, peering at the book spread in front of him. "Certainly not by reading about... What does that even say?"

He wasn't sure. The angel who had written this account had worse handwriting than the last one.

"Something about a..." He squinted at the page. "I believe it says... nymph."

"Are you reading dirty books?" The Third Commander playfully shoved at his shoulder, earning himself a growl as pain flared in it to chase along his nerves down his arm and his back. "You definitely need to bed a female if you are reading second-hand accounts about nymphs."

He rolled his eyes closed and prayed for the strength to stop himself from throttling the male again. "I am not interested in any female you have to offer."

"Ah." There was a decidedly gleeful and triumphant note to that simple sound, one that had him grimacing as he realised why. "So you are interested in *a* female, just not one I can give you."

"Is it the half-breed? Because the demon would probably hang you by your entrails." The Second Commander sounded as amused as he looked when he turned a glare on him. His pale blue eyes were bright with humour that rubbed him the wrong way.

Why did everyone think it was alright to tease and poke fun where he was concerned?

"No, it is not... I have no interest in that female." He should have chosen his words more wisely, because the Second Commander exchanged a look with the Third.

"He definitely has a female in mind."

"No, I do not. Will you both just leave me in peace?" He tried to return his focus to the book.

The Third Commander ripped it away from the text. "Is it that healer angel?"

He lifted his head and arched his right eyebrow as he looked up at the male. "The healer?"

Why would they think he was interested in her?

"I mean... I get it. She is pretty." The Third Commander clapped a hand down on his bad shoulder, again, and grinned as he leaned closer. "Have you slept with her?"

He huffed and batted the male's arm away.

That infuriating grin remained. "You act like it would be reprehensible to do such a thing. I sleep with my healer sometimes. He does too."

He jerked his chin towards the Second Commander.

The male didn't deny it.

They slept with the females sent to heal them?

"I thought everyone slept with them from time to time. You have slept with her. Come on, admit it." The Third Commander looked as if he was going to poke his shoulder again and then thought the better of it. He waggled an eyebrow instead. "I have seen her once or twice, leaving your apartment, her cheeks flushed and eyes bright. You definitely paid her back a little for her services."

He slammed the book, stood so fast the chair shot backwards, toppling to land with a loud bang on the floor, and turned on the male.

"I do not, and will not ever, sleep with my healer." He ground each word out slowly, making sure the male heard them and got the message.

He wasn't interested in the female.

He pivoted on his heel and stormed towards the exit, because he was getting nowhere and the males wouldn't leave him alone if he remained.

"She will be upset to hear that," the Third Commander muttered as the door closed behind him.

He paid the male no heed as he strode along the corridor, his boots loud on the white marble floor. Anger swirled, heating his blood, tearing at his control. He growled as he ploughed his fingers through his black hair and tugged it back. He was wasting time. Reading the accounts was pointless. There was only one way of learning the knowledge he needed in order to track the dragon down swiftly and without endangering himself too much.

Emelia.

He needed to see her again, and not only because she could tell him the things he couldn't find in the books. He needed to see her again because he needed her to soothe him as she had last time, giving him the strength to resist the constant, pressing need to go to Hell.

Or he was going to do something reckless.

Like rushing in where angels were meant to fear to tread.

CHAPTER 8

Emelia grunted as she heaved backwards, her grip slipping on the thick root despite the gloves she wore. She gritted her teeth until they hurt and strained harder. When that didn't succeed in pulling the tangle of roots free from the earth, she wriggled it side to side, up and down, anything to jimmy the damned thing free.

It still didn't give.

She huffed and surrendered, breathing hard as she released the twisted root of the sapling that had decided to make itself at home in the centre of the lawn. It wasn't the only one. This was only the first birch she had decided to tackle. She was beginning to wonder whether a copse of them might look attractive in the sprawling green.

Which was another painful task awaiting her, but one she might actually relish.

The lawn had become overgrown since she had last visited the old manor in the Cambridgeshire countryside. The grass stood over a foot tall, had reached its natural maximum height in the five years since she had stepped foot on the property.

It was going to take a strimmer first and then a mower, or possibly a damned tractor to get the grass back to a semblance of what it had looked like when she had been a child.

She looked off to her right, at the elegant sandstone Georgian manor.

Back when she'd had a family.

She dragged her gaze away from the building, not wanting to see the sad state it was in because of her neglect, and sighed as she stared down at the unholy mess she had made in the lawn while trying to dig up the first sapling.

It had seemed like a good place to start at first. Now she regretted it. She couldn't leave it as it was, with the stub of a trunk poking up at a jaunty angle and the winding roots sticking into the air. Maybe if she dug around the other side of it, she could wriggle it free, or chop enough of the major roots to pull it out of the ground.

She swiped the back of her glove across her sweat-dampened brow and grimaced as gritty dirt ground against her forehead.

A huff burst from her lips as she lowered her hand and looked at her filthy gloves. Fantastic. Well, at least it was only her at the mansion. No one would see the mess she was making of herself.

Electricity charged the air.

She whirled on her heel to face the mansion and then the trees that surrounded the entire garden. As her gaze panned across the empty tiered circular fountain in the centre of the cross junction of the two paved paths that intersected the overgrown formal garden, it caught on a spark of blue-white light.

That arc grew, snapping and twisting, spreading until it was unmistakable.

He was coming.

Just as that thought crossed her mind, the light blazed so bright it blinded her and thunder rolled across the land. She raised her arm to shield her eyes and flinched away, keeping them shut until the light had faded.

Keeping them shut long after then.

Awareness washed over her, his familiar power that charged the air chasing over her skin and shortening her breaths as she fought for calm and control.

She no longer feared that he would hurt her.

Now she feared him for another reason.

Because she couldn't stop thinking about him.

She slowly lowered her arm and opened her eyes, fixing them on him.

She had even dreamed of him.

His bright silver gaze traversed his surroundings, a critical and assessing edge to it. Her gaze traversed him, leisurely roaming over the sculpted planes of his face and his firm mouth, down to his broad shoulders. Her pulse accelerated as she found a tight navy T-shirt hugging his chiselled chest. The morning light accented every honed muscle of it, playing across it in a way she had imagined her fingers doing.

She shut down that line of thought as adrenaline spiked, her heart pounding for another reason, and forced her eyes away from him.

Panic closed her throat and she fought it, didn't want it to overcome her, not now, not when she had been doing so well recently.

"You are not where I expected to find you." His warm baritone rolled over her, as smooth as whisky, smoky and decadent.

When she had wrangled her fears back under control and found the courage to look at him again, he was staring at her forehead.

"Shit," she muttered and quickly rubbed her brow with her bare arm, trying to clean the dirt off. "I was gardening."

"You work here now?" He tossed a puzzled look at the manor house and took a step towards her along the path that ran parallel to it.

He rocked sideways, frowned as he caught himself, and looked down at his feet, lifting one heavy boot off the paving slabs and causing his black jeans to stretch tight over his thigh.

"Some of them are a little wobbly." Another thing she had to fix.

Still, it was good to be busy. Sometimes, she was so worn out at the end of the day that she slept like the dead.

Other times, she dreamed of him.

He arched a black eyebrow at the slabs and tested each one with his foot before trusting it with his weight. It wasn't as if they were going to just fall out beneath him and send him plummeting to his death.

"You did not answer my question." He stopped at the edge of the path, where it met the wild lawn.

Question? She frowned as she tried to remember it.

"Oh." Her eyes widened. "I don't work here."

"So you just thought you would do some gardening at a place where you do not work?" He cast another look at the mansion. "Or is it abandoned? It appears abandoned."

"It is not," she snapped, the hardness of her tone surprising them both judging by the way he arched an eyebrow at her now. She tore her gloves off and jammed them into the pocket of her dark grey sweatpants. The action drew his gaze down, and it lingered, brightened in that way that always sent a hot shiver through her. She cleared her throat and his eyes lifted to meet hers again. Her stomach tightened, squirmed even as she struggled to get the words lined up on her tongue. "I... sort of... own it."

That eyebrow lifted again and he swung his gaze back to the house. "You do not appear to be looking after it very well."

He didn't need to tell her that. She had her reasons, though. Being here was painful, and if she'd had more money saved, she might have gone abroad for her sabbatical, to somewhere sunny and tropical, with turquoise seas and lots of cocktails.

"It is a large house for one female. Do your family not share it?"

She shook her head. "No, they're... gone."

Which was an understatement. Wrenched from her was more appropriate.

"I need a drink. Do you want a drink?" She didn't wait for him to answer.

She waded through the knee-high grass, heading towards the long patio that lined the entire length of the back of the house, stretching over one hundred feet wide. She took the steps up to it and stopped at the rickety cast-iron table she had found in one of the outhouses. It only had one chair, and the last time she had sat on it, her backside had come away covered in rust flakes.

She crouched and opened the lid of the cooler she had set on the flagstones this morning and grabbed a soda from the myriad of cans. The beer was tempting, but it was far too early for drinking. Unless he started probing about anything. Then, she might self-medicate a little.

Emelia cracked the can open and straightened, twisting to face the way she had come and expecting to find him there right behind her.

He wasn't.

He stood by the copse of saplings, peering at her handiwork.

"It's a bitch." She shrugged when he glanced at her, and it hit her that she didn't mind him looking at her now. She actually liked the way he would look at her from time to time, would even let his eyes linger if she didn't disturb him. "I think the roots are tangled with the other trees. I can't get the damned thing out."

He leaned forwards, gripped the sawn-off trunk with one hand, his biceps flexing beneath the sleeve of his tight T-shirt, and casually pulled.

Her eyes shot wide as the entire root system popped free, cutting through the earth in places to leave streaks of dirt in the grass she had trampled down.

He looked at the mass of roots as he held the remains of the tree aloft, and then turned his head towards her and hit her with a killer smile.

"Show-off," she muttered and sank to her backside on the first step. "Don't suppose you want to give the others the same treatment?"

He dropped the vanquished tree at his feet and assessed the other ones. "Why do you want them removed?"

The more she looked at them, the less she was sure of the answer to that question.

Because they hadn't been there when life had been good here, when she had lived here and had been happy?

She couldn't get those days back, not even if she put everything back to how it had been then. Maybe change was a good thing and would allow her to come to love this place again as it entered a different era, similar to how it had been in those halcyon days, but different enough that she could be here without it constantly reminding her of everything she had lost.

"Leave them," she said as he looked as if he might pull the other trees up.

He nodded and moved away from them, striding towards her across the lawn, his long legs devouring the distance between them.

When he reached her, she jerked her chin towards the cooler. "There's drinks if you want one."

He shook his head and sat a short distance from her, and the few feet between them felt like an ocean. When had she started wanting a man to be closer to her than arm's length again?

She reminded herself he wasn't a man. He was an angel. His wings might be hidden, but she had seen them, and she couldn't allow herself to forget they existed. It would be so easy to pretend he was just a man, not an immortal, but she would be a fool to do such a thing.

He was powerful and dangerous.

Pretending he was anything other than that would be a mistake.

"Why do you keep hiding your wings from me?" She let the question slip from her lips and took a sip of her drink as his gaze landed on her profile.

He was silent for a long minute before he sighed. "I thought perhaps it would make you more comfortable."

It did, but she didn't want to be comfortable around him. She needed to remain distant from him. She needed to protect herself. To do both of those things, she needed to see him as the angel he was.

The warrior he was.

"Let them out." She took another mouthful of her soda.

"No." The firmness of that denial surprised her, and she glanced out of the corner of her eye at him.

His black eyebrows dipped low, the corners of his mouth twisting downwards as he turned his cheek to her.

She had pissed him off. Because he knew she wanted to use what he was as a barrier between them, a reason to keep him at arm's length.

"Why are you here?" She swirled the drink in her can, staring at it now, and tried to push away her negative emotions and the fear that she was beginning to despise.

She was weak. Not in mind, apparently, but she *was* weak. She kept letting fear get the better of her.

She sighed and tipped her head back to stare at the blue sky.

She had let fear get the better of her long before now. It was the reason she had stayed away from her family estate. She feared she would end up like her parents if she came to this place, had convinced herself there was some sort of curse on it, one that would drive her to take her own life too.

"Why are you here?" he parroted softly, and she had the feeling he was trying to get her to talk again, to reveal things to him that would only bring him closer to her.

On a long sigh, she let her chin fall and looked out over the grounds as she rested her arm on her bent knee and let the can dangle from her fingertips.

Talking about what had driven her away from this place was always painful, but it was better than the alternative. If she didn't talk about her family and her reasons for letting the house fall into neglect, he would want her to talk about the dragon.

"I took a few weeks off. Paid leave. Mark thought it was a good idea." Would he let her leave it at that?

Of course he wouldn't.

"You do not seem to visit this place often. Because your work at the hunter organisation keeps you busy?"

She could have nodded at that and he probably would have let it go, but her mouth had other ideas.

"I don't like it here." She frowned at her can as she rocked it back and forth, feeling the contents slosh side to side. "I love it... and I hate it at the same time."

"So, why keep it?"

A reasonable question.

She shrugged. "It's all I have left of them."

"Your family?" He edged closer.

Her chest tightened at the thought of answering that question and she swiftly turned to face him, planting her free hand on the paving slabs that separated them. "Can't you just do that looking-into-my-eyes thing and see it for yourself?"

She stared into his eyes, convinced that if she did, he would spare her the pain of speaking about her past.

The corners of his lips curled slightly, a regretful edge to that half-smile as he shook his head. "Your mind is a little... *closed*."

It was?

"So open it." She wasn't sure how it worked, but the last time he had looked deeply into her eyes, he had seen things. "Like you did last time."

"Your mind was open to me that time."

It had been?

She didn't like the idea she had been walking around with her mind open to anyone who possessed his talent.

"Why is it closed now?" She swigged her soda. "I don't remember closing it."

"You are more certain of yourself. Stronger now. Your mind is falling back into order. It was in chaos before." He leaned back, planted his hands behind him, and stared at the sky, his noble profile to her.

He did that whenever he wanted her to be relaxed around him, to make himself non-threatening. She had figured out that much about him. She wasn't going to complain. It was strange, but nice, feeling so at peace and calm in the presence of a man.

A relief.

She had thought she would always be jittery around them now.

But being around him felt... good.

It felt normal.

He didn't poke and prod her, or make her feel as if she was liable to break. He didn't treat her as if she was fragile or weak. He didn't pity her or look at her as if she didn't belong, or something was wrong with her.

He just looked at her as if she was another person.

No, that wasn't strictly true.

There was heat in his eyes at times, an edge to them that made her feel he liked looking at her, that he found pleasure in it and in her presence. It made her feel as if he cared little about others, but she was different. Special.

Special enough that he wanted to slay a dragon for her.

"My mother would have loved you," she said as she dragged her eyes away from him, and surprise washed through her when a smile teased her lips, unfamiliar warmth rising inside her with it. She felt his gaze land on her, a hot caress that had her blood heating in a way that had panicked her the last time they had met. "She was always a sucker for romantic white knight shit."

"White knight?" He looked as puzzled as his tone had sounded when she risked a glance at him.

"Slaying a dragon for me? It doesn't get more white knight than that." Or more romantic. Maybe this wasn't a good subject. "It's the focus of many fairy tales."

"This is not a fairy tale, though."

It wasn't, and Emelia didn't expect any happy endings in life. Her past had taught her that much.

"My folks thought they'd been living a fairy tale." She set her can down, brought her knees up, and hugged them to her chest.

She picked at a frayed patch on her grey sweats as she stared at the garden and remembered it in its heyday, back when her mother had spent hours each day working on it with the gardener.

"There were roses in that area once, beyond the wall." She pointed to the golden dry stone wall that cut across the end of the lawn, where the path that started from the patio and cut past the fountain led. "I used to play in there while she worked, and she tried to teach me things. How to care for different flowers. How to grow herbs and vegetables and tend to the fruit trees in the orchard. I never listened."

"But you do share her affinity for nature." His soft voice drifted around her, and she nodded, relaxing again as she remembered little things about her past.

"I started helping out when I was a teen. Every summer, I would come home and work in the garden with my mum. There was always something that needed doing. The boxwood hedges in the formal garden would need pruning to stop them from growing higher than a foot around the displays. Or new flowers would need to be planted. Or the roses would need pruning. Every day I was doing something." She rested her hands on her knees. "I think it was good for Mum to have company."

"Your father was absent?" He edged closer, and she didn't mind, actually found herself wanting him a little closer still.

"He was always working. Running the company in London. He would come home on weekends." She used to hurl herself into his arms every time.

"You mentioned you came home each summer. You did not live here?"

She shook her head, frowned as a strand of her dark hair fell down and tucked it behind her ear. "I went to boarding school, so I was away from home most of the year."

"They send children away from their homes?" He sounded horrified by that.

"What, angels don't have boarding schools?" She almost smiled at him. "It was a good education. The best, really. My parents just wanted to give me the best shot at being happy in life."

"But you do not seem happy. Being here saddens you. Why?" His gaze left her, and she ached for it to come back, for him to look at her again, because it had been comforting to know she wasn't alone here, in this place.

In this world.

"I think I had rose-tinted glasses on my entire life before my parents died. I had everything I wanted... a horse... a pool... all the things a rich kid needs... except for independence. Looking back, I can see how controlling my parents were, my father in particular." She rubbed at the frayed patch again, needing to do something with her hands to distract her from what she was saying. "Don't get me wrong, I loved my parents... but they demanded too much from me. I was sent to study at Cambridge, and both the teachers and my parents expected me to do great things."

She wanted to laugh, or maybe cry, as she thought about what university had been like.

"I busted my backside, but doing great in the subjects my parents had all but picked for me was impossible."

"Did you fail?"

She nodded. "But not because I had bad grades. I failed because I had to ditch uni when my father's company went bankrupt... and he took his..."

She couldn't say it after all.

She tugged at the threads on her knee, fiercer now as her past crept up on her, the pain that refused to fade rising back to the fore.

"Emelia," he murmured, as soft as a whisper, and she shook her head, because she didn't want his pity or condolences.

"He took the easy way out." She ground the words from between clenched teeth as the backs of her eyes burned. "He gave up, and my mother's fairy tale turned into a horror story. She... It was gateway drugs at first... to calm her or take the pain away, but soon it was the harder stuff. I went back to uni to get my things so I could move back in with her and help her through it. I wanted to get her off that shit and show her life could go on. We still had each other."

Her voice cracked. She sucked down a shuddering breath and shook her head again when she felt him move. Not because she didn't want his comfort, but because he couldn't touch her. Her throat closed at just the thought, and panic gripped her. She tried to breathe through it, covered her fear of being touched by a man with the fact she was upset and struggling to talk about what had happened to her family.

"I came home, and she... I found her..." She wasn't sure she could say the rest, but his gaze rested heavily on her. Expectant. He wanted to know what had happened. She gathered her strength and forced the words out so he wouldn't make her talk. "It was a coke overdose."

She had lost both of her parents just months apart. Her mother had gone downhill so quickly that Emelia had been left reeling. She didn't remember all the meetings with lawyers, or anything people had said to her. At the end of the roller coaster, when things had finally slowed down and smoothed out, she had been left with only the house and a small amount of money.

"Look at me, Emelia," he husked, and she sucked down a breath before she slowly turned her face towards him and lifted her eyes to his.

They were bright silver again, shining and swirling, with gold edging his irises.

"Relax. Breathe slowly, evenly. Fall into each breath and do not fight the pull."

She did as instructed, and with each breath, she seemed to fall deeper into his eyes, just as she had that night at Archangel. The world around her dropped away as she lost herself in his shimmering eyes, let herself go, and did something she had thought impossible.

Trusted him.

Warmth filled her, as comforting as when she woke wrapped in a duvet that was just the right temperature, sated from a restful sleep but unwilling to leave, savouring every moment beneath the blanket.

Light followed, flooding her in a way that left no dark spaces in her heart.

She swayed closer to him, fell deeper still.

"You have had a difficult life. I see that now." His voice was distant, swimming in her ears as if he was speaking to her while she was underwater.

Heat streaked her cheeks, a terrible sense of loss welling inside her, but she couldn't blink, couldn't take her eyes away from his.

"Emelia."

She tensed as she felt the nearness of his hand, the gentle warmth of it close to her face, and reared back.

The connection shattered.

She gripped the hem of her dark-grey T-shirt and scrubbed her cheeks with it, wiping away the tears.

"I apologise." He drew back and turned away from her.

Silence stretched between them.

Emelia twisted around, reached, caught the handle of the cooler, and dragged it to her across the paving slabs.

He glanced at her as she flipped the lid open and rifled through the contents, heading towards the bottom where she had stashed the beers.

She didn't look at him as she cracked one open and took a large mouthful. She needed something to take the edge off and she didn't care if he judged her for it.

"Can we talk about something else now?" She gulped down the ice-cold beer and reached for another. "Pick a subject."

"The dragon."

CHAPTER 9

"No." Emelia's flat denial rang in the early afternoon air as she crushed the can she had been drinking and tossed it into the container beside her.

She had asked him to choose another subject and he had. He had learned more about her, had seen how her parents' deaths had broken her, and how she had been forced to fend for herself. He now knew why she often practiced boxing.

After losing her parents, she had moved to a small apartment above a shop in Cambridge and had started working at a nightclub. In order to keep herself safe from the males who had frequently bothered her while she tended the bar, she had taken to boxing, using it both to train her body and as an outlet for her feelings.

But he was here to learn about the dragon too.

"I don't want to talk about him." She opened another can and took a sip, drinking it slower than the last.

He could smell the alcohol in it, and the thought he had driven her to drink didn't sit well with him.

"So let me see what you did."

She refused to look at him.

"Emelia, I need to know more about him. Where he lived. His powers."

"You want to know one power a dragon has?" she snapped and her hand shook as she lifted the drink to her lips again. "They can use it to make a woman compliant by looking into her eyes."

He reared back. "Emelia, I would not do such a thing. I cannot do such a thing. Your mind is strong, and you can easily shut me out if you want. I cannot manipulate you, so I cannot hurt you."

"Would you do it to another woman?" She flinched at her own words and cast him an apologetic look. "I'm sorry... I just... thinking about him..."

She shook her head.

Fire rolled through his blood as he ran back over what she had said. The air around him darkened as the urge to call his blade to his hand and form a bridge to Hell surged through him. He breathed through it, taming the dark need to hunt and kill, afraid it would terrify her and she would come to view him as a monster too.

After how well he had been doing with her, such a blow might kill him.

He held back his temper so it wouldn't affect his surroundings, but he couldn't keep the growl from his voice. "Did *he* use such power against you?"

She briefly shook her head, causing that rogue strand to slip from behind her ear again. He followed her fingers as she swept it back, gently hooking it behind her ear, mesmerised by the action and wanting to know what it would feel like to do that for her.

He was glad the dragon hadn't manipulated her in that way, but he didn't like what he saw in her eyes as he shifted his to meet them.

She had drawn a parallel between him and the bastard, and it had rattled her, shaking her trust in him.

"You should go." She set her can down near the container and rose to her feet. She dusted her backside down and muttered, "I need a nap."

"You are making excuses now. If you want me to leave, just demand that I leave. Do not lie to me. I know you have not been sleeping well. I doubt you are going to have a nap."

Her pulse went off the scale.

She twisted to face him, her green eyes widening as realisation dawned in them.

Her eyebrows dipped, a wrinkle forming between them as she narrowed her gaze on him. "How did you know where I was?"

He stood, because he could see where this was going. It had been a mistake to casually comment on the fact she hadn't been sleeping well.

"Emelia—" he started, holding his hands up by his sides.

"Have you been *spying* on me?" She spoke over him, the horror that filled her eyes lacing her voice too.

Damn.

He wrestled with how to word things, what to tell her, aware that the longer he let the silence stretch between them, the angrier she would be and the less likely she was to understand.

"I do not mean harm by it," he blurted to shatter the tense silence, and she planted her hands on her hips, an expectant edge to her expression. "I can turn my gaze to anyone, and I look at you from time to time. I need to know you are safe, Emelia… and I cannot… sometimes I cannot… I…"

He sucked down a long, deep breath.

"Seeing you calms me."

She frowned.

He raked his fingers over his short black hair and turned away from her, needing room to move without frightening her, because he couldn't keep still. He needed to pace, or he feared his nerve might fail.

He couldn't bring himself to look at her as he confessed this either, because there was a chance it might drive her away from him, and he didn't want to see her looking at him as if she despised him.

He didn't want that to be his final memory of her.

He wanted to remember her as she had been just minutes ago—relaxed, almost smiling, calm around him and trusting him.

"Sometimes I am a breath away from teleporting to Hell," he confessed and scrubbed his left hand over his face as he stopped with his back to her, every muscle in his body cranked tight and his heart pounding. This would either be a colossal mistake, one that would destroy whatever fragile bond they shared, or it would be a good move, one that might bring her closer to him. "So I turn my focus to you… I watch you going about your life… and I see you are safe and well… and it gives me the strength I need."

Her pulse accelerated, the acrid scent of her fear swamping her sweeter perfume.

Damn. Colossal mistake it was.

"You can't… Sometimes I'm… I'm…" The rising note of panic in her voice had him wanting to turn towards her, to comfort and reassure her somehow, but he couldn't muster the courage to do it. "You can't look at me then. I'm… *exposed*."

It struck him that she thought he looked at her at times when she was nude.

Was there a level above colossal mistake?

He gritted his teeth and clenched his fists, and forced himself to face her, because he needed to fix this, couldn't let her imagination run wild and paint him as some kind of pervert so she could draw another parallel between him and the dragon.

"I have never seen you like that, Emelia," he murmured, hoping the softness of his voice would calm her as it had before and make her listen to him. "I would never—"

"You can't know what I'm doing!" She picked the can up in a lightning-fast move and hurled it at him.

He grimaced as it hit him square in the chest, splashing the sharp-smelling liquid all over him so his T-shirt stuck to his skin.

He sucked down a subtle breath to keep his temper in check and held his hands out in front of him, because she was in a full-blown panic now, her green eyes wild and pulse off the scale as she faced him.

"The process of turning my gaze to someone is twofold, Emelia." He kept his voice calm and even, somehow managing it despite the turbulent emotions that battered him, ones that were strange and powerful, had him desperate to make her listen. She couldn't breathe because she was panicking, and he couldn't breathe because he feared she was going to tell him to leave and never return. "I connect with you in a way that allows me to sense the way of things before I connect in a visual manner. Think of it as a sixth sense angels possess."

It didn't calm her as expected.

"So you *know* when I'm naked?" She backed away from him and looked ready to pluck another can from the container and launch it at him.

He shook his head and clawed his hair back with both hands as frustration got the better of him. "No... I am not explaining this well. I am not aware of exactly what you are doing or how you are dressed. It is not like that. I can feel... your mood, perhaps. I can feel what you do—"

"And what do I feel in the times when you don't look at me?" she interjected, a flicker of fear in her eyes now that made him want to brush his fingers across her cheek in a touch she wouldn't welcome.

One that would only make things worse.

He swallowed and murmured, "Vulnerable... and it angers me now that I know the reason for it. I hate that you feel at risk whenever you are undressed."

She cast him a black look, one laced with hurt, and shook her head as she turned towards the house and walked away from him, her hands balled into fists at her sides.

"I am sorry, Emelia." Pointless words, ones that would get him nowhere, but ones he needed to say.

She stopped.

"I will not turn my gaze to you again," he said, the last threads of his hope hanging on her believing him and accepting that, and allowing him to visit her again because of it.

She hesitated.

Murmured.

"You can look."

Surprise washed through him, carrying away some of his fear, and he stared at her, unsure what to say.

"Why?" It fell from his lips, filled with the need burning inside him, a desire to understand why she would allow him to watch her whenever he needed the sight of her to soothe him after she had reacted so violently to the thought of it happening.

"Because the alternative is something I don't want." She shyly glanced over her shoulder at him. "I don't want you to go to Hell."

That touched him, together with the fact she would allow him to do something that unsettled her in order to keep him away from a place that might be the death of him.

"But I do really want you to leave… because I have a lot of work to do and I'm getting nothing done with you around." She smiled faintly. "Unless you want to pitch in with the gardening?"

If it made up for upsetting her, he could get his hands dirty, although he didn't know what he was doing. He hoped she was a good teacher.

"What would you like me to do?" He ventured a step towards her, trying not to look too eager to hear his punishment for upsetting her.

She walked to the house and picked up a tool that was leaning against the creamy stone. He wasn't sure what it was. A long pipe attached the bulky end she held to a flat plastic disc at the other. She checked that end, did something that allowed her to tug more thick red string out of the device, and then walked to the table, where she picked up another item. She waved the padded semicircle with two weighty-looking plastic cups attached to each end at him.

"Since you slowed me down, and might have pissed me off, you pulled strimmer duty." She strolled over and shoved the tool at him.

He took it, careful to avoid brushing her skin with his so he didn't spook her. It smelled strongly of gasoline to him. He was still inspecting it when she tossed the other item at him, and he reacted with all the speed of his kind, easily snatching it out of the air without even lifting his head.

"Those go over your ears." She pointed to the cups, and then at the tool. "And that… well… you don't get to leave until this lawn is tamed."

He looked around at the enormous expanse of tall grass he had presumed was a meadow. With such a paltry tool, he would be here all night. It would be quicker to burn it with the flames of his sword, although he doubted Heaven would approve of him using angelic fire to tame a wilderness. He also doubted Emelia would approve.

Although it saddened her, this place meant a lot to her, and she would be distraught if anything happened to it. The fact she hadn't sold it in the years since her parents' deaths was proof of that.

When she moved closer to show him how to use the tool, her scent invading his senses and filling his lungs, he forgot about doing things quickly.

If it took days to cut the grass, he wouldn't care.

Because being near her was fast becoming his own personal heaven.

CHAPTER 10

It had been three days since Emelia had last seen him. What was he doing? She couldn't keep her thoughts away from him as she packed up her gardening tools, tossing them into the large purple plastic bucket she had bought on her last supply run into the nearest town. Was he alright?

When he had confessed the reason behind why he watched her sometimes, she had seen the strain in his eyes, how the need to go to Hell and fight on her behalf weighed on him. She had seen it whenever she had looked into his striking silver eyes since then. He could smile, frown, glare, and even laugh, and she would still see it, lurking in the depths of his eyes, a need he couldn't shake.

Could only deny.

Had he watched her since leaving? She tilted her head back. Was he watching her now?

She stilled and stared at the porch that stretched the length of the rear of the sandstone mansion.

At the steps where they had sat and talked.

He had come back to finish the task of strimming the lawn the day after, and had even mown it without complaining, stopping from time to time to make a passing comment or enquire as to what she was doing. He had a keen mind, seemed to enjoy learning new things, and she appreciated that he had kept things light between them, especially since she had seen in his eyes that he wanted to ask her again about Zephyr.

She rubbed her right shoulder where her T-shirt concealed the worst of her scars, a habit she couldn't quite shake. Cold slithered down her spine as she brought her fingers away and risked a glance at them, and she gritted her teeth as she mentally berated herself. She wasn't there now. Blood wouldn't be staining her fingertips. It was over.

She was home.

She lifted her head and took in the building that held her favourite memories, the best days of her life, using the sight of it to purge the fear that still gripped her from time to time.

She didn't dream of the dragon anymore.

She dreamed of the angel.

And each dream was hotter than the last.

Emelia grabbed the two handles on the soft plastic bucket and carried it in front of her as she ambled across the neat lawn.

A sigh escaped her lips.

She wasn't sure what to do.

There was no denying she was attracted to the angel, felt a pull towards him whenever he was near, and found it difficult to keep her eyes off him. There was no denying he felt that same pull towards her. He had tried to gloss over his reasons for wanting to hunt Zephyr and avenge her, giving her a multitude of excuses that she had seen straight through.

She knew the truth.

He needed to kill the dragon because he had hurt her.

"What am I going to do with you, TeeDeePee?" She shook her head, and a faint smile danced on her lips. "We need to give you a better name, that's for sure."

But not George.

And definitely not Jorge.

The way he had said it, rumbling 'hor-hay' in his delicious deep voice, had stirred a wicked and shocking heat in her that had made her curse him in her mind. It had sounded far too sexy, something an angel shouldn't be.

Although, there was no denying he was sexy.

Handsome.

Charming in his own strange way.

She had learned things about him in the two days he had spent with her at the mansion. He liked new challenges, was devoted to his duty, and could burn a demon to ashes with a mere touch thanks to the fancy black cross on the inside of his right wrist that had been there since birth. The last one was getting filtered straight to Sable, just in case her friend didn't know the power of her mark.

He didn't have a family that he could recall, and had worked with the Echelon for most of his life, having spent his formative years learning and carrying out other tasks before ascending to the rank of Echelon in order to replace an angel who had fallen in combat.

His mention of an angel falling had distracted her enough that she had forgotten to ask him about his age and had instead asked if he had meant fallen, like the Devil, or fallen like dead, which had prompted a conversation over a cold soda that had stuck with her, haunting her at times when she was alone and her mind drifted to him.

Echelon could fall.

In Hell, she had heard the rumours of fallen angels. The demon king, Thorne, had tried to prepare the Archangel hunters who had assembled under Sable's lead to assist him in his war. He had told them there was a chance the Fifth Realm, their enemy, might have employed fallen angels in their ranks, and that if they saw one, they were to immediately retreat to the castle.

Apparently, fallen angels were extremely powerful and even demons didn't like to tangle with them.

TeeDeePee had gone one further and told her they weren't only extremely powerful, they were the most powerful beings in Hell.

"I really need to give you a better name," she muttered. "You're tall and dark, and were a little pompous… but TeeDeePee sounds stupid."

EffSee for Fourth Commander didn't sound much better.

Thunder rumbled in the distance and she glanced in the direction it had come from. Black clouds filled the horizon, slowly rolling towards her. For a moment, she had feared he had heard her and had come to argue with her again about his name.

For a moment, she had hoped he was back.

There was a flash this time, and she counted the seconds in her head between it and the next ominous growl of thunder. It wouldn't be long before it reached her. It looked like she was calling it early today, and it was only just past four. She had hoped to get at least some pruning done in the tangle of thorny brambles that had once been the rose garden.

She sighed and let her mind run with finding him a suitable name she could call him, at least in private, as she dumped the bucket near the back door of the mansion, tipping it upside down to provide some shelter from the rain for her tools. She made her way along the rear of the building, heading towards the east side, where her father had constructed a more modern pool house.

Her current home until Archangel called her back into service.

Mark had allowed her all the time she wanted on the proviso that if they needed her, or if she felt she was ready, she returned to London. She had agreed, because she wasn't ready to leave Archangel. It was still her family.

She skirted the empty outdoor pool and opened the door of the pale stone building that most people would have thought was an expensive detached home rather than an area for changing, with a hot tub on the ground floor and a guest apartment on the upper one.

The hot tub tempted her as she passed it, but she headed up the stairs instead, into the small kitchen-diner. She walked through it, shedding her clothes as she went, her steps slowing as a desire formed, one that would have startled her just weeks ago and sent her into a panic.

He couldn't see her when she was vulnerable, when she felt exposed.

What if she could let him see?

Her hands shook at the thought as she halted in the middle of the cream-and-red living room.

Did she want him to see?

The answer hit her like the thunderbolt that struck outside.

Yes.

She wanted him to see her, not naked—she wasn't ready for that yet—but she wanted him to see *something*. A sign that he wasn't alone and she wanted him too? Was it dangerous to let him see such a thing? She shook that fear away. It wasn't. She had noticed more than once that he was careful to avoid skin contact with her, that he distanced himself whenever he wanted to touch her to reassure her when she was in danger of drowning under the crushing tide of her memories. He didn't want to frighten her.

He wouldn't act on whatever she was brave enough to show him.

He would let her be the one in control, as he always had.

She would set the rules.

It was thrilling in a way.

She strode through the bedroom to the bathroom and ran the water into the clawfoot tub in the middle of it. Her pulse fluttered, nerves trying to get the better of her as the water ran and bubbles laced the surface. All he was going to see was a hint of shoulder, nothing he probably hadn't seen before, and the fact she was having a nice relaxing bath.

How would he react to that?

Her heart skipped a beat for a different reason, heat flashing through her as her mind traversed the same paths as her dreams had been recently. A sense of power rushed through her as she imagined him turning his gaze to her, as she pictured his fierce reaction to the sight of her in the bath, how his eyes would gain that gold shimmer as they brightened, the one she had realised was sparked by more than anger.

Desire turned his eyes gold too.

Would he ache to see more? Would he grow *hard*?

Panic crashed over her at that thought, and she breathed through it, chanted in her head that he wouldn't hurt her and that this was different. She wanted him too. She couldn't let what had happened to her control her anymore. She didn't want to be caged by her past, despised how deeply the things Zephyr had done affected her and how they had changed her.

She didn't want to be that Emelia.

She wanted to be her old self.

The Emelia who had been happy, who had felt strong, and who had been brave.

Three things she would feel if she went through with this.

She twisted the taps and paused as she stared at the bubbles. Was tempting an angel wrong? He had been tempting her since the moment she had met him, and he hadn't once said it was a sin for him to desire her, or her to desire him.

She pushed that fear aside. If he wasn't allowed to desire her, he wouldn't be looking at her in the bath, that was for sure. He was a man of rigid principles who obeyed the laws of his kind. She doubted he would go off the rails because of her. Besides, Sable was a half-breed, and he hadn't been fazed by that at all. He hadn't seemed to care that she was the product of an angel breeding with a human.

God, she was thinking too much.

She stripped off the last of her clothes, stepped into the water, and sank into it.

She could do this. She wanted him to see her. She wanted to show him that she trusted him and that she did want him too.

She paused again.

She just wasn't sure how.

Emelia focused on what he had said to her—that she felt vulnerable, and that was why he never saw her when she was naked.

"I'm not vulnerable," she whispered, feeling like an idiot.

He probably wasn't looking at her anyway. This would probably be for nothing. No, not nothing. Even if he didn't see her, it was helping her. She felt stronger already, more in control of herself and her life. She was being brave again, taking command and doing what she really wanted, without letting her past hold her back.

She closed her eyes, sucked down a deep breath, and let it slowly flow out of her as she relaxed against the back of the white tub.

She wasn't vulnerable.

She was in control.

She wanted this, and she was allowing it. It was her decision. Her choice. She slowly opened her eyes and fixed them on the ceiling.

Because she had all the power now.

CHAPTER 11

He pushed the book away from him with a sigh and rose from his desk in the office of his apartment. His back ached as he stretched his arms above him, clasping his hands together. The books were still yielding little information on dragons, although he had learned a few things about Hell in the new tomes he had borrowed from the library, bringing them to his quarters so he could be alone with them.

Mostly because he was tired of the Third Commander harassing him whenever he set foot in the library. He was beginning to suspect the male was waiting for him just so he could prod and poke and tell him about all his recent conquests in the city.

The Third Commander wasn't exactly the sort of angel who took study seriously, and normally, the male was more likely to be found in the common area of the building, sharpening his sword.

He felt sure that if it wasn't for the Second Commander's influence, the male would have been kicked out of the Echelon centuries ago and would probably be off whoring himself in a fae town somewhere in the mortal world.

He pushed thoughts of the male away just as he had shoved aside the book, and grimaced as he rolled his neck and spread his white wings. His wing sockets cramped in protest and he gritted his teeth and carefully shifted his wings, trying to loosen the tight muscles. Sitting for hours was definitely a bad thing.

Although, he ached far less than he had on returning from helping Emelia with her gardening. If the constant bending, stretching, and lifting took its toll on him, he couldn't imagine how fiercely it took its toll on her more delicate mortal body.

Leaving her alone the past few days had been one of the hardest things he had ever done, but he had wanted to learn more about Hell and the effects it had on his kind, and that was something she couldn't help him with. Plus, he hoped that if he left her alone, she wouldn't turn him away when he returned to question her about the dragon again.

He dreamed of the bastard whenever he slept now, witnessed the male through Emelia's eyes as he relived twisted versions of her memories, ones far darker than she had revealed to him.

His hand twitched at his side, the urge to call his blade to him strong as he thought about the male. Zephyr. A name was a good lead, and he knew more about what to expect when he entered Hell now. It was as good a time as any to venture there and see if he could locate the dragon.

Sense told him to hold back and wait, to give Emelia more time to recover in the hope she would be able to tell him where to find the dragon. It would cut down the amount of time he needed to be in Hell, reducing his exposure to the darkness infesting that realm and the dangers it possessed.

The more he considered that, the less it seemed like a good thing. The need to hunt the male was growing stronger each day, but that wasn't the only reason he wanted to step foot in Hell as soon as possible.

Part of him wanted to know if he could grow accustomed to the effects it had on him if he had enough exposure to it.

Getting the dragon's location from Emelia would be useful, but if he rushed straight there, the drain Hell would have on him would still be fresh and new, stripping him of his strength and leaving him vulnerable to the male.

Could spending small amounts of time in Hell be beneficial to him? It would spare Emelia the pain of talking about the dragon, would assuage his need to do something about the bastard by making him feel he was finally making progress, and it might allow him to acclimatise to the effects that realm had on him. Three very good reasons to do his own investigation in that realm, leaving Emelia out of it.

Emelia.

Was she well?

Did she think about him as often as he thought about her?

His sleeping hours might be filled with the dragon, but his waking ones were filled with her. It was impossible to keep his mind off her, his thoughts away from running over every facet of her, all the things he had learned and how her expression and eyes changed with every emotion she experienced.

His beautiful little mortal.

He glanced at his bare feet before he could consider what he was doing, driving through the layers of the building to the mortal plane, his gaze fixing on her location. She wasn't in the garden. Rain lashed the grounds, lightning striking around the manor. Was she in there?

His eyes shifted unerringly to the smaller house beside the pool.

He focused on it and moved through the roof, to the top floor, and stopped dead.

His mouth went bone dry.

Heart thundered.

He swallowed hard, but it did nothing to ease either of those things.

Emelia lay reclined in a bath, her eyes closed and her wild chestnut locks tangled in a messy damp knot at the back of her head. White bubbles clung to her chest, spotting her creamy shoulders in places, and her hands glistened with moisture as she rested them along the sides of the tub.

His breaths came faster as he tried to tear his eyes away but found he couldn't.

Because she didn't feel afraid, or vulnerable. She was relaxed, and that was the reason he was able to view her this way.

With those bubbles slipping over her skin as she moved her arms beneath the water, parting as she lifted her hands to flash a hint of a knee and her thigh.

He groaned, the low sound rising unbidden into his throat as she raised her hands and gently scrubbed her neck, the action causing her chest to lift and her breasts to crest the surface of the water. The infernal bubbles covered them, but his breath hitched as they began to slide down from the peaks.

He growled as she sank back under the water just as the bubbles were about to slip off her breasts entirely to reveal the buds of her nipples to him, stealing the pleasure of seeing them from him.

What was she doing?

Did she know he could see this?

She tilted her head back, her eyes still closed, a smattering of suds on her rosy cheeks as she sighed.

Her lips moved silently.

Sent him reeling as he read them.

Are you watching?

Any desire to look away dissipated in an instant, a new feeling replacing the shock of seeing her in the bath. He wanted to keep watching. He felt like a voyeur, knew this was wrong of him and he should look away, but he didn't want to. He wanted to keep his eyes on her, couldn't breathe as he anticipated her next move, silently willed her to flash another hint of pale skin at him.

It was torment, but damn, it pleasured him like nothing else could or ever had.

Anger surged through him, aimed at himself for a change. What was he doing? He curled his hands into fists and clenched them so hard his arms shook as his muscles tensed. This was wrong of him. He had to look away. He was violating her by doing this.

She mouthed something else, something that shattered his entire world and all his restraint with it.

I wanted you to see.

He swallowed thickly at that, was instantly cranked tight by a swift and powerful need, one that startled him, because he felt sure he had never experienced it before now.

He scrubbed a hand over his face and tried to ignore how hard he was in his trousers. His cock throbbed, bucked, and screamed for him to palm it, to relieve the staggering ache that was bordering on painful. It took all his considerable will, but he resisted the urge to touch himself, because this moment wasn't about that.

This was about her revealing that she trusted him.

It was about her taking a leap that was brave and bold after everything she had endured.

He wouldn't ruin the sanctity of it.

When she slowly opened her green eyes and seemed to look right at him, even when that was impossible, he sensed her mood shifting, the nerves rising inside her.

He found the strength to look away, to shut the link between them and give her privacy.

His aching erection still demanded attention.

He dropped his hand to it and was on the verge of stroking it through his white trousers when he stopped himself. His hand hovered over it, his entire body trembling as he pictured her in the bath. The image was stamped on his mind so deeply that he wasn't sure he would ever forget it.

It would be his new torment.

One that might prove dangerous.

He couldn't let that hunger she ignited in him build into something he couldn't control. He couldn't let the vision of her and his imagination collide to push him over the edge. He needed to be careful around her, no matter how fiercely he needed her.

He hadn't had much experience with females beyond interacting with the angels he met in the city and the healers who were sent to him whenever he returned injured. He had been too focused on his duty to court them, had little time for socialising because of that duty, and wasn't exactly a good companion on the best of days. His temperament took care of that, although something about Emelia mellowed it.

Still, he was better suited to hunting and killing than wooing.

What if his lack of experience with the gentler sex allowed the hunger he felt whenever he was around her, the urges he had a difficult time controlling, to overwhelm him when he was around her?

He didn't want to frighten Emelia, and he feared he would be too rough when lost in the throes of his passion, rather than being gentle with her as she needed.

Just the sight of her taking a damned bath had him treading the very edge of control, in danger of being overwhelmed by his need of her.

Worse than the thought of scaring her was the thought of harming her.

She was mortal, fragile in comparison to him. What if he lost awareness in the heat of the moment? His hunger for her might result in him hurting her, or being too rough, or holding her too tightly, or being too demanding. It was a minefield of dangers, and just one of them would be enough to drive her away from him forever.

He scrubbed his hands over his black hair, tousling it as he growled.

She had been through a lot at the hands of a brutal male, one who was a warrior too.

She had already drawn parallels between them, ones that had made him aware of his size when he was around her, and that he was as quick to anger as his superiors said. Sometimes, his rage got the better of him before he could get himself under control. If that happened around Emelia, would she see him as a monster?

He didn't want to make her relive the events that had traumatised her, and he certainly didn't want her to come to view him as someone to be feared—someone as dangerous to her as the dragon warrior had been.

He chuckled mirthlessly.

For the first time in his long life, he felt his temperament was a bad thing, and it had taken a slip of a female to make him see it.

All the centuries of his superiors teasing him about it, all the times others had witnessed it, he had never felt it was a negative. But now he did, because he was aware of how easily it could push Emelia away from him.

The side of himself he harnessed in battle to give him the advantage, the rage and darkness that gave him focus and determination, now felt like a weakness, one that might make him lose his fight for Emelia.

He was unpredictable, even to himself. Emelia didn't need that. She needed someone stable, calm and gentle, and kind. He was none of those things.

Not really.

He tried his best when he was around her, but it would only take one slip.

He shifted his gaze back to her where she lazed in her bath, letting him see her, wanting him to see her.

Wanting *him* to see her.

She had faith in him at least, more than he had in himself. He couldn't trust himself around her, constantly worried he was going to do or say something wrong, but she trusted him. He could see that now. She trusted him not to scare her. She trusted him to help her. She trusted him enough that she had talked to him.

If there was one thing he knew about Emelia, she hated talking about herself.

But she had talked to him.

And now she trusted him enough to let him see her like this.

He still couldn't believe that.

He drank his fill of the sight of her now that she was calm again, watching every subtle shift in her features, and felt his eyes changing, growing golden.

What had she told him when he had looked at her like this the second time they had met?

He frowned as he sought the answer.

She had said he looked like a wolf.

He was a wolf for her. He burned with a need to hunt her, stalked her whenever the urge struck him and he wasn't strong enough to deny it, and hungered to taste her. She made him wild, and a little dangerous, roused a fierce desire to protect her and a need to fight for her.

A startling new desire swept through him as he gazed down at her.

He wanted to claim her.

He wanted her to be his female.

His only one.

If that made him a wolf, then he was a wolf for her and only her.

Her Wolf.

Her eyes remained closed, her face peaceful as she lay with her head tipped back, everything below her shoulders beneath the foamy water. He wasn't the only one who looked at another with hunger in his eyes, though. Her green ones had revealed need to him, had shone with heat and desire that he had sensed in her.

But she was still afraid, still scarred by what had happened to her.

If it took all the time in the world for her to trust him further, he would gladly wait. Seeing her growing bolder, coming out of her shell more each time they met, and how colour would stain her cheeks sometimes when she looked at him, or dared a smile in his direction, was enough for him.

He would bide his time, would learn to master the emotions she roused in him, the deep and wicked needs she stirred, and hopefully, one day, she would take the next step.

Although he wasn't sure what he would do then.

He only knew it would be explosive and wild.

And it would change them both.

CHAPTER 12

Wolf strode through the grand foyer of the elegant white marble building, passing the gold-accented columns that supported the enormous dome. Resembling numerous stately buildings in the human world, the headquarters of the angels who ran the realm known to the mortals as Heaven was an exercise in opulence, designed to show the wealth and power of those who called it home.

He had no time for this, but ignoring his superiors' summons before had ended with a rap on the knuckles. Refusing to attend the meeting they had set up this time, and had sent several messengers to him to ensure he couldn't deny knowing of it, would result in a far worse punishment.

His white boots were loud on the faintly veined marble floor, his dress uniform drawing glances from several females and some males who passed through the foyer with him or were working in the area behind the many desks that lined the open-plan rooms of the wings of the building that flowed outwards from the dome.

He adjusted the hem of the thick white jacket, conscious of the eyes on him. This was the reason he hated having to wear his best clothing. He preferred to remain unnoticed, blending in with everyone else so he could move unhindered through the crowds of the city whenever he had to visit it.

But being called before his superiors meant wearing the appropriate uniform.

Which meant drawing slack-jawed stares and whispered comments from all around him.

He flashed a glare at one pair of twittering females.

They stiffened, paling a little, and scurried away. A satisfying reaction.

He made a game of it as he took the stairs up through the building and walked with purpose down the wide corridor that would lead him to his superiors, pinning every male and female who dared to gawp with a black look and cataloguing their reaction.

His reputation always preceded him. Only the Echelon had single-coloured irises, and only he among them had silver ones. Murmured words about his temper, his victories, and his strength passed between the angels as he neared them.

A slight compression of his jaw, a lowering of his black eyebrows over his eyes as they narrowed on the offenders, was enough to have them falling silent. Very satisfying. Flexing his power was always pleasing.

It certainly took his mind off the meeting ahead of him, providing a nice distraction from mulling over the reasons his superiors might have called him.

He didn't need another mission right now.

He had been a breath away from forming the bridge between Heaven and Hell and teleporting there to begin his reconnaissance and acclimatisation to the dark realm.

He knew what he had promised Emelia, but he couldn't stand idly by and let the dragon continue to breathe, not anymore. Seeing the scar on Emelia's shoulder that was still pink, still fresh, and how she had struggled at times to relax in the bath, even when she hadn't been aware he was watching her, had sparked his anger, igniting his rage and the need to do something.

She had been brave to show herself to him, but it had taken a lot out of her. Even though she had been covered entirely by the bubbles, no more exposed to his eyes than she was in clothes, it had still stirred feelings inside her, ones she had struggled with before he had finally turned his gaze away from her for good.

Knowing that she suffered still, that the pain of her captivity and Zephyr's abuse was still raw inside her, affecting her deeply and hindering her ability to live the life she wanted, was enough to have his mood blackening and the air around him darkening.

He dragged down a deep, stuttering breath and reined in his temper before anyone noticed. It refused to calm, and he had to pause in a quiet spot in the corridor to lean against the wall and brace himself against his turbulent emotions. Almost a thousand years of feeling little other than the hunger to do his duty, the fury born of a desire to eradicate demons to cleanse the world of their filth, had left him ill prepared for feeling other emotions.

The rage was still there, but emotions fuelled it now, not dark needs and desires, but feelings he had always expected to be light, to provide a sense of warmth and goodness.

Like love.

He was slowly beginning to suspect that love was the fuel for his rage this time.

He cared about Emelia, so much so that the sight of her in pain, the sight of her scars, was enough to have a black need to bloody his sword blasting through him.

Anger born of love?

He had been led to believe that love was the opposite of hate, that it bred only positive effects, made couples coo over each other and brightened the world.

The love that burned inside him was powerful, controlled him far more easily than the natural darkness he held within him ever had. His temper had nothing on this new emotion. Love had him seething with a desire to destroy, to hunt and kill, to slay the dragon in cold blood. He would fight without honour for the sake of love, would drag the bastard kicking and screaming to the mortal world to shackle him with the curse, and would take pleasure in tormenting him before he finally ended him.

Love made him dark.

Not light.

"Fourth Commander?" A male voice shook him from his twisting, dangerous thoughts.

He blinked and lifted his head, reeling for a moment as darkness washed from the air, warmth rushing in to swiftly replace it as his mind cleared.

The angel standing before him cocked his right eyebrow, his short blond hair matching the golden wings furled against the plates of his equally as gold armour.

Amber-to-silver eyes narrowed on him as the male's expression shifted to curiosity tinged with cautiousness.

Wolf pushed away from the wall. "My apologies. I was…"

He wasn't sure what to say in order to explain his behaviour. The Second Archangel had an annoying gift for being able to see through lies.

"Come, come." The male ushered him towards the white double doors of the office at the end of the hall, one of which was ajar.

The Second Archangel must have come out when he had sensed Wolf going off the rails. Wolf glanced over his shoulder, past his white wings to the surprised faces of several males and females who had stopped a distance away.

Another rumour to add to the pool. By tonight, angels across the city would be discussing how the Fourth Commander of the Echelon had lost his temper in public.

He sighed and followed his superior, relief washing over him when he entered the office and closed the door behind him.

It was short-lived.

The moment he turned and realised that only the Second Archangel occupied the office today, the three other males who were normally present at any meeting startlingly absent, cold snaked down his spine.

"What is this about?" Wolf edged into the room, remaining near the door as he scanned his surroundings.

Tall windows on either side of the long white room allowed light to flood in and revealed the garden of the building, and the city that crept up the hill towards it. At the far end, bookshelves held multicoloured tomes, some so ancient that only magic was holding them together. Records of the previous Archangels and the slain Powers.

Rumour had it that Echelon had been born of the Powers, angels who had been the first order to protect the world from demons.

Archangels had mounted a war against the Powers to take control of the realm.

Now, only four Archangels were in existence.

Five if you counted the one that had been banished to Hell.

Satan had fomented the rebellion, and the fathers of the four current Archangels had sided with him. Satan had been banished and all Archangels executed.

And four young Archangel offspring had been spared and ordained as the ruling house.

Wolf had always found that little titbit interesting.

Did he suspect the current Archangels of being behind what had happened in some way? If he did, he wouldn't be the only one. The underground of the realm often whispered rumours of what had really happened, that it had all been the plot of four young angels hungry for power.

He stared across the room at the Second Archangel where he leaned with his backside against the enormous white circular table in the centre of it, his furled golden wings brushing his greaves and his arms folded across his chest.

"I asked what this was about."

The male unfolded his arms and stood. "We need you to relay a message to the Fifth Commander."

His reason for being summoned didn't surprise him. He was the direct contact for the Fifth Commander. The male sent reports to him, and he passed them on to the Archangels. He had little contact with the male other than issuing orders to him and receiving reports, wasn't sure what the Fifth Commander was doing, but he knew the mission was deemed important.

"In person," the Second Archangel added.

That was concerning.

He had never been asked to personally deliver a message to the male before. Was something wrong?

"You will find him in the fae town near London." The male paused, his sandy eyebrows drawing down. "I think it will do you good to get out. It has been noted that you have been struggling with something recently."

"I am not struggling with anything." He wasn't struggling, so it wasn't a lie. He was drowning. Doomed already. He had no more fight to give.

But he still tilted his chin up and straightened his spine, stared the male down and waited because he didn't want his superior to see it.

The last thing he needed was them meddling just as he was about to go completely off the rails. They wouldn't condone what he was going to do, he knew that, but if they suspected he was up to something, they were liable to invoke a barrier to prevent him from travelling anywhere. He couldn't let that happen.

"It was raised by several angels. Most notably, the Second and Third Commanders brought it up in their reports several days apart." The angel's gold-to-silver eyes dared him to deny it.

Damn it.

"The Third Commander is simply annoyed with me because I argued with him about how inappropriate it was to wear his dress uniform when seeking female company in the city." Deflecting? A low tactic, but one that might save his neck.

The Second Archangel didn't look pleased to hear that.

Wolf jumped on that. "The Second Commander was in on the plan with him, and they tried to convince me to do the same. I refused, of course."

"Because when have you been interested in female company?" the angel drawled, a teasing note to his deep voice that had Wolf frowning at him.

He was interested in female company. *Very* interested. He just wasn't interested in whatever wares the city females might attempt to peddle to him.

There was only one female for him.

"You *have* been distracted recently." The male pulled Wolf back to him the instant his mind started wandering, thoughts and images of Emelia filling it. "Ever since we sent you to retrieve the female half-breed."

Wolf leaped on that too, because what better excuse was there?

He sighed wearily for effect. "I admit, I am irritated that I failed to apprehend her before her... *demon*... placed her beyond my reach. I do not like to fail in my missions, as you know. She was more troublesome than I had anticipated, and I lost my temper, and my chance to bring her in with it."

All the truth.

It still annoyed him that he hadn't been able to bring Sable to Heaven to serve as the Sixth Commander, a replacement for her sire the Echelon badly needed.

"We will surely get another chance." The male approached him and placed a heavy hand on Wolf's shoulder.

"If I were to go to Hell, I could—"

"I will not hear of that," the angel interjected, and Wolf mentally cursed him.

Retrieving Sable was a viable excuse for heading into that realm, one he had failed to see before but shone at him like a beacon now, luring him to it.

"The Echelon need her strength. She has gone to ground. It would only take—"

"It would only take you running into a strong demon, one like her apparent mate, or worse, a fallen angel, and we would be down two Echelon," the Second Archangel countered, his expression darkening as his eyes brightened.

Wolf couldn't dispute that.

A strong demon would be enough to kill him if he was new to the effects of Hell. Running into a fallen angel didn't bear thinking about. He wouldn't stand a chance against one. Angels could renounce their realm and their kind without any ill effect, becoming what mortals thought of as a fallen, with black wings that looked the part.

A true fallen was something else.

Something evil.

Everything good in an angel was extinguished when they fell, the darkness that caused the fall consuming them to eradicate their softer feelings, leaving them as vicious and twisted and as power hungry as the Devil. It was rare for a fallen angel to retain any shred of good. Angels had tried to study fallen angels in the mortal realm to discover how some had survived the transition with their personality intact. So far, none of them had been able to figure it out.

Probably because a lot of them had ended up paying for their curiosity with their lives.

While a fallen angel was weakened in the mortal world, they were still extremely powerful.

"I will not hear another word about this. Understood?" The male gripped his shoulder so hard, Wolf almost flinched, his bones aching under the pressure.

A flex of the angel's strength and power to put him in his place.

He bowed his head and nodded, playing the meek Echelon as the male desired. The Second Archangel might be stronger than he was, but it wasn't going to stop him.

He would go to Hell.

He just hoped he would come back again.

CHAPTER 13

Wolf despised fae towns and avoided them as much as possible. The number of demons who either inhabited or frequented them had the rank-and-file angels staying away from them, let alone the Echelon. Whenever he had reason to enter one of the secret marketplaces that were home to a myriad of immortals, from witches to shifters to lesser-known fae, his Echelon mark always felt as if it was on fire, the sheer number of demons present stirring it into a frenzy that had him constantly wanting to call his blade and cut them all down.

Regardless of whether or not they were deemed dangerous to the humans.

All demons in the mortal realm were monitored, their behaviour recorded by a specialist team of angels. Many of them were no more a threat to humans than other humans were, so they were allowed to live.

His Echelon mark didn't distinguish between 'good' demons and the ones he needed to eradicate. It fired up whenever he was near one, burned beneath his white-and-gold armour like a brand, making him itch to summon his sword and rousing the black need to spill blood.

It probably didn't help that he viewed all demons as something to be wiped from the face of the Earth.

Which was why he was so surprised when he landed quietly on the roof of a low square white building in the witches' district and found the Fifth Commander facing off against a demoness in the street below.

And looking for all the world as if he didn't want to kill her.

The heat in the Fifth Commander's eyes changed to vast coldness as Wolf stepped closer and bright golden light burst from the cross emblazoned on the inside of the Fifth Commander's right wrist, Wolf's presence in the sprawling town that occupied a cavern in the English countryside triggering it. Their gifts fed off each other, easily sparked to life when they were in close proximity, even when demons were a long distance away.

With the demoness, one of the Devil's spawn judging by her gender since the wretch had destroyed all females of the mutinous demon breeds when they had turned against him, so close to him and the Fifth Commander, the hunger to hunt and destroy her was ruthless and relentless.

Wolf was tempted to call his sword and end the female, but the way the Fifth Commander reacted to his mark triggering had Wolf stalling.

Fascinated.

"Get away from me." The blond angel gripped his right wrist, clutching it hard and visibly straining against the black urge to do battle that ran through Wolf too.

The Fifth Commander's shoulders shook beneath his mortal clothing of a tight black T-shirt paired with equally as dark jeans and heavy soled boots.

He loosed a low growl of frustration as he wrestled with the mark and the urge, and Wolf canted his head, curiosity running as rampant in him as the hunger to kill.

The demoness leaped back a few feet, her blue eyes wide with shock that showed on her face.

Why was she surprised that an angel of the Echelon was reacting badly to her presence?

Why hadn't the Fifth Commander ended her the moment he had crossed paths with her?

"What's wrong?" she murmured, voice throaty with the fear Wolf could feel in her.

Fear she had every right to feel. She had set foot in the mortal world and was in the presence of the Echelon. While demons from the numbered realms were tolerated if they weren't a danger to the mortals, no demon of the Devil's spawn was allowed to live if it entered this realm.

She nervously brushed a gold-to-red stripe down the right side of her long black hair, her fingers shaking as she studied the Fifth Commander.

For a heartbeat, she looked as if she was going to move towards him rather than opting to run away.

And then the angel's huge white wings burst from his back as his fight against the urges boiling inside him faltered.

She gasped and stumbled backwards, the heel of her knee-high black stiletto boots snagging on the gap between one of the cobbles and almost sending her onto her backside. As it was, she flashed black lace-trimmed panties as she jerked to regain her balance, causing her red pleated tartan skirt to flip up at the front.

Wolf curled a lip at her manner of dress. What sort of female wore tartan-trimmed black corsets and stockings, heels that looked more like a weapon than footwear, and impossibly short skirts that had to expose her undergarments whenever she moved?

An image of Emelia dressed that way flashed into his mind, and he quickly shoved it out, not giving it a chance to affect him. While his white armour covered him from neck to toe, giving him modesty, he didn't need to get a hard-on. No one would see it, but it would be as uncomfortable as hell.

What was Emelia doing now?

His focus drifted.

The Fifth Commander dragged it back.

"Run," he gritted out, his face crumpling as he fought the urge to slay the demoness.

Fear tainted the air, stronger now, coming not only from the demoness. The Fifth Commander feared too.

He feared killing her?

She stood her ground, courage lighting her features as she faced the male, the small black horns that protruded from her fall of dark hair flaring slightly as she tipped her chin up.

"Asteria," the Fifth Commander whispered.

A revelation struck Wolf like a thunderbolt.

The male *knew* this demoness.

Wolf focused on him, exerting some of his indomitable will on the male, stoking the hunger to destroy the demoness. She was not allowed to be on this plane. If the Fifth Commander didn't cut her down now that Wolf had twined their gifts together to increase the power and influence of it, then Wolf would cut her down in his stead.

His mind filled with pleasing images of battling her and crushing her under his boot heel.

She shattered them.

"Rey." She held her right hand out in front of her, her palm facing his comrade. Speaking to him with that name. "You don't want to do this."

The Fifth Commander closed his eyes, his jaw muscles clenched, and his wings trembled as he tightly gripped his wrist.

There was a pause.

And then the male shook his head.

Wolf narrowed his silver eyes on the angel.

Avenged by an Angel

Rey.

Someone had given him a name. Had he chosen it? Or had it been the demoness who was now breathing a sigh of relief, some of the fear washing from her blue eyes as her shoulders sagged, the tension draining from her?

Wolf moved a step closer.

Her spine stiffened and she sharply looked up to her right.

At him.

The colour drained from her face and her heartbeat accelerated.

He slowly shifted his gaze from her to the one she had called Rey, his eyes narrowing as they traversed the distance between them.

"Fifth Commander of the Echelon," Wolf said in a deep commanding voice, one he normally reserved for demons and those who had irritated him because it got him the results he wanted.

More often than not, it was the sight of them looking ready to relieve themselves against their wishes.

The male straightened, inhaled hard and calmly released his right wrist. The mark glowed faintly, slowly darkening against his skin, and Wolf marvelled at the fact even his had settled, the desire to slay the demoness nothing more than background noise in his mind now.

Rey's doing, or someone else's?

Did someone want the demoness kept alive?

Only his superiors had such command over the Echelon gifts.

What reason would they have for wanting to stop him and the Fifth Commander from eradicating the one called Asteria?

Rey nodded and looked up at him. "Fourth Commander of the Echelon. What brings you here?"

Wolf ran an assessing glance over the people who had gathered to watch the furore, including the witch who had come out from the store beneath his boots to glare up at him with her hands planted against her hips, tugging at her drab black dress. More than one demon skulked in the shadows of the narrow alleys that branched off from the main cobbled avenue like streams from a river, feeding the hotchpotch buildings with customers.

What brought him here indeed?

It certainly wasn't the demon-infested tavern that crawled up the wall of the cavern to his left, where several taller buildings tracked the curve of the end of the town.

He glared in that direction, sending a few of the weaker demons scurrying inside. Several of the larger males stood their ground, staring right back at him, their eyes beginning to glow the different colours of their breeds and their horns curling from behind their ears to follow the curves of them, growing larger and more pointed as aggression flared in them.

He turned his gaze on the female demon.

Curled his lip at her, unable to hide the disgust that crawled through him whenever he thought about the fact he was in the presence of one from the most fiendish and despicable of demon breeds and had clearly been issued a command not to do anything about it.

His gaze darted to the inside of his right wrist and then to the black cross on Rey's. No urge to hunt and kill flowed through him. It wasn't even background noise now. Someone had shut off their Echelon gift, meaning someone had declared this demoness was no danger to the mortal world.

Someone was up to something.

He blocked out the female and focused on Rey. "I relay a message. There is a male you must question in regard to your mission. He resides in the Rozengard coven."

"I am aware. The reason I work with the demoness is to question said male." Those words sounded distinctly like an excuse for being around her.

Did Rey know something about why the female had been struck from the list of demons they were allowed to slay?

Wolf sighed and ignored her. "I have no interest in your reasons for aligning yourself temporarily with a demon. You can explain them to the council when your mission is done and you return, after you have dealt with her once she is no longer useful."

"I'll fucking deal with you, how about that?" She strode towards him, all spit and fire, her pupils starting to glow gold.

She slammed to a halt when Wolf turned his glare on her and unleashed a fraction of his power, and the black need to spill her blood crashed over him, filling him with an urge to obey it regardless of the consequences.

He didn't give a damn if she was whitelisted.

She was a demon and he would kill her if she dared to step any closer to him.

Rey held his hand up and blocked her path to Wolf.

Protecting her?

She edged back, settling for glaring at Wolf.

How many of her kind inhabited Hell?

She was weak in this world, her power diminished. He could easily best her here, but it would be a different outcome if he met her or one of her kind in Hell. He would be the weak one, wouldn't stand a chance against a single demon of the Devil's ranks.

But he still had to go.

He had put it off long enough, had formulated a plan and would see it through now that an excuse for heading into that dangerous and dark realm had materialised.

A reason his meeting with the Second Archangel had revealed to him.

Sable.

It was a good excuse to venture into Hell. His superiors wouldn't be surprised that he had disappeared, that he would enter Hell in order to track down the half-breed and make another attempt at retrieving her for the Echelon.

He always saw his missions through.

He curled his lip and turned away from the demoness again as thoughts crowded his mind, doubts and fears jangling his nerves, tinged with excitement. It was the perfect excuse, and if he got into trouble for doing it, he wouldn't care, because it would mean he was safely back in his world and he had been to Hell.

He had taken his first step towards avenging Emelia.

It was a struggle to resettle his focus on Rey and hide his churning emotions from the male. "I will be out of contact for a short time. If the council ask where I have gone, I am heading south on personal business."

With that, he disappeared.

CHAPTER 14

It took all of Wolf's focus to teleport quietly through the bridge he had formed between the fae town and Hell. Other Echelon could silently teleport with ease, but it was affected by their mood.

Which meant, more often than not, Wolf teleported in a flash of thunder and lightning that shook his destination, announcing his arrival.

Drawing attention to himself like that when he wasn't sure where in the vast realm of Hell he was going to land would be a death sentence. He only knew how to form the bridge between him and Hell. He didn't know the topology of the realm first-hand. He had studied maps of the realm held in the Echelon library, cobbled together from information given by various species the former Echelon had met during their lifetimes.

None of the Echelon had been crazy enough to venture there themselves.

Wolf realised why when he landed in a bleak black valley roofed by a drab grey sky.

Pain hit him like a tidal wave, rocked him to his knees on the loose gravelly ground, and had him close to vomiting. He leaned forwards, braced his hands against the dirt, and tried to breathe through it, sure it would pass given time.

It only grew worse.

Tightness formed in his breast and his muscles knotted, spasming so hard as pain wracked him that they felt as if they might crush his bones.

His eyes watered and he blinked hard, struggling to clear his vision so he could check he was alone. His normally sharp senses were scattered and dulled, the agony that crashed over him in increasingly strong waves making it impossible to detect whether anyone was nearby.

He scanned the endless dark lands, a vast plain that stretched to mountains in all directions, and swallowed hard on repeat as he fought to keep from retching.

He was alone, as far as he could tell.

The realm was darker than anticipated and he couldn't see clearly beyond a few hundred feet.

The urge to roll onto his side and lie on the ground was strong, almost overpowering, but he pushed back against it and the earth. He slowly eased up onto his knees, inch by agonising inch, until he was upright at last, sitting in the middle of a featureless valley in a realm where he didn't belong.

He sat there, time drifting past him as he sucked down increasingly deeper breaths, fighting to master his own body. His muscles gradually relaxed, but they felt weak, watery beneath his skin, and they ached. If he tried to move, he would fall.

So he remained on his knees, just breathing, battling to lock down the pain that still ran rampant through him, had him wanting to lean over and vomit from time to time.

He catalogued his body's reaction to the realm, using the study to give his mind something to focus on other than the fact he was a damned sitting duck in a world where most of the beings would kill him on sight.

If someone found him, he wouldn't have the strength to fight them.

He didn't even have the strength to teleport back out of Hell.

The debilitating pain coupled with the intense drain on his powers left him far weaker than he had anticipated. He fought another wave of nausea and tried to muster enough strength to stop his hands from shaking against the armour protecting his thighs. The rattling sound was loud in the still air, was probably carrying for miles and could easily alert anyone in the vicinity to his presence.

He drew a deep breath, gritted his teeth, and moved his arms. A grunt burst from his lips as his muscles screamed in protest but he kept going, gradually shifting them so his hands fell from his thighs to the dirt beside his hips. Better.

But now he wanted to vomit again.

Pain blinded him, darkness encroaching at the corners of his vision.

No.

He couldn't pass out. Not here. He stopped battling the effects of Hell and sagged, letting all the fight flow out of him so his muscles loosened and he was just sitting there again, breathing.

The pain receded a little, enough that the darkness disappeared and he could focus again.

Had he been a fool to think he could master this if he had enough exposure to it?

He tilted his head slightly and looked down at his right hand, at the Echelon mark that glowed faintly through the sections of his white armour. He was strong. One of the strongest angels in existence. He could bear this pain. Maybe not overcome it, but he could bear it enough that he could move.

Could fight.

He could learn to cope with it so it was no longer a weakness.

He focused on his body again, felt a glimmer of his powers, and took it as a sign that he was right. With enough exposure, he could grow accustomed to this realm. He could use his powers here and be strong enough that he could slay a dragon.

For a beautiful female.

His Emelia.

Just thinking about her eased the pain and poured strength into his muscles, and he seized on it.

He focused on his apartment and forced a teleport. His entire body shook as the bridge between him and his destination formed, his strength fading so rapidly that he feared it would give out before he could complete it and leave Hell. He had to return, and not only because he needed to see Emelia again.

Now that some of his power and strength had returned, fire arced down his spine in a constant rolling wave, a command from his superiors that reinforced his strength so it held steady as the bridge completed.

Pale light engulfed him, and he had never been so relieved to be summoned.

He landed in a heap on the white marble floor of his superiors' office instead of his home.

"What do you think you were doing?" the Second Archangel bellowed.

Wolf gasped as power surged through him, the suddenness of it making his head spin. It was as if a floodgate had been opened and all he could do was weather it as he knelt on the floor, his ears ringing. The pain that had wracked him faded under the onslaught, and his strength returned as his body purged the effects of Hell.

Gold metal boots appeared in his vision.

He slowly lifted his head, tracking up the seven-foot height of the Second Archangel. The blond glared down at him, his eyes more gold than amber-to-silver now, revealing his displeasure. His pale golden wings arched high above his head, furled against his armour, shifting as he bent over and grasped Wolf by the neck of his breastplate and hauled him onto his feet.

Wolf's legs threatened to give out under his sudden weight, but he locked his knees, gritted his teeth against the ache in his bones, and refused to fall.

"You know what he is like." A familiar deep voice drawled the words, a lazy edge to it that the owner used as a ruse to disarm angels, making them believe he cared little about what was happening, when in fact he was charting everything, remembering it all and mentally weighing up the angels in the process.

Deeming them worthy or unworthy.

Angels had lost their lives by underestimating the First Archangel.

Wolf wasn't going to be one of them.

The black-haired male liked to tease him, using it as a way of finding faults in his armour, exposing the softer parts of him that could be manipulated in order to force him to do whatever the male bid.

He didn't even take his purple-to-blue eyes off the maps spread across the large circular white table in the middle of the room as he casually commented, "We gave him a mission."

The Second Archangel huffed as he shoved Wolf away from him and looked over his shoulder at the First Archangel. "I did not expect such behaviour as a consequence, though."

"We were not to know the female had mated with a demon. This consequence could not have been foreseen." The First Archangel did look up now, his long black ponytail slipping from the shoulder of his golden armour as he straightened. His multihued eyes narrowed on Wolf, piercing him and leaving him feeling as if the male was seeking answers from his soul.

Or was demanding an admission of guilt.

"It is true," Wolf said without hesitation, aware that if he wanted his superiors to believe he had wanted to go to Hell in order to seek Sable, he had to speak the truth. "I did venture into Hell in order to test the limits of my abilities and the effect it would have on me."

"And what were the results of this *experiment*?" The First Archangel moved around the table, casually shifting some of the pieces of parchment on it to reveal a crudely drawn map.

The same one Wolf had studied in the Echelon library.

Had the male known all along that he had been intending to go to Hell against the Second Archangel's wishes?

"The effects of Hell were far worse than I had expected." Another truth, one that still irked him.

He hadn't quite believed the stories about Hell and how it stripped angels of their powers, part of him feeling they were only cautionary tales told to the young and foolish in order to keep them away from that dangerous place.

The Second Archangel scoffed. "It gets worse the longer you are in it."

"You have been there?" Wolf couldn't quite believe that.

The blond nodded, his expression grim. "And I have the scars to prove it."

Wolf bit back the questions that rose to crowd his mind and clamour for attention as both males eyed him. The First Archangel's purple-to-blue gaze narrowed, shrewd and calculating as he stared at him in silence, idly walking his fingers across the map he pinned to the table, traversing realms Wolf wanted to explore.

Where had he landed in Hell?

"I was young, and you are strong. It is possible in time you could come to cope with the curse," the Second Archangel said, and for a heart-stopping moment, hope bloomed. The male cut it down. "I will not condone you entering Hell again, though."

Wolf frowned at him.

The First Archangel spoke before he could demand the male change his mind. "Now, now... with the right intelligence, it is possible he could limit his exposure to the curse and complete his mission."

The blond angel turned wide amber-to-silver eyes on his comrade and barked, "There is also a chance we lose another Echelon rather than gain one."

"That is a risk I fear we will have to take. I do not think he is going to give up on this mission. It is not in his nature."

It definitely wasn't in his nature to give up on a mission, but this was different. This was about Emelia. He would never give up where she was concerned. They could lock him away and he would find a way to escape and hunt the dragon. Nothing would stop him from avenging her.

"He must give up." The Second Archangel rounded on the First, gold flashing in his eyes as he narrowed them on the male.

"I will not," Wolf said with all the conviction he felt burning in his breast. "I cannot."

If he did, it would destroy him.

The blond sighed. A hint of a smile curled the First Archangel's lips on hearing it. The male wanted him to go to Hell. Why? He had expected both males to argue against his desire to go to that realm again.

"Going to Hell made you stronger, Second Archangel. Think of the strength the Fourth Commander could gain if he was allowed to be exposed to the darkness of that realm. We need our warriors to be the strongest they can be." The First Archangel glanced down at the map, his voice dropping to a whisper. "The time is drawing near."

What time?

Wolf wanted to ask, but kept his mouth shut. Rumours had been circulating for centuries that the First Archangel could see events in the future given the right conditions, but the cost of his gift was high. Angels with such a power often lost memories dear to them whenever they used it, and there was always a darker price to pay too.

The rumour mill had speculated about the specific conditions required to trigger the First Archangel's gift.

The latest one had been born in a time when the First Archangel had been holed up in his apartment for a lunar cycle, apparently recovering his strength, and his mind.

The First Archangel's gift demanded a high price indeed if those rumours were true.

Not only did the male have to suffer great physical pain in order to trigger it, he had to endure tremendous emotional pain too.

The whispers in the city said he achieved that by torturing an innocent female in order to feed the beast that was his gift and sate it.

If that was true, and not little more than the wild fancy of bored angels, then the male would do better to avoid using his gift. He was risking black feathers for each sin he committed, each one that corrupted his soul. A corrupted Archangel had no place being in a position of power.

"I will grant you access to any records you might need." The First Archangel held his gaze, a dark edge to his purple-to-blue eyes that had Wolf shaking himself out of the grip of his thoughts before the male grew suspicious.

It wouldn't do to anger the First Archangel. Wolf didn't need to hear the rumours about his temper. He had witnessed it first-hand. The male had a darkness inside him that matched Wolf's own, which he was sure was half the reason the angel liked to tease him about his personality.

They were alike in too many ways.

Reflections of each other, but different in one critical way.

Wolf would never torture an innocent.

He wanted to avenge one.

He bowed his head. "The map I found was not of much use, and the accounts of Hell I found were few and far between, and more fanciful than anything helpful. I think many of the angels who penned them made up details."

The Second Archangel shook his head. "That much I can tell you is true. What I saw upon entering Hell did not match the image that had been painted for me in the records. It was a bleak, black wasteland, not a verdant, green world filled with life."

"You probably landed in Hell proper. The elves have brought nature and light into their corner of the dark realm, and there life flourishes under their care." The First Archangel frowned as he scanned the map and then jabbed a finger against a point on the left of it. "It is said the sky near the elf kingdom is always brighter, the light from it bleeding over into some of the demon realms."

As far as Wolf knew, the elves were neutral. Perhaps if he visited them, he could get information about the dragons. He was sure that with the constant wars in Hell, the elves would know of them, would have fought them.

He frowned as he recalled what he had seen in Emelia's mind.

There had been flashes of tall males dressed in black armour formed of scales that moulded to their bodies, revealing their physiques. Males with pointed ears.

And no horns.

She had fought on the side of the elves.

If he could discover their location or even the signature of the pathway that would allow him to teleport directly into their lands from one of the many portals in the mortal world, he wouldn't need to explore all of Hell in order to discover the location of the dragons. The elves could give him all the information he needed.

He strode past the Second Archangel, and the male's gaze landed on his back.

"Where are you going?" the blond said.

"To get started." He paused and looked over his shoulder at the male. "The elves fought on the side of Archangel in a recent war in Hell, a war in which the half-breed also fought. If I locate the elves, I can locate the stronghold of the demon king."

The Second Archangel smiled coldly. "And the female."

He nodded. Not a lie.

Only he didn't intend to retrieve Sable and bring her in to serve the Echelon.

He intended to convince her to help him avenge Emelia.

He just had to convince the demon king not to kill him first.

CHAPTER 15

There were rumours circulating in Hell. In every village he visited in the dragon realm, and every town he passed through in the free realm, those rumours followed him.

An angel was in Hell.

And that angel had been asking about elves.

And then he had been asking about demons.

And now he was asking about dragons.

Zephyr patrolled the ledge of his cave high in the black mountains, far from his clan's village, his mind churning with thoughts of the angel. He had questioned every person he had met who had spoken of the angel, had pieced together the truth from among the rumours.

An angel was looking for one dragon in particular.

A green one.

Him?

Why would an angel want to find him?

His mind conjured only one answer to that question.

Emelia.

Just thinking about the petite brunette had him furious and aroused, aching with a need of her that he had little control over. She had been taken from him what seemed like a forever ago now, ripped from his grasp by that interfering huntress and her demon king.

His claws extended and he curled his hands into fists, so they bit into his palms. The sting was pleasant, comforting even, and he relished it as his anger spiked again, flooding him with a need to shift and hunt.

But with the anger born of the hole she had left in his chest upon slipping from his hands came another anger, a rage so deep it threatened to tear him apart.

It made him want to rip himself to pieces with his own claws.

Because he had realised too late what Emelia was to him.

His fated one.

On a low, vicious growl, he raked claws down his bare chest, unable to stop himself from cleaving his own flesh open and spilling blood. Green scales rippled over his skin and his teeth sharpened as physical pain became emotional agony so vast and endless, it felt as if it was going to consume him.

He sank to his knees on the edge of the ledge overlooking a fork in the valley and stared at the horizon, beyond the cragged peaks of the black mountains.

He slowly lifted his eyes, tilting his head back as he raised them to the grey vault of Hell, and that ache that burned inside him worsened, scouring his chest and hollowing him out.

"Emelia," he whispered, and then threw his head back and roared, unleashing every drop of his rage and despair in it until his voice gave out and he had no more breath in his lungs.

He sagged and clawed at the black rock beneath him, on either side of his green-leather-clad knees.

"Emelia."

He idly stroked the ground, rock she had slept upon, that had carried the scent of her long after she had been taken from him. That scent had faded now, the last piece he had of her gone.

He needed her back.

He had been cruel to her, but from the very start, he had been aware on some primal level that she was different to the other females he had been given as a spoil of war, free to do as he pleased with them. The desire to treat her as he had treated his prizes in the past had been muted, the carnal hungers, the thought of taking a female against her will, breaking her mind and her body non-existent. He hadn't understood why until it had been too late.

He had teased Emelia, had toyed with the little mortal in ways he could never forgive himself for now that he knew what she was.

His fated one had deserved better treatment, should have been shown respect and tenderness, wooed until she surrendered to him and consented to be his.

He had made mistakes with her, but all was not lost. After realising what she was to him, he had taken steps to make amends, to show her that he could be a good male for her.

"And it had been working," he snarled, anger surging through his veins to burn away the softer emotions that had been building inside him, stirred by merely thinking about his mate.

She had been softening.

He shoved his bloodied fingers through his wild green hair and pulled it back until it hurt, his lips peeling off his fangs in a grimace as the despair he tried so hard to deny pushed to the surface inside him.

She would never be his.

She would never look at him the way Loke's female, another mortal huntress, had looked at the blue dragon that day she had been brought to the clan village and Loke had come to rescue her from their chief's grasp.

Acid had flowed in Zephyr's veins that day, anger so fierce, he hadn't been in control of himself, hadn't been able to stop himself from poisoning her mind against Loke when he had been given a chance.

He had lied to her, painting a terrifying picture in her mind, wanting her to see the darkness male dragons were capable of so she would believe Loke was the same at heart, that given the chance, he would take her against her will, would abuse her as he had Emelia.

He had lied to everyone that day.

All because he had realised Loke had something he never would.

He had his fated mate.

Zephyr wanted his.

Emelia was beautiful, strong, and drew him to her like nothing else in this world. He wanted her as his female. Attempting to break her will to make her want him had gotten him nowhere with her, although he was sure he had been close at times, when she had looked at him with soft green eyes and had spoken sweetly to him.

He had gone to the village for her sake, desperate to make amends after they had argued, seeking a way to make her happy.

To please his female.

Witnessing the way the blonde huntress had behaved, how she had fought for Loke and had clearly wanted him, had aggravated him.

So he had fought Loke for the right to the huntress.

He had wanted to take her from him, to slake his urges on her while he worked to wear down Emelia, stopping himself from making advances toward his mate by satisfying them with the other female in secret. He had wanted an outlet for his anger.

But he had failed in that too.

He stroked his fingers across the fading slashes on his stomach and chest, feeling an echo of the pain that had burned inside him that day.

When Loke had defeated him.

But his defeat had only been the start of his suffering.

He had returned to his cave with a present for Emelia, the carcass of an animal he had managed to kill despite the injuries Loke had dealt him. He had hoped the present would calm Emelia, an olive branch that, in his mind, she would accept and would then be pleased to see him.

He had found her crying, and gods, it had destroyed him, because he had known her suffering was his fault.

He had wanted her to look at him with those soft eyes again, the way Loke's female had looked at him, so he had tried his hardest to be gentle with Emelia, compelled to tend to her wounds, injuries he had caused. She had allowed him to take care of her, and he had thought he had been making progress with her.

So he had tested her.

He had offered to let her leave, hoping that she wouldn't take the chance to escape him.

That she would want to remain with him.

When she had made a break for the ledge, something inside him had snapped, and he had stopped her, had restrained her and forced her to stay, his heart breaking at the thought she wanted to leave him. She had lashed out at him, had battered his chest as he had restrained her, gently holding her so he didn't hurt her again, taking her blows and her cruel words, even though every one of them had cut at his heart.

He needed her to love him.

She *had* to love him.

He shook his head.

He hadn't considered the consequences of his actions, though, his instinct to keep her with him so powerful that it overruled everything else. She had grown quiet, distant, and had refused to eat. She had withdrawn from him, and the thought he had broken her had terrified him.

He had grown to want her fiery attitude and defiance, her barbs and blows, anything other than the dreadful cold silence.

So he had tried to be kind to her again, sure that it would make amends and bring her back to him.

Bring her closer to him.

When she had begged him for something she could eat, something familiar to her, he had gone on a mission to get her what she needed.

Because he hadn't been able to bear watching her fade away, drifting towards death little by little.

He had wanted to make her strong.

Happy.

But in doing so, he had sentenced himself to pain, to a life that felt hollow, empty without her.

Because he had returned to find Emelia gone.

He needed her back.

She belonged to him.

She would come to want him too. He just needed to get her back. He just needed her, and he would stop at nothing to have her.

She would be his mate.

CHAPTER 16

Things were not going according to plan. It had taken Wolf days of scouring the records in his superiors' library to piece together enough information to pin down the location of the elf kingdom. Upon attempting to enter that kingdom, he had found the way barred. Every time he had tried to use a portal in the mortal world to reach it, or had attempted to teleport into it by using his own powers to form a bridge to that realm, he had been bounced back.

The closest he had come to the elf kingdom was standing at the border with his hand pressed against an invisible force. His knees had given out shortly after that, and while the pain had been less intense, the drain on his strength and his powers had been just as fierce as before.

So he had adjusted his plans.

He had taken to charting Hell, roaming unseen through the lands dressed as a traveller in a dull grey cloak that covered fawn trousers and a black shirt suited to the region known as the free realm. A few well-placed questions to the locals had revealed the elves had locked down their lands against selected breeds of immortals close to a month ago.

Around the time Sable had slipped from his grasp.

Apparently, the elves wanted nothing to do with him.

Understandable given what he had learned.

The elf prince was mated to a mortal female who was a friend of Sable's. The two had frequently been seen together in some of the towns in the free realm, where a multitude of breeds gathered to form their own unique society. According to those he had questioned, the two females always travelled with an entourage of at least a dozen elf warriors and demon guards, and neither female had been seen since the elf kingdom had done something to close the doors in Wolf's face.

Still, he wasn't going to be deterred.

Each visit to Hell provided him with new information, and he was slowly growing acclimatised to the dark realm, was able to move around with only a little pain now, and had even managed to endure the effects of the curse for a full hour before having to retreat back to his apartments to recover.

His strength was still a shadow of itself, and his wings were not to be trusted—a close call with the jagged side of a mountain had proven that, bringing him close to being skewered around thirty times when he hadn't been able to control his ascent—but he was making progress.

He had given up on the elves, and had charted several demon realms instead, hoping to find the right one.

None of them had belonged to the Third King and all of them had seen him chased from the lands by a horde of warriors intent on cutting him down.

He had learned that hearing the demon tongue in Hell was far more excruciating than hearing it uttered when he was in the mortal realm, and had decided that gaining an audience with Sable might not be a sensible course of action after all.

He had the feeling it would end in his death.

So he had adjusted his plans.

Again.

The last two visits to Hell, he had settled himself in three different taverns in two different towns and had made subtle inquiries about dragons.

Which brought him to now.

The female sitting across a tacky ancient oak table from him, her back to the enormous obsidian brick fireplace, smiled winsomely and leaned forwards, flashing a lot of cleavage in her tight violet corset. Her jaw-length black hair swayed with her, brushing rosy cheeks.

"After that, he just sort of left, you know?" She swirled a pewter tankard around, and he was tempted to pinch his nose closed as another potent wave of alcohol threatened to singe it. She looked down into her black drink, pulled a face, and swayed it towards him, missing how he reared back to avoid getting splashed with the foul brew as she slurred, "Fucking bastard."

Indeed.

Apparently, the delicate fae female had experienced more than her share of dragons. Only, she had experienced them in ways he hadn't quite anticipated when she had told him she knew plenty about the breed he was seeking.

A slow grin spread across her painted purple lips and a wicked light flashed in her aqua eyes. "Of course, he got what was coming to him."

Wolf wasn't sure he wanted to know what she had done to the male.

He imagined it was something terrible, and that was enough for him.

She peered closer at him, leaning even farther over the table, so her breasts were in danger of spilling out of her corset as they pressed against the wood. "You're not a dragon, are you?"

He shook his head.

She pushed up on her toes, sliding closer still, and reached up with her free hand. He tensed as she brought it up to his face, in danger of brushing his cheek with her violet nails, ready to shove her away if she dared to touch him.

He wasn't sure what she was, but he knew she was trouble.

Several of the males at the bar had been eyeing her since she had entered the tavern, dressed as wickedly as the demoness Asteria had been.

They had been eyeing Wolf with a different sort of look from the moment she had taken the seat opposite him. He was fairly certain that if she didn't speak with them after spending time with him, he was going to get lynched and possibly murdered upon exiting the tavern.

She casually flicked her hand, and his hood fell backwards, revealing his face to her.

Her eyes widened and brightened, and her smile grew pleased. "Why, aren't you sex on a stick?"

He reached over his shoulder and pulled his hood up.

"Aw, handsome, don't cover up." She tried to push his hood back again.

Wolf snapped his fingers around her wrist, pushed it away from him, and gripped it hard.

It didn't stop her from gawping at him as if she was suddenly starving.

Which made a whole lot of sense when she next spoke, her voice a lazy, seductive drawl.

"Darling, I could dine on you for days." She raked her glowing eyes over him, her fine black eyebrows rising as she took him in. "Shame you're not into me."

Succubus.

He froze. Wait. She could see that he wasn't interested in her?

"Sugar, don't be shocked." She smiled and hiked her bare shoulders in a small shrug. "It comes with the territory. Kinda like how I can see that passion flaring in you whenever you think about someone. She pretty?"

He nodded before he could stop himself.

The female leaned closer and whispered, "She the reason you here? 'Cause you know... angels shouldn't play in the Devil's backyard."

He shot backwards in his seat, his eyes locked on hers, seeking the truth in them.

"Don't act surprised. There's rumours all over Hell about you, darling. Not many folk asking about dragons in these parts. I'd recommend you go home, before it's too late."

"I cannot." He planted his palms against the table and leaned towards her. "I will find the dragon, and I will kill him."

"Fighting words. I love it." She picked up her tankard, drained it as she sat back in her seat, and held it aloft as she said, "You're gonna need some serious balls, though. You do know where the dragons live, right?"

He schooled his features, hiding the truth from her.

She laughed. "Oh dear Lord… you, sugar, are in for a shock. You want to know where the dragons live?"

He leaned closer before he managed to get the better of himself. "Where?"

Her violet lips curved into a slow smile. "Just about exactly where you really don't want to be."

His face fell.

She couldn't mean…?

She drew on the table, using the drops of moisture that had collected on it from the several tankards of brew she had consumed. Jagged lines formed borders, and those joined to form realms, some of which he was familiar with from the maps and charts he had purchased from several stores in the towns he had passed through.

The succubus stopped when she reached a point far to the right of the lands he could recognise.

"There be dragons." She tapped a violet nail against a wide curving kingdom before sliding it to the adjoining one. "There be the Devil."

"Shit," he muttered.

"That's what you'll be in if you go there, darling. I really wouldn't recommend it."

But he had to go.

The effect of the curse grew stronger whenever he ventured closer to the Devil's lands, which had led him to realise that the first time he had landed in Hell, it had been close to that realm.

He stared at the fading map on the table.

That close to the Devil's kingdom, the drain on his powers and his strength would be immense, the debilitating effects of it more severe than he had experienced since his first visit to Hell. There was a chance he wouldn't be able to cope with it and would be left vulnerable again, unable to defend himself as he battled the pain and the weakness.

"Never seen an angel with that look in their eyes." The female eased away from him and took the fresh tankard a male offered her.

"What look?" He kept his eyes on the table, battling the urge to go to the dragon lands now. He could fly across any flat ground, covering it swiftly, but he would have to climb any mountain he came across. He could scout the border of the area she had indicated was the dragon realm before he had to return to recover from being exposed to the darkness of Hell and regain his strength.

"Your eyes are as black as a demon's."

He stilled right down to his breathing.

Lifted his gaze to lock it with hers.

Cold slithered down his spine beneath his dark shirt.

She was lying.

He pushed to his feet and threw a glance around the room. It settled on the mirror above the fireplace and he turned towards it, slowly approached it, his heart pounding at a sickening pace in his throat as the light from the flames chased over him, highlighting his face.

Dark silver eyes stared back at him, swirled like oil mixed with mercury.

Fear drove an icy spear through his heart.

He unleashed his wings, ripping startled gasps from the occupants of the tavern as they tore through his shirt and burst from beneath his cloak. His fingers shook as he spread his left wing and took hold of it, scoured every damned white feather for a black one. His pulse accelerated as he found none and he twisted to his right to give that wing the same treatment, desperation flooding him as fear tightened its grip on him.

The breath he had been holding burst from his lips as he saw all his feathers were still white.

But the relief he had hoped to feel didn't come.

This realm *was* affecting him in ways he had feared.

The dark need for vengeance grew stronger whenever he was in Hell, becoming a relentless force that drove him onwards, had him spending more and more time in the realm with each visit. Pushing himself harder.

Was it opening him to corruption?

He backed away from his reflection.

His panic spiked to new heights.

He needed to see Emelia.

He teleported without thinking, landing in the bright garden of the mansion.

"What's wrong?" Emelia's voice was soft, compelling him to look at her as fiercely as fear of the darkness that was growing inside him had compelled him to come to her in the hope she could loosen the hold it had on him.

She rounded on him, discarding a pair of pink-handled shears at the same time, her eyes probing his as they locked.

Worry shone in them, making him regret coming straight to her from Hell. He should have rested first to regain his strength and shake off some of the fear, but he hadn't expected her to notice how tired he was, or how afraid, not with her limited mortal senses.

"Where have you been?" Her tone turned soothing, as if she knew how close to the edge he was and that he needed her to be gentle with him right now, craved her softness and tenderness to wash away the darkness of Hell that tainted his soul. "I've not seen you in a few days."

A blush climbed her cheeks as she said that.

One that had him recalling the last time he had seen her and how she had looked in the bath with those white bubbles clinging to her creamy skin.

He felt his eyes change again and hoped it wasn't darkness that flooded them now.

Her blush deepened and she fidgeted with the hem of her black tank, smoothing it along the waist of her dark blue jeans. "Where were you?"

When he didn't answer, she bravely lifted her eyes to meet his and the heat and embarrassment in their jewel-green depths gave way to a darker emotion. Her mood shifted, turning colder as she released the hem of her top and straightened, staring into his eyes as suspicion coloured hers.

"You wouldn't."

Wolf looked away from her as her anger hit him like a physical blow.

She looked him over, her gaze trailing fire in its wake as she took in his clothing and then his wings. She shook her head and folded her arms across her chest, and he couldn't tell whether she was disappointed or finding it hard to believe him, or both.

"You said you wouldn't," she bit out, no trace of softness in her voice now. Anger laced it as strongly as it laced her scent. She wheeled away from him, her steps clipped as she began gathering tools and hurling them into a large plastic bucket, looking for all the world as if she would rather be throwing them at him. "Leave it. This... this vengeance isn't yours to take. It's *mine*."

Wolf wanted to growl at that. "What do you mean?"

She paused with a pair of secateurs in her hand and stared at them, her voice distant and barely there as she whispered, "I've been training."

Hell, no.

Just no.

Anger burned in his veins now. "Why?"

She boldly cast the tool into the bucket with the rest of them and faced him. "Because you're not the only one who thinks about what happened to me. You're not the only one who wants to make Zephyr pay."

"And exactly what do you intend to do?" He strode towards her, determined to get an answer.

She briskly walked away from him, a vain attempt to keep the distance between them steady. His legs were longer, allowing him to easily close the gap by the time she reached the steps of the broad patio that lined the rear of the elegant sandstone mansion.

"Emelia," he husked, and she finally turned to look at him again, her expression solemn.

"Something," she murmured and then put strength into her voice. "I'll do something."

Like hell she would.

"I may be weaker in Hell, but I am still stronger than you are," he bit out and then felt like a bastard when he added, "Can you really return to that realm?"

She paled and tossed him a wounded look, one that cut him to his soul as he sensed the fear and pain in her.

An apology for bringing up her past balanced on the tip of his tongue.

Other words came out instead.

"Let me go in your stead. I am happy to be your sword."

She snapped, "At what cost to yourself?"

"The cost does not matter," he said and resisted the need to reach out and take her hand, to hold it to stop her from running. The need was there in her eyes, steadily building. "I will pay whatever price needs to be paid."

"Why?" she croaked, her brow furrowing as she searched his eyes, an edge of confusion mixed with despair in hers.

He couldn't answer that, not without pushing her too hard.

Her face crumpled a heartbeat before it darkened.

"I don't want you to go. I don't want it!" She shook her head, causing tendrils that had fallen from her messy bun to sway and distract him with how she had looked in the bath with her hair pulled up like that, strands of it sticking to her damp skin. She took a hard step towards him, shattering that vision of her. "I won't sanction such a thing. I won't be responsible for whatever happens. I can't."

She choked on that last word.

He had pushed her too hard.

"Emelia, I am sorry."

She cast him a pained glance and turned away from him.

Instinct screamed not to let her walk away, fear bellowing that he would lose her if he did.

He reacted in a heartbeat, had his fingers wrapped around her trailing wrist before he could consider the consequences.

Emelia shrieked and twisted towards him, smashed her fist into his jaw with enough force to send him swaying sideways, the suddenness of her blow catching him off guard.

She clawed at his hand and he released her the moment he realised what he had done.

"Emelia," he started, and she stared at him, visibly shaken. His apology faltered again, the need to protect her pushing it out of his mind as he seized on how badly she had reacted to him touching her. "Do you really believe you can enter Hell and face the dragon when a simple touch from a male terrifies you?"

Disbelief danced across her face, but it rapidly morphed into resolve as she straightened her spine, tipped her chin up, and stared him down.

"I can."

She believed that.

For some reason, it irritated him more than the fact she had reacted so violently to his touch.

"I cannot allow it." He held her gaze, refusing to look away when the disbelief returned and mingled with horror, and a whole lot of anger. "You will get yourself killed."

"You don't get a choice." She jabbed her finger in his direction. "It's my decision to make."

"Then you do not get to say what I can or cannot do either." He backed off a step and folded his arms across his chest as he set his jaw.

Her green eyes narrowed on him, the anger in them flaring hotter.

He refused to take his words back. She didn't know how fiercely the need burned inside him, how it controlled him. He couldn't deny it. He had tried. He looked at Emelia, at how she was still shaking despite how rigidly she held herself in an attempt to quell her trembling.

It hit him hard in the gut.

He let everything else fall away, all his anger and the need that pounded inside him, and whispered, "I am sorry for touching you. I never intended to frighten you."

His gaze dropped to her hand as she moved it, and his stomach twisted tighter as she rubbed her wrist with it. The one he had held.

Hope bled from him, his strength flowing out of him with it. What hope was there for him if just his touch was enough to terrify her? She would never accept him as her male, was never going to be his. Her scars ran too deep.

He rubbed his tired eyes, the drain of his time in Hell catching up with him as his emotions evened out.

"I truly am sorry." With that, he turned away from her and focused on his apartment, on the place he should have gone to instead of coming here when he was raw from being in Hell, on edge and weak to his emotions.

They had gotten the better of him, and he had ruined everything.

"You don't need to apologise." Emelia's softly spoken words filled his heart with light, had him closing the connection between him and his home and looking over his shoulder at her instead of teleporting.

"I do." He smiled tightly, the light she caused in him stuttering out when he thought about what he had done. If he had rested before coming to her, he wouldn't have made that mistake. He would have been strong enough to resist that urge to grab her. "I reacted on instinct. I try so hard…"

She frowned.

Was quiet for so long that he felt sure she wasn't going to speak again and was waiting for him to leave.

Wanting him to go.

But then she murmured, "What do you try so hard to do?"

Wolf didn't want to say.

When he didn't answer, she spoke again.

"Do you try hard not to… touch me?" Her voice grew strained, and he felt her nerves returning, the fear she tried so hard to master.

They both hated feeling weak.

He turned to face her, struggling to find his voice to answer that question. He wanted to deny it, but the look in her eyes told him not to do it, told him that she knew the answer he wanted to hide from her.

She pulled down a deep breath, swallowed hard, and flexed her fingers at her sides before lifting her right arm. It shook as she held it aloft between them, a flicker of fear lighting her eyes.

"You can…" Her throat worked on another hard swallow. "You can touch."

His heart thumped against his chest, his mind spinning so rapidly, he was sure he had misheard her.

Avenged by an Angel

But she kept her hand held out to him, and her eyes beckoned him, lured him to her, and he was powerless to resist her invitation.

He took a slow step towards her, aware that this was a difficult and monumental moment for her. She had allowed him to see her at a time when she normally felt vulnerable, and now she was bravely allowing him to lay his hands on her. He fixed his focus on her, monitoring her emotions and the tangled scents that swirled around her for a sign of fear, and vowed he would stop if she grew frightened.

Wolf carefully lifted his hand and brought it towards hers, stopping just short of contact. His gaze flickered to her. No trace of fear shone in her eyes. They were calm, accepting pools of green as she waited. The only outward sign of her nerves was the way her fingers continued to shake slightly.

He held his breath and gently eased his fingers towards her, his pulse pounding faster and faster as he stared at the gap between their skin, watching as it narrowed. The second his skin brushed hers, electricity arced through his blood, and he tensed as it lit him up, flooding him with heat. His gaze leaped to hers, sure he would see fear in it now.

There was only fascination.

Why?

Because he was touching her and she wasn't afraid, was enjoying the feel of his skin against hers as much as he was?

He looked down at their hands as he skimmed his fingers along the lengths of hers, towards the back of her hand.

His eyes widened. Or it might be because a trail of rainbow-coloured light shone in the wake of his touch.

He stared at it as it slowly faded, unable to believe his eyes.

"Is that normal?" Emelia's low-spoken question barely registered as he moved his fingers, painting more rainbows over her skin.

He couldn't find his voice to answer her.

It was far from normal.

He had heard of angels doing such a thing when they were experiencing strong emotions, but he had never seen it happen. It filled his head with a thousand questions, the loudest of which demanded an immediate answer.

How did he feel about Emelia?

He gently stroked her hand, his eyes fixed on it and that dazzling trail of colours as he probed the depths of his feelings for her and found them endless.

"It happens all the time," he murmured, lost in how the colours pulsed and chased his fingers, lost in his feelings for her.

Ones that made him feel like the vulnerable one now.

Because it was clear he was falling for her, and he was falling hard.

He still wasn't sure how she felt about him, and damn, that unsettled him, had him thinking up excuses to give her in case she asked him any more questions about what was happening as he touched her.

Not only because he wasn't sure of her feelings.

But because he was certain that if she knew the reason why he left rainbow trails of light when he touched her, she wouldn't understand, not after everything she had been through.

And he wasn't sure he could handle the rejection.

He stared at their hands, the emotions she stirred in him surging stronger as he surrendered to them, to the deep and consuming love he felt for her—love that felt as if it might destroy him if she turned him away.

He had never felt anything like it.

It was empowering, and debilitating. It made him brave and a coward at the same time. It was beautiful and terrifying.

He couldn't bring himself to risk his heart, not yet, but he would walk into Hell and face all it had to throw at him. He could do that, could risk his life without fear in that shadowy plane, but the thought of her rejecting him was terrifying.

The amount of power she had over him was humbling.

Had he thought her a weak, delicate little thing?

She had the power to break him, a warrior, with only a look.

With a word, she could slay him.

"Fourth Commander?" she murmured and then made a small noise of frustration. "I feel so stupid calling you that… but it's better than TeeDeePee."

"Wolf," he said without taking his eyes off their hands.

The intensity of her gaze on him increased, burning into him as she stood in silence that stretched around him, demanding an answer to her unspoken question.

He managed to find the strength to drag his eyes away from the swirls of colour he had been painting on her skin and lifted them to meet hers. Confusion crinkled her brow, and he mirrored her expression for a split second before he realised he hadn't spoken with her since he had decided upon a name.

"I am Wolf now."

Her Wolf, if she would have him.

"Why?" She looked as if she wanted to chuckle at his choice of name.

Her face instantly sobered when he answered.

"Because of what you said about me. You said sometimes when I look at you, I look like a wolf." He eased closer to her, holding her gaze and refusing to let her look away. "I am a wolf, Emelia, and I want to devour you."

Crimson coloured her cheeks and nerves shone in her eyes, but she didn't pull away from him, neither physically nor emotionally. She remained close to him, her hand brushing his, heat building in her bright green eyes.

Was he finally making progress with her?

CHAPTER 17

Emelia told herself to look away, but she only fell deeper into his shifting silver eyes. Wolf. She held back her smile. The name did suit him. He was a predator, a hunter. He was patient when he needed to be, calm and still. Calculating. He was quick to explode with violence, though. Powerful. Hard to read, which made him unpredictable. And he preferred the shadows, stalking, watching, and studying his prey.

Like he was studying her now.

The gold emerged in his irises as he held her gaze, his eyes hooded and framed by his long black lashes, filled with hunger that both frightened and thrilled her.

A wolf.

And he had been hunting in Hell.

Not successfully, judging by the fact he wanted to go back.

The thought of him in that dark place terrified her more than the fact they were touching, his hand still moving against hers, as if he couldn't stop himself from stroking her skin. The rainbow light that chased his fingertips was bright in the fading light as afternoon gave way to evening, illuminated his face and reflected in his eyes.

She didn't want him to go back to Hell, not when she could see it was taking its toll on him. He was paler than before, and dark shadows circled his eyes. He was tired. Something deep inside her told her that. He was tired and needed to rest, or he would be in even more danger in Hell.

She couldn't stop him from going back there, but perhaps she could convince him to rest before he continued his hunt for Zephyr.

Perhaps she could help him in the only way she could.

Because he was right and she wasn't brave enough to go to Hell. She had trained twice a day, every day, since she had last seen Wolf, but her physical strength failed her whenever she thought about returning to that realm to face the dragon.

If just the thought of seeing him again was enough to have her on her knees, what would actually seeing him do to her? It would be all too easy for him to capture her again.

But she didn't want to rely on Wolf, sending him to a place that was dangerous and was clearly taking its toll on him, asking him to fight her battles for her.

"Emelia?" He closed his hand around hers and she welcomed the lightness of his grip, took comfort from it as his deep voice rolled around her, chasing away her fears.

"Wolf?" She lifted her eyes to his again. "Stay awhile?"

Surprise shifted across his handsome face before he nodded.

She slipped her hand free of his, walked over to the steps that led down to the gravel path that cut through the formal garden, and sat on the top one.

Wolf eased down beside her.

"You look like a hobo," she said without looking at him and felt his gaze leave her.

She snuck a glance at him, a touch of heat climbing onto her cheeks as she thought about what she had done. Had he seen her in the bath?

She thought about it a lot.

Dreamed about it.

"I am in disguise." He stated in a matter-of-fact tone, as if she should have known he was dressed to conceal his true identity. "It did not work as well as intended. A succubus could tell what I was."

"Hold up, buddy." She frowned at him. "A succubus?"

There was a glimmer of something in his silver eyes that looked a lot like pleasure, and she was sorely tempted to box him. She froze. She was on dangerous ground. First she had missed him, then she had let him see her in the bath, and then she had fantasised about him most nights.

Nothing good could come of where this was leading her.

Or could it?

She studied his eyes, trying to see whether he had been pleasured by the succubus or was pleased she was annoyed at him for talking to one.

"The female was giving me information about dragons," he explained, an innocent edge to his expression.

That had better be all the bitch had been giving him.

Emelia paused again, struck by that dark thought.

She had never been the jealous type.

So what was it about Wolf that had her ready to claw a stranger's eyes out? He wasn't hers, and she certainly wasn't his.

She wasn't.

Was she?

She shoved that line of thought firmly out of her head as her throat closed, a trickle of panic running through her veins in response to the thought she might be falling for the angel sitting beside her.

Or worse.

She might have already fallen for him.

"Was that all she was giving you?" she bit out, unable to stop the words from lashing from her lips.

Wolf arched an eyebrow at her.

"What is that supposed to mean…" His eyes widened as both eyebrows shot up. "Oh. No. She knew I was not interested."

She frowned again. "How?"

He unfastened his cloak, curled a lip at it in a way that told her he didn't like his choice of clothing either, and set it down beside him. "My aura."

"That isn't really an explanation." She looked over her shoulder, towards the cast-iron table and the cooler sitting atop it, wishing she had brought it with her so she could have a drink.

She needed something to do with her hands, because she was in danger of touching Wolf, and the thought of where that might lead her had her throat closing up again and that trickle of panic turning into a flood.

Wolf glanced past her in the direction she had been looking, pushed to his feet, and strode over to the cooler. He grabbed it by the blue plastic handle and carried it over to her, setting it down beside her before resuming his position next to her on the step.

"Thanks." She popped the lid, grabbed a cold can of soda, and sighed as she pressed it against her overheating cheeks. "This doesn't get you out of answering my question."

He gave her a look that said it had been worth a try. "Succubi can see emotional auras, especially around males. I believe it helps them… well… you know."

She could guess.

It was probably nifty being able to see the mood of the men in the room, and she didn't doubt it made picking dinner far easier for the succubi.

"And your aura was flashing a big nope at her?" She cracked the can open and swigged it. The ice-cold cola was bliss as it slid down her throat, just what she needed after a long day working in the garden.

"Apparently." He averted his gaze, letting it run over the low boxwood hedges that enclosed the four sections of the formal garden. "You have been busy. The place looks far more like a garden now."

He was evading again.

"Because you want me?" She posed the question to her can, too nervous to ask him directly.

His gaze zipped to her and he cleared his throat.

"Well... I mean... my aura was... it has nothing to do... I was just..." He heaved a sigh. "Yes."

And braced himself.

His entire body tensed, muscles flexing beneath his black shirt, and he gripped his knees through his brown trousers, hard enough that his knuckles burned white.

Did he expect her to explode at him over that?

The thought that he wanted her might have scared her weeks ago, but now it sent a quiet thrill through her. She had wanted confirmation of his feelings, and she was finally getting it. The last few weeks spent wondering what he was doing, whether he was watching her, and whether he had seen her in the bath, had taken their toll on her, but now that weight lifted from her shoulders.

She reached into the cooler, snagged another can of soda, and offered it to him.

He surprised her by taking it, fumbling with opening it as badly as he had with admitting he wanted her, and cautiously tasted it. He shivered, every feather on his enormous white wings quivering.

Emelia arched a brow at his reaction.

He scowled at her. "I was not expecting it to be... tingly."

"Fizzy," she offered and his scowl deepened. "It's called fizzy. The drink is carbonated."

"Carbonated?" He studied the can with an arched brow of his own and then looked at her.

Emelia held her hands up. "Don't ask me to explain carbonation. I think it involves pumping gasses into the liquid."

He gave a slight nod, as if that explanation was more than enough for him to comprehend what science was at work in the can, and took another mouthful, grimacing as he swallowed it and losing a battle against another shiver.

She giggled.

He glared at her again.

"Sorry, it's just... your wings quiver when you drink." She idly brushed her hand down one and stilled with her palm against the soft, satiny feathers as gold instantly bled into his irises and his pupils dilated to devour it.

Her heart pounded in her throat and she eased her hand away.

"I... wasn't... *thinking*." She sounded as surprised as she felt as she spoke that word and it struck her that it wasn't that she hadn't been thinking, it was that she hadn't been overthinking things.

It had been instinct to touch his wings, even when she knew they were a part of him and it was no different to touching his hand or his thigh, or his face. She hadn't fought the instinct, or questioned it. She had just rolled with it, and damn, it felt good.

She had *touched* him.

They had been talking, and then she had been *laughing*, and then she had touched him, and it had felt good.

She wanted to laugh again at that.

But the way Wolf was watching her made that laugh catch in her throat.

He remained motionless, his eyes locked on hers, dark with desire she had roused by simply touching his wing. There was a battle in his eyes too, a war he was waging as he stared at her, his chest straining with each heavy breath.

His firm lips parted.

His tongue swept over them, sending a wave of fire rushing through her blood.

"Touch them again," he husked, anguish rolling across his face as he uttered that demand.

Because he thought he would frighten her, or because he feared she wouldn't do as he needed?

Her stomach somersaulted and she had to pull down a slow breath to steady her racing heart as her mind screamed they were moving too fast. Her body cried they weren't moving fast enough.

She lifted her hand and brought it to his wing, waged a war as violent as the one in his eyes as he tracked her hand with them, turning his cheek to her. She could do this. He was asking her to touch him, not ordering her. He needed this, and damn but she needed it too. She wanted to feel his feathers again, to explore their softness and learn the differences between them all, from the long feathers at the tips of his wings to the downy ones that covered the inside near his shoulder.

She swallowed to wet her dry mouth and throat.

Eased her hand forwards.

Made contact that sent a thousand volts bolting through her and ripped a gasp from her lips.

And his.

His eyes closed and his nostrils flared as the black slashes of his eyebrows dipped low above his nose.

"Sweet mercy," he muttered, strained and raw sounding, as if she was overloading him with her exploration of his wings.

Emelia slowly stroked her hand down the curve of his wings, memorising the way the feathers near the top were softer than the longer ones. Those felt firmer beneath her palm.

"What's it like to fly?" She focused on his wings, on what she was doing as she carefully skimmed her fingers outwards from the central rigid spine of one feather. "Do you moult like a bird?"

She almost smiled at the image that popped into her head, one of him tossing disgruntled looks at feathers he was shedding in his wake. She could just imagine how sour he would be.

"I do not know any different. It is natural to me, so I do not even think about it. Flying is just flying." He opened his eyes and tracked her hand with them. Their silver depths were swirling again, almost as mesmerising as the feel of his wings. "As for moulting, I do not go through it in the same manner as a bird does. There is no set season and time. I lose feathers throughout the year, purging weakened or damaged ones. Sometimes they require intervention on my part."

She lifted her gaze to meet his as the meaning of that hit her. "You pull your own feathers out? Sounds a little sadomasochistic to me."

His eyebrows dipped low again, narrowing his silvery gaze in a way that screamed his displeasure. "It is necessary."

"Does it hurt?" She couldn't imagine what it would be like to tug a feather loose. Like pulling a nail from the bed? Or ripping a hank of hair out? Or maybe it was more like a wobbly tooth and it was a simple twist-and-yank procedure that only hurt for a short time.

He shrugged, shifting his wing beneath her palm. "Depends on the feather. If I pulled a pinion feather out, that would hurt. Move back a little."

"Why?"

"Because I do not want to hurt you." His expression turned deadly serious and she did as he asked because she didn't want him to hurt her either.

She scooted back on the stone step, placing some distance between them, and her eyes widened as he twisted away from her and stretched his wing forwards so it formed a barrier between them and his feathers spread.

His wings were far larger than she had expected.

When they were furled against his back, they were imposing, distracting in a way, but like this, they were incredible. His wing easily reached twelve feet across, close to twice his impressive height.

"The longest ones are flight feathers. Secondaries nearest my body and primaries at the tips of my wings. The dozen or so nearest the tip are also called pinions. They hurt if they are pulled out." The way he said that made her wonder if he had ever had one pulled out by an enemy. His wings were an advantage against many immortals, and she would probably target them if she was fighting an angel. He curled his wing towards him a little and reached over to poke at the shorter feathers above the primaries and secondaries. "These are coverts. They hurt less. I have probably pulled thousands of them out over the years."

"How many years?" It struck her that she didn't even know how old he was.

He looked like a man in his late thirties, close to her age. She didn't know anything about angels, other than what popular culture and mythology made them out to be. Archangel had never been able to study his kind. How long could he live? What powers did he have? What was his world like? She suddenly had a thousand questions she wanted to ask him.

He peered over his wing, his silver gaze locking with hers, as if he wanted to gauge her reaction. "Nine hundred and twenty-four."

"Fuck, you're old." She smiled when he looked affronted. "Puts my thirty-six years into perspective. I thought I was getting old. Now I feel like a spring chicken."

He glowered at her and went back to his wing, evading again. "These tufts at the bend are alula, and these are scapulars."

"They look soft." She reached up and ran her hand over one, delighted when they were as soft as they appeared, and over the fact she was finding it easy to touch his wings now, as if it was perfectly natural for her to be doing such a thing.

Which was such a relief that her throat closed up. She picked up her soda again and took a mouthful, hiding in the can as she swallowed it because she didn't want him to see how this was affecting her. She had been so convinced she would never know normal again that it was all a little too much for her to handle.

Wolf furled his wings against his back, so they draped across the paving behind her, and swigged his drink, his feathers quivering less this time. He stared off into the distance, mercury eyes reflecting the sunset as it intensified, the entire sky above the distant woods turning pink and gold.

Emelia studied his profile, unable to take her eyes off him. They were so different. He was closing in on a thousand years old, was an immortal warrior, and his seven-foot frame made her feel like a damned dwarf, but she had never felt closer to anyone in all her limited years.

She had never felt so comfortable around a man.

"It is beautiful here." He sighed and rested the can on his knee.

It was, and she appreciated it more for having been in Hell, a world without colour and light, and life. Did he feel the same way now that he had been there?

"Wolf?" She swirled her can around in her right hand, her eyes on it now as she thought about that realm and his reason for going there.

Not the dragon.

He was doing it for her.

"Yes?" His gaze landed on her, sending heat dancing over her skin.

She tripped on her words. "I... could you... just... I won't tell you not to... but know that I don't want you to go back there."

He was right, and she couldn't tell him what to do any more than he could tell her what to do. His need was as strong as the one that beat inside her whenever she was feeling brave, was able to think about Zephyr and facing him without crumbling into a pathetic weak little thing that just wanted to hide and cower somewhere.

He wanted to make the dragon pay.

He just wasn't afraid as she was, not even of going into a place that apparently hurt him. He faced that pain and bore it, endured it so he could fulfil the desire drumming inside him.

"Emelia," he started and then looked away from her, and she appreciated him not lying to her. Telling her he wouldn't go just to please her and offer her relief, and then going back to that place would hurt her more than the thought of him entering Hell again. She didn't want him to lie to her. "Would you like to fly? I mean, if you wanted, I could—"

"Hell, no!" She weathered his glare as his head swivelled towards her. "It's just, no thanks. I don't like flying in planes... The thought of flying... Can your wings even support the weight of two?"

He casually hiked his shoulders. "I believe they could. They can easily carry me, and you cannot weigh much. You're such a slender, petite thing."

She mirrored his glare. "I'm not petite."

She supposed she was compared with his seven-foot frame, but she had managed to hit the average height for a woman. Just. Considering her mother had been petite, she was counting her blessings. If she had come out five or six inches shorter, she would have felt ridiculously tiny when standing near Wolf and not just tiny.

"It's not my fault immortal genes make men stupidly tall," she grumbled into her can.

The corners of his profane lips curled into a shadow of a smile. "All male angels are tall, but the warrior class are the tallest."

"You're considered warrior class?" She glanced at him out of the corner of her eye, could easily see why he would be with his carved muscles and impressive physique and the calluses she hadn't missed on his hands that said he wielded weapons a lot. "Like me?"

That shadow of a smile became a full-blown grin.

It devastated her.

Tore down her defences in a skipped heartbeat.

He was gorgeous when he smiled like that, his silver eyes shining brightly with it.

"A warrior?" He chuckled as he looked at her. "Perhaps in your world. In mine, the males would think you play at being something you are not."

"Well, that's nice," she snapped with a frown. "Now I know Heaven is severely lacking in equality, I definitely don't want to go there."

He shrugged again. "You could not venture there anyway. The entry points into my realm have been sealed to all outside my breed for centuries, since long before I was born."

"You couldn't even sneak me past the pearly gates?" She swayed towards him and stopped herself when she realised she meant to nudge him with her arm, a silly gesture meant to cajole him into playing along with her, but one that probably would have had his eyes glowing gold again.

And her heart missing another beat.

"There are no pearly gates, and Heaven is what mortals call it. Like Hell. Mortal terms, used to make it easier to communicate with your kind."

"Is it made of white fluffy clouds?"

He chuckled, the warm sound of it like a shot of the finest whisky, smoky and decadent, and filling her with a gentle heat that melted her worries away again.

"It is mostly white, that much is true, but it is not clouds. Like Hell, it is a solid plane, with mountains and forests that surround the cities. Creatures roam it. There are roads and farmsteads and many things you have in this world."

"So it's nega-Hell?"

He arched an eyebrow.

"Like a negative version of Hell? Hell is all black, and Heaven is all white?"

He rolled his shoulders again. "The sky is blue."

She tilted her head back and looked at her sky. It was growing dark now, and faint pinpricks of stars were emerging.

"You have stars there." It was a statement, not a question, and he looked at her, a flicker of a frown dancing on his dark eyebrows. She pinned her gaze back on the heavens again. "When we met on the rooftop of Archangel, you said you preferred the view of the stars from my world."

"I do." He leaned back, resting his elbows on the flagstones, and stretched his legs out, crossing them at the ankles. "The days are longer where I come from, and I am always busy when I am there. Here in this world, I have time to stop and look."

"It's important to do that." She lowered her gaze to him and didn't look away when their eyes locked. "To stop and look. To take a breath to see the world around you... The leaves as they emerge in spring, or flowers that blanket a summer meadow, the snow as it falls, or the stars in the sky. We only get one life. It's important to take in as much of the world while we can and not rush headlong through our years only to end them never seeing anything."

She chuckled and shook her head.

"Look at me... lecturing an angel on the importance of taking a moment to take in the world before it's too late. You're a bloody thousand years old."

"Nine hundred and twenty-four," he corrected as his eyebrows dipped low above his swirling mercury gaze.

"That's probably eight hundred and fifty more than I'll ever see."

Something crossed his eyes, a shadow that darkened them, and she wanted to know what he was thinking as he looked away from her, gazing up at the emerging stars again.

The air between them cooled like the day as it turned to night, and she wished she could take back what she had said, because it clearly troubled him. He wasn't the only one who had thought about the fact he was immortal and she was just mortal. He wasn't the only one it troubled.

Even if they were to end up together, how long would it be before he moved on? She was going to age, and as far as she knew, he wouldn't. Or at least he would do it extremely slowly. She gave it no more than ten years before he traded her in for a younger model, probably one who was immortal like him.

For some reason, that made her heart sting. She rubbed the sore spot between her breasts, trying to ignore the ache and how hopeless she suddenly felt, deflated when just a moment ago, she had been filled with life and light, and everything had felt wonderful for the first time in what felt like forever.

"Emelia?" he murmured, his voice distant in her ears. "If you could live forever, would you?"

She pursed her lips as she considered that. "Who wouldn't want more years? All those things you wanted to do and never found the time... You could do them. You could see the world change, explore it all, touch a thousand lives. What human wouldn't want more time? I'd be crazy to say no."

"But I mean... if it was possible for you to become immortal."

That sounded less pipedream and more serious, so she looked down at him, studying his face as he studied the stars, diligently keeping his eyes away from her. Did he know a way to become immortal? Would she want to go through with it if he did?

She returned her focus to the stars, thinking about it as she traced patterns in the sky, linking the brightening pinpricks.

If she had a chance to live forever, would she take it?

Sable had become immortal when she had mated with Thorne. Olivia had gone through the same transition.

But they had been fated mates.

Born for each other.

"I don't know." Because she honestly didn't.

If she remained mortal, Wolf might leave her when she grew old or got a few wrinkles and things started sagging, but that pain would be short-lived, over in a matter of years when her life came to a close.

If she became immortal and Wolf left her for some reason, she would have to face centuries of living with the idea the man she loved had abandoned her.

She tensed.

The man she loved?

Was it already too late to save herself?

She had wanted to find a way to guard her heart against him, had thought she had more time.

She traced the noble lines of Wolf's profile, heart hitching as she thought about her feelings and how deep they ran.

She loved him.

This wasn't good.

She couldn't love him, couldn't love an immortal. Their relationship was doomed from the start. She fought to stifle the hurt that caused, but it bloomed in her chest, swift and fierce, stealing her breath. He said he didn't want to hurt her, and she didn't want that either, but just the thought of falling harder for him and having him leave her when she was too old cut her deep. It wasn't the only source of her pain, though. Even if he didn't leave her, their love would only destroy one of them. The thought of him having to watch her age, seeing her change and fade, knowing he would lose her in the span of only a few decades, tore at her too.

"I fear I have outstayed my welcome." He pushed to his feet, the air around him cold and darker than before.

Emelia struggled to find her voice to ask him not to go, not to leave her, not yet.

He took a slow step backwards, and the pain in her heart grew as she realised he was distancing himself from her, bringing up a wall between them to shut her out. Why? It wasn't the first time he had done it, but that didn't make it hurt any less. Why did he feel the need to close himself off to her?

Or perhaps he just closed off the softer parts of himself.

She looked at him, studying the hard planes of his face and his impassive silver eyes as he stared down at her.

"Emelia." He dipped his head, those cold eyes slashing her heart to pieces, and then he was gone.

She blinked, stared at the spot where he had been, and wasn't sure whether she wanted to scream out her frustration or curl into a ball and hold herself.

"What makes you pull away?" She tugged her knees up to her chest and held them.

She thought back over everything that had happened today, how he had reacted at times, darkness emerging in his eyes and sucking the warmth from the air, and how withdrawn he had become whenever she hadn't been speaking, holding his focus.

Cold danced down her spine, chilling her blood.

Was Hell affecting him worse than he had let on? Had he left because their conversation had pained him, or because he needed to go back to Hell and continue his hunt?

Was he hiding things from her?

She didn't want that. She worried about him enough as it was without him concealing things from her. How badly did Hell affect angels?

Enough to turn him from good to evil?

Fallen angels roamed Hell and called it home. Could spending too much time in that realm, exposed to all the darkness it contained, cause Wolf to fall?

A fiery lance speared her heart at that thought and she shot to her feet and strode over to the table, her eyes on the phone resting on top of her fleece.

She needed answers.

And she knew Wolf wouldn't give them to her, would skirt around the issue to keep her from worrying and from demanding he give up his mission to avenge her.

So she would get them from Sable.

Her friend had mentioned an angel in London, one she had been to see when her, Thorne and Bleu had been shut out of the Third Realm during the war. One who Sable had been frequently visiting in the past few weeks as she tried to learn more about the world her father had been part of. Sable would be able to answer her questions, and if she couldn't, Emelia would ask her to introduce her to the fallen angel.

She dialled Underworld, the nightclub where Sable had been hiding out between her visits to Hell and the angel.

"Yello," a deep male voice growled at the other end of the line.

Kyter. The big jaguar shifter owned Underworld and had seemed nice enough the few times she had met him.

"It's Emelia. I need to speak with Sable."

Glass clinked and someone muttered obscenities in the background. Kyter covered the receiver, and she couldn't make out what he said as he shouted at them.

She gripped the phone harder, waiting impatiently as an argument erupted. As it subsided, the line crackled again, and Kyter's voice came through loud and clear.

"She's not here right now, but I can relay a message when she drops in."

She let out the breath she had been holding and sucked another in for courage when she thought about how angry Wolf might be with her for meeting her friend and probing into his life as an angel, let alone the fact she was going to meet Sable when he probably still wanted to fulfil his mission to bring her in for the Echelon.

He could be mad at her all he wanted.

Sable was her friend, and she would protect her.

Wolf was her everything, and she would protect him too, even if it was from himself.

"Tell her I really need to meet her."

A loud crash sounded at the other end of the line.

Kyter growled something at someone else and then gruffly spoke to her.

"Tell her yourself. Her idiot mate just landed on one of my tables with her."

CHAPTER 18

Emelia sat at the long black bar of Underworld, the music quiet as the place dialled down for the evening. She had driven straight from her home to the heart of London, the thought of seeing Sable and getting everything off her chest while learning more about angels too alluring to deny.

For once in her life, she wanted to talk to someone. She needed it.

She sipped her whisky, savouring the smokiness and smoothness of it as it reminded her of Wolf and the way he had laughed. That laugh had been just as intoxicating as the drink, and she wanted to hear it again, and feared she wouldn't if she let him continue his vendetta.

"Another?" Sherry asked as she reached her and stopped cleaning the bar top.

She had a lot in common with Sherry. They were both human and they both knew that immortals existed, and neither of them were particularly bothered by it.

The blonde swept her ponytail behind her as she straightened, and grumbled something as she pressed her hands into the small of her back and arched forwards, causing her white shirt to tighten across her breasts.

Her warm blue eyes turned cold as a man hollered something in her direction.

Sherry saluted him with her middle finger. "Rowdy fuckers."

Kyter paused as he came out from the back of the bar with a box in his arms, his face darkening and eyes brightening to a shade of gold that matched his wild short hair as he looked from Sherry to the man.

"He bothering you?" he growled and narrowed his gaze.

His muscles tensed beneath his tight white shirt as he flexed his fingers against the cardboard box.

The man made a fast exit.

"Nah." Sherry waved her hand down through the air. "Just tired of getting catcalls whenever I stretch. It's not my fault I'm blessed with boobs."

Emelia wished someone had blessed her with them. She looked down at her own meagre offering, hidden beneath the loose black T-shirt and leather jacket she had thrown on before jumping in her car.

She shut out the voice at the back of her mind before it could wonder whether Wolf liked large breasts or not.

Sherry and Kyter both looked towards the entrance of the club. Emelia glanced there too, the hope building inside her turning into something else as she saw it wasn't Sable.

It was Anais.

And she had the feeling the fair-haired huntress wasn't here for a nightcap.

Anais pulled a face that was half apology, half grimace as she slid onto the stool beside Emelia.

"Sable isn't coming," Emelia said for her, sparing her the job of having to break the news to her. "She sent you."

"Yeah." Anais accepted the whisky that Sherry poured for her and offered another apologetic look, her dark blue eyes overflowing with it and concern. "She said you wanted to talk about a problem."

She had, but Anais wasn't going to be much use to her. What had Sable been thinking by asking Anais to come to her instead?

"It's nothing. I needed some information she could give me, that's all." She waved away the drink Sherry slid towards her. "I came all the way from Cambridge to see her."

"Sorry." Anais pushed a rogue strand of blonde hair back into the loose knot at the back of her head. "She said there was trouble at the border. Thorne had to take her back. She really wanted to speak with you."

Trouble at the border.

Emelia suspected that Thorne had dragged her away because she had wanted to talk about angels, and he wanted to keep his mate out of Wolf's hands.

"Dammit." She pushed her glass away, frustration mounting inside her as she tried to figure out what to do now. Could she speak with the fallen angel herself?

Apparently, the woman lived at a vampire theatre somewhere in London. How many vampire theatres were there in the city? It couldn't be that hard to find one. She knew where to find vampires who were talkative for the right price, although normally she wasn't the one offering up her vein.

Could she let a man bite her and take her blood for the sake of learning more about Wolf and what might be happening to him in Hell?

It felt too intimate, as if she would be cheating on Wolf by letting a vampire get that close to her, closer than he had been.

"Emelia?" Anais leaned forwards, coming into her field of vision, and Emelia shook herself out of her thoughts.

She couldn't let a vampire bite her, and not only because she didn't want to do that to Wolf.

She couldn't go through with it because she couldn't bear a man being that close to her, holding her, restraining her while he took from her.

Just the thought of a strong man gripping her arms, caging her against his body, his lips on her neck and her at his mercy was enough to have her throat closing and muscles clamping down on her bones.

"Emelia." Anais touched her arm.

Emelia batted her arm away, breathing hard as panic flashed through her. It quickly subsided, leaving her staring at her friend's hand as she realised what she had done.

"Sorry," she mumbled and pulled her glass back to her, lifted it to her lips, and drained the last of her whisky.

"Do you want to talk about it?" Anais's soft voice, so tentative and careful, had Emelia's hackles rising, but she fought back against the instinct to push her friend away.

"Not really." She sighed and pushed the empty glass away instead, and reached for the full one Sherry had left for her after she had refused it. "How's Loke?"

Anais's expression grew guarded and Emelia couldn't blame her for being wary after everything Archangel had put the dragon shifter through.

"I'm asking as your friend," Emelia said, wishing things with Archangel were different and she hadn't needed to distinguish.

But they weren't different. They were all messed up. Her friends were all leaving that place behind and she wasn't blind, she could see it wasn't only because they had found men they loved. Archangel was shifting course, starting to tread a darker path, one she wasn't sure she could follow it down.

"He's fine. He'll be a nightmare when I get back. He was against Thorne bringing me here."

"Because he can't be here?" When Anais nodded, Emelia added, "What's it like for him when he's here?"

"He's weaker, drastically weaker. He can't shift, and I think that only makes him feel even weaker. It's different for him now we're bonded, but he's still drained if he comes to this world."

"How weak?" She couldn't stop her mind from traversing paths almost as dark as the one Archangel was treading. "As weak as a mortal?"

Anais's eyes narrowed. "Where's this leading?"

She could see what her friend was thinking and she was way off the mark. "It isn't about Archangel. I just... If a... *dragon*... came here, would I be able to kill it?"

"You mean, if Zephyr came here, could you kill him?" Her friend's tone was hard as she stared into her eyes, and Emelia forced herself to remain looking at her, to let her see that was the question she was really asking. "With the right weapons... probably. Why? Do you have a reason to think Zephyr will come after you?"

She swallowed hard, nerves crashing over her as she fought to find the words, ones she hadn't told anyone, not even Wolf.

"Emelia, what is it?" Anais leaned closer, concern washing across her delicate features as she looked up into Emelia's eyes, her blue ones filled with worry. They darted between hers as her voice failed her and awareness dawned in them. "You think he's going to try to take you back."

She didn't think it. She *knew* it. Some deep, primal part of herself knew that Zephyr wouldn't let her go. She had seen the need in his eyes, one that wouldn't die unless he did.

She wasn't sure how much longer she could go on knowing that at any time, he could appear before her and take her back to Hell.

"I'd be strong enough to kill him, right?" She searched her friend's eyes, hating how her voice wobbled, lacking the belief she knew she would need if she faced him.

She had to believe she could kill him, or it would be game over. She would never manage to defeat him if part of her was convinced she was going to fail and he was going to force her to become his.

"You are... in this world. Tell me you're not thinking of doing something crazy here, Emelia." Anais placed her hand over hers on the black bar top. "You can't go to Hell to find him."

"I know that," she bit out, fear for Wolf sharpening her tone as it gripped her, squeezing her heart until she felt it might burst. "He'll come for me... if Wolf doesn't find him first."

"Wolf?" Anais canted her head, causing her messy tangle of blonde hair to slip to one side. "Who's Wolf?"

How to put it? Did she keep it straight and nothing more than the basics, or did she admit what was in her heart?

"Remember the angel?" she said.

Anais frowned.

"The bastard who wanted to kill Loke... oh..." Blonde eyebrows rose high as her blue eyes widened. "Wolf is the angel. He has a name now."

"I sort of... might have... might be responsible for that. But that's not the point." She really wasn't going to get into why he had called himself Wolf, because it would only lead to more questions. "I needed to speak with Sable because Wolf keeps going to Hell."

"Hang on. The angel who is after Sable keeps going to Hell, a place he said he couldn't go? A place where Sable thinks she's safe?" A flare of panic lit Anais's eyes. "We have to warn her."

"He's not there for her. He wants to kill the dragon." Her face crumpled as she thought about that. "I think he's weaker in Hell, though. It affects him like this world affects dragons. I'm worried he's going to get himself killed, or worse."

"Worse?"

"What if there's a reason angels aren't meant to spend time in that place? We know there are such things as fallen angels in that realm. What if angels fall if they're exposed to it for too long? He's already changing." She pushed her fingers through her dark hair, pulling it back as she thought about Wolf roaming that bleak land, coming into contact with forces that might corrupt him and ultimately lead to his downfall. "It's why I need to speak with Sable."

"Okay, okay. I'll tell her when I get back. If she had known it was like this, she would have come. I promise."

"Like what?" Emelia tensed.

"Oh, Emelia... It's clear you have feelings for him. I don't know what's been happening between you two, but if he's doing this for you... well, he must have feelings for you too."

Emelia schooled her expression, even when she knew it was too late to hide how she felt about Wolf.

"Emelia?" Anais started, a low note of caution in her voice that had Emelia tensing for a different reason, bracing herself for the question she could feel coming. "What did Zephyr do to you? I don't want to probe, and tell me to shut up if you want. It's... When I was taken to their clan chief, Zephyr said some things."

"Things?" She frowned, afraid of what the dragon might have told everyone about her.

"He said he had broken you, that you did nothing but cry now because he had been…" Her friend paled. "I can't say it. I can't… if he… God, Emelia, I can only imagine what he did. Loke told me he's cruel, refuses to use his powers to make a female want him… that he likes to hurt them and do things against… I'm sorry, I shouldn't be saying this."

"It's fine." And it was, because now she understood why everyone at Archangel had been smothering her so badly. "You told Sable about all this, didn't you?"

Anais nodded.

And Sable had told the medical team, Mark and Linda.

Everyone thought Zephyr had been violating her, had broken her mind by abusing her body.

He had damaged her, there was no doubt about that, and what had happened to her was terrible, but it could have been so much worse, and it was nowhere near to what everyone thought had happened.

It wasn't even close to what Zephyr had said had happened.

Why had he lied?

She shoved him out of her head, but he refused to go, kept looming in it, tormenting her even now.

Why hadn't he treated her like he had treated so many other women, judging by what Loke had told Anais about him?

He had been different with her, but he had still been cruel. A leopard couldn't change his spots, and Zephyr's were black blemishes on his soul that tainted him, coloured his actions and controlled him. He might not have broken her as he did other females, but he had been vicious at times, had lashed out at her, revealing what sort of man he was.

Still, she felt lucky as she thought about what Loke had told Anais about Zephyr. Which was weird. She wasn't lucky at all. Zephyr had put her through hell.

But it could have been so much worse.

Unspeakably worse.

"It isn't the truth." She sipped her whisky for courage, because she wanted to talk at last, but it was still difficult. Anais wouldn't judge her, not as others at Archangel would if they knew what had really happened to her. She kept telling herself that as she lined up the words. "He was cruel, and he did… touch me… over my clothes… sometimes not… and he made me touch him once, but I hurt him."

Surprise flickered in her friend's eyes. "What happened then?"

"He was angry with me. He said something vicious sounding in the dragon tongue and hit me so hard, I almost blacked out. He left me alone for a while after that, went to the ledge of the cave and ignored me for a day straight." Which had been heavenly because she had needed the reprieve, the space to think about how he had changed and to wonder why. She hadn't imagined the cause of his change to be anything close to what had fuelled it—that he wanted her to love him. "Another time when I lashed out at him, he retaliated by splitting my lip and twisting my arm behind my back, forcing my front against the wall of the cave. He pressed against me from behind, and I was so scared... But rather than... He ended up trying to soothe me."

"That doesn't sound like the Zephyr I met." Anais shook her head. "No... he said that he..."

"I don't know why he lied." She honestly didn't. She was having as much trouble trying to comprehend that as Anais was.

"What happened after he tried to calm you?"

She swallowed another mouthful of whisky, needing the liquid shot of courage. "He left and was gone for some time before he came back with a dead creature."

"He left?" Anais's eyes widened. "As in... you were alone? Unguarded?"

She nodded, hating herself all over again for missing her chance. "I was too afraid to attempt an escape, and in too much pain. Maybe he did break me a little. I had been too busy crying to even think about running."

"That's nothing to be ashamed of, Emelia." Anais curled her fingers over Emelia's hand and held it gently. "It's only natural. My strength left me at times too, but we're both still here. Still fighting."

She wished she could smile at that, but she felt too heavy inside, weighed down by what had happened. She needed to get it off her chest, to spill it all and hope it would free her as she believed it would.

"When he came back, I was terrified. I thought he was going to try again." She shook her head, remembering how he had looked, his expression hard and his green eyes more than a little crazed before his entire face had softened, all the tension draining from him as he had looked at her arm where she had been holding it to her. "He came back... different. I wasn't sure what to make of him."

"Different how?" Curiosity mixed with suspicion tinged her friend's voice.

"He took care of my arm, was gentle with me, which confused the hell out of me." She closed her eyes as she remembered what had happened next. "He was so grave that when he told me I could leave, I believed him. I reached the cave mouth before he grabbed me from behind."

"Bastard," Anais spat, the venom in that one word flowing in Emelia's veins, eating away at her like acid.

She gripped her glass harder, glaring at it. "I couldn't take it anymore, so I lashed out at him. He was weak, injured, but he didn't fight me. He just kept saying that he couldn't let me go. That I couldn't leave him. I sank into myself... I... gave up."

And she was ashamed to admit that.

She had prided herself on being strong, capable, and a warrior.

Depression had defeated her so easily, had revealed the truth of her. She wasn't strong. She was weak.

She didn't want to be weak again, and if it took slaying a dragon to make her feel strong once more, she would do anything to achieve Zephyr's death.

"He tried to make me eat." She wanted to vomit at just the thought of the food he had tried to give her, meat she still wasn't sure which creature it had come from. "I refused, and when I felt sure I might finally die of hunger, I... I was scared. I didn't want to die, but I couldn't eat what he was offering. I begged him for fruit... something familiar to me. Something from my world."

"What happened?" Anais grabbed the bottle of whisky Sherry had left and poured them both another, and Emelia looked around, only just now realising they were alone.

The club was empty, as quiet as that cave had been. Almost as dark.

"He swore he would get me anything I wanted and mentioned a town in the free realm where he could get some. He immediately left to get it. I thought about escaping, but when I tried, I passed out." She took a large gulp of the whisky and forced it down. "When I came around, I was in the medical wing with Sable standing over me."

She had been so relieved to see her friend, to see the familiar surroundings, and so afraid that it was nothing more than a dream, that she had broken down.

"So Zephyr never...?" Anais said.

Emelia shook her head. "No."

Her friend looked relieved to hear that.

"He touched me a few times, and was vicious and hit me, hurt me... and he kissed me once... but I tried to bite his tongue off, so he didn't try again after that." Even though her stomach had turned at the thought of actually biting it off once she had sunk her teeth into his tongue, she had still tried to go through with it. Zephyr had been too quick for her, and too strong. He had easily broken free of her, and had struck her for her efforts, almost breaking her jaw. "I think he tried hard to be nice to me."

Which was the most confusing thing of all and one that still haunted her to this day, had her thinking about it from time to time, trying to decipher why he had been attempting to be kind.

"I don't know why he changed. Do you have any idea?" She couldn't get answers or insight into angels without Sable, but she could certainly get some answers about dragons from Anais.

"Nope." Her friend studied her drink. "According to Loke, Zephyr is known for taking females against their will and taking pleasure from it."

Emelia shuddered at the reminder. "Why didn't he do that with me, then?"

Not that she was upset he had tried to be nice to her instead of completely breaking her.

"I don't know."

There was wariness in her friend's voice and a guarded edge to her blue eyes that rang alarm bells in Emelia's head.

Her voice was a touch too bright when she said, "I can ask Loke."

Emelia frowned.

Anais knew something and was hiding it from her.

That feeling was compounded when her friend stood, hurriedly gathered her things, and barely spared her a glance. "I had better get back. I'll tell Sable to get in touch with you about the angel."

As she watched her friend go and silence rose around her, a question spun around her mind.

What wouldn't Anais tell her?

CHAPTER 19

Wolf paced the garden, wearing a trench in the grass as he fought a constant battle against the darkness writhing inside him. His lips peeled back off his clenched teeth as he pivoted and strode back the way he had come, his steps clipped as his entire body tensed. The air around him cooled, the evening light growing dimmer. He rolled his shoulders, trying to shake off the invisible force that was irritating the fuck out of him. When that didn't offer the relief he needed, he flapped his wings, hoping the feel of the wind in his feathers would soothe him.

Where was Emelia?

He needed to see her.

Black thoughts surfaced, wicked ones that goaded his mood into traversing darker paths. She should have been here. Where had she gone without him? To see someone? A male? He growled, the inhuman sound pealing from between his teeth as he glared at the mansion. She wasn't here, that was for sure.

The air around him darkened further, turning towards night despite the sun that skirted the horizon.

His fingers twitched at his sides, the urge to call his blade to him and hunt her down growing stronger inside him, almost overwhelming him before he wrestled it back under control, tamping it down enough that he remained where he was.

His heavy white armour clanked with each rough stride that carried him across the grass.

He flexed his fingers again as his gaze settled on the rose garden, and his lips twisted in a cold smile as a hunger to go there and tear it all down surged through him. Images played across his mind, a vision of him ripping every rosebush from the ground, destroying that place Emelia held dear.

Because she wasn't here.

She had to pay for that.

He caught himself as he pivoted towards the walled garden, froze as cold swept through him as he realised the path of his thoughts and how much pain it would cause Emelia if he followed that urge that beckoned him with promises of relief and retribution.

Retribution?

He had no reason to desire such a thing where Emelia was concerned.

She had done nothing wrong.

He growled again and shoved his fingers through his black hair, clawing it back with both hands. He clamped his palms down against his skull and squeezed as his growl turned pained, a hollow sound that bore every drop of the frustration and confusion welling up inside him.

What was wrong with him?

He had seen Emelia only yesterday. It should have been enough to calm him, to give him the focus he needed. But when he had teleported into Hell, the effect she had on him had instantly dissipated, replaced by degrees with other feelings.

Rage.

Despair.

A hunger to kill any who strayed into his path.

Wolf sank to his knees on the grass, breathing hard as he continued to fight those emotions, to overcome them and rein them in to regain control over himself.

That urge had only grown in strength as he had scouted the dragon realm, charting several small villages nestled among valleys surrounded by high, dangerous black peaks. Several caves had been visible, opening on ledges high on the sides of the mountains. He had wanted to investigate them, but had managed to focus on taking stock of the entire area, aware that landing at the entrance of what was likely the home of a dragon might be seen as an act of aggression.

Although, apparently, entering one of the villages to politely inquire about any green dragons was an act of aggression too. The dragons had turned on him, and he had been forced to teleport to avoid a fight he knew he would lose. It had been difficult, a struggle when he had wanted to fight, had craved the violence the dragons had promised as they had closed in on him. For a brief moment, he had imagined the battle, and had found it glorious.

He still found it glorious.

He had left Hell three hours ago, but still the effects lingered, had him close to losing himself to the dark needs that burned in his veins.

Hunt. Kill. Destroy.

He could return to Hell and fulfil those needs.

Or he could venture somewhere else, somewhere less dangerous, where he would be strong enough to win any fights he started.

He slowly turned his head, his eyes unerringly fixing in the direction of a place where he could sate those needs.

A fae town.

He was swift to lose himself in the images that built in his mind, a glorious vision of mayhem and destruction, blood-soaked and beautiful. How many demons lived in a fae town? One hundred? Two hundred?

A shiver wracked him at the thought of slaying two hundred demons, a ripple of pleasure chasing down his spine that had him pushing to his feet and spreading his wings, aching with a need to fulfil that vision.

He paused as he twisted towards the fae town.

His eyes dropped to his left wing.

To the tiny cluster of black feathers nestled close to his side.

A sign he had been sinning.

He didn't recall committing a sin.

Was Hell corrupting him to the point where he was in danger of falling?

His strength bled from him as the answer to that question hit him, rocking his world on its axis.

Yes.

It was slowly but surely destroying him.

His mood was testament to that. The black needs and darkness he could normally keep under control were slipping their leash more often, and during his last trip to Hell, he had come close to fighting everyone who had failed to provide him with useful information. He had wanted to kill them.

Those dark urges weren't born of the fact he felt he wasn't making progress with his mission to avenge Emelia.

They were born of the fact Hell was tainting him.

Turning him.

"Wolf?" Emelia's soft voice cut into his thoughts, and he whirled to face her, shock tearing through him as he found her standing close to him.

He hadn't sensed her.

Her eyes dropped to his left wing.

He quickly furled it against his back, but the sorrow that danced across her delicate features said he had been too late.

She had seen his black feathers.

"What do they mean?" she whispered, her eyes leaping up to meet his before they darted back to his wing.

"Nothing," he bit out more harshly than intended, and she flinched away, recoiling from him.

He growled and reached for her, wanting to pull her back to him, needing her close because she was already calming him, soothing the sharper edges of his temper.

She curled into herself, closing her leather jacket over her loose black T-shirt and frowning at him. "It's because you keep going to Hell, isn't it? You know what sort of angel has black wings? A fallen one."

"That is not happening to me." He tried to say it with conviction, but the look she gave him said she had seen the doubts and fears he held locked within his heart.

"It is." She shook her head, her dark eyebrows furrowing as she looked up at him. "I don't want this, Wolf. I don't want you to ruin your life. It isn't worth it!"

She meant that. He could read it in her. She honestly believed what he was doing wasn't worth it. If he found the dragon and killed him, wouldn't she be happy?

Of course she would be happy. So why was she denying him, trying to make out that what he was doing was pointless, a waste of both their times, when he knew it would please her?

His mood darkened, and he couldn't stop his voice from darkening with it. "I think it is. I think you are worth it."

Her expression shifted, delicate features softening as the anger he had sensed in her faded, giving way to emotions that put sorrow back in her eyes.

She solemnly shook her head, her green eyes pleading him as she lowered her arms to her side and took a step towards him. "Never go there again. Let it go."

He stared at her in silence, the darkness inside him writhing like a living being as he considered what she was asking, growing stronger with each passing second.

"I cannot," he husked and curled his fingers into tight fists beside his hips. "What that bastard did to you is unforgivable. I will not rest until I have punished him for it... until he is dead, Emelia. I will do this for you... I must."

Because the alternative was just as unacceptable as the fact the dragon was still breathing.

She lowered her head and whispered, "It won't change what happened. It won't take it away."

"I know." His right hand itched at his side, the need to lift it and cup her pale cheek, to comfort her so powerful that it was difficult to deny it, even when he was aware his touch would frighten her. "I wish I could do that for you, but your mind is too strong… your memories too painful."

She slowly raised her head and her eyes locked with his again, the emotions that swam in them mingling together to make them unreadable. "You want to make them go away for me?"

He nodded.

"Maybe there is a way… no… never mind." An emotion he could decipher danced across her eyes.

Fear.

What was it she was considering that had her suddenly afraid?

"Tell me the way, Emelia." He forced himself to remain where he was, even when the need to step closer to her drove him to surrender to it. "I would do anything to help you. Whatever it takes."

"Whatever it takes?" She searched his eyes and he nodded again.

Shock flashed through him when she suddenly took hold of his right hand, followed by a surge of heat that set his blood on fire. A thousand desires sprang to life inside him, clamouring to be the one he gave in to, but he held them all in check.

Because she was trembling.

Her hand shook against his as she slowly raised it, bringing his up with hers, and he tensed as she brought it to her face. His breath hitched in his throat, lungs squeezing tight and heart hammering a fast beat against his breast as she gently unfurled his fingers and placed his palm against her cheek.

Wolf stilled.

He could feel how difficult this was for her, could see it in her eyes as the fear he had sensed in her collided with panic and her shaking worsened.

The emotions colouring her eyes had them shifting, though, her pupils dilating to devour the rich green of her irises as she leaned into his touch.

The heat that stirred in him blazed into an inferno, had him aching to brush his palm across her cheek and feel the softness of it, the warmth that turned it a pretty shade of rose.

When she calmed, her emotions levelling out, he risked it.

Smoothed his palm against her cheek.

Her eyes slipped shut.

Shot wide open as her panic spiked right back up.

She hurled his hand away from her and stumbled back a step, her breathing laboured and eyes wild as she stared at him.

"I would never hurt you, Emelia," he whispered, meaning every word, feeling the strength of them in his heart. To hurt her would be to hurt himself. "Never."

She looked as if she needed to believe that, wanted to believe it, but couldn't.

Because of the dragon.

His mood blackened in an instant, the air around him darkening and chilling as rage roared to the fore, the need to destroy the dragon blazing so fiercely in his blood that he couldn't contain it. He growled and focused on his hand as he imagined killing the male. A slow death. He would make the bastard suffer for what he had done to Emelia. He would draw out the pain, would torment him, let him heal his wounds only to inflict new ones. He would take pleasure in watching the male bleed, in seeing his fear as he begged for mercy only to be offered none.

He would tear the male to pieces, from the inside out, breaking his mind before he broke his body.

He sank into the darkness that swirled around him, chilled his insides and clouded his mind.

His sword materialised in his hand and he gripped it hard, a smile stretching his lips as he shifted his focus to Hell.

He snarled as shadows wrapped around him, climbing his limbs like vines, and spread his wings as he surrendered to the hunger for violence, bloodshed and death that called to him.

He would find the dragon and he would kill it.

Soft warmth pressed against his cold cheeks and light shone before him, so bright it blinded him.

"Let it go!" A voice reached through the darkness, drove it back as it struggled to keep its hold on him, the tendrils of shadow desperately trying to twine around his armour.

A face materialised, the most beautiful he had ever beheld, her eyes swimming with concern and warmer emotions, ones that tugged at his heart and pulled it up from the black abyss.

"Wolf," she whispered, a name that meant something to him.

His name.

"Let it go."

He looked down at the shadows, at the darkness that still clung to him and was trying to twine around her now.

No.

He couldn't let it touch her.

He lifted his eyes to meet hers and fell into them. He would never let the darkness reach her. She was his light.

The air around him warmed and he warmed too as he realised she was touching him, her small hands framing his face, steady against him. No panic touched her features now. Only fear. Not fear of him, but fear for him.

"Emelia," he croaked, aware of how close he had been to the abyss, that the darkness had almost pulled him under this time.

He didn't need to look to know there were more black feathers in his wings. He could feel the corruption, a black stain on his soul that would never be erased, would only continue to fester and spread until he completed his mission.

Only killing the dragon could free him from the darkness now.

He stared down into Emelia's green eyes, memorising every paler fleck in them, and all the feelings they revealed to him as the darkness surrounding them both faded. There was love in her eyes, and it stole his breath.

The need to kiss her was strong, almost overwhelming, but he somehow managed to hold it back, to remain where he was, savouring the feel of her hands on him and all the feelings she was showing to him.

She wasn't ready for him to kiss her. Not yet. This was only another step forwards by her, but it was an important one. He could see how it affected her as she gazed at her hands, seeming surprised by how easily she touched him now and that it hadn't shaken her.

His focus lowered to her lips, his mind fixing on what they would feel like against his. Soft. Yielding to his. Intoxicating. Just the thought of kissing her was a drug that had him hazy, hot all over and losing awareness of anything but her.

He needed to do something to unleash all the energy boiling inside him, the raw hunger and need, or he was going to surrender to that ache to kiss her, even when he knew it would only drive her away.

Something made an abrupt jangling noise.

His gaze whipped towards the source of it.

A pale blue bag sat on the grass a short distance away.

"Crap," Emelia muttered and hurried over to it, unzipped it and fished out a phone.

She glared at the screen.

"What is wrong?" He inched closer to her as she glanced at him and then returned her gaze to the phone.

Her fingers danced over the screen that highlighted her face and the furrow in her brow. She shook her head, but he could feel she was drawing away from him. Whatever message she had received, it had rattled her.

"Emelia, what is it?" He ventured another step closer and she finally looked at him.

"My superior. He wants me to come in for a meeting." She huffed and scrubbed a hand over her face, suddenly looking tired. "I was just in London, dammit. He couldn't message me then?"

What had Emelia been doing in London?

He pushed his curiosity aside and tried to get a look at the screen of her phone. She pressed a button and it went dark before he could read the message she had received. He only caught the name.

Mark.

She pocketed her phone and loosed a long sigh. "I should go."

"You should rest," he countered but she wasn't paying attention, was too busy gathering her things and looking for something else on the grass.

He spotted what she wanted and was tempted to hide them, but no good would come of that. If her superior was anything like his, she would get into trouble for ignoring the summons. As much as he wanted to spend more time with her, he couldn't be so callous. He wouldn't enjoy the time with her anyway, not if she was fretting about missing the meeting.

So he stooped and picked up the keys that lay discarded on the lawn a few feet from her bag.

He held them out to her and she hit him with a dazzling smile.

"Thanks." Her fingers brushed his as she took the keys and she stilled, her skin lingering against his as her eyes slowly lifted to meet his again.

That need to kiss her stirred inside him, growing stronger again, rousing other desires, ones that had him thankful he was wearing his armour so she couldn't see the effect she had on him.

"I should go," she whispered, voice as distant as the world around him as he stared down into her eyes.

She didn't want to go. He didn't want to go either.

But she had to, and so did he.

Because if he stayed here any longer, he would end up kissing her.

CHAPTER 20

Emelia couldn't get her mind off Wolf. She had felt sure he was going to kiss her, and some secret part of her had been willing him to do it, even when the rest of her had screamed they were going too fast again.

But then he had bid her goodnight and had teleported out of her life, leaving her standing on the lawn aching for his kiss.

Would his kiss be gentle, a bare brush of his lips over hers that would send thrill after thrill chasing through her?

Or would his kiss be firm, a hard meeting of mouths that would ignite her blood?

She lost track of her surroundings as she imagined a mixture of both, a gentle exploration that would lead to a hard kiss that would have her toes curling in her boots.

She marvelled at how she felt only a deep ache in her belly at the thought of that happening, at how badly she wanted him to come to her right now and kiss her. It didn't frighten her now, although the thought of him taking that next step had panicked her at the time. Now she wanted it. Needed it with a ferocity that startled her.

Someone cleared their throat.

She zoned back into the world and offered Mark an apologetic smile. "Sorry. I was in London last night and had only just got back to Cambridge when you messaged me."

"Unwinding with friends?" He offered a smile that reached his grey eyes as he leaned his backside against the large oak desk in the centre of his office.

She nodded. "I have to admit the time off has done me good."

"You look better for it." Mark folded his arms across his chest, causing his dark grey tailored suit to tighten across his shoulders and biceps, and then uncrossed them and planted his hands against the desk on either side of his hips. "If you're not ready to come back to work yet, that's fine. I just wanted to speak with you about a matter I think you'll be pleased to hear about."

It wasn't like Mark to mince his words. He hadn't risen through the ranks by being diplomatic, or a soft touch. He had gained the position of station chief in the London headquarters of Archangel by being a hard-nosed, take-no-shit hunter who didn't know when to quit.

So why was he dancing around whatever he wanted to tell her?

"Is this about what happened to me?"

He shook his head, causing threads of his sandy hair to fall down and brush his brow. He swept it back and scrubbed the back of his neck before loosening his black tie and undoing the top button of his white shirt.

"It's about you getting what you deserve."

Emelia wasn't sure whether that sounded ominous or not. Coupled with the vague text he had sent her that had only asked her to come back to HQ immediately for a meeting, she was leaning towards ominous.

Did he know she was having doubts about Archangel? Did he know she had been meeting Wolf and keeping it secret from them because she didn't want them turning their sights on him?

"What would you say if I was to show you this?" He pushed off the desk and rounded it to the other side, and her heart began a painful rhythm in her throat as he opened a drawer and looked in it.

Her mind conjured photographs of her with Wolf. With everything that had been happening recently with Sable and Olivia, and now Anais, she could only imagine how badly Archangel would react to discovering she was growing close to an angel.

One who had entered their headquarters twice without authorisation and had attempted to take their best hunter from them by force.

But it wasn't photographs that Mark pulled from the drawer.

It was a rectangular black box.

He held it out in front of him and opened it, revealing the contents.

A gold pin.

Her pulse shot into overdrive as recognition hit her, and her gaze leaped up to meet his. "You're kidding."

His grey eyes remained serious. "I assure you, this is real. In light of your recent achievements, dedication to our cause, and continued hard work, we reviewed your position and decided you were the right choice for the role that just opened up."

A commander.

It was everything she had ever wanted, but as she stared at the gold pin nestled among the black velvet, she couldn't help but feel she was only being offered the position and the chance to lead her own squad of hunters because Sable was leaving.

And because her superiors pitied her after everything she had been through.

Not only that, but she was one of only a handful of experienced hunters left after the war in the Third Realm of the demons and several incidents in Hell and this world.

Mark pulled the pin from the presentation box and walked around the desk to her. She stared at it as he held it out to her, unsure what to say.

Did she care that she was getting this role now, when she was probably one of only a few suitable candidates?

Not really.

Did she care that she might be getting chosen for it over the other hunters because of what she had been through in Hell?

Absolutely.

"This isn't about that," Mark said on a sigh as he withdrew the pin, clearly catching her train of thought. "I can understand why you might think it, Emelia, but it isn't. This promotion has been a long time coming, and you deserve it."

She raised her eyes from the pin to his. Belief shone in their depths. Mark had always championed her, putting her forward for the role of commander more than once. The committee had always decided in favour of another. She guessed persistence won, though, or whoever had been against her had been removed from the council.

Or maybe they pitied her.

Mark certainly didn't.

He curled his fingers around the pin. "You can take it or not. It's up to you, Emelia. You earned this based on your merits, not on anything else. Never think that. You've worked towards this moment the entire time you've been with Archangel, so don't let those doubts I can see in your eyes ruin it. You've been the best candidate for promotion for the last few years, but the idiots are only just seeing that now that two of the people they chose have screwed up."

He wasn't talking about Sable now. One of the hunters in question had gone rogue, using his team to take out targets not on Archangel's list. The other had gone mercenary, dealing death in exchange for cold hard cash and using Archangel's resources to make it happen.

There was corruption in every corner of Archangel these days.

It was getting hard to see who was still loyal to the organisation and its creed.

Emelia reached out and took the pin. It was warm in her fingers, far heavier than it had appeared, and she felt the weight of it as she looked down at it.

A commander.

This small pin gave her the power she had always wanted, the ability to help shape Archangel and keep it on the right path, and she would do her best to serve it and make that happen. She wouldn't let the bad seeds steer it wrong or destroy it, turning it into something evil.

"Return whenever you're ready, and we'll have the squad picked out for you. I'm afraid you'll have to handle some new blood. Think you're up to the task of wrangling some rookies?"

She nodded, her eyes still locked on the pin. "They won't know what hit them."

Mark grinned at that. "Hazing the rookies always was the best part of being on the front line."

He looked as if he missed being in the thick of the action whenever he smiled like that with a wistful edge to his grey eyes.

"Get out of here." He waved her towards the door. "Before I start telling tales of the days when some of the serving members of the council were greenhorns and the shit we pulled on them."

Emelia rose to her feet, nodded and drifted towards the door, her focus fixed on the pin she clutched in her palm.

She couldn't wait to tell Wolf.

She paused outside the office as that thought hit her, rapidly followed by another. She was so comfortable around Wolf now, had enjoyed the time they had been spending together and she hadn't been afraid when she had touched him.

The feel of his strong jaw beneath her fingers, the light dusting of dark stubble that coated it scratching at her palms, and how warm his skin had been had thrilled her.

And how he had looked at her.

Damn, his silver irises had been glowing, gold edging them as he had stared deep into her eyes, his holding her immobile, unable to move a muscle as she fell into them.

Desire had darkened them, pulling her deeper under his spell, and she had ached for the kiss they had promised.

Still ached for it.

She wanted to see him again.

Avenged by an Angel

Tired as she was from so much travelling, she made her way back down through the building in the heart of London and exited it. She strolled through the courtyard, taking in the cool night air as she made her way to the other side of the building. A few of the hunters she passed that were relaxing in the courtyard, taking a break from their work, nodded and she returned it, a new bounce in her step as she clutched the pin.

She hadn't realised how badly she had needed this lift until it had happened. Now, her outlook had changed, her future seeming brighter and her past further away.

She pushed the door to the other wing of the sandstone building open and made her way down to the underground parking lot. It was quiet, only a few of the black fleet vans and SUVs out on patrol. She walked past the two lines of spaces reserved for them and tiptoed as she tried to remember where she had parked her car.

When she found it, her thoughts shifted back to Wolf while her feet carried her over to it. She didn't notice as she entered it, or as she drove it out of London. Didn't notice the songs that were playing on the radio as she thought about Wolf, part of her hoping he would be waiting for her.

And that he hadn't returned to Hell.

She wasn't sure how she could convince him to give up his mission, but she knew she had to do it, before it was too late. Hell was affecting him. He couldn't hide that from her, not anymore. She had seen the black feathers and how dark he had grown when his mood had shifted.

She had seen the shadows that had writhed around his legs.

Now more than ever, she needed to speak with Sable, but she wasn't sure her friend could help her. Not anymore. What was happening with Wolf was probably beyond the limited knowledge of angels her friend had gained and into the territory of her fallen angel contact. If Emelia could speak with the female angel, maybe she would be able to find a way to halt the spread of those black feathers. She didn't know much about angels, but she knew fallen ones had black wings, and something told her she needed to stop him from gaining any more tainted feathers.

Was there something she could do to slow their spread?

He had told her once that she calmed him, that he came to her whenever things got too tough for him and he needed her to soothe his darker side, to ground him and give him the strength to fight back against his urges.

If she asked him to stay for a while with her, would it purge the darkness from his soul?

Would he even consider it?

He was bent on going to Hell and hunting down Zephyr. She had watched that need as it had grown inside him like an infection, a disease that had stolen control from him, making him a slave to his desire to kill the dragon. Now, she wasn't sure whether he would stay if she asked it of him.

He had denied her the few times she had tried to convince him to leave the dragon alone and stay out of Hell.

Talking to him wasn't going to make him change his mind, that much was clear.

Her heart started a hard pounding against her ribs as she pulled to a halt on the gravel drive of the manor house.

If talking wouldn't convince him to let it go, to at least take a break and stay with her for a while, would something else?

Her hands shook against the steering wheel, conflict flooding her as her body heated at the same time as her mind shrieked at her to not even consider it, she wasn't strong enough to do it. He would hurt her. Be cruel to her.

She closed her eyes and rested her forehead against the top of the steering wheel, between her hands.

Wolf would never hurt her.

She knew that in her heart and she had to listen to it, not to the instincts Zephyr had created in her.

She had wanted that kiss, and she wanted so much more too. She wanted to be brave again, to seize the moment and the object of her desire and not let go. She wanted to take the risk, make the leap, and she knew it would be worth it.

Wolf would catch her.

She just had to keep her nerve and not listen to that damned voice.

Zephyr had hurt her, physically and emotionally, mentally, but he hadn't broken her. She was still strong. Still brave. Wolf had shown her that and so much more. He had shown her she could still laugh. Still smile.

Still love.

She switched off the engine and pushed the door open. The gravel crunched under her boots as she stepped out of the car and closed the door. It slammed, the sound loud in the still night.

Emelia stared at the old mansion. Her home. Strange how she had always avoided it, and now she couldn't wait to return here whenever she was away.

Because of Wolf.

Part of her felt this was more than her home now. It was becoming theirs, the place where they always met, where he was relaxed around her and she was at peace. A world away from their own ones. Here, she wasn't a hunter for Archangel. Here, he wasn't a warrior of Heaven.

They were just Emelia and Wolf.
Two people fighting against falling in love.
It was time she gave up that fight.
And she would make him give up too.

She skirted the illuminated sandstone building, following the path that led around the back. The lights were on inside the pool house and she frowned, an uneasy feeling trickling through her.

She hadn't left the lights on.

Her steps slowed and she had half a mind to return to her car and get the weapons she kept in the boot.

But then the most glorious sight she had ever seen strolled out of the open door, seven feet of pure masculine beauty in nothing more than a pair of tight black trunks.

CHAPTER 21

Wolf froze mid-step, his silver gaze wide as it swung to land on her.

"Making yourself at home?" Emelia couldn't stop the words from leaving her lips, and the teasing way they came out startled her, bringing a smile to her lips as that sense of comfort she always felt around Wolf chased away her momentary panic that it was a burglar.

Or worse.

Emelia shoved the dragon out of her head.

He wasn't here, and he would be dead if he came to her now. Wolf would see to that.

So she was safe.

Although, there was a barely clothed warrior staring at her as if he wanted to tangle with her.

Every muscle on his powerful torso tensed and flexed as he breathed, a mesmerising symphony that kept drawing her eyes downwards.

"I was… I came back and you were not here, and I was bored waiting." He looked down at his tiny shorts that left very little to her imagination and the white towel he clutched in his left hand, and then at her. "I thought I would swim."

The bolder part of herself thought that sounded like a good idea.

She'd had the pool cleaned only a few days ago and hadn't had the chance to test it out.

It didn't seem fair that Wolf got to be the first to swim in it when it was her hard-earned money that had paid for it to be cleaned and filled, and the heater fixed.

"Stay right there." She pointed to his feet.

He had big feet. They shifted as she stared at them, one lifting and then the other, and she realised she was making him uneasy with her gawping, so she hurried inside. She stripped off her jacket as she climbed the stairs and tossed it onto the couch in the small living room area.

She looked down at the pin in her hand, a slow smile curling her lips. She was a commander now. The same rank Wolf held. She was going to tease the hell out of him about that, because she felt she was going to need to do something to lighten the mood when she walked out and jumped in that pool.

Her swimsuit was modest as two pieces went, but the thought of wearing only the plum-coloured shorts and halter-style top in front of a man had her nerves threatening to rise to panic point.

She breathed through it as she dug the swimsuit out of her bags in the bedroom.

When she laid the top and bottom out on the dark wine covers of her double bed, nerves shot to panic so fast, she felt ready to pass out. She fought for air, battling her emotions at the same time, wrestling to get herself under control.

It was only a swim.

She had wound herself up thinking about kissing Wolf, but now that wasn't necessary. He was here, and he looked as if he meant to stay. The pressure was off. She could keep him here by swimming with him, giving him a chance to relax and hopefully recover from the effects of Hell, at least enough that those black feathers stopped spreading.

She switched off her emotions by focusing on her task, removing her T-shirt, boots, and jeans, and then her underwear, and stepping into the shorts of her swimsuit. She tugged them up and smoothed them over her backside and hips, and followed them with the top. She did up the front fastening and left the cups barely clinging to her breasts as she twisted her dark hair into a knot at the back of her head. Her hands shook as she grabbed the two long thick ties of her top and pulled them up, tying them at her nape in a bow.

Glancing at herself in the mirrored doors of the built-in wardrobes was a mistake.

She froze, her breaths coming faster as she stared at her reflection.

At the scars on her thighs and over her right shoulder.

Emelia tore her gaze away, squeezed her eyes shut, and just breathed.

She wasn't the only one with scars. Wolf had them too. They criss-crossed his chest and darted across his thighs, visible beneath the dusting of dark hair. He wouldn't see her scars and judge her. He wouldn't.

She forced herself to move as she opened her eyes, through the living room and down the stairs, and hesitated for only a moment in the lower room of the pool house. She flicked on the underwater pool lights and grabbed a towel from the pile, giving herself a second to draw up her courage and seize hold of it so it wouldn't fail her, and then strode out of the open door.

Wolf's eyes immediately leaped to her, sending a hot shiver cascading over her as he raked them down her, from her head to her bare toes.

"I thought I would swim too." She scurried past him, deeply aware of his gaze on her, how he tracked her as she moved towards the illuminated pool.

She tossed the towel on one of the wooden loungers beside the pool, twisted, and dived into the water. She swam as far as she could beneath the surface, letting her breath out little by little as her tight lungs relaxed.

Wolf continued to track her, hunting her through the water.

When she breached the surface and drew down a deep breath, her panic faded to a trickle, nothing more than background noise as the water lapped around her. She kicked her feet and moved her arms, swishing them back and forth to keep herself stationary.

Wolf prowled along the front of the pool house, the lights on the outside of it chasing over him as he stalked towards her, his eyes on her the entire time.

"So you'll never guess what Mark wanted." She kept treading water, fighting the heat that began to build in her veins as he continued staring at her.

He stopped at the edge of the pool, towering over her, imposing even without his wings. "What did the human want?"

She frowned at the way he said that. Was he trying to distinguish himself from Mark by pointing out her boss was human? She could see no other reason for it. He wanted her aware that Mark was a mortal and he was an immortal. Did he believe she would think he was better than a human because of that mere fact alone?

Or was he just jealous because she was talking about another man and he wanted her to be more impressed with him, wanted to keep her interested by playing on his strengths and pointing out differences between him and Mark?

She sighed and leaned back, letting her feet rise towards the surface.

Tension bolted through her when Wolf's glowing gaze dropped to her body and she fought it, refusing to listen to that voice and listening to her heart instead. Wolf wouldn't hurt her. He was immortal, and a man, and he wanted her, but he wouldn't force her.

He had shown her that.

He could have kissed her the last time they had been here together, but he hadn't. He had held back for her sake, restraining himself and denying the hunger that had shone in his eyes.

Her gaze drifted from his face, falling to the broad flat slabs of his chest and his dark nipples, to the thick ropes of his stomach and the rigid arches of muscle that cut over his hips in an enticing vee that lured her eyes downwards to the dusting of dark hair that trailed below his navel, heat stirring inside her as she drank him in.

"You have to come in the water, or I won't tell you." She shrieked when he dived into the water, cutting through it so close to her that she was rocked to her right.

He came up behind her and swam around her, circling her.

Like a shark.

Emelia frowned as she tracked him and caught sight of his back. Two long thick ridges of scar tissue ran down his back, parallel to his spine.

"Are they where your wings are?" She jerked her chin towards the scars as he arched an eyebrow at her and kept swimming.

She kept turning with him, spinning in the water so he couldn't get behind her.

"You were meant to be answering my question." He ducked beneath the water in a fluid motion, barely disturbing the surface as he disappeared.

Emelia twisted and frowned when she scanned the pool and couldn't find him.

Shrieked when he came up behind her.

"Goddammit," she bit out and whirled to face him. "Stay where I can see you."

He looked as if he wanted to ask why, but then the light of amusement that had been in his eyes faded, his expression turning serious again as he nodded.

Because he realised he had scared her.

She was struggling enough as it was, without him sneaking up on her and surprising her. She wanted to stay in the water with him, needed this moment to prove to herself she was strong enough to do this, to wear such little clothing and be this close to a man without what had happened to her affecting her.

"I am sorry." He swept his arms forwards, propelling himself backwards. "I forgot myself."

Because he had been having fun, hunting her and enjoying himself. She could understand that, because she had been having fun too.

She corrected herself.

She *was* having fun.

Wolf slicked his black hair back and the itch to do that for him had her splaying her fingers as she pushed them through the water, maintaining her position. His silver eyes reflected the lights of the pool and she lost herself in them, found herself just treading water opposite him, bobbing up and down.

While he was perfectly still.

Her eyebrows pinched. "Are you standing on the bottom?"

He looked down and nodded.

Emelia couldn't remember how deep the pool was, but she felt sure that standing on the bottom shouldn't be possible. She dropped her feet, trying to see if she could reach it, and went under, keeping her eyes open as she sank close to a foot beneath the surface before she could touch the bottom with her toes.

She kicked off and scowled as she broke the surface. It wasn't fair that Wolf could just stand and relax in the water and she had to keep moving.

Although, she didn't necessarily have to keep moving. She did have other options. One was boring—moving to the side of the pool. The other was far more enticing, if not a little nerve-wracking.

Either resting her feet on Wolf's thighs or taking hold of his shoulders.

She opted for what she thought was the safer one, scooting towards Wolf until the soles of her feet hit his thighs.

He immediately took hold of her ankles.

Panic lanced her, the feel of him gripping her ankles with both hands and the thought he could easily move his body between her legs making her kick at him.

"Shh," he murmured and released one ankle, then moved to her side so he was on the outside of her legs. "Just float."

"I can't." She hated to admit that and pulled a face when he looked at her. "I suck at floating. My dad sank like a stone whenever he tried, and I think I got the sinking gene. Can you float?"

"Another question? I'm still waiting for you to answer my first one." He teased her with a mock frown.

"Oh, shit." She had forgotten she hadn't answered him, and he had done as she wanted too, diving into the pool with her. The problem was, he was more of a distraction in the pool than he had been outside it. She wanted to tempt and tease him, to play around with him, and wanted to run for the hills at the same time. She focused on the tempting and teasing, hoping to shut down the part of her that wanted to do the running. "I'm a commander now."

"A commander?" He turned with her as she finally managed to relax and slowly lifted her ankle, bringing her as close to floating on the surface as she had ever been.

She stretched her arms out at her sides, aware of his eyes on her and how her breasts crested the surface, her nipples beading on contact with the colder air. She was not going to panic. Wolf wouldn't do anything she didn't want. He wouldn't hurt her.

"Emelia, you might want to breathe," he murmured, a hint of panic in his deep voice as he moved closer.

She sucked down a breath, unaware she had been holding it while she had been trying to relax and fighting her fears.

"Do you want me to let you go?" he said and she looked at him, catching the concern as it washed across his face. "You are in absolute control here, Emelia."

Those words settled her panic faster than she had ever been able to manage alone. They rang in her mind, backed up and strengthened by the honesty his gaze held. He meant that. She was in control. She made the decisions.

Did she want him to let her go?

"No," she whispered. "I think I like floating. I don't want to stop yet."

"Just tell me if you change your mind." He eased back, his deep voice soothing her as it rolled over her like a gentle wave while she floated close to him. "I could take you for a spin?"

"A spin? Floating and spinning?" She found she liked the idea of that, so she nodded before the damned voice could poison her mind against it.

Wolf took hold of her wrist, cradling it gently in his large hand, and slowly turned with her so she was moving through the water, the hazy stars spiralling above her.

Damn, it was relaxing.

"So you are a commander now?" he prompted.

She nodded and smiled, still a little giddy over her promotion. "A commander just like you. I'm as powerful as you are."

"A title does not give strength to the bearer of it."

She frowned. Was he belittling her again because she was mortal?

He continued before she could call him on that. "You were always strong. You just lost sight of it. I have never met a female as strong as you."

Did he honestly mean that? She looked at him and found him staring at her body, his silver eyes darker than she had ever seen them, filled with hunger as he raked them over her. He tensed and they leaped to hers, a sheepish edge to them that said he knew she had caught him checking her out but he wasn't going to apologise for it.

She didn't want him to apologise for it.

She had been enjoying it.

"Not even Sable?" She wasn't sure why she put that one out there.

Setting herself up for disappointment? Of course Sable was stronger than she was. Her friend was half-angel.

She waited for him to admit it.

He shook his head, his handsome face solemn and serious as he said, "Not even Sable."

"Liar."

His eyes narrowed, darkening with something other than desire now. "Never. I would never lie to you, Emelia."

Her stomach squirmed. She knew that. She had only meant to tease him, not upset him.

After a long silence, he relaxed, his stern features softening by degrees as he turned with her. She drifted in his arms, not really feeling anything, not aware of anything other than the peace that flowed through her as he spun her in lazy circles in the water.

"Yes and yes." His luscious baritone cut through the silence, warming her and luring her gaze to him again. When she frowned, confused as to what he was talking about, he said, "The scars are where my wings should be, and I can float."

She had forgotten she had asked him those two questions.

"Is it weird not having wings?" She peered at his shoulders, eyes catching on his pectorals as they flexed.

It seemed she wasn't the only one who felt a little tense when the other was looking at their body.

She tried to convince her eyes to leave him, but they lingered, absorbing the hard slabs of his chest, the sinewy muscles of his shoulders that screamed of strength, and the enticing bulge of his biceps. He was every inch the warrior, cut from steel and made for battle, and other things.

That heat bloomed in his eyes again and stirred inside her, and awareness of where he held her rippled through her. Her wrist and ankle felt hot beneath his fingers, burning despite the water that washed over them. His gaze shifted, slowly and leisurely drifting over her body, taking in every inch of her just as she had taken him in.

"It is strange, I suppose," he murmured, distant as he traced the length of her body with his eyes. "But necessary. Many species do not like angels."

"Demons in particular," she offered, a little breathless as the heat he was stirring in her reached a new crescendo, setting her blood on fire and filling her with a need that startled her.

She wanted him to touch her.

She wanted to feel his hands on her, caressing her the way his eyes were.

"We are born of the same stock," he muttered with a twist to his lips that told her what he thought about that. "The liar produced demons, moulding them from his blood and feathers, breathing life into the fiends."

Now she understood why he hadn't liked it when she had called him a liar. He viewed the Devil as one and must have felt she was comparing him to that male.

"Is the Devil as dangerous as the demons believe?" She averted her eyes when his leaped to meet them, fixing them on the stars to avoid his curious gaze.

If she kept looking at him, she was going to get distracted again, and she wasn't sure where that would lead. Did she want to be distracted? Heat climbed onto her cheeks when she thought about kissing him and the nerves she expected to rise inside her didn't come. Could she kiss him without panicking?

She forced herself to focus on their conversation rather than the wicked fantasy building in her mind.

"Thorne warned us about the Devil, and some of the elves spoke of him as if he was the big bad of Hell, and one you didn't mess with if you wanted to continue breathing. Is he like that?"

Wolf's voice was gruff as he spoke. "He is dangerous, unpredictable and vicious. A cruel being. It is unwise to venture near his realm."

"The dragons live near his realm," she whispered, her throat tightening with each word and every memory that threatened to surface, pushing at the corners of her mind. She fought them, not wanting them to ruin this moment. They persisted, but other thoughts overshadowed them, awakening a fear worse than they ever could. "Wolf... What happens if you go close to that realm?"

He tensed, his fingers tightening around her ankle and wrist.

He didn't want to tell her.

She twisted in his arms, forcing him to release her and lowering her legs so she was facing him, treading water again. She stared at him, waiting for him to look at her, but he seemed overly fascinated with the pool, the house and everything but her.

"It's dangerous for me to be near there, but it has to be one hundred times more dangerous for you... and don't lie to me," she said, and he finally glanced at her, resignation crossing his features as his eyes met hers. "Is it dangerous for you?"

He swallowed and nodded, regret dancing across his eyes before they hardened again, his jaw tensing as he tipped his head up and straightened his spine. "It will not stop me."

"I know," she whispered, unable to keep the hurt from her voice as she let those two words slip from her lips, filled with the pain the thought of him venturing so close to the Devil's lands caused in her. "I still don't want you to go."

"I must."

She knew that too. She had learned a lot about Wolf, and one of the things she had discovered was that he didn't give up when he was given a mission, whether it had been assigned to him or whether he had chosen it himself. He was determined, courageous, and a dash of foolish. She was stubborn too, but even she could recognise when letting go was the wiser course of action.

"I don't want you to go to Hell... or at least I don't want you to go alone." She hesitated as his eyes drilled into her, narrowing as he stared at her, and she caught the flare of darkness in them. She had caused that, but she wouldn't apologise and she wouldn't back down. "I can go with you."

"No," he barked, "I will not allow it. The risk to you is too great."

"The risk to you is greater." She closed the distance between them and pressed her hand to his chest.

His heart thundered against her palm, a powerful beat that soon echoed in her breast as she looked up into his eyes, struggling to find her voice as pain flowed through her in strengthening waves that evoked images in her mind. Each vision of him in Hell was worse than the previous, from him being caught by demons, to facing Zephyr, to him being pressed to his knees before the Devil.

"I cannot risk you, Emelia," he husked, the pain that drummed inside her lacing his voice as he gazed down into her eyes, the dark slashes of his eyebrows furrowing above them. "I cannot."

He lifted his hand from the water, droplets of it rolling down his arm as he eased it towards her, and she didn't stop him when he brushed his knuckles across her cheek. Colourful light shone from that side of her face as he searched her eyes, his darting between them, and her breath hitched, a need surging to life inside her, pushing her to obey it.

She wanted to kiss him.

He closed his eyes and withdrew, turning his face away from her as he lowered his hand back into the water.

"If you won't let me go with you, can you not take another angel? It isn't safe for you, Wolf. You know that." She wasn't only talking about the dangers that awaited him in Hell, she was talking about the black feathers he was gaining. Maybe if another angel went with him, the effect on him would be weakened, the darkness kept at bay. Even if it was only by a little, it was worth it.

Although she wasn't sure how she felt about two angels risking their lives for her.

Wolf said she was worth it, but she didn't feel as if she was.

"I might have an ally in Hell." Those quietly spoken words drew her out of her thoughts and she looked up into Wolf's steady silver gaze. "I returned to my realm after you left and there I received an interesting, but disturbing, report."

She was glad he hadn't gone off to Hell again.

He sighed, frowned, and rubbed the bridge of his nose, his voice gaining a pained note as he muttered, "The damned idiot."

"What happened?" She scooted closer to him, so she could peer up at his face, wanting to see his eyes because she could feel his hurt and confusion, could sense it somehow.

Whatever had happened, it had been to a friend, and he was conflicted by it.

"The Fifth Commander..." He gave a slight chuckle. "Although he calls himself Rey now. He chased a demoness into Hell, and he... if the reports are correct, he fell to save her."

"He fell?" She blinked, shock washing through her as she ran back over everything he had said. "This Rey... He chose to fall because of the demoness?"

"According to the report he sent back, it was the only way to save her." His expression soured.

What was he thinking? She found the idea of an angel falling to save the woman he loved romantic. He looked as if it had been blasphemy of the highest order. Or stupidity.

Would Wolf fall for her?

She immediately kicked that thought from her head and her heart. She didn't want Wolf to fall. His duty meant too much to him and she knew it would devastate him if he lost it. Just as it would devastate her if she lost her duty.

She frowned as she thought about that, and her heart answered differently, whispering that she wouldn't be devastated.

She wouldn't be?

She thought about Archangel and what it meant to her. It was her home. Her family.

But now that the high of being made a commander was beginning to wear off and reality was settling back in, she was gaining perspective again. She wanted to keep Archangel on the right path, but what if she couldn't save it?

Like Sable and Anais, she thought Archangel had been wrong to capture Loke. She could understand why they had done it, thinking he had harmed Anais, but he had done nothing wrong. Even when they had realised that, they had still wanted to experiment on him, learning all they could about dragons.

What if that was only the tip of the iceberg and they were doing other terrible things?

Could she condone that and remain with Archangel, hoping she could change it for the better again, or would she choose to walk away like Sable and the others?

"Do you think he can help you?" She skimmed her hand up to his shoulder and held on to him as he lifted his head, his eyes locking with hers again.

"I believe he can, and that he will." Conviction rang in his words, bringing sweet relief to her.

"I thought angels turned... evil... when they fell in Hell?"

A crinkle formed between Wolf's black eyebrows, his expression turning pensive again. "He does not seem like a normal fallen. He sent a report. I do not think a normal fallen would send a report."

She didn't think so either. It seemed a very angelic and noble thing to do. She wasn't even sure how she would word such a note. How did an angel inform the world they had served that they had fallen? It sounded a lot like switching sides to her, and that made the notion of sending a report about it to the former side all the stranger to her.

"Somehow, he has retained his good, although I am not sure how." That furrow between Wolf's eyebrows only deepened as a troubled look flitted across his handsome face. "A score of angels in Heaven want to study him to find out."

Emelia bet that had gone down well with Rey. Wolf looked as if he was going to ask Rey in order to find out for them, and for him. Because he was worried about falling?

She didn't want to think about the danger of that happening.

A fallen angel would be a powerful ally, and she felt better knowing that Wolf would have Rey on his side. He wouldn't be alone in Hell now. If she couldn't go with him, then his friend was a good substitute, one she definitely approved of given the strength fallen angels had at their command.

"You will be careful, though. I mean, not to diss your friend, but even if he did send a report saying he was fallen, you need to be careful. It might be a trap." Which turned her stomach and made her heart flip in her chest.

Wolf's eyes shifted to meet hers again. "I will be careful, Emelia. I promise."

His gaze grew distant, and she could see he was already thinking about heading back down to Hell to see Rey. She didn't want him to go, not yet. She wanted him to stay a little longer, and not only because he was relaxing again, the darkness lifting from his eyes and his mood calming.

"Wolf?" she whispered, and he blinked, his eyes clearing as he came back to her.

"I should go."

No. He couldn't. Not yet. She needed him to stay. Just for tonight.

"You're sure you can't delay a little longer?" She searched his eyes as she eased her hand higher, cupping the rigid muscle that ran from his neck to his shoulder, heading towards his nape.

He looked down at her hand out of the corner of his eye and then back at her. "What for?"

Emelia steeled herself.

Shifted her hand to his nape.

Pulled herself up to him and whispered against his lips.

"This."

CHAPTER 22

Emelia pressed her mouth to his, fifty thousand volts racing through her like a lightning bolt as his firm lips met hers. She tilted her head, drew him closer, and crushed the nerves threatening to rise inside her as she kissed him, her lips playing across his, a barely there brush that had her feeling lighter inside, as if she was floating.

Wolf made a low noise in his throat and returned the kiss, his mouth gentle as he met hers, lips grazing and sending wave after wave of thrills chasing over her skin. He was holding back. Afraid of scaring her.

She held her nerve and stroked her tongue along the seam of his lips.

He opened for her on a ragged groan, and she slipped her tongue inside, shivered as his met it, the warmth and taste of him drugging her.

His hands clamped down on her waist.

Panic spiked.

She broke away from his mouth and shoved backwards, breathing hard as she stared at him, wrestling to get her fears back under control.

He held his hands up at his sides, water rolling down his arms as he looked at her. "I will not hurt you, Emelia. You are in control here."

She was.

She sucked down a steadying breath and clung to that.

She was in control.

She had this beautiful, intoxicating warrior at her command, and she didn't want to stop. She didn't want fear to keep ruining things, stopping her from doing as she wanted.

Emelia held her hand out to him, beckoning him, and a deeper thrill ran through her as he obeyed, cutting through the water towards her.

She was in command.

Damn, that was empowering.

She licked her lips and he groaned, the sound strained as his eyes fell to her mouth and darkened, the hunger that lit them tugging at her, luring her back to him. He looked like a man starved, desperately in need of her. She couldn't stop herself from kicking off and floating backwards, keeping the distance between them steady as she glided towards the broad steps at the end of the pool.

He prowled towards her, following her, his gaze dark and locked on hers.

She wanted to moan as the water shallowed, sluicing off the broad slabs of his pectorals and running down the thick ropes of his abdomen, revealing them to her hungry eyes. She devoured every inch of him, the need inside her growing as she took him in, admired her warrior.

Her Wolf.

His hips breached the surface, the ridge of muscle that arched over them combining with the trail of dark hair that spread down from his navel to lead her gaze to his tiny black shorts.

Her mouth dried out.

The rigid outline of his hard cock was impossible to miss, curved up towards his left hip as he waded towards her.

Heat pooled lower in her belly, a flood of desire making her slick in her shorts, and she swallowed hard and resisted the temptation to rub her thighs together as she tingled, her need of him growing. She wanted to touch him. Wanted to explore every delectable inch of him with her hands and maybe even her mouth. She wanted to savour him.

Her fears drifted away as the hunger built, need she had been denying for too long, that had tormented her each night when she had closed her eyes. She wanted to fulfil those fantasies now, wasn't afraid of where this was heading because it was Wolf prowling towards her.

And she was in control.

"Stop," she said, needing to prove that to herself.

Wolf halted, the water lapping around his hips, keeping her gaze on his shorts.

She swallowed her nerves and walked towards him, aware of his eyes on her as she closed the distance between them again. Her breathing shallowed, speeding up as she approached him, her hands shaking as she thought about what she wanted to do. She was in control. She was the one instigating this and she wanted it. He wasn't doing anything against her will, was doing everything she desired instead.

Emelia stopped close to him, raked her eyes over his muscles again, fingers itching rather than shaking as she devoured him with her gaze. His flat nipples beaded in the cold air, skin turning to gooseflesh as he waited.

Waited for her to make the next move.

Anticipation swirled inside her, a thousand fantasies colliding, making it difficult to decide what she wanted to do with him because she wanted to fulfil them all, right now, this instant.

She lowered her gaze, following the line of his eight-pack, past his navel, and down that trail of dark hair.

She wanted to start there.

She raised her hand out of the water and brought it towards him, shivered in time with him as her fingers brushed above the sexy dip of his navel and water cascaded over his muscles in tiny tempting rivulets that pushed her to follow them. She wanted to follow something else.

She swallowed to wet her parched throat and let her fingers drift lower, so they brushed the start of that treasure trail. She followed it downwards, intensely aware of his eyes on her, how they tracked her, and how his breath hitched. His entire body tensed beneath her touch and the thought she was affecting him gave her the courage to continue because she liked it.

She liked how he reacted to every little thing she did as if it was killing him, as if he couldn't bear it but still wanted more.

The trail of hair thickened, crisp beneath her fingertips, and her heart pounded as she reached the tight waist of his shorts.

His breathing quickened, chest heaving as he remained still, letting her explore him despite the fact he had to want to join in, to touch her too. She rewarded him by skimming her fingers along the waistband, dipping it lower as she went. Her hand brushed his hard length.

He hissed in a breath.

Damn, he was like steel beneath her palm as she swept it over his shaft. It kicked, pulsing against the tight material, and she bit her lower lip, stifling the moan that bubbled up her throat in response. How many nights had she fantasised about this? How many times had she woken aroused and frustrated, aching for him to come to her and chase away her fears so she could have this moment with him?

Now it was becoming real.

"Emelia," he murmured, strained and low.

She was killing him. She could see it in his eyes as she lifted hers to meet them. He needed more than this innocent touch.

And, damn, she needed that too.

Avenged by an Angel

She kept her eyes on his as she fought another wave of nerves and focused on what she wanted next. The same thing he wanted judging by how his face crumpled for a heartbeat before his eyebrows dropped in a frown that narrowed his eyes as she brushed her fingers along the waist of his shorts, dipping them behind the elastic.

"Take them off," she whispered, shocked by how throaty her voice had gone.

Wolf groaned and did as she had ordered as she stepped back. She wanted to purr as he discarded the shorts and rose to stand before her, his long cock jutting out of the water, the broad head dark with need. A moan slipped from her lips instead and Wolf groaned in response, his brow furrowing as he stared at her, stood before her naked and glorious, his hands at his sides.

At her mercy.

The heat pooling between her thighs grew hotter.

She licked her lips again and wriggled, just enough to have a thrill chasing over her thighs. Her aroused nub pulsed, sending a stronger wave through her, and she closed the distance between them again, grabbed him around his nape and dragged him down to her for a harder kiss.

He moaned and moved closer, his shaft jabbing her belly. Emelia pressed closer to him, trapping it between them and savouring the heat of it, the way it flexed and pulsed, demanding attention as she stroked her tongue against his, losing herself in the kiss. She couldn't stop her hand from slipping between them and curling around his cock, couldn't bite back the moan that rolled up her throat as she stroked him, felt all that velvet on steel and how hard he was for her.

His breaths quickened again, panting against her lips between each fierce meeting of their mouths, but his hands remained pinned at his sides. She could sense his need to touch her. Or was that hers?

She ached all over, couldn't keep from wriggling as she stroked him, as she thumbed the tip and smeared the moisture gathering there into his skin. He groaned into her mouth, the low, guttural, and oh-so-masculine sound sending a shiver through her. His body tensed, straining now, and she couldn't take any more.

She wanted to scream at him to touch her, to palm her bottom and her breasts, to thumb her nipples, but her voice seized, and panic began to rise.

"Not going to hurt you," he murmured against her lips between rough kisses, his words a heady drug that had her nestling closer to him. "Might make a fool of myself if you keep doing that, though."

She realised she had been stroking his cock harder, her need for him to touch her controlling her actions. She slowed her hand, teasing him instead, feathering her fingers over his flesh as she stepped back. He groaned and leaned towards her, keeping his mouth fused with hers.

"Tell me what you want," he husked. "Say it and it's yours. Whatever you need."

What didn't she need?

"You," she whispered, brushing her lips across his, teasing them with her tongue and savouring the way he shivered in response, a moan tumbling from his lips. "I want you."

Three words that should have terrified her, but only made her burn hotter.

"Where?" He kissed her harder, a brief flash of dominance that she relished rather than feared.

She wasn't sure she could make it to the bed, not this time. She needed him too fiercely, was too wound up, beyond ready for the next step as her desire and passion drowned out all her fears. She wanted him now, before her nerve failed, before the voice dared to poison her mind. She wanted to take the leap, to prove to herself she could do this, she could be with a man.

With Wolf.

She was taking back control.

She seized his hand and pulled him towards the steps of the pool, heart beating harder with each stride she took towards them. She was doing this. A thrill bolted through her, a wave of tingles in its wake. She was doing this, and nothing would stop her, because this was what she wanted. She wanted Wolf, and she was damned well going to have him.

When they reached the steps, he tried to pass her, heading towards the pool house.

She tugged on his hand to stop him, moaned as he twisted to look at her over his shoulder, giving her a side-on view of his perfection.

Emelia pulled him in the other direction, over to the wooden lounger, and turned so his back was to it. She gripped his shoulders, heat sweeping through her at the feel of his muscles flexing beneath her touch, and pushed him down onto the lounger. Dark silver eyes locked with hers, the hunger in them pulling at her own, bringing it to the surface.

She couldn't resist stroking her fingers through his hair, pushing them through the tangled black locks as he gazed up at her. He tilted his head back and she lowered hers, captured his lips again and moaned as he kissed her, as softly as before, each sweep of his lips over hers adding fuel to the fire blazing inside her.

She grew wetter as she stroked her hands over his broad shoulders, explored his powerful muscles, and thought about what came next. He read her mind, twisting so his back was against the rear of the recliner, luring her down with him. She followed, too mesmerised by his kiss and the feel of his body beneath her fingers, and where they were heading, to feel even an ounce of fear or doubt.

She flattened her palms against his chest as he brought his legs up, stretching them along the recliner, and she straddled his thighs. The heat blazing inside her burned hotter as she settled against him, and he raised his arms, lifting them above his head to drape them over the back of the lounger.

Emelia sat back, devoured the sight of him as he lay at her mercy, every muscle of his torso tensed as he held his arms above his head, showing her that he wasn't going to touch her. Not unless she asked it of him.

She raked her gaze down the line of his body to his erection.

It kicked against his stomach.

Jerked again when she skimmed her fingers down the length of it, from the dark plum that tipped it to his balls. He groaned as she teased them, tilted his head back, and closed his eyes as his big body shuddered.

He needed her. That thought had a fresh wave of desire rolling through her, dampening her shorts. She needed him too. Ached for him too fiercely to stop now.

Just the thought of him filling her was enough to have her close to climax.

"Keep your eyes closed." She shimmied off him, loving the way he frowned at that, his nostrils flaring as he fought to do as she wanted.

She pushed her shorts down her hips, excitement bubbling in her as she thought about what she was about to do, as she imagined it and let her mind run wild.

She tossed her shorts aside, straddled him again, and took hold of his cock. He was big, thick in her grip. She lowered her other hand, moaned as she pressed it between her thighs and felt how wet she was, so damned ready for him despite his size.

She brought her hand to his length, and a moan tore from his lips as she stroked it, slicking it with her arousal. It kicked and jerked, pulsed and gave up another drop of seed. She smeared that into his skin too and kept stroking him as she eased up on her knees, as she moved forwards and planted her other hand against his hip, holding him down.

Her breaths came faster as she positioned him, as the blunt head slipped down through her folds, teasing her with what was to come. She looked down and then at his face, torn between watching him enter her and watching his expression as he filled her. She flickered between the two as she eased back and he breached her. He shifted his hands, gripping the back of the lounger as his brow furrowed, his lips parting and breath sawing from between them as she sank onto him, slowly taking him into her.

She wanted to rush and wanted to savour it, couldn't decide which was more important as he filled her, stretching her so much she was aware of every inch of him. Bliss pulsed through her, pushing her close to the edge already. She moaned and couldn't stop herself from rocking her hips, rotating them as she took him into her.

"Emelia," Wolf bit out, his deep voice shaking as badly as his body. "I need to see."

The thought of him watching them joining sent a sharp thrill through her and she whispered breathlessly, "Look."

His eyes flicked open, swirling gold as they leaped down to his cock. He groaned, the strangled sound filling the air as his eyebrows pinched hard above his nose. His muscles flexed as he gripped the rear of the lounger harder, causing his hips to rise and pressing him deeper inside her. She moaned as he filled her, sank deeper on him, and pressed both hands into his stomach, clutching his hips as she swirled hers.

"Sweet… mercy." He tilted his head back again, the corded muscles of his neck tightening as he groaned. "Emelia."

She surrendered to him and her desire, sank back on him so he was as deep as she could take him, and rose off him, building a pace that would have her shattering before long. She didn't have the strength to ease back on the throttle, to savour each plunge of his cock into her, every meeting of their bodies. The need was too strong, had her rocking on him faster and faster, in time with his breaths as he began shifting his hips beneath her, driving his length into her.

Pleasure built, twisting tightly in her belly, and she closed her eyes and hung her head forwards, moaning as she reached for the bliss she needed. The ecstasy. She leaned over him, sought his mouth, and kissed him hard as she bounced on him, as his pelvis struck hers and tore another groan from her. He moaned with her, pumped her harder as she kissed him deeper, clutching his shoulders and then his arms. She skimmed her hands up his triceps to his elbows, curled her hands over his biceps, and clung to him as she rode him, losing awareness of the world.

There was only her, Wolf, and this incredible pleasure that was building inside her.

And a burning need that wouldn't be denied.

She had that look again, the one he had come to know well during the time he had known her. She hated that he had seen her suffering, that he knew the things that had happened to her still haunted her.

Still had power over her.

He opened his gauntleted hand and cupped her cheek, grazed his thumb over it, and gently lifted her head so her eyes met his.

"I will make the dragon pay, Emelia. For you." He searched her eyes, seeking out whether that vow pleased her.

Would she argue against it today, or would she reluctantly accept it? He was never sure which Emelia he would get whenever he promised her vengeance—the one who didn't want someone fighting her battles for her, or the one who was willing to lean on him and let him be the strong one.

She surprised him by tiptoeing, pressing her hands against the breastplate of his white-and-gold armour, and kissing him softly. He fought the urge to claim her lips, keeping the kiss light and gentle rather than passionate and hard as he wanted it. That urge slowly faded as heat spread through him, and he felt as if he was floating with every tender sweep of her mouth over his.

She eased back, and her eyes met his, holding him immobile as his lips tingled from their kiss, warmth suffusing every inch of him to chase away the darkness that had been plaguing him.

There was magic in her kiss.

She tamed the darkest part of him with it.

Enslaved him with it.

"Be careful," she whispered as her eyebrows furrowed and she lifted her right hand to place it against his cheek, mirroring him. "Come back."

He nodded, stepped away from her, and focused on his destination, a point close to the most dangerous kingdom in Hell.

A place he felt strong enough to set foot in now because he knew what she was really asking of him and it touched him.

She wanted him to return to her.

He took one last, lingering look at her and teleported.

When Hell materialised around him, the effect the grim bleak lands had on him was instantaneous. All the strength Emelia had inspired in him dissipated, and a weight pressed down on him, making his limbs heavy as he struggled to breathe.

He kept still, giving himself time to adjust to the realm again. It always took a few minutes to acclimatise to the curse and regain enough strength to move without falling on his face.

But he wanted to stay too, needed to remain near Emelia while she slumbered, vulnerable to all the evil in this world. He wanted to wait until she woke and he could speak with her, didn't want to leave her without a word after what had happened between them, because he was sure it would be the wrong move. He had limited experience of females, but he wasn't an idiot. If he left before she woke, she would take it badly, would read into it and convince herself of things that weren't true.

He wanted to be with her, had loved every second of last night, and ached to do it all over again a thousand times and then some.

"Wolf?" Her sleepy voice came from behind him and he slowly pivoted to face her, the sight of her hitting him hard in the region of his heart.

She was beautiful.

Rumpled from sleep with her rich brown hair tangled and wild, and a cream robe cinched at her waist.

She rubbed her green eyes, stifled a yawn with her hand and then offered him a sweet smile that held a hint of shyness.

"Couldn't sleep?" She slowly approached him, narrowing the world down to only her.

He shook his head and drifted towards her, unable to fight the pull of her, and tilted his head to keep his eyes on her when she stopped close to him.

A thousand things danced on the tip of his tongue, clamouring to be the one he said. Mentioning her nightmare. Confessing he needed to go to Hell. Detailing the way he was going to make the bastard suffer for what he had done to her. Telling her how incredible last night had been for him.

Admitting he was in love with her.

In the end, he settled for saying, "You are beautiful."

He lifted his hand and tucked a rogue strand of hair behind her ear as she averted her gaze, rose staining her cheeks.

"I look like hell." She looked herself over, felt her hair and pulled a face. "I should have brushed it before coming to find you."

But he had panicked her.

He could see it in her eyes and feel it in her. She had woken alone and had panicked, had thought he had left her without saying a word.

"I needed air." When she looked as if she needed a better explanation than that, he added, "You had a nightmare."

The brightness in her green gaze faded. "Oh. I'm sorry you had to see that."

He shook his head. "Do not apologise. You have nothing to apologise for."

CHAPTER 23

Wolf had carried Emelia to her bed when he had felt how chilled her skin was and had spent the night beside her, tucked beneath the covers and holding her, awake and aware that at any moment, she could stir and panic at the feel of his arms around her. He had savoured every second he had been able to hold her, every minute she had slept soundly in his arms, her breaths skating across his bare chest, heat warming his side.

Just before dawn, she had begun twisting and turning, making noises in her sleep that had torn at his heart, panicked and scared sounds. She had pushed at him and clawed at his chest, leaving long red marks on his skin, and he had released her, had rolled onto his side to face her and whispered to her, hoping the sound of his voice would soothe her and chase away whatever nightmare had her in its grasp.

When she had settled, he had stayed with her until he had felt the sun break the horizon and the birds had begun to sing.

Until the burning need inside him had driven him from the bed and the comfort of her.

He paced the length of the pool, his wings furled against his white armour as dual needs warred inside him. The hunger to hunt the dragon was back, blazing stronger than ever in his blood, roused by the nightmare Emelia had suffered and the time he had spent staring at the vicious scars on her shoulder and chest in the aftermath of it when he had been soothing her.

Scars he knew that bastard had given her.

He wanted to teleport to Hell right now and locate Rey, was wound tight and restless with the need to find the dragon and make him suffer as Emelia had.

Still did.

She moved faster, longer strokes that had her moaning breathlessly, muttering whispered pleas as she took him. He shifted his left foot, pressed it into the lounger, and angled his hips, using the leverage to give her what she needed. His long length filled her over and over, pushing her right to the edge, until she was sagging against him, rocked by the force of each thrust, hazy and lost as she reached for her climax.

It exploded inside her in a blinding flash. She cried out against his chest, shuddering from head to toe as she quivered around his cock, heat and light flooding her. She shook as she collapsed against him, moaning as he continued to thrust, drawing out her climax as he sought his own.

He tensed beneath her, grunted as he drove deep into her and stilled there, his cock kicking and throbbing, seed scalding her and tearing another moan from her lips as her body responded, clenched and pulsed in time with him as another wave of bliss rolled over her to carry her away.

He was still for a long time, his big body tensed and trembling, and then he sagged against the lounger, relaxing beneath her, his breaths stirring the drying strands of her hair.

Emelia nestled into his chest, listening to his heart drumming against her cheek as she drifted in a daze, warmed from head to toe, sated and savouring the feel of him beneath her.

She didn't fight him when he curled his arms around her.

She sank into his embrace.

Feeling safe and protected for the first time in a long time.

Trusting Wolf would take care of her.

Because she knew she wasn't the only one falling in love now.

His gaze roamed over the mountains surrounding him, a valley he had only seen from a distance during his travels. He hadn't dared to venture this close to the Devil's lands before. The drain on his powers was intense, had his legs wobbling beneath him as he focused on his breathing, making a vain attempt to keep it even and level.

How long would it take to grow used to the devastating effects of the curse enough that he could move?

He kept scanning his surroundings, his senses slowly sharpening as his body adjusted. His heart hammered a staccato rhythm against his ribs, blood thundering as awareness of the danger he was in, how vulnerable he was standing in the middle of the valley, drummed inside him.

Demons no doubt roamed these lands and he was a sitting duck, and a very obvious target in his white armour. Even if he concealed his wings, he would still stand out at a distance, a bright streak against the black of Hell. It was dark, the sky a strange shade of amber and the valley lit only by the distant volcanoes that lined the horizon to his right, but he could see perfectly well.

Which meant demons could see him too.

He had to move.

He shuffled one foot forwards, scuffing it through the loose black basalt, and then the other, following his instincts. The mark on the inside of his right wrist itched and burned, irritating him, warning there was a demon nearby.

He was banking on it being the demon he had come here to see.

If it wasn't, he was in serious trouble.

The intelligence he had uncovered on hearing of the Fifth Commander falling had pointed to this valley, though, rumours that a fallen angel lived here and a demoness killed any who attempted to get near him.

His left boot snagged on a stubborn rock, and he stumbled a few steps, struggling to keep himself upright as his legs weakened beneath him. He spread his aching wings, a vain attempt to regain his balance that had the opposite effect. Pain ripped through him, blinded him, and sent him to his knees.

His Echelon mark blazed.

Fire shot down his spine, an order to return. It stole his breath, the pain of it so intense as it combined with his foolish attempt to use his wings that his vision tunnelled.

He leaned over and clutched the dirt, clawing it with his gauntlets.

He couldn't return. He had to be close if his superiors were demanding he leave Hell. Rey had to be here, somewhere, and for some reason, they didn't want him talking to the fallen angel.

Or was it because they knew he was in danger?

Warning bells jangled in his mind, his senses stretching far and wide around him to chart everything as his instincts warned he wasn't alone. Someone was here. Stalking him. Hunting him.

The instinct to survive so he could return to Emelia drove him to his feet and had him focusing on her as it flooded him with the urge to teleport.

He barely suppressed it and called his sword instead. It was heavy in his grip as it materialised, threatened to send him back to his knees as it drained him, the power it contained desperately feeding off his limited strength as it sought to overcome the curse that affected it too.

He couldn't leave, though. He needed to speak with Rey. If there was a chance the male could help him, he needed to take it, even if there was a risk that male might no longer recognise him as a friend.

If the fallen angel attacked him, he wouldn't be strong enough to defend himself.

He wouldn't be quick enough to teleport.

His life would end here.

The sensation of danger grew stronger, the pain from the command to return to Heaven intensifying with it, pushing him into obeying.

He gritted his teeth against it, refusing to do as they wanted, part of him hoping that if he resisted them enough, they might send someone to retrieve him and might pluck him from the maws of death if Rey attacked him.

"Shit on a stick. What the fuck are you doing here?" The female voice lashed at him, her crude words ringing in his buzzing, blurry mind.

Not Rey.

A demoness.

He inched his eyes up until they hit pointed boots and black plates of armour moulded over a pair of long legs. He forced his gaze higher, beyond the exposed vee of creamy skin where her leg armour dipped from her hips to a point below her navel, and up to the matching tiny breastplate that hardly concealed her breasts.

"Ew, are you ogling me?" She kicked him in the face, sending him flying across the rough black ground.

A bellow ripped from him as his wings twisted beneath him and he rolled, tumbling across the dirt to come to a halt at her feet. The bitch had teleported. He pushed his hands into the dirt and shook off the blow, struggling to get his senses back online before she could attack again.

Too late.

She caught him in the stomach this time and swept her leg upwards, hurling him high into the air.

He stared down at the enormous drop to the ground, a strange sense of emptiness filling him as he looked at it and knew there was nothing he could do to prevent what was coming when his wings were useless and he was too weak to teleport.

It was going to hurt like hell.

Someone grabbed him around the waist, stopping him from falling.

The demoness?

No, she was glaring up at him and whoever had ruined her fun by stopping him from hitting the ground.

"Asteria." The familiar baritone held a chiding note, one that had the demoness's expression souring into a pout.

Wolf had never been more glad to hear that voice.

Relief poured through him as all his fears flooded out of him. Rey sounded no different to when he had been an angel, and Wolf could sense the light that remained inside him. How had he fallen and retained some of his goodness?

"I was only having some fun," Asteria said in a sweet, sing-song voice as she twirled the gold-to-crimson stripe down the right of her onyx hair around her fingers. Her lips pursed further, and she blinked her blue eyes up at him. "The stupid big black bear wasn't hurt. Much."

Rey huffed and beat his black wings, their feathers appearing in the corners of Wolf's vision as the male lowered him towards the ground. Wolf reached for it with his toes when he was close, eager to touch it again and not enjoying the way Rey's arms around him were a constant reminder he had needed to be saved from a tiny demoness.

The fallen angel released him as they touched down.

Wolf's legs were surprisingly steady beneath him.

Was he acclimatising?

Rey stepped aside.

Wolf collapsed to his knees, the impact with the ground sending pain shooting up his spine. "Dammit."

"Sorry." Rey stooped, grabbed his arm, and hauled him back to his feet. "I thought you had it there."

Had the male been holding him until the moment he had moved aside? He cursed again, aiming it at the damned weakness infesting him this time.

He aimed one at the demoness too as she approached them, a swagger in her step that had her hips swaying side to side. He had been doing just fine until she had attempted to kick him out of Hell.

She hit Rey with another sultry pout. "Forgiven?"

Rey heaved a sigh. "Not everyone who comes near me is out to kill me, Asteria."

"But... but he's a bloody angel!" She flung her hand to her right, pointing at Wolf. "He wasn't exactly friendly with me either. Don't think I've forgotten how he looked at me back in that fae town. He wanted to incinerate me."

"I still want to incinerate you," Wolf grumbled and rubbed the armour above his Echelon mark.

It was going crazy now that she was close to him again, burning so hot, he was finding it hard to breathe.

"See!" She turned wide, horrified eyes on Rey.

The fallen angel just rolled his crimson eyes. "Sometimes, Asteria, I want to do that too."

She glared at him and planted her hands against her hips. "No sex for you."

Rey's gaze narrowed on her, his blond eyebrows dipping low. "You will be begging for it within a couple of days."

She shrugged, lifting her black breastplate. "Probably."

A slow grin spread across Rey's face and his red irises blazed like hot coals, his elliptical pupils dilating as he stared at her.

She loosed a wistful sigh and fluttered her long black eyelashes as she murmured, "Definitely."

Wolf rolled his eyes and shrugged off Rey's grip, staggered a little but managed to remain upright this time. Definitely making progress.

"Why are you here, Fourth Commander?" Rey finally stopped looking at the demoness as if he was about to rip off her armour and take her right there in the middle of the valley in front of Wolf.

Some things about Rey had changed. The male seemed more confident now, far surer of himself. A positive effect of being a fallen angel? Or did this newfound confidence stem from his love for Asteria?

He looked at the fallen angel and noted that, while the demoness wore her armour, Rey wore a pair of tight black jeans and heavy leather boots paired with a charcoal-grey T-shirt. Fallen angels possessed armour similar to that which Wolf wore, only it was as black as sin. Why hadn't Rey come dressed for war like his demoness?

He took it as a sign that the male had known it was him and that he had no interest in fighting him.

He would have changed his own armour to show the male he wasn't here to fight either, but the drain of Hell was too strong and he could barely stand, let alone muster the strength to call fresh clothes to him.

Avenged by an Angel

"Put your wings away." Rey jerked his chin towards them. "And the sword should go too. It makes it easier."

Wolf focused, forcing his wings away first and then dematerialising his weapon. At first, he didn't notice much difference, but as he stood there with Rey staring at him and Asteria giving him killing looks, he began to feel stronger. Calmer. He could breathe more easily. Was no longer in danger of collapsing, his legs steadier beneath him.

"Better?" Rey said, and when he nodded, the male continued, "So why are you here, Fourth Commander? Did they send you?"

"Wolf," he corrected and removed his gauntlets, flexed his fingers and ignored the burning in his mark. "And I sent myself."

"Wolf?" Asteria regarded him with curiosity. "Who gave you that name? They should have called you Bear."

What was it with this female and calling him a bear? He glared at her and she gave him a look that said he had just proven her point.

"You know, when you look at me that way, I can really see the demon in you."

"Asteria!" Rey hissed as he gave her a pointed look, one that had her blinking at him as if she wasn't sure what she had done wrong this time.

Wolf frowned at the female. "*What?* Demon in me?"

He was about to point out that he was obviously an angel, something she had mentioned earlier when she had been kicking him around Hell, when Rey spoke.

"Fourth Commander… Wolf… You should probably be sitting down for this one."

He didn't like the sound of that, or the grimace the male gave him when his eyes leaped to him for an explanation.

"The skinny is that your holier-than-thou bosses have been lying to you for centuries and the reason you can sense demons is because you are one. Or at least a little itty bit of one." Asteria earned another black look from Rey. She shrugged this one off. "Look, it's easier if you do it quickly. Like ripping off a Band-Aid."

Wolf wasn't sure what a Band-Aid was and he wasn't sure hitting him with something this big, this shocking, in a single blow was better than breaking it to him gently.

He looked to Rey as his knees gave out again, sending him to the black ground, hoping despite everything his instincts were screaming at him, that the demoness was joking. This was all some twisted joke, meant to shake him. Wasn't it?

Rey's crimson eyes were deadly serious as he lowered them to Wolf. "I did not believe it at first either... but it is the truth. The Echelon are born half-breed, from a union between a demon and an angel. We are hunted down by one from both factions and given a choice, serve Heaven or serve Hell."

Wolf's ears rang as he stared at the fallen angel, struggling to comprehend what he was saying.

If it was true, it had to be the reason the Archangels were still attempting to call him back to Heaven. They hadn't wanted him to find out about this.

"Who told you this?" Because maybe they had been joking.

Rey sighed. "The half-breed I was sent to bring in. She knew what her parents were and what she was. She exposed the game between our world and the Devil."

Wolf leaned over and swallowed hard as bile rose up his throat. He wanted to deny it, to laugh it off and declare they had all gone mad, but it made a sickening sort of sense and all he could do was stare at the ground as everything suddenly fell into place. All those questions that had plagued him when he was younger, answered in the blink of an eye.

Or the rip of a Band-Aid.

He could sense other angels, and demons could sense other demons. It wasn't unreasonable that his gift to sense demons could come from demon blood in his veins.

Rey eased to his haunches beside him and offered a sympathetic smile that was at odds to his dark appearance now. Was it possible that Rey had retained his good when he had fallen because of the demonic side of his blood?

"I wanted to break it to you gently." His crimson eyes shifted to Asteria. "I said we were going to do it gently."

She shrugged. "It was more fun this way."

He sighed and tilted his head back as he closed his eyes and muttered, "Give me strength."

"You love me really." Asteria wrapped her arms around Rey's neck, pressing her front into his spine, and rubbed her small black horns against his temple.

Rey didn't deny that. He kept his eyes on Wolf. Waiting for him to have another meltdown? He was taking it in, little by little, as his mind offered up all the times he had wondered about his origins, about his gift, and other things. They all made sense to him now, and it was strange how that made him feel. Not confused or conflicted. Not even angry he had been lied to all these years, made to believe he was fully angel.

He felt calm.

Numb?

Or just at peace because all the things that had bothered him, everything he had questioned, had just been answered?

And in their place, a new question arose.

Demons had fated mates. He looked from Asteria to Rey, not missing the way they were looking at each other as if they would die without the other. Were they mates?

What if the reason Emelia drove him so wild was because his suppressed demon blood recognised her as his fated one?

Was that the reason he felt an overpowering need to protect her, to keep her from harm and from other males? Was that why he so desperately needed to avenge her and punish the one who had hurt her?

It was a lot to think about and take in.

He sat back on his knees and looked at his dirty hands, the next question that pinged into his head chilling him.

If Emelia learned of his demonic blood, would she look at him differently?

Would the fact one of his parents had been from Hell affect her opinion of him—her feelings for him?

He didn't want her to fear him because there was a part of him that came from the same realm as the one who had harmed her.

"What's going on in his head?" Asteria said.

"I am not sure." Rey placed his left hand against Wolf's shoulder. "Are you alright?"

No. He was far from alright. He had just made love with Emelia and everything had been wonderful, his future had seemed so bright and sure, one where she would stand by his side and be his forever. Now, part of him feared she would turn on him if she discovered he carried demon blood in his veins.

"Wait," he muttered and frowned at the featureless valley bottom and the mountains that speared the amber sky in all directions around him. "If I have demon blood, why does the curse affect me so badly?"

"We think it affects Echelon worse because my dark lord is pissed you chose the wrong side." Asteria smiled sweetly, as if she was delivering words of encouragement that should please him rather than another blow.

Damn.

He had hoped there would be some sort of psychological reason the curse affected him more than it should have, some barrier he could overcome by tapping into his apparently demonic blood, or a method he could employ to weaken the curse's hold on him.

Of course the Devil would ensure his curse affected those who had picked Heaven over him more than angels who had been born in service of that realm. It was just the sort of spiteful thing that male would do.

His thoughts turned to Emelia. What was she doing? He imagined her swimming, wearing that sexy little two-piece she had been wearing last night. A grand mistake. He shifted his hips as he shot hard as stone.

"Is the bear having naughty thoughts?" Asteria edged away from him. "Or is he thinking about killing me again?"

He realised his eyes had changed, blazing gold in response to the desire that rushed through him, a wicked ache that urged him to return to Emelia.

He tamped it down instead and looked at Rey, right into his bright scarlet eyes. "I need your help."

"Anything you want." Small fangs flashed between Rey's lips, another mark of his fallen angel status.

What was it like to fall? Rey still seemed to be Rey, the same collected and level-headed angel he had always known. Only his wings were black now, his eyes red, his canines were fangs, and his armour would be obsidian.

Shadows swirled around Rey's legs, and he casually swept them away, an irritated look crossing his face as he brushed his hand through them. Such shadows had wrapped around Wolf's legs when he had lost his temper in the presence of Emelia. Was it a sign he was changing?

Falling?

Another question shoved to the front of his mind, pushing aside what he had wanted to ask Rey.

"You are not like other fallen. Because of your demon blood?" The weight of hope that hinged on the answer to that question was crushing as it pressed down on Wolf.

He was growing darker, had black feathers already and Hell was affecting him, changing him. He needed to know what would happen if he fell.

Rey shrugged. "I do not think so. Perhaps."

"How did you fall?" Wolf leaned towards him a little, eager to hear the answer.

"I cut off my wings."

The pain that crossed Rey's features said that was the truth and that doing such a thing had been hard for him.

Was that the only safe method of falling if an angel wanted to retain his personality? His light?

If it was, it was little wonder the angels in Heaven hadn't figured it out yet. No angel in their right mind would cut off their own wings. The way Rey looked at Asteria, desperation mixed with love and fear in his crimson gaze, said he had been far from sane when he had taken a blade to his wings and had chosen to fall for her sake.

She sidled closer to Rey and brushed her palm across his cheek, a wealth of love and gratitude in her eyes as she stared into his.

Wolf's shoulders itched at just the thought of severing his wings, a spark of pain skittering down his spine. Never. No matter what happened, he could never cut off his own wings. They were sacred. Even though they were marred with black feathers, he would do all in his power to keep them safe.

He looked at Asteria and imagined Emelia in her position, in danger in this bleak realm where he was weaker than most, unable to protect her.

If Emelia was in danger, could he cut his wings off for her sake, to gain the power he needed to save her?

The answer shocked him.

In a heartbeat.

If the choice was sacrificing her or his wings, he would pick his wings.

He could live without them. He couldn't live without her.

Although he wasn't sure he would retain any shred of good if he did fall. The darkness had always been strong in him, constantly attempting to push out the light. If he fell, there was a danger he would turn evil.

And Emelia would leave him.

He added that to his list of reasons for keeping her out of Hell and away from the dragon. She was growing stronger though, more confident. If he didn't slay the dragon soon, there was a chance she would finally find the courage to hunt Zephyr down herself.

"I need to hunt a dragon." He gripped Rey's arm when the male offered it and stood with his assistance.

"A dragon? What business do you have with a dragon?"

"It is personal." He wanted to leave it at that, but the ever-astute Asteria was eyeing him again, a flicker of suspicion in her steady blue gaze.

"He totally has a woman," she announced, and when Rey frowned at her, she waved her hand towards Wolf. "Look at him. He's a little less grizzly bear than before. My verdict is he got some sack time with a hottie and now he's a boner-fide bad boy. See what I did there? Boner-fide."

She wagged her fine black eyebrows and chuckled to herself.

"*Boner-fide.*"

Rey just sighed. "Is she right?"

Wolf's instinct was to deny it, but he forced himself to nod. If Rey knew he was doing this because of a female, he might be more inclined to help him.

"It is true. Emelia is a hunter for Archangel."

"The hunter group?" A thoughtful furrow marred Rey's brow as he pursed his lips. "I had heard some of them had been in Hell recently."

"She is a commander in their headquarters in London, and was here as a member of a party sent to assist a demon king." He tried his hardest to keep the contempt from his voice as he mentioned the brute. If Rey and Asteria were right, he was hardly in the position to judge demons anymore. "She was captured by a dragon clan and given to one of their warriors."

Asteria's eyes blackened. "Given?"

"The dragon held her captive as a spoil of war and... *mistreated*... her." And the dragon would pay for that.

His mood took a nosedive, the darkness swift to rise as his mind filled first with Emelia's memories and then with pleasing images of what he was going to do to Zephyr when he got his hands on the bastard.

"You sure he's not more demon than angel?"

He shook himself back to Asteria and found her staring at his legs.

His gaze dropped to them.

To the shadows writhing around them.

Concern flickered across Rey's face as he studied them. "You have been in Hell too much. How long have you been hunting this dragon?"

"Weeks."

The fallen angel lifted his eyes to lock with Wolf's. "And how many black feathers do you already have?"

He swallowed and allowed his wings to emerge, stretching them out at his sides to reveal the cluster of dark feathers. Asteria's eyes widened and she gasped, her hand flying up to cover her mouth. A chill skated through him and his gaze zipped to his wings, fear pounding in his veins as he imagined the worst.

The patch of black feathers was still small.

Hadn't spread as he feared.

The demoness laughed. "Oh, you should have seen your face!"

"Fuck off," he barked and sent his wings away again, his hands shaking as he fought the panic that had flooded him at the thought he might have gained more black feathers.

She clutched her hands to her chest. "My delicate ears. Are you going to let him speak to me like that?"

Rey loosed another weary sigh. "I know where the dragons live. I can fly you there directly and we can end this male."

Asteria pulled a face at Rey for ignoring her.

"I have visited the dragon villages. Many live there, and they are protective of their kind. It is better we locate the male and tackle him when he is alone. Would you be strong enough to kill him?" As much as Wolf hated the thought of his friend having that honour rather than him, he was aware he was no match for a dragon.

"Or you could do the romantic thing."

He looked at Asteria as Rey pinched the bridge of his nose, looking for all the world as if he was stifling another sigh.

She beamed at Wolf. "What better way to say you love her than to tie a big old bow on the bastard and present him to her? I know if it was me, I'd want to end the fucker myself. It's all very macho killing him for the one you love, but she's a hunter. Don't tell me she doesn't want to castrate this dragon herself."

He thought about that.

Emelia had been training, had told him she wanted to track the dragon down herself, and had even spoken of entering Hell before her nerve had failed her. What if he could bring the dragon to her? The male would be weakened in her realm, unable to shift, and Wolf would be stronger.

They could end the bastard together.

Would Emelia like that?

"He's totally considering it, isn't he?" Asteria nudged Rey's arm with her own, her face filled with delight as she looked up at him. "And I thought you were the bad boy. Are all Echelon this wicked?"

"You are not going to find out." Rey chucked her under her chin. "Wolf is the only one I would trust near you."

And Wolf was glad of it, because he was no match for Rey.

He wasn't even a match for Asteria right now.

And he definitely wasn't a match for the demons who landed just beyond them.

Asteria slowly turned towards the three towering males who wore armour similar to hers, black metal plates moulded to their legs and hips. Their chests were exposed, their black leathery wings enormous as they furled them as one, a regimented air to their action that warned these males often fought as a team. Black horns curled from behind their ears, curving downwards before they flared forwards into deadly spears beside their temples.

Bright golden elliptical pupils shone in the centres of their black irises.

"Elite," Asteria breathed, and he didn't miss the note of fear amidst the awe in her voice.

Wolf knew of the elite of the Devil's demons, warriors who were kept in a permanent state of rage in order to protect their master and deter any would-be enemies with the formidable show of power.

The one in the middle, a male who stood at least two inches taller than Wolf's own seven feet, lifted a gauntleted hand and pointed a clawed finger right at him.

Wolf didn't know what the male said. He only knew pain as it crashed over him, blinding him in an instant as the demonic tongue sent a thousand white-hot spears piercing his skull.

"Teleport... now!" Rey's words wobbled in his ears, distorted and distant, watery sounding as Wolf fought to remain standing.

The three demons charged.

Wolf could only stare at them, numbness sweeping through him as he thought of Emelia and how foolish he had been.

Had he really thought himself strong enough to enter Hell and survive all it would throw at him?

A single demonic word was enough to render him useless.

His lips curled into a cold smile.

But they weren't the only ones with power in their voices.

Rey intercepted the first demon, tackling him head-on as Asteria threw a panicked look over her shoulder at Wolf.

"Cover your ears," Wolf said.

She frowned and then her eyes widened, her hands leaping to her head. She jammed her fingers into her ears and flinched.

Wolf said the only word he knew in the ancient angelic tongue.

The three demons fighting Rey roared and staggered backwards as it hit them, and hope soared in Wolf's heart. He was going to make it out of this alive.

The biggest of the demons grew even larger as rage lit a fire in his eyes, and he casually tossed Rey aside, sending the male flying through the air towards him.

"I'm guessing the rumours are true, then." Asteria kicked off, launching upwards to catch Rey in the air before he could fall. She spread her leathery wings and drifted down with him to land near Wolf. "The Devil keeps them pissed off by speaking the angelic tongue at them."

Wolf stared at the enormous, now ten-foot-tall demon that was charging him, all the fires of Hell raging in his eyes as he snarled and growled, flashing huge fangs.

"Oh, *fuck*."

The demon collided with him.
All hell broke loose.

CHAPTER 24

The Fourth Commander of the Echelon was back. The Third Archangel had sent a message to her, ordering her to go to the Fourth Commander and heal him.

She smoothed her golden hair in the twin braids she had gathered into a sort of bun at the back of her head, and then the two wavy lengths of loose hair she had allowed to flow beside her cheeks today. A last-minute decision she had made upon looking at her reflection in the mirror.

It had taken a few minutes to rearrange her hairstyle, and she was sure the Fourth Commander wouldn't be happy with the delay, but she wanted to look her best for him.

He had been distant recently, distracted by something. The last time she had been sent to him, he had barely looked at her, had been focused on the floor of his apartment, clearly watching something unfolding in the mortal world.

She had heard rumours he had been sent to retrieve a half-breed for the Echelon and that he had failed and was now seeking her, had even gone against the orders of the Archangels and had entered Hell.

Had he been injured there?

She knocked softly on the double doors of his apartment in the Echelon headquarters and waited, nervously retying the twisted band of gold rope that held her white robe closed at her waist. She licked her lips, a vain attempt to settle herself. She healed others, but the Fourth Commander always made her nervous.

She was always the healer the Archangels sent to him. There had to be a reason for that. A purpose. She had thought about it often when she was healing him, tending to his wounds after his battles.

Avenged by an Angel

Now, she felt certain they had chosen her for him.

He was powerful, handsome, but a little dark. She was sure she could grow used to that aspect of him if he sired her offspring, though. If one of them was born with the mark, they would be as important as he was, and she would rise in the ranks because of what she had done.

There was a chance she might even be selected to lead one of the healing houses.

She knocked again. Her senses said he was in his rooms, and he was moving around them. The Archangels were never wrong about who needed healing, and she could smell blood. When he didn't answer this time, she twisted the handle and gently pushed the door open.

"Forgive my intrusion."

Her eyes widened.

Blood tracked over every inch of his bare chest, drying in thick rivulets down his muscular arms, and stained the armour he still wore on his lower half. Vicious gouges streaked across his chest, as if some wild beast had gored him with its horns.

It wasn't her place, but she couldn't stop herself from asking, "What happened?"

He glared at her and turned away, revealing the horrific injuries on his back and the two long scars where she hoped his wings were hidden.

"Demons," he muttered, his voice blacker than his expression as he resumed his pacing, leaving a red smear on the white marble tiles in his wake.

"You must keep still." She picked up the basket of healing items, closed the door, and hurried over to him.

He didn't do as she bid. He kept pacing, taking long strides across his apartment, leaving blood everywhere. It was stark against all the white, turned her stomach with fear as she took a closer look at him and saw all the wounds on his body, all the slashes and punctures that still seeped crimson.

"What sort of demon has the power to do this to you?" she whispered, unable to hold that question back too.

"Elite." He practically growled the word.

She wasn't familiar with that sort of demon. Was it powerful? It had to be powerful in order to wound the Fourth Commander like this.

"And I did not say demon, I said *demons*," he snapped and glared at her, and she shrank back, curling away from him as the air around him darkened and chilled. He frowned and sighed, his big body relaxing as he looked himself over. "I apologise. Just fix this. I have somewhere I need to be."

He was mad if he was planning to return to whatever battle he had come from. She didn't press him for information. It wasn't her place. She set the basket down, opened it, and took out everything she was going to need. She wasn't sure the large canister of healing water she had would be enough to wash all his wounds, but she would make it work somehow, because she was sure that if she left him for any reason, he would be gone when she returned, whether he was healed or not.

"You must keep still." She tried not to flinch away when he turned dark eyes on her again, ones that warned he didn't like her ordering him around.

He had been warm towards her once, and she had thought they were growing closer, that he was coming to desire her as someone who could bear him offspring. She wasn't expecting him to pledge himself to her. She wasn't a fool. Echelon were revered, and many of them had offspring with multiple females. Only the strongest of those offspring would be chosen to follow in their footsteps.

She was sure she could bear that child for him.

He stilled at last and stared at the floor again, his silver gaze distant and troubled as he watched something in the world beyond their realm. She carefully removed his armour, stripping it from him piece by piece, struggling to ignore the curiosity that built inside her as she set the limited parts of it aside. What had happened to the rest? Had the demons stripped it from him?

When the last of his armour was gone, she set to work, unabashed by his nudity. She had seen him naked countless times now, found his body quite alluring. She would go as far as saying his powerful physique delighted her, and would never admit it to anyone, but she had thought about it sometimes when she was alone in her small room. She pictured him to be a gentle lover despite his strength, attentive and tender.

His expression hardened, his black eyebrows dipping low above the straight line of his nose as he narrowed his gaze on something.

"What is it you watch? The demons?" She had never been so bold before.

Normally she remained as silent as possible so as not to disturb him. The fact she was speaking with him made her a little giddy, had the nerves she always felt around him rising to the fore to make her hands shake. She hoped he didn't notice.

He shook his head. "The demons are dead... though I was not the one to kill them."

Anger flared in his eyes, giving them a golden shimmer. It faded a moment later, his face softening in a way that drew a frown from her as she carefully cleaned his chest, moved closer to him than usual, so their bodies almost touched. What was he watching that calmed him so easily?

She didn't possess the power to see the things he saw. If she turned her gaze to the mortal realm, she wouldn't be able to locate the object that fascinated him and held his focus so completely.

She sponged over his hip, chased the watery rivulets of blood across his stomach, so low her palm brushed the trail of hair above his penis. Her heart thundered, courage faltering as her eyes leaped to his to measure his reaction.

He frowned.

Not quite what she had expected.

The females in her healing house spoke of the other Echelon, how they had been bedded by some of them, their touch arousing the males as they worked. She glanced at the Fourth Commander's manhood. It hung flaccid and evidently uninterested in pursuing such wicked pastimes with her.

Perhaps it was because he was distracted by whatever he was watching.

"Is it your mission objective you are watching?" She weathered a curious glance from him and the following frown.

"No." He returned his gaze to the floor. "Just do your work."

She nodded, her courage failing her completely as his tone lashed at her, as he put her in her place with only a look and a handful of words. She moved behind him, finishing bathing him. When she was done with the healing water, she carefully dried him off, tending to *every* inch of him. Still no reaction.

He didn't even acknowledge she had touched him this time.

She was sure the Archangels intended her for him, so she wasn't going to be deterred. Since realising their reasons for always choosing her for the Fourth Commander, she had been faithful to the male, had refused the advances of many others. She had saved herself for him.

She held her hands over the wounds on his back, using her gift to aid his healing process. The shallower slashes and punctures closed instantly, leaving his skin smooth and perfect again. The deeper ones drew grunts from him, his muscles tensing as his flesh stitched back together. She controlled the flow of her power, even though it drained her to do so, making it easier on him by slowing the healing so he didn't experience the pain of it all at once.

And so she could spend longer with him.

Even though he wasn't with her.

His gaze remained fixed on the floor. On something else. *Someone* else?

There were rumours about him floating around, ones spread by his own comrades. The half-breed wasn't the reason he had been so distracted and distant recently. She pushed the painful thought of him with another female out of her mind. She had been chosen for him. He would sire her offspring, and she would make him love her. Somehow. She didn't want him to be with other angels. She wanted him to need only her.

She moved around to his front, and he frowned and leaned to one side, peering past her. Staring at the damned floor.

"What holds your attention so fiercely?" She regretted that question the second it left her lips.

He didn't look at her. "None of your business."

"I need to heal your neck. Could you raise your head for me?" And break his gaze with the mortal realm in the process.

"No." He tossed her a black look, one that chilled her as the air around him seemed to darken again. "Continue your work."

She bit her tongue to stop herself from demanding he look at her and not whatever held his attention in the human world. Pain blossomed in her heart and she did her best to ignore it and the whispered taunts in her mind as she worked to heal his neck. It wasn't a female. The rumours were lies. He was meant for her.

She was meant for him.

She leaned a little closer as she lifted her hands higher, attending to a cut on his earlobe. A frown flickered on his brow as she brushed her fingers over it, touching his skin. She trailed her hands down his strong neck, keeping contact with him for a change, something she had never done before when in the healing stage of tending to him.

He huffed, but didn't order her to move away.

Her hands drifted lower, healing the smaller wounds on his chest first, and then skimming across the flat slabs of his pectorals to the gouges. She hovered her palms above the deep grooves, gentling her power so she was healing him slowly, painlessly. Not that he noticed.

His eyes were still locked on the infernal floor.

But they were brightening, turning gold as his pupils dilated.

Was she affecting him?

Emboldened by the thought she might be, she eased her hands lower, focusing on the wounds on his stomach, grazing her fingers over the relaxed muscles that were still pronounced beneath his skin.

His pupils dilated further.

Was this what her fellow healers had told her about? Surely that was desire in his eyes. Passion he might give to her if she continued to be brave.

She swallowed hard and forced her hands lower, to a wound that cut across his stomach below his navel.

His penis twitched.

Heat washed through her, startling and swift, and her pulse accelerated.

He lifted his hand, ran it over his mouth, and muttered, "Swimming again."

He said those two words as if they were a curse, and she frowned as she tried to make sense of them. Swimming again?

"That damned two-piece." He almost groaned the words as his manhood twitched again.

It hit her that he *was* watching a female. A human female. He was watching her while she was here with him, throwing the human and his evident desire for her in her face. No. No way. She was not going to let a human take him from her.

She stepped back, hastily untied the gold rope at her waist with trembling fingers, and tried not to shake as her white robe fell open, baring her curves to him.

His gaze finally shifted to her.

She pushed on, determined to conquer her fears, to overcome them because she couldn't let that female have him. He was meant for her. She had been chosen for him. She let the robe fall from her shoulders, the soft material sending a shiver through her as it brushed her skin to pool around her feet.

The Fourth Commander stared at her. "What do you think you are doing?"

She was tempting him. She was going to win him. That was what she was doing.

She stepped close to him, pressed her body to his and gripped his shoulders, pulled herself up on her tiptoes and kissed him. Electricity arced through her, the taste of him divine and the heat of his lips against hers a drug she wanted to indulge in forever. She moaned and kissed him deeper, sweeping her lips over his, stroking them with her tongue, a fever wracking her as she worked her body closer to his.

His hands clamped around her hips.

To draw her closer?

She shivered at the thought, aching for it.

He shoved her away from him.

To take her to his bed?

She looked up at his face, sure she would find the heat of desire in his eyes now.

They were glacial, the coldness of them hitting her hard, destroying the courage that had been blooming inside her.

He stooped, picked up her robe, and looked as if he wanted to hurl it at her as his expression blackened, his lips compressing into a thin line and his eyes growing dark. He hesitated, drew down a deep breath, and then carefully wrapped the robe around her instead, pulling it closed over her chest.

She caught the sides of it, her eyes burning and shame eating away at her as she slipped her arms into it and tied it over her body.

That shame became anger, rage as she had never known it, when he spoke.

"Leave and forget this foolishness." His voice was as cold as his eyes.

She obeyed the order to leave, gathering her healing items and racing for the door, trembling from head to toe, but she wouldn't forget him. She wouldn't give up on him.

She couldn't.

He was meant for her.

And she wouldn't let the mortal bitch have him.

CHAPTER 25

Zephyr turned the demon away, tempted to rip him to pieces for bringing him no new information on Emelia. He had four in his service, all mercenaries from different kingdoms, all after his gold. He had promised the one who found her that he could take whatever he desired from the hoard hidden deep in his network of caves. The incentive had been enough to have six demons pledging themselves to him.

Two had died. One in an altercation with the angel in Hell when he had been attempting to listen in on a conversation. The other after he had returned to report that fact to Zephyr and had admitted to not assisting the male and allowing the angel to leave.

The angel wanted Zephyr dead.

Zephyr wanted the angel dead.

The demon had been given a chance to eliminate the male and had fled instead. So now, the demon was dead. The message it had sent to the remaining four demons had certainly spurred them into action, although apparently none of them had personally encountered the angel since their comrade had been reduced to a smouldering pile of ash by him.

Wilhelm, a demon from the Third Realm, had balls as big as they came as he strode forwards with purpose, his dusky horns flaring into twin daggers through his thick chestnut hair as he exchanged a look with the demon Zephyr had just dismissed. The male's deep red eyes tracked his opponent, not leaving him until the other demon, one from the Fifth Realm, had teleported.

That demon had a problem with Wilhelm that stemmed from what Wilhelm called 'ridiculous loyalty to a pathetic kingdom'. The two realms had been at war recently and although they were mercenaries and neither had fought in the battle between the Third Realm and the Fifth Realm, the demon bore a grudge against Wilhelm.

Zephyr couldn't really understand that. He had fought in that war, his dragon clan hired by the Fifth Realm. He felt no anger towards Wilhelm and was inclined to agree with the male's view of the kingdom. The Fifth Realm was pathetic. It had lost the war despite having a larger force, and the clan had lost many dragons in the process.

At least Ren had demanded the coin up front. It had been enough to add to the hoard of every warrior.

On top of that, Zephyr had found his mate.

That was worth almost as much to him as the gold.

Wilhelm brazenly strode towards him, not stopping at a meek distance like the others had. He didn't stop until he was almost toe to toe with Zephyr and refused to cower, kept his chin tipped up and shoulders straight. In a fight, Zephyr could take the male if needed, but the demon was strong, broad bare chest packed with muscle and legs like tree trunks in his tight mahogany leathers. The male had twice his build.

In this form.

As a dragon, Zephyr would stand fifty feet taller than the demon even if he entered a rage state, and could crush him like a bug beneath his paws.

Wilhelm reminded Zephyr why he was his favourite.

"I found her."

Just like the demon to announce something so important in a brusque, blunt way. The others would have embellished a little, built him up with a tale of their travels before announcing their success. Not Wilhelm. He said things straight.

The demon offered another reminder.

Sometimes, that wasn't a good thing.

"She was fucking an angel at some fancy country estate."

Zephyr growled and bared his teeth as they all sharpened into points.

"Think it's his?" Wilhelm pulled a thoughtful face.

"I don't give a shit if the house is his, or hers," he snarled in the demon tongue and stepped up to the male, glaring right into the bastard's eyes. "Tell me where this was."

"Mortal realm."

"I figured that out for myself." He curled his fingers into tight fists and his claws cut into his palms, the sting of them slicing into his flesh strangely calming as he stared the demon down. "Where in the human plane?"

"Hundred miles or so north of London."

"And is she still there?" Zephyr raised his right hand, curled it around the front of the demon's throat and held him. "Can you take me to her?"

"But—"

"No fucking buts," he barked.

He knew the risks. He had been aware from the moment he had lost Emelia that getting her back was going to be dangerous, involving a journey into a realm where he would be weak and vulnerable, and would die if he wasn't careful.

That was the reason he had hired the demons.

He had needed to reduce the amount of time he would be exposed to the curse. If he could get in and out, the curse wouldn't have time to kill him. He would be weakened, but he would still be strong enough to retrieve Emelia.

He would still be strong enough to make her belong to him.

He tightened his hold on the demon's throat, lost in the vision building in his mind, spurred by the constant ache in his chest. He needed her back. He had to get her back, and then he would make her want him and only him.

"I will give you every drop of gold I possess if you take me to her. It will be yours once she is safely back here, in this cave, with me."

He didn't care that he would be a dragon without gold.

She would be his prized possession.

He had been mistaken earlier. She was more valuable to him than gold.

He could get more treasure, but there was only one of her. She was unique, had been born for him. His fated mate. If he could have her, he would want for nothing else.

But it had to be now.

If the demon was right and she had slept with the angel. He growled, and emerald scales rippled over his skin, causing the demon's eyes to widen. It didn't bear thinking about. He would forgive her indiscretion, because she would be his. He would cleanse her of the angel's corruption.

He would make her love him.

He looked into the demon's eyes and saw his reflection in them, barely recognising the crazed male staring back at him.

"Take me to her."

CHAPTER 26

Emelia finished drying off and tugged on a pair of black panties and then her jeans. She fastened them, enjoying the buzz in her muscles as they recovered from her swim. The forty lengths she had forced herself to complete had been just what she had needed to unwind after working in the garden.

She didn't bother with a bra, just pulled on a purple tank and brushed her wet dark hair from her face.

Now it was time for a glass of wine on the patio as the sun set.

Would Wolf come by tonight?

Her blood heated at the thought he might and the images that popped into her head, ones that no longer frightened her. She wanted him again, ached to feel his hands on her now, had fantasised all day about what it would feel like to be touched by him. She had proven to herself that she could handle being intimate now, with him, and she wanted to take the next step. She needed his hands on her as they made love, his lips caressing her flesh as he took command.

Panic rose, but it was only a trickle now, a brief flare that she easily conquered as she thought about how gentle he would be, how he would never hurt her.

She took the rosé from the refrigerator, placed it in an ice bucket, and selected a glass from the cabinet. She paused and added another one, just in case Wolf did show. It would be rude not to offer him a drink.

Emelia walked barefoot down the stairs to the ground floor and pushed the door open with her hip.

The sun was still warm on her skin, the patio toasty beneath her feet, as she stepped out and let the door swing closed behind her.

"Is that to celebrate our reunion?"

Her eyes leaped to the owner of that voice.

Her heart stopped.

The ice bucket and glasses fell from her hands, smashing on the stone paving. She didn't feel the shards of glass as they cut into the tops of her bare feet, didn't hear the sound of everything breaking as she stared into the dark green eyes of the man opposite her.

All the rage she had expected to feel, the strength she had always believed would surge through her in this situation, failed to come.

Numbness swept through her and fear stole her strength, had her legs quaking beneath her as she fought for air.

Rather than launching herself at him to fight him, to take him down while he was weakened by her world, she wanted to run as far as she could. She wanted to escape.

Zephyr's gaze roamed over the pool and the loungers, the house, and then her. She shivered as he raked his eyes over her, heat blooming in them, and swallowed hard as he held his right hand out to her.

Bloody crescents marked his palm.

"Let us go home." He smiled, flashing all-sharp teeth that had her backing away another step and searching his eyes.

Panic flared as she saw the darkness in them, the same crazed look he'd had whenever he had been about to hurt her.

She shook her head and somehow found her voice. "I am home."

His face blackened and he took a hard step towards her, his strange accent thick and his English stilted as he hurled the words at her. "Here? Where you fucked another male?"

She blinked.

He roared at her and closed the distance between them so quickly, she didn't have a chance to react. He was stronger than she had anticipated, the pressure of his grip more than humanly possible as he grasped her throat and choked her.

"I did not want to believe it," he snarled in her face, his eyes glowing brightly now, shining like deadly emeralds as he leaned over her, easily bending her to his will. "You fucked him."

She clawed at his hands as the instinct to fight finally kicked in, scratching him with her short nails and drawing blood. He flicked a glance at the marks and glared into her eyes as he tightened his grip, squeezing so hard she couldn't breathe.

Couldn't fight.

"You are *mine*, Emelia." The longer strands of his green hair fell down to brush his brow as he brought his face close to hers.

His breath washed over her skin, warm and sickening, and she sagged in his grip as tears filled her eyes.

"You will come to want me as I want you." He loosened his grip on her throat, frowned as he smoothed his fingers over the bruises she could already feel, his face softening and eyes losing their wild edge as he looked at them. "I hurt you again. See what you make me do?"

She blinked back her tears and stood still, too afraid to move, sure that if she tried, he would turn violent again.

She stared at his hand out of the corner of her eye, trembling as she tracked it, gut twisting as she imagined the worse. He knew she had slept with Wolf, that Wolf had touched what he clearly viewed as his. He hadn't forced her before, but she had never seen him so crazed.

Maddened by the thought a male had tasted what she denied him.

What he viewed as rightfully his.

He chuckled low in his throat, "You make me so... mad. Why do you make me hurt you?"

She wanted to spit in his face and say that she didn't. He hurt her because he was cruel, because he wanted to break her because some part of him knew it was the only way she would ever come to want him. As long as her mind and her spirit were intact, she would keep denying him.

But he didn't want to break her.

She could see that in his eyes as he stroked her throat, his focus on the bruises he had caused, wounds that hurt him too. He honestly wanted her to love him and choose him, as Anais had chosen Loke.

Why?

The reason Anais had grown solemn just before she had left when they had met at Underworld suddenly hit her.

Rocked her and almost sent her to her knees.

Zephyr was obsessed with her, craved her and wanted her, couldn't live without her, and there was only one possible explanation for it.

She was his fated one.

"We are meant to be together." He dipped his head and brushed his cheek against hers, sending a cold shiver through her. "You will come to want me."

"Never," she bit out, echoing the word she had thrown at him in Hell when he had tried to convince her to be his, that she would come to feel something for him if she only gave them a chance. She shoved her palms against his bare chest, forcing him off her. "I will never want you."

"Because of the angel?" The crazed glimmer was back in his eyes. "I will remove the angel from the equation, and in time, you will forget him. He comes to Hell looking for me, but he will never find me. I move constantly. We will do the same."

Which meant if he took her to Hell, Wolf would never find her in time.

She couldn't let that happen. Zephyr was weaker in her world, she had felt it when she had pushed him away, could feel it as her palms pressed to his bare chest. His heart raced against them, but it wasn't steady. It faltered at times, and whenever it did, his lips quirked, as if he was fighting a grimace.

Because he didn't want her to see he was already weakening.

"I'm not going anywhere with you." She pushed with all her might, sending him staggering and falling onto his backside.

She pivoted, breaking to her left, not feeling the pieces of glass as they cut into her soles. She sprinted as hard as her tired muscles could manage, cutting around the pool and through the formal garden.

Zephyr growled, and she resisted the desire to look over her shoulder. He was coming. She didn't need to see it. She just had to keep running. If she could keep running, he would keep chasing her, and the longer he chased her, the weaker he would become. Once he was weak enough, she would fight him.

Although she didn't have a weapon.

Her eyes leaped to the patio table and the bucket of tools she had left there. She changed course, heading towards them, aware that Zephyr altered direction with her and she was closing the distance between them now rather than opening it up.

A distance that was only going to get narrower when she stopped to grab a tool she could use as a weapon.

She reached the bucket and bit out a curse when the leaf scoops were on top, blocking her way. She tossed them aside, losing precious seconds, and grabbed the first two things that her hands hit.

A pair of shears and a hand fork.

She twisted to run.

Zephyr made a triumphant noise as he grabbed her trailing wrist and spun her to face him. Emelia turned it into a bellow as she drove the fork into his right thigh, shoving it deep through his green leathers.

When she gave it a vicious twist, he released her on a roar to grab at it.

Emelia started running. No looking back. She just had to keep running. If she was lucky, the pain and blood loss would slow him down.

She reached the end of the patio that ran the length of the rear of the house and kept running, heading towards the meadow.

Zephyr snarled something, closer than she had expected.

Pain shot over her skull like lightning as something struck the back of her head and she staggered, missing a step and barely keeping her balance as she flung her arms forwards, bracing for a fall. She reached up as she regained her stride, stomach twisting as she felt her wet hair, and her scalp stung where a warm patch was spreading.

The fucker had thrown the hand fork at her.

Anger poured through her veins like acid, and she stopped dead and turned to face him. She was done with this. She clutched the long shears in her grip like a dagger and stared him down, using every ounce of her experience as a hunter and her knowledge of him to calculate what he would do.

As predicted, he came straight at her, a flare of victory in his eyes.

Pain shimmered in them a heartbeat later, twisted his lips and had him scowling. He slowed to a halt, keeping his distance instead of making an attempt to seize her, and glared down at the wounds on his right thigh. Thick ribbons of blood chased over his green leathers, coating the entire side of his leg.

"It is not nice to hurt your mate, little one." He ran his fingers through the blood and curled a lip at it, exposing his sharp teeth.

"I'm just extending you the same courtesy you've shown me," she bit out and tightened her grip on the shears.

She would have preferred a distance weapon, one she could use without having to get close to him, but the shears would do. At least she hadn't grabbed the trowel or the secateurs.

The shears were a ten-inch dagger. They were strong, sharp, and she could use them. She kept telling herself that as he stalked towards her, his face darkening as he closed the distance between them. Just a few more feet and she could attack.

His gaze lowered to her weapon, narrowed on it, and then tracked up her arm to lock on her face.

"Think to hurt me again, mate?"

She nodded. "I dream of it every damned night."

His eyes narrowed further, his lips compressing as he glared at her. Hurt that she dreamed of dealing him all the pain he had given her? It was dangerous to anger him, to wound him in a way she could manage without getting close to him, but it was also an advantage she would be a fool to dismiss.

When he was angry, he was easier to manipulate, his emotions fuelling his actions. Anger clouded his judgement and his mind, turned the skilled warrior into a male who reacted to his emotions before he could think things through. She was counting on that happening and giving her an opening she would take to bring him down.

"I dream of crushing you under my boot heel," she snapped and flashed her makeshift blade at him. "I had an army at my disposal, ready to go to Hell and hunt you down."

He frowned. "So why did you not come to me?"

She smiled and canted her head, looked him over with a critical eye that held no emotion, gave away none of the fear brewing inside her as she made her final move.

One she knew would push him over the edge.

"Because I knew you would come to me." She weighed the blade in her hand.

"I will always come for you, mate," he murmured, a hazy edge to his gaze as he looked at her, one that turned her stomach.

"You're weak here, dragon. I can see it in you. You hide it well, but you're weakening. It's only a matter of time now before you'll be begging me to end you."

He flashed sharp teeth at her, his green eyes glowing as they narrowed on her. "I am not weak and you will be the one begging me once I get you home. You will be aching to have me between your thighs."

Her stomach rebelled, heart lodging in her throat despite her attempt to let those words roll off her without affecting her. "I told you. I *am* home, and I will never want you. I will never love you. I love—"

He was right in front of her, barely space for air between them. She gasped and reacted on instinct, thrust her hand forwards and relished his grunt as the blade plunged into his side. She went to pull it out and he grabbed her wrist, gripping it so tightly her bones ached and pain shot up her arm. She cried out.

"Enough of your games," Zephyr snarled from between clenched fangs. "You will want only me. Once you have tasted me, only I will be able to please you."

Her eyes widened as he struck hard on the side of her throat, sinking fangs into her flesh.

Electricity whipped through her as the world around her faded, her body growing numb as he pulled on her blood. Pain arced along every nerve ending, a static charge that raised the hairs on the back of her neck as her mind screamed at her to do something.

Before it was too late.

But fear locked her in place as he pulled his fangs from her flesh, as he eased back to stare down into her eyes, his lips coated in her blood.

He shoved the arm he held, forcing her to pull the shears free of his side, and the numbness that had overcome her faded as he lifted them.

As he licked the blade, tasting his own blood.

As he lowered his mouth towards hers.

She had to move. She had to fight. If he forced his blood on her, she would be his mate, and she feared he would be right and she would be blinded by the bond between them, convinced she felt something for him when she would be nothing more than a slave.

Zephyr's mouth neared hers and she still couldn't move.

His breath washed over her face.

She closed her eyes.

Mustered the remnants of her strength to put it into one last attack as his grip on her wrist loosened.

Zephyr reared back and howled in agony.

Only she hadn't moved.

And it wasn't her blade held above his shoulder, blood rolling down its white length.

She looked to the male towering behind the dragon, rage burning in his golden eyes, and all her strength flooded out of her, sending her sagging to the ground as Zephyr released her.

Wolf.

CHAPTER 27

Wolf returned his gaze to Emelia as he finished cleaning the blood from his apartment, the ache to see her too strong to ignore any longer. The layers of his realm whizzed past him, and he felt as if he was leaving it behind, escaping whatever madness had come over the healer and the gnawing fact his superiors had lied to him.

Everyone had lied to him if Rey was correct and he had been born of a union between a demon and an angel, a half-breed who had chosen to serve Heaven and had been given a clean slate, his memories removed as his demon genes were suppressed.

What would Emelia think of him if he told her about that? He was finding it hard to take in himself, had struggled with it the entire time the healer had been tending to him.

And then she had tried to seduce him.

Had kissed him.

He hadn't kissed her back, had been quick to push her away, but he still felt as if he had betrayed Emelia. He should have forced the female to leave the moment she had removed her robe, but he had been distracted by Emelia and it had taken him a second to realise what the female had done. She had taken full advantage of his distracted state. His fingers flexed at his side, eager to call his blade.

He should have cut her down for daring to touch him.

He belonged to Emelia—body, heart, and soul.

She came into view, running across the grounds of the mansion. Strange. He had watched her exercising in the pool, and she wasn't dressed for a workout. Her dark jeans and tank were form-fitting, too tight for her to be comfortable as she sprinted.

Something flashed across the grass and collided with the back of her head. She stumbled, and his heart missed a beat as she barely caught herself and threw a panicked look behind her.

His gaze zipped there and darkness surged inside him as he spotted the male pursuing her.

Green leathers hugged his legs as he chased her, his longer strides allowing him to close the distance between them. Sweat glistened on his bare back as he slowed and raked fingers through his wild green hair, preening it back as he said something.

Because Emelia had stopped running.

Wolf focused on the pathway that linked him to her and summoned all his remaining strength. His body ached, protesting as his muscles tensed, and he pushed through the pain.

Because Emelia needed him.

The dragon had come for her and the foolish female looked as if she was intending to fight him.

The air around him charged with an electrical current that rapidly built as the dragon closed the distance between them down to nothing and grabbed hold of her.

Lightning struck all around him as the fiend bent his head to her neck and she cried out.

Wolf snarled and unleashed his wings as he teleported, sparks of electricity snapping over his fingers as his blade materialised in it. He landed in a crouch in a seismic blast that shook the ground, causing a few of the windows in the house to explode, and lightning struck all around him.

The dragon stiffened, his shoulders going rigid as he stopped his attempt to kiss Emelia.

Wolf didn't give him a chance to process what was happening.

Blue flames erupted along the length of his white blade, flickering black at the hilt as his anger got the better of him, and he roared as he swept it upwards in a devastating arc. The dragon bellowed as blood spurted along the diagonal path of Wolf's blade, swift to cascade down his back as he released Emelia.

She collapsed to her knees, as pale as the moon, visibly shaking as she stared at Wolf.

Her fear pounded inside him, her relief bittersweet on his senses as all her fight drained from her.

Not quite all of it.

As the dragon turned on him with claws and fangs bared, his green irises glowing with rage as his pupils thinned into narrow slits in their centres, Emelia lunged towards him.

Buried what looked like an oversized pair of scissors into his left calf muscle.

The bastard roared again, whirled towards her with a vicious twist to his expression, darkness rising in his eyes. Wolf didn't give him the chance to hurt her. He beat his aching wings and slashed at the male, forcing him to dodge and stealing his focus away from Emelia.

She sagged forwards, hands braced against the grass as she breathed hard and tears streamed down her cheeks.

His temper snapped when he saw the ragged wound on her neck.

The dragon had bitten her.

Violated her again.

He should have come quicker, should have shaken himself into teleporting sooner. He berated himself with every swipe of his sword that drove the dragon away from Emelia, blaming her pain on both the male and himself.

She had been hurt because of him.

The voice of reason said he couldn't have teleported here sooner even if he had reacted instantly to the sight of her in trouble. The drain of Hell combined with the fight against the demons had left him weak, and he was barely able to dodge the dragon's attempts to slash him with his claws, his movements sluggish and slow as he countered each attack with one of his own.

"Wilhelm!" Zephyr hollered.

Who was Wilhelm? Another dragon?

The answer became apparent when the cross etched on the inside of Wolf's right wrist burned, blazing gold and warning him of the presence of a demon.

He couldn't let the demon fight him. In his current state, he was no match for a demon, not even one from the mutinous realms.

A male with dusky horns and crimson eyes appeared a short distance behind the dragon, eyeing Wolf warily. Wolf smiled coldly. The demon didn't want to get close to him. The male knew he was an Echelon.

He used that to his advantage.

When Zephyr looked over his shoulder at the male, a scowl hardening his features, Wolf lunged at him.

Drove his sword through the male's side where a smaller puncture wound was already bleeding down his leg. He grabbed the dragon by his throat and squeezed hard, digging the tips of his fingers into his flesh as he savoured the pain that rolled across his face, the grunt that tore from his lips as Wolf slowly twisted the blade.

Zephyr bit out something in the dragon tongue.

Whatever it was, it motivated the demon. The male cast him a calculating look and Wolf knew what was coming, braced himself for it. It didn't make it any less painful when the demon spoke, using his native tongue to send fire ricocheting through Wolf's mind.

His grip on the dragon weakened and he looked at Emelia.

For a sickening moment, Wolf feared the male was going to attempt to reach her.

The demon grabbed Zephyr and hauled him backwards, dropping them both into the black void that opened beneath him.

As Zephyr disappeared from view, his eyes locked with Wolf's, the message in them clear.

This wasn't over.

The urge to follow the male into Hell and hunt him down while he was injured was strong, but his need to take care of Emelia easily overpowered it. He sent his blade away, turned from the spot where the dragon had teleported, and looked at her.

She sat on the grass, her hand clasped over the left side of her neck, blood dripping from between her fingers.

His stomach tightened as he approached her, the darkness fading as concern replaced it, the need to ease her pain and comfort her driving it from him.

"Emelia?"

She tensed, threw him a panicked glance before the fear in her green eyes cleared. "Wolf."

She was on her feet and in his arms before he could blink, her arms wrapped around his waist as she buried her face in his bare chest. Her fingers twisted the back of his white trousers, clutching them tightly as she sobbed against him.

He wrestled the desire to chase the dragon, fought the rage that spiked inside him as she shook against him, each gasping sob tearing at his control. She didn't need him to fight the dragon, not right now. She needed something else from him.

Wolf lifted his left hand, buried his fingers in her loose brown waves, and held her head to his chest as he wrapped his other arm around her, tucking her close to him. He folded his wings around her, cocooning her as she cried. His beautiful, strong, female. The sight of her so shaken utterly destroyed him.

He lowered his head and smoothed a kiss across her hair, unsure what to say to her, inexperienced in handling females in this sort of situation. His instincts said to tend to her, to stem the bleeding and steal away her pain. They said to hold her until she found her feet again, until her strength returned and she calmed.

He could do neither of those things in the middle of the meadow.

So he carefully stooped until he was eye level with her.

She hid her face from him, and new rage lit his blood on fire as he realised she was ashamed of breaking down in front of him. She had no reason to be embarrassed. He could never think her weak. Even now, he could see her inner strength. It was still there, a constant fire inside her that not even the dragon could extinguish.

"May I carry you to the pool house?" he whispered as he kept his hands still against her trembling shoulders, deeply aware that she could react badly if he made even the slightest mistake with her.

Forcing her into his arms would probably result in her lashing out at him, and that would only cause her more pain.

Her green eyes were haunted as she finally lifted them to meet his and he didn't need his gift to see she was reliving everything the dragon had done to her in Hell.

Her chin dipped slightly.

She eased closer and even went as far as wrapping her arms around his neck, showing him that she wasn't as lost in her memories as he had thought. She was still here with him, aware it was him with her and not the dragon. He hoped she knew she was safe too, that he wouldn't allow any harm to come to her now that he was here.

He was careful as he scooped her into his arms, closely monitoring her in case the act of being close to him, restrained by him in a way, caused a negative reaction in her. She shocked him again by nestling her head against his neck, her tears dampening his skin. He held her close, tucked her against him and carried her towards the pool house.

"I should have come sooner," he muttered, fire burning in his blood as he replayed what the dragon had done to her. He lowered his head and pressed a kiss to her brow, whispering against it, "I am sorry."

"Don't be," she murmured and rubbed her nose against his neck. A sigh escaped her as she settled more heavily against him. "You're here now. You saved me."

But he could have spared her the trauma had he been faster at summoning the bridge between them and teleporting.

He should have been here when she needed him.

He had failed her.

First he had allowed the female angel to kiss him, and now he had allowed the dragon to bite her.

He had a lot to apologise for, and he would do all in his power to make up for his mistakes.

"Did you find Rey?" Her voice was distant, a little hollow.

"I did. He and his demoness were where my intelligence placed them." He could feel she wanted to take her mind off what had happened. If talking about where he had been did that for her, he was happy to answer any of her questions.

She perked up. "He's living with his demoness?"

Wolf was surprised she liked the sound of that, given what she had been through in Hell. "You are not afraid of demons?"

She shook her head. "Some demons have been nice to me. Is she nice?"

"She is irritating." An accurate description in his eyes. "But Rey obviously loves her, despite the fact she vexes me at every turn."

"She sounds fun." And Emelia sounded sleepy.

"Stay awake," he murmured and jostled her enough to keep her with him. She moaned, and he felt her face move, pictured her pulling a moody one at him. "You lost blood. Sleeping might be a bad thing."

Although he wasn't sure. Being immortal, losing blood was more of an inconvenience than anything else. The only thing that would kill him would be removing his head or his heart.

They reached the pool and he frowned at the glass scattered all over the pavement twinkling among the melting ice.

Emelia emerged from his throat and stared blankly at it. "I dropped the wine."

She didn't need to say any more than that for him to put the pieces together. The dragon had frightened her, and she had dropped what she had been carrying and had run.

Wolf looked at her bare feet, each tiny laceration that peppered them adding fuel to the fire blazing inside him. For every laceration, he would cut the dragon and make him bleed as Emelia had.

He carried her into the pool house, and she remained sitting up in his arms, her eyes on his chest now.

She absently fingered the healing scar that darted across it. "You're hurt."

"I am healed now. Do not worry about them." He turned with her at the top of the stairs and headed to his right, crossing the living room to the bedroom.

"Who did this?" She lifted her gaze to his face.

"Demons. The Devil felt my presence and sent them to intervene. Rey and Asteria dealt with them. I owe them a great debt."

"So do I," she murmured, distant again.

He glanced down at her. "Why?"

She leaned her head against his shoulder. "Because you were able to come back to me."

And she had put two and two together and realised that without their intervention, he wouldn't have survived.

"Don't go back there." She curled closer to him as he went to place her on the end of the bed, clinging to him so fiercely that he didn't have the heart to make her release him.

He turned and sat on the burgundy bedclothes with her, just holding her and letting her hold him as he sifted through the feelings he could sense in her, naming each one and charting the depth of them. Fear ran deepest as she desperately clung to him, and he wavered.

But only for a heartbeat.

He couldn't do as she asked, no matter how much he wanted to. If he didn't go to Hell and deal with the dragon, the dragon would come back for her, and he wouldn't be alone. He had seen the look in the bastard's eyes when the one called Wilhelm had crippled Wolf by speaking the demon tongue. Zephyr intended to use it against him, would probably bring an entire army of demons with him when he returned, ensuring his victory.

Rey and Asteria could come to the mortal plane, but both of them were weaker in this realm. In Hell, the dragon would be no match for either of them, especially Rey. Fallen angels were the most powerful beings in that land.

He didn't want to leave Emelia, hated the thought of causing her pain, but Hell was the better choice of battlefield.

"Let me take a look at you," he whispered and gently took hold of her hands where they linked behind his neck.

He coaxed them open and leaned back so she was sitting on his lap and he could get a good look at the wound on her throat.

It was still bleeding.

"I need to take care of that." He carefully lowered her hands into her lap. "Can I?"

She fingered the wound and flinched, her eyes watering as she touched the puncture marks.

"Come. Sit." He lifted her from his lap and set her on the edge of the bed.

When he went to stand, she caught his wrist, her small hand tightly locking around it.

He looked down at it and then at her. "What is it?"

Fear coloured her eyes. She opened her mouth and then closed it.

Wolf bent and smoothed another kiss across her brow. "I am only going as far as the bathroom. Do you keep medical supplies there?"

She nodded, brushing her forehead against his lips. He went to ease back, but she refused to let him, and when he looked down at her, she brought her head up.

Captured his lips in a soft kiss.

He cupped her cheek and returned it, as softly as he could manage, giving her what she wanted. He wasn't sure why she felt compelled to kiss him, but he wasn't going to complain. He swept his mouth across hers, savouring the warmth and taste of her.

The only female he wanted to kiss.

She was it for him. Forever. Even if she turned her back on him when she discovered he was part demon and when he told her what the damned healer had done, or at some point down the road, she would always be the only woman he wanted.

The only one he loved.

He broke the kiss, feathered his thumb across her reddened cheek, and gazed into her eyes. "Let me take care of you now, Emelia... and then I will run you a bath, pour you some wine, and kiss you some more."

"I like the sound of that." Her eyes darkened, her pupils dilating, stirring his own desire as he forced himself to break away from her.

He wanted to kiss her some more right now, but tending to her wound took priority, and helping her relax came after that.

He found the stash of medical supplies she kept in the cabinet beneath her bathroom sink, came back to her, and crouched before her. He spread the items out on the bed and set to work, cleaning the wound first.

The more he focused on the bite mark, the more the unsettled feeling inside him grew.

His gaze leaped to her face, studying her eyes as they locked with his. They were brighter now. Was she up for answering some questions? Because he needed answers.

"What happened, Emelia?" He returned his gaze to his work, giving her time to process that question and what he was asking. Why had the dragon bitten her?

Her voice was hollow. "I'm his fated one."

For some reason, his chest felt as if those words had just carved it open. Because he had hoped to be that for her? Or was it because he hadn't just been hoping? He had convinced himself that she was his fated one, the female who had been made for his demonic side, just as Asteria was Rey's one true mate.

He swallowed hard to settle his nerves, not wanting to ask but needing to know. "Did he give you blood?"

"No." She was quick to bite that word out and he glanced at her, caught the flare of anger in her eyes as her eyebrows knitted hard. Her expression softened a heartbeat later and her eyes darted to his. "What does that mean?"

"That you are safe." As far as he knew, anyway. A bond required an exchange of blood.

Taking blood often had other benefits, though. There was a chance the dragon could use the one-sided connection to locate her even if she went into hiding. She wouldn't be safe until the dragon was dead.

"Emelia," he said and she looked at him again. "I want you to return to Archangel. You will be safest there. The bastard would not dare attempt to reach you when you are surrounded by so many hunters."

She was still for a moment and then she nodded. "I can leave tomorrow."

"Why not tonight?" He frowned at her, pausing at his work

Her smile hit him hard. "Because you're here. I'm safe when you're here."

Damn, that made him want to stay at her side forever, but he couldn't. Even if she asked it of him, he wouldn't be able to do it. Not because he had a duty to perform, but because he needed to hunt the dragon before he could amass an army. He couldn't delay any longer.

Rey and Asteria would be able to help him convince any dragon they met that it was in their best interest to give up Zephyr's location.

He opened a dressing that looked large enough to cover the puncture wounds, placed it over them, and smoothed the sticky edges down, careful not to hurt her. His focus drifted down to her feet, and he shifted back to reach them, gently cleaned each tiny laceration on the top of her feet and carefully checked the deeper ones on her soles. He placed more sticking plasters over the deepest of the cuts and couldn't stop himself from unravelling a bandage he found, cutting it in half and wrapping the two pieces around her feet to protect them while they healed.

He tore off two strips of white tape and used them to keep the ends in place.

"There." He stroked his hands over her feet, his touch light. "Do you want a bath?"

She shook her head.

"A glass of wine, then?"

Another shake.

He searched her eyes, a frown knitting his eyebrows as he tried to figure out what she wanted. Whenever things had become too much for her before, she had always turned to a hot bath and a glass of wine. She needed to relax and find her calm again.

"What do you need, then? Name it, and I will make it happen." He took hold of her hands, lifting them from her lap to brush his thumbs across her knuckles.

Her green eyes held his, clear and serious, sharp and focused. "You."

He frowned again. "Me?"

She nodded, shuffled to the edge of the bed, and wrapped her arms around his neck as she gazed down at him, her eyes darkening as they dropped to his lips and she murmured, "I need you, Wolf."

"Why?" He was an idiot for questioning her, should have been leaping at the chance she was offering, but he needed to know.

She had been terrified, she had been wounded, and she had been violated. He had expected her to be afraid of him after the trauma she had suffered, to want him away from her as quickly as possible, not want him as close to her as she could get him.

"Because you're the one I want, Wolf. I won't let him ruin this... take this away from me. I need you to make love to me... to erase what happened. I just need you." She hesitated and then quietly added, "I feel like I'm using you. I'm sorry."

He shook his head. "You are not using me. I want to make love with you."

He hadn't understood her line of reasoning, but now he did. She wanted to focus on something good, something that made her happy and gave her the strength to look forwards and not dwell on the past. He was apparently that something for her. Being with him had helped her cope with the things that had happened to her, and he was honoured that he had been able to do that for her, and that even after everything she had just been through, she still turned to him.

Still wanted him.

Just the thought of being inside her again had him hard as stone in his trousers. He stood, and her eyes dropped to his waist, widening slightly as they settled on his erection, burning it through the white material. He groaned as he remembered the last time they had made love, his heart drumming harder as images popped into his head to torment him.

Emelia's light touch feathering down his concealed shaft had all his focus narrowing on her.

Her eyes darkened by degrees as she stroked the length of him, and her nipples beaded in her tank, beckoning him. He wanted to taste them, imagined himself suckling them and eliciting soft cries from his female. Every one of them would be a sweet reward of its own, and he would savour them all.

Just as he wanted to savour her.

She had other plans, made fast work of the ties of his white trousers, and pushed them down his thighs, freeing his cock.

"Where do you want me—" His question cut off in a strangled groan as she wrapped her lips around his flesh, the heat of her mouth scalding him as she took him deep. "Sweet mercy."

He clenched his fists at his sides, a foolish attempt to stop himself from taking hold of her as she stroked him with her tongue, pressing it hard into his cock as she sucked it.

"Emelia," he breathed, "you do not have to—"

Another groan escaped him as she sucked harder and released him, looked up at him with hooded eyes.

"I want to," she husked before dropping her head again to flick her tongue around the blunt crown.

"Fuck," he muttered and gripped her shoulder, breathing hard as his heart thundered, blood rushing south so fast, he felt dizzy.

She moved to kneel on the bed and took hold of his hips, her palms scalding his flesh as she wrapped her lips around him again. He grunted and threaded his fingers in her hair, thought about telling her she didn't have to do this, they didn't have to do this, but it was lost on him a moment later when she took him deeper, the pleasure so intense, he forgot everything but the feel of her.

Just as he was on the precipice, she pulled back. Dark eyes flooded with desire held his as he bent his head to beg her to keep going. He had been so close. Every inch of him was hard, every muscle tensed as the pleasure that had been building inside him ebbed again.

He could only stare as she stepped from the bed, as she stripped off her jeans and panties, and followed them with her tank.

He swallowed hard to ease his dry mouth, groaned as his brow furrowed and he looked at her.

She was beautiful.

She stepped towards him, skimmed her fingers over his chest and down his stomach, holding his gaze the entire time. He shivered as she raised her hands and brushed them over his wings, couldn't contain the moan that ripped from him when she teased his feathers.

"You like that." A throaty statement of fact he couldn't deny as she broke away from him and knelt on the bed again, flashing her backside at him.

She twisted to face him, held her hand out, and smiled.

He took it, followed her onto the bed, and wasn't sure what to say when, rather than making him lie on it, she did.

She wanted him to be in control?

Fear shot through his veins, but the thought of making love to her, of worshipping her body with his, had it fading into the background. He could be gentle with her, had proven that the last time they had made love. He hadn't hurt her then, and he wouldn't hurt her now.

She reached for him. The moment his gaze fixed on her hands, she lowered them, and he groaned and his cock kicked as she feathered her fingers around her pert nipples and eased her other hand lower, dipping it between her thighs. She was wet, glistening with her need. His balls ached at the sight of her, the hunger in him mounting as he lowered his body towards her.

She beckoned him, a sultry smile that promised pleasure dancing on her lips.

He wanted to give her pleasure too.

He dipped his head between her thighs rather than covering her body with his. Her cry was sweet music to his ears as he stroked her flesh with his tongue, tasting her honey, and he did it again, rapidly losing himself in how she reacted to him, learning everything that made her tense and moan.

When he skimmed his fingers down to her core, he was the one moaning. She was so wet, ready for him. Colourful light shone in the path of his touch, revealing her to him as he stroked her. His cock jerked against the bedclothes, and he lowered his hips to them and rubbed against them as he licked her, waves of sparks skittering through him as need built inside him.

She moaned and arched her hips, pressing against his mouth as he wrapped his lips around her sensitive flesh and suckled her and slipped his fingers into her. Her cry and the way her delicate features crumpled as she tilted her head back into the pillows in response to him filling her had him aching with a need to replace his fingers with his shaft.

He focused on giving her pleasure instead, savoured the way she reacted to every lick and swirl of his tongue, each thrust of his fingers as he added another, stretching her with slow strokes that had the pads of his fingers rubbing a soft spot inside her.

She writhed, wantonly uttering his name in a passion-drenched plea.

A groan escaped him as he buried his face in her, licking her harder, stroking her deeper as she clenched and bucked, as her left hand came down to clutch his head. She twisted his hair into her fingers, gripped it tightly as her breaths shortened and came faster, and he sensed her need rising.

She was close.

He plunged into her, and she shuddered, his name bursting from her lips as her thighs quivered and her core pulsed, growing slicker as her climax took her.

He licked her, kept stroking her with his fingers to ease her down, his cock aching as he felt her trembling and savoured her quiet gasps and soft moans, putting the sound of her shattering because of him to memory because he loved it.

When he finally pulled his fingers from her and lifted his head, her eyes opened and dropped to him. Her hooded gaze held his, spoke of the need he could feel in her, one that echoed inside him.

He rose to his knees and carefully covered her with his body. She arched to meet him, her thighs soft against his hips, and he groaned as he took hold of his cock, meeting her hand as she gripped him. A shudder wracked him as he edged it downwards with her, a wave of bliss rolling through him as her wet heat scalded him. His balls tightened, and he breathed through it, determined not to make a fool of himself.

She moaned and pressed her hips higher so the tip of his shaft met her core, and he held her gaze as he eased into her, feeling how tight she was around him, gripping him like a glove as he filled her. Her eyes slipped shut, her head tipping back on another soft sighing moan as she clutched the pillows. A moan of his own fell from his lips as her breasts jutted upwards, his mouth watering for a taste of them.

He clutched her hip in his right hand, painting rainbow light over it, and pressed the other to her back, drawing her up to him as he settled his weight on her. He dipped his head and captured her nipple as he pressed deep inside her, savouring the feel of her around him.

A little moan was his reward, together with a roll of her hips that demanded more.

He gave it to her, setting a slow pace as he worshipped her breasts. Each long thrust of his cock was bliss, each moan she surrendered like heaven to him. He relished them all as he drove into her, gaining speed as she shifted her hands to his shoulders and gripped them hard.

"More," she murmured and buried her fingers in his black hair, pulled him down to her, and kissed him.

He tried to keep it soft, but she was fierce as her tongue clashed with his, demanding as her body moved against him. Her right hand shifted, and he shuddered as a thousand volts lit him up, striking down the line of his spine as her fingers brushed the delicate feathers that coated the arch of his wing. He thrust deeper, unable to stop himself from plunging into her as need rocked him, gathering into a tight ball inside him that had control slipping through his fingers. Every brush of her fingers over his feathers, each time she dared to grip his wing and hold on to it as he filled her, had that need cranking tighter.

Control slipping faster.

He tried to be gentle with her, but it was impossible as she moaned and writhed, working her hips against his as she explored his wing, as she clutched it and kissed him. He shifted his right knee, pressing it to the bed beneath her leg, and curled his hips, groaning into her mouth as pleasure built inside him, had his balls drawing up and his shaft thickening. The bliss of her touching his wings collided with it to magnify it, pushing him to dizzying new heights.

Her sweat-slicked skin stuck to his, and she moaned, her nipples beading against his chest, abrading his skin in a delicious way as she wrapped her left leg around him and dug her heel into his backside, spurring him on.

"More," she uttered, breathless and wild as she strained for another release, rocking her hips to meet each thrust of his cock.

Her grip on his wing tightened, her fingers tugging at his hair as she kissed him deeper, harder, each clash of their mouths relaying the need he could feel inside her, the desperation that flooded him too.

He groaned and held her closer, thrusting deeper and faster, giving her what she wanted because he needed it too.

He hadn't realised it until now, though.

The sight of the dragon close to taking her from him, the thought he might have lost her, filled him with a need to stamp his mark on her, to feel she was still here with him and she wasn't going anywhere.

A grunt fell from his lips as she whispered throaty pleas at him, rocked her hips, and wrapped both legs around him. Her heels pressed into his buttocks, and he obeyed, took her harder as his senses screamed that she was close now, needing one last push.

He gripped her hip and pumped her harder, using her moans as a guide as he curled his hips, trying to find that one sweet spot that would send her over the edge.

She cried into his mouth, her entire body stiffening, jerking against his for a heartbeat before she quivered, every inch of her trembling as her core clenched him, pulsed, and gripped him.

Pleasure shot down his spine, tightened his balls, and had his shaft aching as release rose to the base of it. He buried his face against her neck, tried to keep going, but it was too much. He grunted against her damp skin as pleasure detonated inside him, rolled through him in a devastating wave that left every inch of him shaking and weak. He held her to him, sure he was hurting her but unable to do anything about it as bliss swept over him with every pulse of his cock inside her.

Her fingers stroked the line of his spine, and he tried to move, but it was impossible as he struggled to piece himself back together. He had never experienced anything like that, had never felt so wild, so desperate. He focused on Emelia, felt those same feelings echoing inside her, together with other emotions, ones that beat inside him too.

Ones neither of them were ready to admit yet.

"Wolf," she murmured sleepily against his cheek, then stroked his wings and held him.

He sagged on top of her, his breath leaving him in a rush, and rolled as he sent his wings away. They were gone by the time he landed on his back with her on top of him. Her slender weight felt good against him. Right.

He brushed a kiss across her cheek as she sighed and he pulled the covers over her, swearing to her that he would watch over her.

He wouldn't let anything bad happen to her.

He had failed her tonight.

He would never fail her again.

Tomorrow, the dragon would die.

CHAPTER 28

Wolf gently swept a rogue strand of Emelia's chestnut hair from her face so he could see it clearly as he lay on his side facing her. Her nose wrinkled and a frown danced on her brow, and then her eyes slowly opened. He hadn't meant to wake her.

An apology balanced on his lips.

But then her green eyes met his and his gift fired, transporting him from this world into her memories.

A village consisting of round huts surrounded him as he knelt on the dusty black ground, his hands bound behind his back, the ropes biting into his aching wrists. He glanced to his right and left, at the other females lined up beside him. A few were crying. Others were pleading for mercy. He remained quiet, holding his nerve and refusing to let the blond male sitting on a raised platform in the centre of the circular courtyard scare him.

Dark golden leathers stretched over his powerful legs, his honed torso bare and packed with muscles that tensed as he gripped the arms of his throne. Bright golden eyes flickered over the line of captives, and he resisted the urge to avert his gaze when they briefly landed on him.

The scenery swirled, and rough black walls replaced the village, ones that curved up to form a ceiling above him. He listened hard, heart racing as he tried to hear if the dragon had moved away from him, deeper into the tunnels. Sure that he was alone, he pushed to his feet and sprinted for the cave mouth. The ledge was broad and deep, jutted out over a valley far below. His eyes scanned the horizon, fear pounding in his veins as he wondered what was beyond them.

How far was he from the demons?

From going home?

An arm banded around his waist, and he gasped.

It turned into a cry of pain as the world whirled again, the memory shifting to a more recent one. Fangs sliced into his flesh, hot and searing, and fear crawled over his skin. He pushed at the male holding him, stealing his blood and another piece of him. Hadn't he taken enough already? He didn't want to feel weak, hated how afraid he was at times, how his own shadow could make him jump. He wanted to be strong again, and he had been getting there, but now the dragon was back.

Taking that strength from him again.

His vision wobbled from pain and tears, blurred as he frantically clawed at the male, desperately trying to drive him away.

The bastard finally released him, pulled the makeshift blade free of his flesh, and licked it, coating his tongue in his own blood. A terrifying smile curved his lips as the dragon looked at him, and his stomach turned as he realised what he meant to do. He couldn't let it happen.

He tightened his grip on the shears as the male neared him.

The dragon bellowed in agony.

His eyes darted to beyond the male.

To the warrior standing there.

Relief swept through him, laced with softer emotions.

Wolf squeezed his eyes closed, frowning as he shut down his gift and breathed through the assault, the constant flow of memories that swirled in his mind as he fought to get them to settle, to run in an order that wouldn't give him a headache. They slowly eased, becoming background noise again as his mind compartmentalised them.

Emelia had been wide open to him, and he felt as if she had done it on purpose. She wanted him to see these memories because she wanted him to find the dragon, before the male came for her again.

She had wanted him to see her pain and fear too.

That pain and fear goaded him into doing as he had wanted last night. He wanted to hunt the dragon. He wanted to end him.

Rage poured through his veins, and his mind churned, her memories keeping him on the edge, burning with a need to hunt and bloody his sword. He released her and moved away, sat on the edge of the bed and tried to fight that urge. He wasn't strong enough to master it this time.

He had to do something about the dragon.

Now.

Time was up.

He pushed to his feet and tugged on his white trousers.

"Wolf?" Emelia sat up, the covers tucked against her chest as she looked at him, her eyes sleep-filled but growing clearer by the second as they followed him around the room.

"I have to go." He didn't mean for it to come out brusque, but his mind and mood were darkening as he thought about what he had seen and what the dragon had done.

The warrior in him came online, studying everything she had shown him and piecing together the clues. He had seen that village. He was sure of it. He was also fifty percent sure he had seen that mountain range from a distance. A taller mountain stood to one side of it, a peak that had reminded him of the Matterhorn.

The dragon's home had to be in the same valley he had seen.

It just had to be.

"Wolf," she said softly and he paused to look at her. Confusion crinkled her brow.

"Go back to Archangel." He focused on his apartments, unable to waste a second more.

If he was right and he knew where the dragon resided, he could be there within the hour. He could end this. That thought had him drifting away from Emelia, not listening to her as he formed the bridge between him and his own realm.

He teleported, landing soundlessly to avoid anyone hearing him and barging in, attempting to delay him. He gathered his armour and put it on, the need to go to Hell burning stronger in his veins with every wasted second.

As his mind turned to the most recent memory Emelia had shown him, that fire became an inferno, one that threatened to consume him. He growled through his teeth and unleashed his wings as he summoned his blade.

Black flames licked along it, not a trace of blue in them.

The dragon had tried to force a bond on her.

An attempt to enslave her.

Now her blood was inside him, the bastard wouldn't stop until he had succeeded in claiming her. He would keep attempting it, tormenting Emelia. Destroying her.

Wolf wouldn't let that happen.

He focused to form a bridge between him and a place in Hell, and teleported as quietly as he could manage, landing in a brief flare of lightning.

Only it wasn't Rey's valley he landed in.

A great green dragon circled overhead, spotted him, and roared as it swept towards him.

Wolf quickly brought the image of Rey's valley into his mind before the Devil's curse could kick in to sap him of his strength. Lightning arced around him, snapping at the ground, and his heart thundered into overdrive as the enormous dragon neared, flashing long white fangs.

Heat blazed down his spine, an order to return. It shattered his focus, and he could only stare as the dragon neared him, opening its jaws and aiming right for him.

It couldn't end here.

He shook himself at the last moment, threw himself to his right, and rolled across the rough black ground, grimacing as his wings tangled. He came to his feet and focused again, conjuring the image of Rey's valley as he sprinted away from the dragon as fast as he could manage. It wasn't far from this one. The teleport would drain him, but he could make it.

The world around him disappeared.

Pain rolled through him in a sickening wave, one that had his muscles turning liquid beneath his skin and had his head spinning. He growled and staggered as he hit the dirt, threw a panicked glance around to see where he had landed.

It was the right valley.

Relief crashed over him, and he sank to his knees, his vision distorting as the drain on his powers intensified, leaving him breathless and trembling.

Two shadowy figures appeared before him, one female and one male, their wings furled against their backs.

"Rey," he started and then fell silent as his eyesight cleared.

The violet-haired male was a fallen angel, but it wasn't Rey.

The blonde female standing beside him leaned over, planting her hands against her bare knees as she took a good look at him. "He the one?"

She peered up at the male, but he was staring at her backside, his eyes blazing crimson. Heat flared in her own scarlet eyes as she straightened and turned towards him, not bothering to tug her tiny rubber skirt down over her exposed buttocks.

"We can play later." She danced her fingers over the male's broad bare chest and let them drift downwards, over his abdomen as he lowered his head towards her.

A groan ripped from the male's lips as she grabbed his crotch and squeezed it hard, that fire in his eyes blazing hotter, until his irises glowed and his pupils stretched into thin elliptical slits in their centres.

"The dragon says business comes first... and then you can come later." She fondled the male, earning another throaty groan from him.

"Inside you," he moaned and shuddered, then slapped his hand down on her backside and hauled her up to him, his face darkening as he stared into her eyes. He shoved his fingers between her buttocks, tearing a trembling moan from her cherry-red lips. "I'll come inside you."

She sagged against the male's chest, panting as she writhed against his fingers, her black feathers quivering.

The male braced his black-leather-clad thigh between hers and she rubbed against it. She didn't stop him when he yanked the thick band of black rubber around her breasts down and grasped one, squeezing it as tightly as she had squeezed his crotch.

Wolf staggered to his feet, not interested in becoming a captive of the dragon or their perverse display of what he could only imagine passed as affection between them. He would make his escape while they were distracted, caught up in each other.

He stumbled towards the cave cut into the mountainside.

Rey and his demoness would aid him, and the fallen angels wouldn't know what had hit them.

The female suddenly appeared in front of him, her clothing still askew, rose staining her cheeks. She spread her obsidian wings, and her expression went from half-dazed to deadly serious in an instant.

"Nu-huh. Who said you could run away?" She grinned at him and raked her gaze over him from head to toe and back again, a flicker of interest lighting her eyes. She glanced beyond him to the male he could feel stalking towards them. "Can we play with him too?"

Wolf wanted to vomit.

He clutched his blade and mustered his strength, because no damn way he was going to become some sort of slave to this female and male. He would sooner cut off his wings.

"No playing with him. Dragon said." The male's deep voice rolled across the bleak land like thunder.

She pouted, looked down at her exposed breast, and casually covered it. "No fair. I bet angels taste delicious."

The male was behind her in an instant, twisting her arms behind her back as he pressed his thumb between her lips.

He growled, "Only I get to come in here. You best remember that."

She moaned and greedily sucked on his thumb.

When they looked as if they were going to get caught up in each other again, Wolf slowly sidestepped, easing away from them.

He made it ten feet before the male's crimson gaze snapped to him.

The male shoved the female, and she fell on her knees, splayed out on the black ground, a growl peeling from her lips as she hit it face first.

"The fuck was that for?" she spluttered and turned a glare on the male.

He just smiled crookedly at her. "Wanted to see you like that."

She wriggled her backside. "Later."

Wolf definitely wanted to vomit now. He made a break for it, using his wings to speed him across the land and biting back a bellow of agony as they burned, quickly tiring. If he could get close enough, Rey would feel him.

"If you think your fallen friend is going to help... well... they're not home." The female's words made him falter, cost him his focus and sent him slamming into the ground as his wings gave out.

He skidded across it, flinching as small rocks bit into his face. When he stopped, he shoved to his feet as quickly as he could manage.

It wasn't quickly enough.

The male grabbed him by the back of his neck, hauled him off the ground and into the air, so his feet dangled a foot above it. Wolf snarled and lashed out at the male, kicked him in the shin, and tore a grunt from him.

Plan B it was.

He would fight.

"Zephyr sent a message through the Hell grapevine that he had gone after some mortal, of all things. The fallen and his lover were quick to respond. Flew out of here like bats." The female shook her head as she sauntered towards him. "That one has a lot to learn about being fallen."

The male shoved Wolf to the ground, pinned him there by the back of his neck, and took hold of his left wing. Wolf was quick to make them go away, fear spreading through him as he struggled against the male's hold. They could beat him, wound him, torture him for all he cared. If he could keep his wings hidden, they couldn't do their worst.

They couldn't weaken him by removing them.

He had read enough reports in Heaven to know that fallen angels loved nothing more than chopping angel wings off. It seemed to amuse the fallen to watch them suffer, to torment them when they were weakened and push them to the very edge. Removing an angel's wings left that angel vulnerable to darkness, and with darkness already part of him, he was sure to fall.

The female crouched in front of him, thighs spread, revealing a lack of underwear.

Wolf looked away from her, stared at the ground, and slowly gathered his strength. He sent his blade away too, remembering what Rey had told him.

The drain on his power weakened, becoming a trickle rather than a flood. He closed his eyes and breathed steadily, focusing on his body.

"Did you kill him?" The female prodded Wolf in the top of his head, and he wanted to growl at her for believing him so weak that he would die from the way the male was pinning him.

"No," the male snapped. "He thinks to regain his strength. I can feel it in him."

Had the fallen angel retained his angelic powers? The reports Wolf had read had mentioned nothing of the sort, but it was possible. Rey had remained an Echelon on falling. This male had held on to his ability to read people through touch.

Wolf cursed him in his head.

It wouldn't stop him from clawing the scattered remnants of his strength together for one last stand, though. He kept his focus on what he was doing rather than the two fallen angels, didn't respond when the male hauled him back onto his feet and the female landed a solid punch to his gut.

His armour blocked the blow and she grumbled something.

Hope sparked inside him.

His armour was angelic. Strong. Designed to withstand blows from powerful demons. It could hold out against a fallen angel, although he doubted it would last long against two of them.

As the female went to strike him again, he tracked her with his senses, waited until her fist was nearing him and she had twisted at an angle before he called his blade. He instantly swept it upwards the second it appeared in his grip, ripping a satisfying shriek from her when it sliced along her wing.

"Son of a fucking bitch!" She punched him hard, knocking his head back into the male behind him.

The rear of his skull cracked off the male's face and an unholy snarl filled the air. The male shoved him aside and launched at the female, grasped her by her throat and lifted her off the ground.

Wolf twisted onto his feet, kicked off and unleashed a battle cry as he thrust forwards with his blade. It cleaved a long gash in the male's thigh that spilled blood in a waterfall down his black leathers. He couldn't stop himself from following through, barrelling into the male and taking him down.

He spun the blade in his hand, his gaze fixed on the male's chest as the fire that blazed along the length of his white sword turned black.

Wolf brought it down.

The female grabbed him by his hair and hauled him off the male, tossing him across the dirt as if he had weighed nothing. He rolled and bounced, cried out as he hit a rock with so much force that it jabbed hard into his side, shoving his breastplate into his ribs. He sent his blade away as he struggled to breathe, determined to hold on to what little strength he had. The drain on his powers weakened again, allowing the strength that had been flowing out of him to gradually return.

He stared at the male and female, calculating his odds of survival. They were slim. If they didn't kill him here, they would take him to the dragon, and that was a death sentence.

He didn't see the female coming. One moment she was in front of him, the next she was behind him, a blade sticking into his side. It burned like the fires of Hell, and he threw his head back on a hoarse cry, one that emptied his lungs until they burned too.

The male was on him before he could recover his wits, battering him with rapid punches that knocked the wind from his lungs before he could fill them again. His vision wobbled, and a desperate need to fight swept through him. He shoved and clawed at the male in front of him, blocking as many blows as he could manage as he gathered his strength.

His fist slammed into the male's already broken nose, sending blood streaming down over his lips. The fiend licked them, grinned to expose his fangs as he tasted his own blood, and jammed his fingers into the place where the female's sword had skewered Wolf's armour. Wolf cried out as the male tore at his breastplate and the flesh beneath, opening the wound further as he peeled the metal as if it was paper, ripping it from him.

He tried to stop the male from removing his ruined breastplate, but the female grabbed hold of him, pulled his arms behind his back and twisted his right one upwards, forcing him to his knees. The male tore Wolf's chest plate away, exposing his torso, and the female released him and made fast work of removing the arms and the back of his armour.

He couldn't let them take the rest.

He called his blade, roared with all the fury burning inside him as he lashed out at the male. The fallen angel was swift to dodge backwards, using his wings to propel him to a safe distance. Leaving just the female within his range.

He pivoted on his heel as he put all his strength into standing, bringing his blade up with him.

The female cried out as it cut across her chest, slicing from her right hip up to her left shoulder. She staggered backwards, desperately folding her arms over the wound as she looked down at it with wild crimson eyes. Blood covered her in an instant, flowed over her arms and down her thighs.

"You…" She launched at him on a roar, her wings beating hard, and he grunted as she collided with him, lifted him off the ground, and soared into the air with him.

Her hand closed around his throat, and she hit him hard, smashing her fist into his face, her lips peeling back to flash her fangs. His ears rang, mind spinning and vision tunnelling as she hit him so hard, he saw stars. Pain splintered across his cheek and jaw, his left eye throbbed, and he barely stopped himself from passing out.

"You'll fucking pay." She twisted with him, and his stomach rebelled as they dropped, plummeting towards the ground.

He needed his wings.

It screamed in his mind, but he couldn't focus to call them, didn't have the strength to release them as every inch of him burned with pain.

When they were close to the ground, she released him and spread her wings to place a few feet between them so she was hovering above him. He braced himself, even when he knew it wouldn't help.

She shoved her feet into his chest.

Kicked.

He shot downwards, the grim world a blur around him.

And then fire exploded inside him.

A black wave rolled over him.

When it receded, his head was heavy, his hearing muffled, and he could barely breathe. He wheezed with each breath he managed to suck into his battered lungs. Every one he exhaled tasted like copper.

"I want to fuck him up," a female voice sneered, distant as if something was in his ears, blocking them.

Blood probably.

He thought he might be standing, although he wasn't sure how that was possible. He didn't have the strength to stand, was scarcely able to remain conscious as pain burned through him in devastating waves, his body struggling to heal itself. Where to start? He wanted to laugh at that. He was sure every bone in his body had been broken.

"I want to make him fall." She sounded closer now, and angrier, if that was possible.

"The torment of this angel belongs to me," a male answered, his accent strange.

Not the fallen angel.

Wolf tried to open his eyes and grimaced as his lashes stuck together.

Someone helped him by throwing a bucket of icy water over him. He cried out, the sting of it as it hit his wounds almost sending him back into the dark abyss, and sagged. Sagged? He was standing, then. How? He fought to focus on his body and frowned as he realised his hands were above his head and they were numb, his wrists sore.

They had shackled him?

He weakly tried to wrestle against the restraints. Someone laughed. The accented male.

"I have to do something to pass the time while we wait for my mate."

Wolf clenched his teeth and couldn't hold back the growl that rumbled in his chest as his rage kindled, sending strength flowing back into his battered body.

The dragon.

He opened his eyes, ignoring the pain it caused him because he needed to see the bastard, wanted to look him in the eye and make him see that he didn't fear whatever the male had planned for him. He only feared for Emelia.

The male was going to use him as bait.

He was going to lure her into Hell.

He locked gazes with the dragon and saw the sickening truth in his eyes.

And when he had Emelia here, he was going to force her to become his mate, offering her something in return that she wouldn't be able to resist.

Setting Wolf free.

He rallied, gritted his teeth, and grunted as he battled his restraints, twisting his shackled arms and grasping the chain that held him pinned to the black wall of the cave. He couldn't let that happen. He wouldn't be responsible for her condemning herself to a life he knew would destroy her. She would do it. His heart screamed that at him. He tugged on the chain, arched forwards, and tried to use his weight to free himself.

He had to escape.

His strength was returning, the rage blazing inside him fuelling it as he thought about Emelia at the mercy of the bastard standing before him.

Never.

He roared and pulled on the chain.

It gave, the sound and feel of metal grating against stone the sweetest damned music to his ears.

Hope soared.

Zephyr slammed a fierce right hook into the side of his head.

The world went black again.

CHAPTER 29

Sweat rolled down Emelia's spine beneath her tight black tank. She breathed hard, attempting to settle her heart as she tore the gloves off and discarded them on the bench lining the dark grey wall. She sank onto it, grabbed her towel, and rubbed herself down, her focus turned inwards.

The dragon would come again.

She was going to be ready for him this time.

Returning to Archangel had made her feel weak. Zephyr had her running scared, and she hated herself for it, so she had doubled down on her training, spending a third of her day in the gym and the practice room, putting herself through manoeuvres with blades, crossbows, and her tranquiliser gun. She ran circuits and obstacle courses, and sparred with some of the stronger male hunters in the building.

She wished those experienced men had been assigned to her team.

Mark hadn't been joking when he had said she would have to handle a few rookies. It turned out she hadn't exactly taken over Sable's old team. Mark had assigned all the hunters Sable had led to new squads and left Emelia in charge of new recruits.

Eighty percent of her team were greenhorns, and she had the feeling she was being tested. So far, nothing out of the ordinary had happened during their patrol shifts in the city.

Although, some of them were going to get themselves into serious trouble if they continued down the paths they had chosen. She was reaching the end of her tether, and if Carter and Franks didn't heed her advice, staying away from the illicit place she had seen them entering when Archer had been driving her back to headquarters after a meeting at one of the satellite facilities in London, she was going to have to do something.

She didn't want to be a snitch, but she also wouldn't tolerate such behaviour in her team.

Emelia rubbed the back of her neck with the towel and swigged her water, her pulse settling now she was laying off the punchbag.

Her thoughts shifted away from her team to the male that had been on her mind from the second he had teleported out of her life.

Wolf.

He had gone to Hell again. She knew it in her gut. He had distanced himself and then left, and she wasn't sure whether she had done something to cause that cold gulf between them or whether it was just the product of the dragon playing on his mind.

He had told her to run to Archangel, sent her to safety while he threw himself into the lion's den for her. She cursed herself. She should have been stronger, should have rallied more quickly after what had happened and convinced him to take her with him. He hadn't given her a chance, though.

And now she hadn't seen him in over a week.

Was it his vengeance that consumed his every waking moment?

Or was he in trouble?

Her heart ached at the thought he might be, and she rubbed the spot between her breasts, her eyes dropping to the rubber mats beneath her black trainers. She should have made him take her with him. She should have been stronger.

But even now, the thought of entering Hell had her strength faltering. She clamped her hands down on her knees to stop her legs from shaking. It didn't stop the panic that flooded her, had her throat closing and mind hurling images at her, flashes of Wolf at the mercy of demons, or worse.

At the mercy of Zephyr.

What if the dragon had him?

She shoved that thought away because she couldn't contemplate it. The last time she had allowed herself to think that way, she had almost broken down in the middle of a meeting with Mark. He had been worried about her, had even mentioned her taking another sabbatical and returning to her home.

That had made the panic spike, and she had lost control, had begged him to let her stay at Archangel.

He had eyed her closely but hadn't questioned why she desperately wanted to remain in the building, or why she had made excuses about going out on patrols, choosing to train her squad in the practice rooms instead of in the field.

Three nights ago, Mark had ordered her to take her team out for the night. He had reassured her that she was a competent leader, believing her reluctance stemmed from worrying about whether she was good enough to be the commander of her own team. She hadn't told him any differently.

She should have sat down with him the night she had returned and told him the real reason she had come back to Archangel, but she hadn't wanted him to think she was weak. She already thought that about herself. She didn't need others looking at her as if she was liable to break. Not again.

She was stronger than before, even if she wasn't strong enough yet.

Her thoughts shifted back to Wolf. Where was he? Her heart whispered that she knew where he was and why she hadn't seen him. She was only fooling herself if she thought he was anywhere but Hell. If he had returned to Heaven, if he was anywhere but that dark realm, he would have come to her again by now.

Twin needs warred inside her, a desire to find the courage and strength to enter that realm and somehow locate him battling against the fear that gripped her whenever she came close to doing just that. The tiny voice at the back of her mind whispered that Wolf would be safe, that he was fine, that she didn't need to return to Hell.

She cursed that voice and how easily she listened to it and let it sway her, so afraid of stepping foot in that realm again that she was willing to risk Wolf ending up hurt or worse, all because she was terrified of running into Zephyr.

Terrified of becoming a slave to him again.

She aimed her next curse at herself for being so weak.

She loved Wolf, and every instinct she possessed screamed that he was in trouble and he needed her. She had to find a way to help him.

There had to be a way.

Her phone buzzed.

Emelia picked it up and looked at the screen. A message from Sable. She unlocked her phone and scanned it. It was one line.

Can we talk?

Emelia fired a message back. *Sure, call me in five.*

Her pulse picked up, a trickle of nerves running through her as she slung her dark red hoody on, grabbed her things, and exited the gym. What could Sable want?

That question pounding in her mind wasn't the cause of her sudden spike in adrenaline. It was the other one that ran around her head, one she was afraid of in a way, even when it could be the answer to her prayers.

If she asked them, would Sable and Thorne give her the help she desperately needed?

Thorne commanded an army, and he knew the dragon realm. With him and Sable protecting her, she might be able to find the strength to face her fears and head into Hell. Even if she failed to find the courage to go there herself, Sable and Thorne knew where to look for Zephyr, and maybe Loke would help them.

They might be able to reach Wolf before anything bad happened to him.

Her gut clenched, heart squeezing tight as that tiny voice inside her said something bad had already happened to him.

That was the reason she hadn't seen him in days.

She swiftly took the steps up to the roof access door and pushed it open, sucking down a deep breath before she eased out into the late afternoon light. Her pulse ticked faster, heart beginning to thump painfully against her breast as she glanced around the roof and the sky.

She was safe. No one was there, and she needed this conversation to be private. She couldn't risk someone overhearing her. If anything happened, she could be back inside the building in less than a second.

Her phone rang, and she jumped, fumbling as her heart went wild, and brought it to her ear as she swiped her thumb over the screen to answer the call.

"You alone?" Sable's voice rang clearly over the line, a slight echo to it that made her sound as if she was in a large room.

Underworld?

Emelia nodded. "I am. I need to ask you something."

"I need to ask you something too." Sable sounded so serious that the skin on Emelia's nape prickled. Her friend continued before she could speak, "I know this is going to be asking a lot, but I really need your help. *We* really need your help."

"We?" Emelia pressed the phone closer to her ear and glanced around again, listening hard to make sure she really was still alone, because she had the feeling Sable was about to ask her something monumental.

"Me, Sherry, and a tiger shifter called Talon. He broke out of Archangel, and they want him back, which is where you come in."

She frowned at the flat black roof as something hit her. "It sounds a lot like you're asking me to open doors for him."

As in, bring him back through them in restraints.

Damn, it was hard to speak in a coded manner, finding ways to say what she was thinking without saying it straight. She couldn't risk it. If someone overheard her speaking, she needed them to hear nothing out of the ordinary.

"You always were astute." Sable sounded like she was smiling. "That's exactly what I'm asking you to do."

Emelia found that hard to believe. "Why would someone want that?"

She had seen the cell blocks, and they turned her stomach every time. Humans were bad enough at wrongly imprisoning other humans. She knew without a doubt that not everyone who was brought into Archangel should be there. Not all of them were a threat to humankind.

She had always been careful not to pick up a non-human if she wasn't sure whether or not they were a danger to people, had always opted to monitor them instead and do her research before targeting them and taking them down.

Sable sighed. "Because he has friends still in there. He needs to get them out and, hell, I think the bloke is crazy too, but I promised to help him. Archangel... I know you still feel loyal to them, Emelia, and I know this is a huge ask, and if I could do it myself, I would, but you're in good standing with them and I'm on the way out. You know it."

She did know it. Archangel had given Emelia the position that Sable had been removed from once it had become apparent to those in command that Sable had done more than just have a fling with the demon king they had assisted as their first mission in a realm that they hadn't realised existed until a few months ago.

Hell.

"I can still access the building, but no one trusts me there anymore, and my access to certain areas has been revoked. I can't blame them." Sable sighed again as Thorne mumbled something in the background, his deep voice soft, as if he was soothing her. "It was going to happen sooner or later. I'm surprised it took them this long to realise I'm mated to a demon king and my allegiances have shifted because of it."

Emelia tried to stifle that feeling she had been having over the last few weeks, that sense that all her friends were leaving her behind, going off on a new adventure together without her.

Into a realm where she feared to tread.

They had given up on Archangel.

She still wanted to try to save it, to steer it back towards a noble and righteous path, the one it had sworn to follow decades ago when it had changed from hunting all non-humans to capturing and eliminating only those who were a threat to people.

"I don't know. Can't you just *pop* him in?" She hated the waver in her voice as she said that, the note of uncertainty that seemed to echo in all of her, in every feeling she had as she stood on the rooftop, staring out at the city that had been her home for the last five years as dusk fell.

How could she be so unsure of everything?

She loved Wolf. She knew he was in trouble. She knew what she needed to do. She knew, God, part of her knew that Archangel were beyond saving.

Why couldn't she bring herself to admit those things? Why did she want to keep pretending nothing was wrong?

Her gaze fell to the roof at her feet.

Because she was afraid.

Archangel was all she knew now. It was her home. Her family. She had already lost one family. She couldn't lose this one too.

"If I could, I would, Emelia," Sable said, bringing Emelia out of her thoughts. "Thorne can't teleport in without triggering the alarms since they upgraded the sensors to focus heavily on demons, and Bleu is going to help, but he can't teleport Talon in when he doesn't know where to go. Talon says he was being held in a hidden area I've never seen or heard of, which means we need someone on the inside for this mission. Bleu will give you some fancy-pants elf device, you get Talon in and activate it to ping his location to Bleu, and he will get the tiger and his friends out. Me and Thorne will provide a distraction."

"A secret part of the building? Why would they have a hidden facility in HQ?" Those questions left her lips before she could even think about saying them in code, the shock that ran through her tearing them from her.

She found the thought there were hidden areas in the building difficult to swallow, even as a feeling bloomed inside her, a cold and insidious one that ate away at the piece of her heart that still loved Archangel.

Visiting the cell block had always left her feeling off, unsettled, and horrible because of what happened there and the fear some of the prisoners were innocent. What if other hunters felt the same as she did? Sable had never liked bringing non-humans in either. Neither had Anais.

What if there was another side of Archangel? A side where the darker among the hunters could bring non-humans they had captured. A place where the old Archangel still existed and operated, experimenting on non-humans to uncover weaknesses and discover better methods of dealing with each species.

She shook off that thought. She was reading into things again. Archangel had left that method of operating behind decades ago. They were different now. She had to keep believing that and believing in them.

They were her family.

"I don't know why they have a secret area in HQ, but I want to know, Emelia. I want to know what Archangel are doing and why they're suddenly raiding fae towns," Sable bit out, a hard edge to her voice that sent a chill through Emelia.

"They're doing what?" She stared blankly at the roof as that hit her.

"Talon was taken in a raid on the fae town in Scotland. He was a lucky one. Others were killed. None of them were a danger to people, Emelia. They were just going about their business. I need to know what's going on in there. We all need to know… and you can get the answers for us." Sable drew down a slow breath. "They put him through hell. They did terrible things to him and the female tiger who was taken with him. She died. There are four more innocent non-humans left down there, and he's afraid Archangel will kill them if we leave them there."

Another chill swept down her arms and thighs.

Her ears rang.

The part of her that kept trying to deny Archangel were up to nefarious things fell silent.

"You're a commander now. You can access the main archive room with your security pass. You can get Talon in and activate the transmitter thingy Bleu gives you, and then you can help Sherry recover the files on this tiger and his friends, and maybe find some answers for me there too." Sable's voice darkened. "I know my login won't be worth shit now, but yours should be able to grant you access to enough data that we can piece together what's happening."

Part of Emelia still wanted to say she wasn't sure, even as her heart screamed at her to do it.

Because Sable needed her to do this and something had just dawned on Emelia.

Archangel had become her home.

But it was Sable, Olivia, and Anais, and some of the other hunters who had become her family.

And a member of that new family was asking for her help.

It would be dangerous, might end badly for her if Archangel discovered what she had done, but that feeling she had been having since returning from Hell was only growing, and now Sable was saying there was a secret area within the building and that Archangel were doing terrible things there.

Emelia needed answers too.

She needed help.

"I'll do it." Emelia drew her courage up from her toes. "But on one condition."

"Shoot," Sable said.

"You'll help me in return, and when I tell you what I need you to do, you can't turn me down."

"That sounds ominous." Sable paused. Thorne mumbled something. Her friend sounded more cautious when she spoke again. "But I'll do it. Whatever you need, Emelia. I'll help you."

All the tension that had been building inside Emelia suddenly flooded out of her as if a dam had burst, and she sagged against the door behind her.

She closed her eyes, pressed her hand to her chest, over her heart, and willed Wolf to hold on if he was in trouble.

An army was coming for him.

Even if she couldn't find the courage to lead them.

They were coming for him.

Coming to bring him back to her.

CHAPTER 30

Emelia tilted her head back so the spray of the shower cascaded over her hair as she closed her eyes. Nerves threatened to rise again, but she tamped them down.

A trip to the central archive room and a little light research had revealed that Talon hadn't been lying and he had been a captive of Archangel until recently. She had been careful not to probe too deeply, afraid someone might be able to trace her actions and she would get into trouble, ruining tonight's plans, but she had needed proof that the tiger shifter had been telling the truth.

Since Sable's call yesterday, she had been worried that the shifter was up to no good, had lied because he wanted to get into Archangel and cause trouble. Now, her mind was at ease, even if the rest of her was nervous as hell. She was doing the right thing.

Because, according to the records she had looked at, the woman brought in with Talon was indeed dead. Apparently, she had been under observation when she had suddenly attacked the electrified steel bars protecting the window where the scientists had stood on the other side.

And she hadn't stopped attacking them.

It had resulted in her death and Talon's escape.

Had she done it in order to give Talon a chance to break free?

The thought that she might have roused a feeling inside Emelia, a sensation that unsettled her. She couldn't imagine how brave, or how desperate, the woman must have been to do something like that, sacrificing herself for the sake of another.

It made Emelia feel weak.

She pushed that feeling aside. She had been weak, but tonight, she was going to be strong. She was going to see this mission through, and then she was going to face her fears. She was going to be the brave one.

Emelia turned off the water, stepped out of the shower and dried herself off. She grabbed her black underwear and slipped it on, then pulled on her black turtleneck and combat trousers. She tied her hair up in a bun at the back of her head and fixed the collar of her top so it concealed the healing bite mark on her throat. She shoved her feet into her black heavy-soled boots and tucked her combat trousers into the top of them before lacing them tightly. Her pulse pounded, and she breathed steadily, quelling the nerves threatening to race out of control.

No one would suspect a thing.

The plan was sound. Entirely plausible.

It would be a routine patrol along their usual route that turned up an escaped captive. Hopefully, the tiger would play along, because she wasn't sure her team were experienced enough to hold back if he got a little rough with them.

He was going to be the first non-human they had captured, and that made her uneasy. There was a chance their excitement might get the better of them. She had warned Sable about that, and her friend had promised she would relay it to Talon so he didn't put up too much of a fight.

Her focus shifted to her mission as she geared up, slipping her tranquiliser gun into the holster on her hip.

She strode from her apartment, working her way down through the building to the parking garage.

Four male voices sounded ahead of her as she reached the underground lot. Her team were rowdy tonight. She sucked down a secret breath to steady her nerves again, struggling with her mood as thoughts of what was to come and Wolf's continuing absence wore it down, shortening her temper.

She had already snapped at Woods today when his lack of attention had ended with her getting hit in the back with a baton when he had been training with the team, practicing close-quarters combat. A member from one of the other teams in the room had given her a look, one that had left her feeling as if they were questioning her leadership abilities.

She wanted to see them get clocked hard in the back with a steel baton and not react to it. It had hurt like a bitch, and she had a bruise on the left side of her ribs because of it.

As she pushed the doors to the garage open, Carter and Franks mercilessly teased Woods about last night's patrol, when he had fallen flat on his face in the lake after tumbling down an incline in a shadowy area of Hyde Park.

He had stunk to high heaven when she had helped him out of the muddy water. A smile worked its way onto her lips as she recalled how horrified he had looked when she had threatened to make him run back to HQ.

Riley was laughing his arse off over it still, his deep chortle as warm as his smile as his grey eyes landed on her. Out of the four rookies, the built-like-a-brick-shithouse raven-haired Riley was the only one who hadn't done something to test her patience.

Her team's fifth member, Archer, a brunet with some experience in the field, was quiet, leaning against the driver's side door of the black van as he smoked. He watched the others in silent contemplation, his brown eyes studying them with a disapproving air as he pushed his black-rimmed glasses up his nose with his index finger.

Emelia had been able to pick him herself. He had been part of the team sent to assist King Thorne and one of only a few men who hadn't treated her differently since her return. She trusted him, and they worked well together, which was more than she could say for the others.

"Quit fucking around and get in the van," she barked.

Carter, Franks, and Woods jolted and turned towards her.

"Sorry, we were... just..." Woods, the youngest of her team, stumbled over an apology as Franks pushed him into the back of the vehicle, causing him to trip on the step and almost fall flat on his face again.

The fair-haired lad needed some balance training. She made a mental note to request it, even when she knew he would hate it. She had seen recruits going through the training before, and it was gruelling and painful.

She stepped up behind Carter as the blond mounted the step after Franks, pulled the doors closed behind her, and moved to the front of the van.

"Good to go, Archer." She took a seat behind him where he sat in the cab.

He nodded and pulled away, easing the cumbersome vehicle through the maze of parked cars and fleet vans and SUVs, the strip lights reflecting off his glasses.

"Routine patrol. End point is Regent's Park tonight." Where they were going to run into a tiger shifter who happened to be on Archangel's wanted list.

She steeled herself and focused on her duty, handing out orders and pointers to her team as usual. The patrol passed without a hitch, no non-humans making an appearance to hinder her, and her nerves increased as they neared the park.

Would Talon be there?

They drove into York Gate, following the road into the heart of the park.

Her pulse pounded faster, palms sweating as she struggled to keep her cool. She couldn't let her team see she was nervous. This had to look good. Real. Her men needed to think this was a lucky encounter with an escaped captive.

If she didn't hold it together and they noticed something was up, if they grew suspicious in any way, there was a chance they would follow protocol and immediately report it to Mark or one of the other senior commanders.

"Commander?" Archer tilted his head back towards her. "Think we might have a situation."

She leaned over the seat and her heart thundered as she spotted the black-haired bare-chested man crouching on the grass, his back to a thick copse of trees.

"Are those Archangel cell block trousers he's wearing?" She managed to keep the nerves from her voice as she frowned at Talon. Her eyes widened. "Fuck. I know him. He's on the wanted list."

Behind her, the four men got ridiculously excited, filling the van with their voices.

"Shut up!" she snapped and glared over her shoulder at them for show. "That's a fucking shifter out there. You want him to hear us coming?"

They fell silent, exchanging looks that said they wanted to blame each other. Some team she had. None of them wanted to take responsibility for screwing up. She added some trust-building exercises to the list of things she needed to do. They were going to need a lot more training before they worked as a unit, acting as a team rather than a group of individuals. She thanked God for Archer. Without him, she might have gone insane by now.

He remained cool and collected behind the wheel, his dark eyes studying the park and the shifter, cataloguing everything.

"Head to the back, now," she hissed, holding back a smile as the four rookies all crept towards the rear doors.

How many times had she told them they could move around in the van without resorting to stealth?

They were a good distance away from Talon, and even a tiger shifter as powerful as he was wouldn't hear them talking at this distance, when they were inside the van.

It was soundproofed.

It didn't stop them from going full ninja, silent for once as they crouched and waited for her signal.

She looked over her shoulder at Archer. "Get us a little closer."

He nodded, put the van into gear, and eased forwards, rolling quietly along the tarmac.

When they were close enough, she signalled Archer to cut the engine and then the other four to go. They opened the rear doors of the van and spilled out into the dark. She followed them, quickly rounding the vehicle to join them as they crossed the grass, not wanting to risk one of them getting a little overexcited and firing on Talon.

The shifter remained crouched on the grass, his muscular back tensed and shoulders curled forwards. There was a dark patch on his side, streaking his skin. Blood.

"He's injured," she murmured to her team.

Emelia moved in front of the four rookies when Talon looked over his shoulder and bared huge fangs at her, his eyes bright gold in the low light.

She held her left hand out at her side, her palm facing her team, warning them to stay back.

The tiger's golden eyes shifted from her to the men behind her, danced over each one, and she didn't need to be a mind-reader to know he was thinking about how easy it would be to take them all down. He was right. Her team weren't up to the task of taking him into custody.

But she was.

She wasn't strong enough to take him one-on-one in a fight, not even when he was injured, but she had enough experience to employ all the tricks at her disposal. Methods she had used countless times in the past.

Her stomach squirmed as she thought about what she was about to do, as she looked Talon in the eye and realised he wasn't sure what was going to happen but was willing to go through with it anyway.

He was far braver than she was.

He turned and rose to stand in one fluid motion, coming to face her.

She silently apologised, lifted her gun, and fired.

He flinched, face crumpling before darkness washed across it, his eyes narrowing as they leaped to his left pectoral. The dart stuck out from the design tattooed on that side of his chest, one that covered his left arm like a sleeve too, the white feathers bright in the moonlight. He blinked hard, and she could almost see the drug taking effect, and the anger that roared to life inside him.

On a growl, he ripped it from his chest and collapsed to his knees. The dart tumbled from his fingers, and he stared at them, shaking his head as the tranquiliser took hold. His hands fell to his knees, a weaker growl issuing from his lips as he sagged.

His eyes lifted to hers, the caged fury in them clear. She apologised again, but if he had known how it was going to go down, it wouldn't have looked convincing. He might have done something to give the game away. Even the slightest tensing of his body in preparation for the dart would have clued Archer in to the charade they were acting out.

Talon slumped and landed face-first on the grass, his breathing uneven as he stared blankly at her.

Emelia signalled her team.

Archer joined them and broke right with two of the rookies as the other two headed left. The greenhorns remained close enough for her to keep track of them, but Archer melted into the shadows like a wraith. She didn't notice where he went as she eased towards Talon, keeping an eye on both the four members of her team and the big shifter, her right hand still clutching her dart gun.

The tiger weakly bared his fangs at it.

She had his attention.

Good.

She twitched the gun upwards. Once. Twice. A third time.

He finally lifted his unfocused gaze from her hand to her face. She mouthed at him, using small motions that her team hopefully wouldn't see in the slender light. His black eyebrows pinched. She kept on mouthing the two words at him, waiting for him to understand as her team closed in on him.

A flicker of understanding shone in his eyes.

Just a split second before the four rookie members of her team jumped on him.

She held her breath, sure that shit was about to go south.

But Talon just closed his eyes, showing her that he had received her order to 'play dead' as he gave a pathetic growl and didn't resist her hunters.

Carter was a little too enthusiastic as he shackled Talon's wrists behind his back, and Franks looked as if he was enjoying digging his knee into the shifter's spine to hold him down while Woods and Riley checked him for concealed weapons.

Archer emerged from the shadows, another unimpressed edge to his expression as he remained at a distance and listened to Carter and Franks.

"Fucking A!" Franks grinned as he dug his knee harder into Talon's spine, leaning towards the tiger's injured side. "Not so big now, are we?"

Carter tugged on the short chain between the heavy steel cuffs. "Should hold you. You won't be getting away from us again. Should get a pretty prize for dragging your sorry arse back to a cell where you belong."

Emelia was surprised Talon didn't react to that. She studied him, holding her breath as she waited for him to explode in rage. He remained calm, relaxed against the grass beneath the weight of Franks.

Archer tossed the four rookies a black look and moved a few steps towards the van before he suddenly halted.

A flicker of a frown danced on her brow as she briefly lifted her gaze to land on Archer.

Where had he gone?

She had expected him to remain in the thick of things, not do a disappearing trick when the action had gone down. He didn't look at her. His dark eyes remained locked on the shifter, his near-black eyebrows dipped low above them as he tracked everything the rookies were doing.

If she had to pinpoint what he was feeling, she would have called it anger, but that made no sense.

Why would Archer be angry about the way they were treating the tiger?

As far as she knew, he was like most of the hunters in Archangel and didn't give much of a damn about the welfare of a captive. She had seen him fighting demons, and he hadn't held back, hadn't hidden the animosity he felt towards the non-humans, not even when he had been surrounded by the demons of the Third Realm, ones who had been their allies.

Had something happened to change him?

Maybe he was like her now, one of a growing number who found the current change of attitude at Archangel distasteful and hard to swallow.

Or maybe he just really hated demons.

The men hauled Talon onto his feet, snagging her attention.

She focused on him, pushing thoughts of Archer aside as worry she had hit Talon with too much tranquiliser ran through her. She had messed with the dosage in the dart, using one big enough for the tiger but removing a third of the violet liquid. She watched as they dragged him through the park, struggling with his dead weight.

Either he was really out for the count, or he was a good actor.

She hoped it was the latter.

The men loaded him into the back of the van, and she sat opposite him, wanting to keep an eye on him. Carter and Franks flanked him, jostling him upright whenever he lolled to his right or left as the van pulled away.

He rolled forwards so he was bent over his legs as they turned a corner.

Emelia jerked her chin at Franks, and the brunet pulled him up, slamming his back against the side of the van. Talon's lips twitched, a sign that he was still with her.

And wanted to rip Franks' throat open with his fangs, by the looks of it.

She couldn't blame him.

His body grew more tense with each mile through the city, with every huff and shove he received from Franks and Carter.

The van hit a downwards slope and eased around a corner, and she glanced at the windshield. They were back. The first part of the plan had been a success, but now she had to end up alone with Talon and get him down into the containment area where he had been held before.

Which was a problem because she didn't know where it was.

If it existed, it was a secret, just as Sable suspected.

Talon had only been able to tell Sable and the others that he had used a lift to reach the ground floor of the building. There were several service lifts in Archangel headquarters, some leading to storage and others to the lower car parks, and even some that led down into emergency escape tunnels. She needed him to be lucid enough to tell her which service lift was the right one.

As they pulled to a halt, she leaned towards Talon and slapped his left cheek hard enough to have him swaying towards Carter.

The shifter growled and flicked his eyes open. They blazed gold as they locked on her.

"Good. He can walk himself." She rose to her feet and removed the dart gun from her thigh holster. "Don't think about getting feisty."

He continued to glare at her.

Carter and Franks grabbed his arms, pulled him to his bare feet, and shoved him towards the rear doors, where the other two were already waiting outside. Franks pushed him in the back, and he dropped to the parking garage floor, landing silently.

"Think he always lands on his feet?" Franks prodded him in his left shoulder, and Talon obediently walked forwards.

Emelia didn't like the look on his face or that glimmer in his eyes. If Franks and Carter didn't stop poking him, they were going to find out first-hand that it wasn't wise to upset a shifter. Woods wisely kept to one side. Riley was already at the door that led into the building, waiting to move.

Carter grinned. "We could take him to the roof and find out."

Talon bared his fangs and clenched his fists behind his back, his shoulders and biceps rippling and tensing as he pulled his arms apart in an attempt to break his restraints.

"Settle down," Emelia barked before things got out of hand. "Since you're all insisting on pissing me off... you can all piss off. Go on. It's past knocking-off time."

Carter glanced at her, missing the way Talon stared at him as if sizing him up as a meal. "You're sure? I mean... he's a lot of guy to handle alone."

"Are you saying for a woman to handle alone?" Emelia snapped, all warmth leaving her voice as memories loomed, whispered voices filling her head, taunting her with her weakness. "You want me to write that up in my report, Carter?"

He quickly shook his head.

"Jesus, you're all fucking annoying. Get out of my sight before I write you all up for that little stunt you pulled the other night. I'm sure the higher-ups would love to know about you visiting that fae bar to bet on the illegal fights in the basement."

Carter's face blanched. The other three looked as if they might relieve themselves in their combats.

Archer just sighed, closed the van's rear doors, and went back to the front, disappearing into the cab.

Her four rookies hurried into the building, and silence fell as Archer pulled the van away, a blessed relief from their incessant noise. She tried to smooth the rough edges off her mood, but it was impossible as she stood in the parking garage with a shifter she was about to break into the building, the task of grabbing information waiting for her, and her fears about Wolf plaguing her.

Emelia came up beside Talon, grabbed his right arm, and huffed. "Men. Always doing something stupid and reckless."

He glanced down at her.

For a moment, he looked as if he was going to ask whether she was talking about him now, but then something crossed his face as his eyes locked with hers. She turned her cheek to him, not wanting him to see that she was talking about another man, one who was constantly on her mind.

"Move." Emelia nudged him forwards, and he obeyed, trudging through the plain metal door in the concrete wall of the underground parking facility.

She pulled on his arm before he could shoulder the next door open, stopping him in the small space between them. He frowned down at her as she looked around, inspecting all the corners of the ceiling and then closing the door to the car park, shutting them in.

"Hold still." She opened the pocket on her left thigh, pulled out a syringe, and tugged the plastic cover off with her teeth. He eyed the needle. When he tensed, she paused with it close to his arm and looked up at him. "It's an antidote... but you'll need to act like you're still shaking off the drug."

He nodded and turned, offering his arm.

Flinched when she stabbed him with it.

Emelia capped the needle again and slipped it back into her pocket. "Sable owes me for this."

The method of helping Talon that her friend had come up with didn't sit well with her, but she could see why Sable had decided on it. It was the easiest way of getting Talon into the cell block without rousing suspicion.

Still, the fact she had drugged him and captured him had her stomach churning, and the thought she was about to take him back into a building where he had suffered so much had her thinking twice about going through with it.

If Sable was right, Talon had been abused just as Emelia had.

She couldn't believe he wanted to go back to a place where he had been tormented. Tortured. Violated.

She looked up at him as he stared at the door, visibly preparing himself for what was to come. She could see he was shaken by what was happening, but she could see his strength too.

And it was inspiring.

He was doing what he felt he needed to do to save his friends, regardless of the danger and the obvious pain it was causing him.

He was facing his fears so he could have the future he wanted, so he could ease his conscience by helping those who were taken with him in the raid on the fae town months ago.

He was doing it for closure too.

So as much as she wanted to back down, she couldn't. If he was willing to put himself through this, she was too.

She pulled down a sharp breath, exhaled it, and sucked down another before taking hold of his arm again. He glanced at her, a softness to his eyes that said he could feel her shaking. She did her best to hide how badly she was trembling as she opened the door and pushed him through it. He staggered and weakly growled at a passing pair of scientists.

"Fucking torturers," he slurred in their direction, and they both gave him a wide berth.

"Try to keep it more under control," the man said to Emelia.

She nodded and shoved Talon again, not missing how he tensed or how his nails sharpened into claws. She hated them for speaking about him that way too, treating him as if he was nothing more than an object, one they probably wanted to carve open on their inspection table.

He shot her a black look. She hit him with one in return and pushed him harder.

"Try to remember who's helping you here, buddy," she muttered under her breath, and then in a louder voice added, "Keep moving, or I'll hit you again."

He growled and stumbled forwards. When they reached the main cell block, he staggered to his right, and she looked down the white corridor in that direction.

Was that where the secret containment facility was?

Emelia pushed him in that direction, fielding a few questioning looks from several hunters as they passed her by with other prisoners. She glared at them all, daring them to speak to her. A few of them saluted, which was a novel experience. She felt the weight of the shiny pin on the collar of her roll-neck sweater. Being a commander did have a few perks.

Talon tensed.

She looked at him, catching his gaze for a second before he fixed it ahead of them. She tried to spot what he was staring at. There was a branch in the corridor, and then a grey metal door. She looked back at Talon.

That service elevator?

He gave a slight nod.

She struggled with him as she walked him towards it, pretending he was misbehaving. He was kind enough to act up a little, fighting her. When they reached the lift doors, she shoved him against the whitewashed wall next to the panel of buttons.

Nerves surged as she quickly pressed the call button. She angled her body so no one passing could see the light on the button as she checked over Talon's restraints, keeping him pinned face-first against the wall.

A curse rolled through her head when a grey-haired woman dressed in a white coat slowed.

"You brought him in?" The woman looked him over.

His eyes instantly glowed gold.

He snarled at her through his emerging fangs.

Not an act this time.

"Keep back." Emelia held her palm out in front of her, towards the woman, and twisted him to face her. She pressed her other forearm against his chest, pushed his back against the wall, and held him there. He could easily break free of her if he wanted, but he played along as he glared at the woman. Emelia lowered her hand and reached for her gun. "He's coming around quicker than we expected."

The lift to her right pinged, and the doors slid open.

Her heart almost stopped as time stretched, slowing as she glanced at the elevator and then the woman. She waited for everything to go south, sure the woman would demand to know what she was doing and how she knew about the hidden facility.

Sure that she was about to become a captive of Archangel too.

Taken into custody for treason.

The grey-haired woman withdrew a small device from her pocket, swiped across the screen several times and then typed something.

When she was done, she looked up at Emelia.

"What are you waiting for? If he's coming around, I want him contained as soon as possible." The scientist pocketed her device and Emelia immediately relaxed, her fear melting away. "I've notified the others. We'll be ready to continue our research on him before the hour is up. Well done, Commander Emelia."

Fur rippled over Talon's golden skin and he launched forwards, knocking Emelia into the opposite wall. The woman backed away as he snapped his fangs at her, snarling and growling, and she narrowly avoided being caught by them.

"Damn it." Emelia barrelled into him and he grunted as she planted the dart gun into his side and depressed the trigger.

Talon staggered backwards, hit the wall, and sagged against it, breathing hard.

Damn him!

He had to go forcing her hand, didn't he?

"Take him down." The woman edged around him, scanned her pass inside the elevator, and made a fast exit down the corridor.

Emelia kept her features schooled as she checked him over, concern building inside her as he stared at her through dull amber eyes. She silently apologised to him as she pushed him into the lift. The doors closed and it started moving downwards.

Running into the scientist had been both a curse and a blessing. She hadn't considered the area might be protected, sealed off to anyone who didn't have the right clearance on their pass card.

Talon shook his head and almost fell to his knees. She barely managed to keep him upright, leaned him against the wall and waited for the car to stop and the doors to open before she risked moving him again.

The entire floor was gloomy, only a few lights at intervals along the corridor illuminating the dark grey-blue walls.

Talon shuffled along in front of her, swaying from time to time. The corridor opened up into an enormous room, one with close to half a dozen doors coming off it, some of which had a guard outside. Light shone from the left side and she picked that way.

The stale air reeked of the scent of blood, vomit and urine. She eased Talon forwards when he stopped, putting up a weak fight. He shook beneath her hand as she planted it against his back, hoping to comfort him.

It was brave of him to do this.

Incredibly courageous.

And maybe a little crazy.

He struggled against his bonds.

Emelia patted his back and offered him the only comfort she could. "Think about Sherry."

The bartender was waiting for him up on the roof. According to Sable, the two of them were involved with each other, had been practically inseparable since Talon had stumbled into Underworld shortly after he had escaped, half-dead and desperate to hide from Archangel.

He settled, his breathing evening out as she guided him around a corner, into a brightly lit cell block. A black-haired demon in the cell to her left glared at her as she pushed Talon towards an empty cell. She looked up at the camera mounted above the exit and the glass panel that formed the front of the cell whooshed as it opened. Talon tensed and leaned back, threw her a stricken look as she nudged him on.

"It'll be fine," she whispered, hoping it would soothe him. "Sherry is waiting."

He stepped into the cell. She unlocked his restraints and moved back into the corridor. The thick panel closed, forming a barrier between them.

Talon fell to his knees.

Looked over his shoulder at her.

She offered a silent apology and a plea for him to be patient, to hold it together for a little while.

She slipped her hand into her pocket, activating the small magical violet teardrop-shaped device that Bleu had given her. She hoped the elf and his sister Iolanthe had been telling the truth about the device. It seemed incredible to her that they could use the signal it emitted as a sort of beacon to locate Talon, allowing them to teleport to a place they had never been before. She willed them to hurry, because she wasn't sure how long Talon could hold it together and now that she had seen this place, she wanted to get him and his friends out as quickly as possible.

There was something wrong about this whole area.

A guard glanced at her as he walked past, and she forced herself to turn away from Talon. She dropped the odd transmitter that resembled a jewel outside the cell block on her way back to the lift.

What sort of things were happening down here? She cast secret glances around the facility as she strode through it, checking out the closed doors and long hallways and the men who patrolled it, dressed in navy-blue fatigues that were different from the uniform hunters like her wore. And why did they feel the need to guard that one door at the back?

She stepped into the elevator, pressed the button, and focused on the next part of her mission.

One that would hopefully give her the answer to the question now burning in her heart.

What was Archangel's new purpose, and why were they hiding it from their own people?

CHAPTER 31

Emelia met Sherry at the bottom of the steps that led up to the roof access door, trying to keep her mind off when she had spoken with Wolf there just weeks ago. The pretty blonde bartender looked the part in a form-fitting black T-shirt and combat trousers, her usual heels replaced by heavy boots.

"Ready?" Emelia glanced both ways along the cream corridor, watching the men and women as they sprinted past both ends of it, heading for the staircases as alarms blared.

Nerves flashed in Sherry's blue eyes, but she nodded.

Emelia quickly led her to the adjoining corridor to her left, and they fell in behind a group of hunters, using them as cover. She glanced at her comrade, keeping an eye on her as they reached the next level and broke away from the hunters.

Another group of armed hunters rushed past them, joining with the team they had followed.

The walls shook as a male roared on a floor below them. A few of the less experienced hunters who were standing in the corridor, watching the dispatched teams rushing to the scene, paled as their wide eyes darted towards the source of the sound.

Sable and Thorne were certainly making it a convincing performance.

Emelia ducked around a corner and tugged Sherry with her, falling into a brisk walk as she followed the corridor to the other wing of the building, doing her best to look calm so she didn't draw the gazes of the hunters who poked their heads out of the rooms lining the hallway, curious about what was happening.

If luck was with them, Emelia wouldn't be summoned to gather her team and head to the cafeteria too.

Mark would dispatch the more experienced teams first, which was one thing she had going in her favour. She had never thought having a group of rookies under her command would be a benefit, but damn it felt like a blessing as she waited for another team to rush past her, sticking close to the wall opposite a pair of women from the science division.

Sherry looked at her and then at the wooden floor when another roar sounded. A few of the passing hunters muttered comments about the demon.

Emelia hoped they weren't brave enough to attempt to attack Thorne. By now, the male would be fully demonic, towering close to ten feet tall and a danger to everyone but his mate.

A mate he was meant to be abducting, whisking away to his kingdom for the purpose of making little heirs.

This wasn't just a diversion.

It was Sable's grand departure from Archangel.

If the rank-and-file hunters didn't already know she was mated to the demon king, they would after this performance. Sable wanted to leave with a bang and had apparently told Thorne to go all out. The floor beneath Emelia's boots shook, and another roar reached her ears.

By the sounds of things, he was doing just that.

Emelia would be surprised if the building was still standing once he was done.

She held Sherry back at another junction, waiting for a rush of hunters to pass. The bartender stared at her boots, a troubled edge to her eyes.

It hadn't gone down well when Emelia had confessed what she had done with Talon during a brief meeting on the roof, how she had been forced to put him in a cell to make it look good after she had run into one of the scientists in charge of whatever went on down there. Sable had reassured Emelia that she had done what she had needed to do and that Talon would understand it. Bleu and Iolanthe had been quick to go on their way to rescue him and the others, teleporting the moment Thorne disappeared to start the second part of the plan.

Despite their reassurances, Talon still played on her mind.

Shoving him into that cell had been one of the hardest things she had ever done.

She wasn't sure she could condone what Archangel were doing, not now they were veering away from their noble mission to keep humans safe from the dangerous immortals that coexisted with them in the world, and not now she had seen the secret facility with her own eyes.

She was going to cut ties with them.

Even when she knew it would be painful.

She had wanted to save Archangel and put it back on track, but now she wasn't sure that would be possible. They were already too far down that dark path she had feared they were treading.

They banked right along the corridor, and she tried to keep her mind focused on the mission and away from her future. A group of hunters lingered ahead of her in the hall, discussing tonight's patrol and how they wanted to join in with the teams that had been dispatched to the cafeteria to deal with Thorne. She nodded to their commander, a man known to be ruthless, and was glad Mark hadn't called on his team yet.

It was only a matter of time, though.

If Mark was following protocol, ten teams were already there.

Each minute that passed where Thorne refused to leave was a minute where Mark would dispatch another team to bolster the hunter numbers in the cafeteria in an attempt to drive him out.

By now, there were probably close to sixty hunters down there.

Not counting those who didn't wait for the call.

A lot of hunters, especially the newer recruits and the commanders, would head there by choice, neglecting their duties because they wanted in on the action.

Sherry offered a flirty smile to a hunter who glanced her way, one of a team who had just returned from patrol by the looks of things and was watching them closely. The distraction worked, and he grinned right back at her and went on his way.

"Not far now," Emelia said in a low voice.

Sherry tensed, nerves flaring in her eyes again. She breathed slowly, clearly struggling with them. Emelia wanted to tell her that she would be fine and no one would suspect her, but there were too many people coming and going along the corridors, responding to urgent calls for more back up in the cafeteria.

Senior hunters visited the archive all the time, checking the files for information on their latest target. If anyone was in there, they would think she and Sherry were a team doing research on a new mark or perhaps looking up the weaknesses of a demon in case their team were dispatched to the cafeteria.

Fear blasted through her, setting her heart racing, and she tried to tamp it down before anyone noticed something was wrong. It was impossible, though. Seeing Talon bravely hurling himself into danger, into a place where he had been abused, to save people he cared about, and seeing Sherry risking everything to gather information for him and Sable, rattled her.

Revealed her own failings.

Emelia slowed.

Sherry stopped and looked back at her, but Emelia couldn't stop staring straight ahead of her, her lips parted and eyes wide as she gave up the fight against her fears and let them wash over her.

The truth hit her so hard, her legs weakened beneath her.

Wolf was in trouble.

There was no point denying it or pretending otherwise. It wouldn't change what he had done. He had gone to Hell, and this time, he hadn't come back. He was in danger, and she was trying to bury her head in the sand because she was scared of following him into that dark realm.

Even when she knew it was the right thing to do.

If she didn't save Wolf, who would?

Her plan had been to ask Thorne and Sable to do it, but in her heart, she knew that Thorne would be against it, and she wasn't sure Sable would be able to convince him.

In her heart, she knew she needed to be the one to do it.

She couldn't let Thorne and Sable fight her battles for her, not when Wolf had been bravely fighting hers. She needed to be the one to rescue him from whatever trouble he had landed himself in.

It was time she found the courage to face her fears.

She wanted to be brave like Talon, a little crazy like she used to be.

But she wasn't.

The thought of going to Hell left her cold and shaking, had sweat sliding down her spine and her breaths coming faster as her memories threatened to swamp her.

But if she didn't go?

She would fail Wolf.

She might lose him forever.

So somehow, God only knew how, she was going to find the strength and the courage to do what she needed to do, for herself and for Wolf.

"What's wrong?" Sherry closed the distance between them, and Emelia snapped back to her.

"Nothing." Emelia hesitated, not surprised that Sherry arched an eyebrow at her lie because her voice was shaking as badly as her body. "I'm just a bit on edge."

"Because of what we're doing?" the blonde whispered.

Emelia shook her head.

"No." She paused again and stared at Sherry. She had known her years, and although they weren't close, she felt she could trust her because they were both falling in love with an immortal. She sighed and glanced off to her right, to a window there that opened onto the courtyard. "Someone I know... I think he's done something stupid... something that might get him killed. I'm worried about him."

Damn, it felt good to say that, to confess it to someone. Her fear began to trickle out of her, strength she had thought she had lost rising to replace it as she looked at the blonde.

"What do you think he's done?" Sherry edged closer.

Emelia's eyes slipped shut. "I think he went to Hell... to hunt a dragon for me."

"Is he a hunter here?" Sherry sidled closer still, showing Emelia that she was aware he wasn't and was worried someone might overhear their conversation and she would get in trouble.

She shook her head again.

"Is he strong?" Sherry murmured.

This time she nodded.

"Capable of killing a dragon?"

Another nod.

"So you're just worried about him because you feel something for him?"

"No." Emelia opened her eyes and locked gazes with her as a barrage of feelings hit her, swirling like a tempest she had no hope of controlling now she had opened the floodgates. "You don't understand... like dragons aren't meant to come here... he isn't supposed to go there."

Her voice broke.

Sherry's eyes softened with understanding. "Is there nothing you can do?"

Emelia's brow furrowed as she shook her head, her courage failing her again despite her attempt to keep hold of it. She cursed herself. She wanted to be strong. She wanted to be brave. She couldn't keep letting her fears get the better of her. Wolf needed her.

A huge boom rocked the floor, and her gaze shot down to her feet.

It felt as if that boom had been a thunderbolt striking her mind and her heart, a surge of power and energy that had her courage flaring again, the strength she had been lacking sweeping through her to lift her back up.

"Maybe there is something I can do after all."

Something that terrified her, but something she was going to do regardless. Sable wouldn't be the only hunter Thorne was taking back to Hell tonight. She was sticking with the plan.

She was going to make him take her with him too, and she was going to make him help her. She wouldn't take no for an answer. She might not be able to convince him, but Sable would once Emelia confessed something to her.

That she needed to save the man she loved.

The main alarm kicked off, shrieking loudly as the lights dropped and red flashing ones replaced them.

"Is it that fucking demon again?" someone yelled.

Hunters streamed past her, heading for the stairs that led downwards, and she grabbed Sherry's wrist, tugging her in the opposite direction. It was only a matter of time before Mark dispatched her team and all the others. The lower floor would be pandemonium, everyone piling there to help out, leaving the archive room quiet.

No one would see them there.

"Now," she said and Sherry hurried to keep up with her.

They skidded around a bend, almost ploughing straight into two men.

"You're going the wrong way," Archer shouted.

Emelia didn't slow, not even as her pulse spiked and she threw a panicked glance at him. He stood in the hall, staring at her, his left eyebrow arching. Something crossed his eyes as he looked from her to the room at the end of the corridor, and she feared he would say something, but then his gaze narrowed and he turned away.

And in the split second before his eyes left hers, she swore the whole of them turned black.

She stumbled a step, heart lodging in her throat as she almost fell, and shook her head as she regained her footing, attempting to dislodge the thought that pinged around her head.

It had been a trick of the light.

Archer was human just like her.

Wasn't he?

Sherry pulled her up and Emelia shifted her focus back to her mission. Ahead of her, twin closed doors loomed at the end of the corridor, and the sign above them read Central Archive.

They were here.

She slipped her hand into her pocket, reaching for the security pass that would grant her access as her focus fixed on the black scanner mounted on the wall near the doors.

The doors burst open as they reached them, a woman coming out of them with a blade at the ready. Sherry plastered herself against the wall as Emelia swiftly released her.

Emelia dodged, ducking past the huntress to enter the room, Sherry hot on her heels.

She headed straight for one of the computers on the long double rows of desks that filled the middle of the room. All around the edges, huge black cases lined the white walls, the servers stacked in them flashing with green, orange, and red lights.

Sherry moved to the computer on the other side of the desk to Emelia and set to work, using Sable's login to access the files on Talon and what had happened to him and the others during and after the raid on the fae town. Emelia had been against her helping, but Sable had backed Sherry up when she had insisted.

Emelia had her own agenda anyway, wouldn't have had time to find those files and do what she had come here to do too.

She paid Sherry no heed as she searched the files, trying to piece the truth together so she could uncover what Archangel were up to. Her faith in the organisation she had loyally served began to waver as she used her new clearance level to access the files on the raids and hesitated.

If she did this, there was no going back.

Archangel would be able to see who had accessed the files in the logs.

She drew down a deep, steadying breath. She needed to know what Archangel were doing, though. She needed to know what that hidden facility was all about.

She followed several links in the files on the raids.

They mentioned projects, some of them completed and others still in progress. There was an entire section on the war they had fought in for King Thorne, and several reports with a list of names that were denied access to them. Sable was among them. She scanned the reports. They were all about Sable, and some were about Olivia. Someone had been spying on them, secretly documenting their behaviour and interactions with Thorne and Loren, and other immortals.

There were other files too, ones that spoke of succeeding in gaining access to Hell. She clicked the links in those files and read them, cold slithering through her as she ploughed deeper and deeper, following the trail down a dark rabbit hole.

"I don't like what I'm reading here." Emelia lifted her gaze to Sherry over the top of the monitors that separated them. "What the fuck are they up to?"

Because as far as she could tell, someone within Archangel was using captured fae to access Hell through the portal network only certain non-human species could use, and they had been sending teams there.

They were charting Hell.

Every damned inch of it.

Geographical reports. Demographics. Detailed counts of populations across the realm. Some of the locations had been marked with a flag, one she couldn't access. Every time she tried to click on the small innocuous identifier that tied a group of locations together, she was hit with an 'access denied' message.

Emelia backtracked to the files on the raids.

Archangel had been deploying teams to the fae towns across the world. Each one mentioned they had dispatched teams to secure dangerous non-humans, but some of the people listed as being brought in didn't have a file on record before the date of the raid, and a lot of them were from different species.

She scanned file after file, noting the species and gender of each captive.

It was as if Archangel were doing their damnedest to get a female and male from every species, and the only reason they could want to do that was one that sickened her.

Talon was right.

They were bringing in innocent non-humans in secret, taking them down to the facility she had seen to experiment on them.

They were charting their weaknesses.

Were Archangel about to do a one-eighty back to the days when they had hunted and killed any non-humans?

What had prompted them to do such a thing?

Emelia found a list of the raids, using the one in which Talon had been captured as a starting point. They had been increasing in frequency over the last few months. She stopped when the number of raids went from one every few weeks to almost one every other day.

Her eyes slowly widened as she recognised the date when the increase had begun.

Six months ago.

Her finger trembled as she clicked to open the file, hoping beyond hope that she was wrong. Her eyes caught on the first sentence, and that hope disintegrated.

It is proposed in the aftermath of discovering the existence of another plane that Archangel must broaden its knowledge of all non-human species through any means necessary and forge forwards towards ensuring the safety of mankind.

Archangel had learned of Hell.

Someone in the organisation had seen it as an opportunity to steer Archangel towards a more violent future under the banner of protecting mankind.

And now Archangel had also learned of Heaven and the existence of angels.

She couldn't imagine the changes that would prompt, but she was sure whoever was behind the secret facility would use it as an excuse to ramp up the number of raids and the experiments.

"Grab everything you can," she said and pulled a USB drive from her pocket, slotting it into the machine.

Sherry nodded.

Emelia was damned if Archangel were going to launch a war with Hell. Most of the non-humans who lived in that realm weren't a threat to her kind, just as most of the non-humans who shared this world with humans weren't. If Archangel were allowed to start a war between the realms, it wouldn't be only the non-humans who suffered incredible losses.

Her world would too.

She had to find a way to stop this, and she had the feeling she wouldn't be alone.

Sable and Thorne would be right there with her, and so would Olivia and Loren, and Anais and Loke, and even Sherry and Talon. Everyone at Underworld and all those they knew in Hell would be on her side, helping her find a way to put an end to Archangel.

But first, she needed to rescue the man she loved, the one she needed at her side.

The only man she needed.

Another rumbling roar echoed through the building.

It was almost time to go. Thorne and Sable wouldn't be able to keep up the charade much longer. The demon would snatch her friend and disappear with her, and Emelia intended to be there when they appeared to take the information from her and Sherry.

Because she had made a decision.

No more running away.

Wolf had saved her more than once, and she couldn't fail him.

Wouldn't fail him.

This time, she would save him.

And then, they would find a way to save the world.

CHAPTER 32

Emelia paced the quiet nightclub, battling another bout of nerves as she waited for Thorne and Sable to finish their business with the fallen angel Sable had been meeting to learn more about her powers. She had managed to get a message to Sable ahead of their meetup, and the huntress had almost instantly fired one back, saying her husband was happy to take her to Hell when they returned there.

Sable had also said she wouldn't be alone when she went to find Wolf. Her friend was going with her whether she liked it or not.

She wasn't about to turn Sable and Thorne down.

It dawned on her that she had chosen to approach the wrong people when she had originally wanted to return to Hell and hunt down every dragon who had escaped the wrath of Archangel.

Archangel had refused to help her.

Sable and Thorne offered to readily, without even pausing to consider the pros and cons.

Although, Emelia imagined that Thorne wasn't happy about who she wanted to rescue. She would reassure the demon king that Wolf wouldn't take Sable from him when they arrived.

"What's taking so long?" she muttered as she pivoted to pace back along the length of the black bar in the dimly lit room.

She glanced at the brightly coloured optics and bottles that lined the mirrored wall on the other side of the bar.

If Sable took much longer, she was going to sneak behind the bar and fix herself a drink, because she was going to need it. Doubts were filling her mind, fear a constant buzz in her veins, and she was finding it increasingly difficult to deny the memories that wanted to surge to the surface.

Zephyr wasn't going to hurt her.

With Thorne and Sable at her back, she was strong enough to tackle the dragon. But she might have more firepower in her arsenal. Not just her friend and the demon, but a dragon too. Sable was sure that Loke and Anais would help if they stopped by their cave first.

Archangel had refused her an army, so she was damn well going to put her own one together, made of the most powerful immortals she knew.

Even Bleu and Iolanthe had offered their services, and Bleu had gone as far as saying his mate, another dragon and one who knew Loke, might lend a hand too.

With an army of friends at her back, she had no reason to be afraid.

Zephyr didn't stand a chance.

And if he had Wolf and had hurt him?

She lowered her hand to the dart gun hanging at her hip.

It was loaded for dragon, and she was going to use it, and then she was going to kill him with her own blade.

She turned to pace back the other way.

Froze as she came face-to-face with an angel.

The petite blonde stood at the other end of the bar, her hands clasped in front of the gold rope that cinched her white robe in at her curvy waist. Her golden hair hung in loose waves, reaching her full breasts. White wings that were smaller than Wolf's rested furled against her back.

"Do you know something about Wolf?" Emelia took a swift step towards the angel, heart racing at the thought she might have information.

"Wolf?" Her nose crinkled as she frowned.

Emelia had forgotten angels had a stupid tendency to have no name. "The Fourth Commander."

The angel's eyes darkened, something crossing them that set Emelia on edge. "I came to ask the same thing. I am worried about him. He was distant the last time I was with him."

Her blood chilled. "*With* him?"

The blonde's lips twitched faintly, as if she wanted to smile but had contained it. "I am a healer. The Fourth Commander has exclusively requested me for the last few years, but recently, he has been drawing away. He seems troubled by something."

By Emelia and the dragon.

She kept quiet, studying the angel as awareness prickled down her spine, warning her that something wasn't right. This angel hadn't come here because she was worried. The bite in her tone, the way she had looked at Emelia with darkness in her eyes, everything about her stirred a feeling inside Emelia. One she found difficult to deny, even when she had no real proof to back it up.

This angel had come here because Wolf had been drawing away from her, distracted by Emelia, and she didn't like it.

"The Echelon are so complicated, and I have worked with several in my years, but none quite like the Fourth Commander. He is always so... fired up... when he returns to me. It is only a matter of time before we produce his first heir." The angel skimmed her hands across her stomach, and Emelia's rebelled, twisting viciously as she realised what the angel was saying.

Wolf came back from battle all riled and fired up, a warrior with his passion stoked, and slept with her.

She tried to shove that thought out of her head, but she was too weak to shake it. It sank claws into her, tormenting her even when her heart remained constant and steady, telling her that Wolf loved her and he would never lie to her about such a thing.

But she had never asked him if he already had a woman.

"Oh... you think the Fourth Commander desires you as his mate?" The angel pulled a face of mock pity that had Emelia itching to punch her as she wrestled with her feelings, trying to convince herself the angel was lying. The woman brushed fingers across her lip, a heated edge to her eyes as she whispered, "He kissed me the other day, while my naked body pressed against his."

Emelia's hand dropped to the dart gun on her hip, the urge to use it on the angel almost overwhelming her as her heart ached, feeling as if it was about to split in two.

She held it together because she was damned if she was going to let this angel poison her mind against Wolf.

"As an Echelon, he will be expected to sire strong offspring to continue his lineage, providing generations of powerful warriors." The angel smiled. "Strong offspring require a strong mother. The Fourth Commander would never choose one from outside his realm for the task. He is meant for me. He could never love a weak creature like you."

That was it.

Emelia drew the gun and aimed it at the bitch, every barb the angel had thrown at her stinging, shredding her heart to pieces as she did her best to deny them. They were lies. They had to be.

Anger followed in the wake of the pain, blazed in her veins so fiercely that she could barely breathe as she stared the angel down.

"If you're so special to Wolf, why is he hunting a dragon for me?" she spat, venom dripping from her words as her hands shook, making it impossible to keep the gun trained on the bitch.

The angel's eyes widened, surprise shining in them before she shut it down, her fair eyebrows dipping into a frown as she glared at Emelia.

Jealous that the man she wanted had done something for Emelia, or angry that he had put himself in danger for another woman?

Emelia sucked down a breath. The angel was lying. She had to be. It was jealousy that had brought her here, and she was mounting an attempt to drive Emelia away from Wolf.

Although he had been distant when he had left her, had been lost in thought, and hadn't paid attention to anything she had said to him.

Her heart ached.

Because he regretted sleeping with her because of this angel? Because he was somehow promised to her?

No. He had been preoccupied, probably with thoughts of the dragon, knowing Wolf. He wanted the male to pay and had been consumed by that need to avenge her. That was the only reason he had been distant.

It had to be.

She wanted to believe the feelings she had seen in him were true and that the angel was lying, but there had been conviction in her voice and honesty in her eyes when she had said Wolf had kissed her.

That her naked curves had been pressed against his.

The anger simmering in her veins rolled back to a boil, the image of them tangled together provoking it until it became rage blazing in her blood, fury that demanded answers, fuelled by the hurt burning in her heart.

"If you want Wolf so badly, go and get him," she barked, every drop of the rage consuming her exploding in those words.

Her phone vibrated in her pocket. She ignored it, had more pressing matters to attend to than seeing if it was Sable.

"I will. Where is he?" The angel looked around them. "Is he here?"

"He's in Hell." Emelia holstered her gun, savouring the shock that rippled across the bitch's face. "Which is where I'll be in around a minute because I'm going to save his arse, and then we'll see whether I have to kick it or not."

The angel paled.

Opened her mouth.

Whatever words she had wanted to say came out as a shriek as Thorne appeared with his powerful arms wrapped around Sable, his seven-foot frame making her look petite against him as he clutched her to his bare chest.

Thorne turned curious dark red eyes on the source of the scream.

They instantly blazed like hot coals.

"Demon!" The angel shrieked again, the sound more piercing than Archangel's intruder alarm.

Thorne's dusky horns curled through his wild russet locks, following the curves of his pointed ears and flaring around each other as rage lit his rough features.

The angel made the mistake of looking at Sable, a flicker of recognition in her eyes as they landed on the black-haired huntress.

Thorne bellowed something in the demonic tongue.

The angel screamed, face contorting as her hands flew to her ears and she collapsed. She didn't even touch the floor. She disappeared before she could hit it.

Emelia needed to learn that language. "Teach me some words."

Thorne's rough low chuckle echoed around the room as he relaxed. "Does not work like that, little huntress. Only demons speaking it hurts them."

That was a shame.

"What did Small, Pale and Holy want?" Sable extricated herself from Thorne's hold, but the male was quick to pull her back into his arms.

He muttered in his own tongue as he petted her. Sable sighed and didn't resist him, letting him stroke her fall of black hair as she wriggled until she was facing Emelia.

"Apparently, she's Wolf's intended or something." Emelia couldn't keep the venom from her voice.

Sable frowned at her and muttered, "More like she's Wolf's groupie."

"She—" Emelia started.

Sable cut her off. "I saw how he looked at you, Emelia. No guy looks at a girl like that unless he's doomed to go crazy for them. Take it from me. I know."

Her friend petted Thorne's hand where it tightly gripped her shoulder, keeping her back plastered against his bare chest.

Thorne had gone a little mad for Sable. Emelia had noticed that from the moment she had met the demon, and the level of crazy had only increased over the time she had been staying at the castle in the Third Realm, preparing for the war.

Just as Wolf's level of crazy had increased in the time she had known him.

Because he was falling for her as she suspected?

"But still…" Sable continued with a grim expression etched on her delicate features. "If he's been two-timing you, I'm going to kick his arse."

Emelia smiled at her friend, glad she was here and that she would have backup when she found Wolf, saved him, and then confronted him about the bitch.

"Not if I beat you to it."

CHAPTER 33

Emelia had only been in Thorne's grim grey fortress in Hell for a day, but it felt like forever as she forced herself to be patient. Loke had promised to come and help her as soon as he was done with some clan business, and Bleu had sworn to bring his mate to the castle tomorrow. Then they would all head out together.

She stood on a balcony that overlooked the courtyard of the castle. It was more of a garrison really. A heavily fortified outer wall that had several buildings nestled inside it encompassed an equally as thick and fortified inner wall. Towers intersected that wall, spread evenly around it, and a large building stood opposite the one she was in. The armoury.

Braziers blazed around the courtyard, illuminating it, the light dancing over the bare-chested demons as they went about their work. Groups of warriors hung out in front of the low building to her left that hugged the curve of the wall. Her quarters were there, close to Thorne and Sable's rooms.

Thorne grumbled something, his deep voice carrying through the open doors behind her. Sable spoke, soothing words that reassured her mate.

Emelia had left them studying the map of Hell that took up an entire table in the centre of Thorne's war room, charting the location she had given them and how far it was from Loke's cave.

If Loke didn't show up tomorrow, Thorne planned to go there and make the male come with them.

Apparently, she wasn't the only one who didn't like waiting.

Although, part of the reason Thorne wanted to save Wolf was to hammer it home that Sable was off-limits and that if he ever came near her, he would kill him. She had assured Thorne that Wolf wasn't interested in stealing his mate, but what did she really know?

Had Wolf slept with the angel?

The more time she spent with only her thoughts for company, the more she was convinced he had.

And the more she wanted to find him and beat the truth out of him.

The air around her charged. A shiver bolted down her spine.

The hope she had been keeping alive since Wolf had left her soared, and she turned towards the room, her breath hitching as arcs of electricity sparked in the middle of it.

Only it wasn't Wolf who stood before her when the blinding light faded.

"I swear, one day, you're gonna vaporise me when you teleport like that." A female voice rang through the room, a teasing note in it.

A very masculine sigh followed.

"We have been through this, Asteria. I would never hurt you."

Emelia's heart ached as those words echoed in her mind, but in Wolf's voice. He had sworn he would never hurt her, never lie to her, but here she was, standing in Hell, afraid of what was to come and scared he had been keeping secrets from her.

The towering blond male who stood before her, black armour covering him from neck to toe, black-feathered wings furled against his back, casually turned towards Thorne as the demon began to growl and held up a gauntleted hand. "I really would not."

"Down boy," Asteria said to Thorne, a wicked smile curving her cherry-red lips as she flicked her black hair over her shoulder, revealing cleavage that looked ready to burst from the tiny violet-trimmed corset she wore with a pair of black shorts that flashed the bottom curves of her buttocks.

Sable glared at the demoness and moved in front of Thorne. "Back off, bitch."

"Meow." Asteria make a swiping move with her hand, clawing the air. "I'm not interested in your demon, half-breed. You can dial back the testosterone. I only have eyes for my bad boy."

She swayed towards the fallen angel, wrapping her arm around his and clinging to it as she gazed lovingly up at him, her blue eyes shining with adoration. She rubbed her small obsidian horns up and down his armoured chest and over his shoulder, her leathery wings trembling as if it felt good.

He smiled down at her, his expression soft even as he said, "You had better only have eyes for me or you might get a little frazzled next time we teleport."

She pouted at that.

If the demon was Asteria, then the black-winged angel was Rey. Wolf's comrade.

"Um," Emelia started.

The demoness looked over her shoulder at her, released the fallen angel and tossed her a broad smile. "Look. We found her!"

"You are sure it is her?" The fallen angel looked her over. "You said that about the last brunette we found."

Asteria huffed and looked up at him as he turned towards Emelia. "You can't smell the angel all over her?"

Okay. That was far too personal. Emelia's cheeks burned.

The demoness noticed and grinned. "Definitely her."

Thorne growled again. Strong arms suddenly banded around Emelia, darkness washed over her, and she was in the room again, but not where she had been. She didn't have a chance to take in what had happened. Thorne shoved her and Sable behind him, his broad dragon-like wings stretching to form a barrier between them and the couple.

"Speak your business!" he boomed as he grew in size, his temper getting the better of him.

"Oh, he's so antiquated. I love it!" Asteria didn't seem to notice the way her mate sighed again.

"Do not anger the demon. Did I not say that when we followed the trail here? What did I say, Asteria?"

She hummed and then said, "Don't piss the big demon king off?"

"And what are you doing?"

"Pissing the big demon king off." She huffed, her voice losing all the light that had been in it as she muttered, "Fine. Spoilsport. You can take the holy out of the angel, but not the angel out of the... wait... I can do this. You can take the good... the light?"

"I am not here for you or your mate," Rey said as Asteria continued to mutter to herself about angels, good, and other things. "We were trying to find Emelia. You are Emelia, are you not?"

She touched Thorne's back to let him know she was going to be fine, not wanting him to go off the deep end again, and stepped out from behind him, coming to face the fallen angel.

His crimson eyes were soft as they locked with hers, holding concern and a dash of hope, and it was strange seeing a fallen angel in the flesh.

He was nothing like the pictures people had painted for her. There was good in him. She could see it.

"I am." She held her nerve and moved a little closer to him, sure that if he had wanted to kill them all, he probably would have done it by now.

"You are a hard female to find. We looked in the places Wolf told us about, but you were not there."

"I... I came here. I think Wolf is in trouble." She searched his eyes, seeing in them that she wasn't the only one worried about the angel.

"I think so too. When we returned to our home, we found evidence Wolf had been there, and that there had been a fight."

Her heart leaped into her throat. "Did you find evidence of a dragon?"

His grim look said it was far worse than that and she curled her fingers into fists to stop her hands from shaking as she waited for him to speak.

"We found... there were black feathers. Not mine."

Her heart sank and she gripped the table for support as her entire world rocked on its axis.

"We think the dragon has hired fallen angels." Asteria's usually bright voice was sombre for once, her expression serious as Emelia shifted her gaze to her.

"But you could take them. If he has hired fallen angels... you could take them, right?" She refused to let this sway her.

Bleu and Loke, and the others might not be a match for fallen angels, but another fallen angel would be. Surely?

Rey shrugged, lifting the plates of his heavy black armour. "Probably. I am stronger than the average fallen angel because I retained my Echelon—"

Thorne roared and had Rey's throat in his grasp before the fallen angel even knew what had hit him. He slammed Rey's back into the grey stone wall of the war room, pinning him there as he flashed his fangs and snarled, his muscles rippling beneath his tanned skin as he grew in size again.

Rey's irises burned crimson, his pupils stretching into thin slits in their centres as he brought his hand up and gripped Thorne's wrist.

"You want to rethink this?" Rey grunted and her eyes widened when she saw the hand he held Thorne with was bare, his naked palm pressing against the demon's skin.

The black cross on the inside of his right wrist was visible just above the sleeve of his armour.

Thorne looked as if he was willing to risk it.

"Let him go, Demon Boy, or your mate has a date with death."

Emelia looked over her shoulder at Sable. Asteria stood behind her, golden elliptical pupils blazing like fire against her now-black irises as she pressed a blade to Sable's throat. Her friend swallowed, looking as if she was trying to figure a way out of it and failing.

It seemed Thorne wasn't willing to risk that.

He released Rey with a shove back against the wall and growled at Asteria when she failed to release Sable. He stalked towards the demoness, snarling and flashing his fangs, and the demoness wisely held up her end of the bargain, disappearing just as he lunged for her.

He grabbed Sable instead, wrapped his arms around her, and petted her onyx hair as he grumbled, "Echelon cannot have you."

"I am not interested in forcing Sable to serve the Echelon." Rey rubbed his throat. "I am not exactly fighting on that side now, am I? I am here because I am worried about Wolf."

He turned his crimson gaze to Emelia.

"Do you know where he is?"

She held his gaze. "Zephyr said he was constantly on the move now to evade Wolf. Before he bit me, he said we would keep moving, so Wolf couldn't find us."

Rey frowned and pushed away from the wall. "He bit you?"

She nodded, weathering the concerned look Sable gave her. She hadn't wanted anyone to know, was still ashamed she hadn't been strong enough to stop him from attempting to force a bond on her.

"He took my blood because he's my... fated one." She had to force the last two words out.

Asteria gasped. Sable came and wrapped her arms around Emelia.

Rey growled low.

Thorne snarled, "A mate is sacred. How dare he..."

"He dared, alright," she snapped and issued a silent apology when he frowned at her.

She hadn't meant to be rough with him, but she hated that the dragon had done that to her, and that he was linked to her in a way now. She wanted to sever that connection, and then his head from his shoulders.

"He will not be moving, then." Rey's words had her turning a frown on him, because she wasn't following his line of thought. "If he has Wolf... and he wants you... he will be somewhere you can find him."

Her stomach dropped and her mind emptied as it hit her, and she whispered, "Because he wants me to offer myself in exchange."

"That sick fucking bastard!" Sable grabbed her sword from the table, unsheathed it, and looked ready to take out her anger on the bookcases.

Thorne stepped in front of them. "We will deal with him. Emelia will not become his."

No, she bloody well wouldn't. She wasn't going to be blackmailed into becoming his mate. She was going to save Wolf and slay the dragon.

"You know where he is?" Rey said.

Emelia nodded. "I know where he is."

The fallen angel held his hand out to her as Asteria joined him, curling against his side as he wrapped his other arm around her. "Then we must leave now. Are you in?"

She took a step towards him.

"Emelia, wait," Sable barked, and she looked at her friend. Worry shone in her amber eyes. "Just wait for Bleu and Taryn, and we can pick up Loke on the way. We need all the strength we can get if we're going to take down fallen angels and a dragon on his home turf. Just think this through for a second, would you?"

Emelia looked between her friend and the fallen angel. Sable was right, and Bleu, Taryn, and Loke would provide valuable backup, but she couldn't wait any longer. Knowing that Wolf was in Zephyr's hands, and the hands of fallen angels too, was a torment she couldn't bear anymore.

She placed her hand into Rey's.

"I'm in."

CHAPTER 34

Wolf's shoulders ached as he hung from his wrists. He had lost feeling in his hands days ago. Or was it only hours? Weeks? Time had lost its meaning, seconds stretching forever as he slowly weakened, the effects of the curse coupling with hunger and pain to steal his strength from him.

He was tired of it all, sick of the way the dragon relished torturing him, did it slowly to draw out the pain, and sick of the fallen angels.

But each day Emelia failed to show up gave him hope even as it stole it from him too.

He hoped she would stay away.

Just for a few more days.

It wouldn't be long now before he either fell, so corrupted by Hell and the things that were happening that the light in him died, or the dragon ended up killing him in one of his regular fits of rage.

A dry chuckle tried to leave his lips but caught in his throat, no sound leaving him as he wished the bastard would gouge his eyes out and puncture his eardrums again.

That way, he wouldn't have to be aware of what was happening in the cave just a few feet from him.

The overenthusiastic feminine cries and deep masculine grunts, coupled with the slap of flesh against flesh, painted a picture in his mind he didn't want to see.

At least they weren't forcing him to watch this time.

The female fallen angel had been taken six ways from Sunday by the male and took pleasure in forcing Wolf to watch her as the male pounded her. Almost as much pleasure as the male took from pulling out of her and spilling himself all over her and then strutting around with his semi-erect cock bobbing around, ruddy from release.

The two were twisted, had revealed the depth of their darkness at times. The male sometimes let the female take the lead, but only if she choked him during the act. He took pleasure from it, roared loudly whenever he climaxed when she was strangling him. Sick fiends.

The few times she had attempted to get Wolf involved, Zephyr had ordered her away from him. Given what Wolf knew about the dragon, he was surprised he hadn't taken her too. The bastard was intent on getting his hands on his 'mate' though, and spoke of Emelia whenever the female offered herself to him.

As the male fallen angel finished, releasing inside her for once, judging by her throatily murmured comments about his seed and her thighs, wind gusted into the cave, battering Wolf.

The dragon had returned.

"Go fuck somewhere else," he growled, and Wolf cracked his eyes open and fixed them on Zephyr as he approached.

The female grabbed the male fallen angel by his shaft and pulled him towards the rear of the cave. He grinned and stumbled along behind her, his gaze roaming down the bare curve of her spine to her backside.

"Enjoy your break?" Zephyr came to stand in front of him, his emerald eyes impassive and green hair tousled, as if he had been ploughing his fingers through it, tugging at it. Before Wolf could muster the strength to tell the male to fuck off, he continued, "I was thinking while I was out… about the irony of our situation."

Irony?

Wolf focused on his aching body, trying not to grimace as he held his wings inside. He couldn't let the dragon get to them. It was what the male wanted, one of the reasons for his regular torture sessions. The fallen angels had told him that if they hurt him enough, he would weaken to the point where he could no longer conceal his wings.

Zephyr looked him over, stepped towards him to close the distance down to under a foot, and reached a hand up.

Wolf snapped his teeth at it when it neared his face.

The dragon's green eyes narrowed, golden sparks lighting them as he withdrew his hand. "I only meant to clear the blood from your eye. Now I think I will add to it."

Wolf bellowed as the male struck him hard, backhanding him across his left temple. The cut above his eye that had been healing reopened, spilling crimson into it, and he blinked to clear it away.

Zephyr's face blackened and Wolf leaned back on instinct. The back of his head smacked against the rough black rock and another roar tore from his lips as the dragon raked claws down the side of his face. His eye throbbed, pain shooting along the nerve. His stomach rolled in response, and he fought to keep the bile down as heat cascaded over his cheek and dripped onto his bare chest.

He pinned the dragon with his one good eye, pictured getting free of the chains that bound him and butchering the bastard.

Zephyr canted his head, and a slow grin stretched his lips. "I like that look in your eye... because part of you knows how futile it is. You know you do not possess the strength to fight me, let alone kill me. Admit it."

Never.

He spat blood at the dragon.

It splattered across his bare chest and sprayed over his cheek.

The male closed his eyes, his jaw clenched, and he lifted his hand to wipe the blood away. "It really is ironic. You are weak in Hell, just as I am weak in the mortal world. We both have our powers stripped from us by entering another realm. We are so similar, yet Emelia wants you... and that makes me a little mad."

Wolf's head cracked off the rock as Zephyr's fist connected with his face, hitting him with the force of a piston and sending his tired mind spinning. The cave whirled around him. The dragon didn't give him a chance to recover. He struck him again, following it with a crushing blow to his stomach that had black spots winking across his vision.

The dragon's hand closed around his throat, and he pushed Wolf back against the wall, holding him upright as his head tried to loll forwards, too heavy for him to lift now.

All he could do was breathe as the male loomed before him, cold light in his eyes, a hunger to deliver pain and savour his suffering.

Fire erupted in his side, and he threw his head back and yelled as it arced through him, setting every inch of him aflame.

Zephyr laughed as he twisted his hand. Claws ripped through Wolf's flesh, and he could almost feel his strength flowing from him. His wings pushed. He desperately pushed back. They had to stay hidden.

He turned the whole of his focus to keeping them away as the male went to town on him, taking blow after blow from his claws, fangs and fists, growing numb to them as the pain became so intense, he could no longer feel it because it was all he knew.

The fallen angels had returned at some point. He heard them speaking, their voices watery in his ears as Zephyr released him and he slumped forwards, hanging from his chains.

"I... never... so many..." The female voice was patchy, and Wolf struggled to understand what she was saying. "Black... feathers."

Panic speared his chest.

His wings.

He jerked his head up, grimaced as pain splintered across it, and fought to twist it to his right, so he could use his one good eye to see. Fear brewed in his stomach, churning it like acid, and his heart beat at a sickening pace. The female had to be lying. He had been focused, determined. His wings weren't out.

His entire world felt as if it shattered around him as his gaze landed on white feathers, stark against the black wall.

His stomach fell as he spotted all the obsidian feathers that marred his wings, more than a third of them turned dark.

He shook his head, unable to believe what he was seeing, desperately trying to convince himself it was a trick of his mind. His wings weren't out. They were safe.

White-hot fire lanced him, bolting along his left wing to his shoulder and rolling through him so quickly that he almost blacked out. Another followed it. A wet sound reached his ears with each one, every blow that had him wavering at the very edge of consciousness. He arched and screamed as he tried to move his left wing, fear flooding him as he realised what was happening.

The dragon grabbed hold of his wing and bent it.

Bone snapped.

Pain so intense it stole his breath and assaulted every nerve in his body, making him jerk forwards, lashed him.

Wolf vomited.

The female fallen angel laughed, the sound grating in his ears.

She would die first.

He weakly gripped the chain attaching him to the wall, intending to lash out at her with his bare feet.

Fresh agony swept through him, stealing his vision this time, and he sagged in the chains, all his strength washing from him as he felt tendons snap and muscles tear.

He vomited again, unable to stop himself as the world around him twisted and turned. He was going to die here. No. He shoved back against that feeling, even when he knew it was true.

There was going to come a point where the pain was too much for his body and soul to handle and he would wish for death. He would welcome it in that moment.

Possibly even beg for it.

He shook that fear away, refusing to let it poison his mind and weaken his resolve.

He had to remain strong, because he needed to return to Emelia. He needed to keep his promise and come back to her. He couldn't give up.

He needed to see her again.

She was his world. His everything. All he needed, and all he had ever wanted. He couldn't give up. He wanted the future he had dreamed about, one with her at his side, where they were together.

He wanted that so badly.

Even when he knew his life was going to end here.

Now.

"Whatcha doing?" A different female voice wobbled in his ears.

"Fuck off," the male fallen angel snarled.

"You fuck off," she retorted. "I asked a *polite* question. I was in the neighbourhood and thought I would drop in. Are you performing a stick-ectomy? Because I hate to say it, but the stick in question is pretty far up his arse. I don't think you can make him fall that way."

"How would you know?" Zephyr snarled.

Who was this newcomer? She was… familiar? His head turned violently as the mark on his wrist throbbed, a low burning igniting in it. He vomited again, his thoughts blurring as he struggled against the pain burning in his body, emanating from his left wing in crushing waves.

"He might be who I'm looking for." Her voice was closer, and she was looking at him? He thought he could feel her eyes on him. "Didn't recognise him at first… what with all the blood and vomit. Looks like you were having fun… but… I'm afraid it's over now."

The dragon laughed and yanked on Wolf's wing, almost severing it.

"Now…" she snapped, her tone darkening, gaining an edge as hard as diamonds and the sharpness of a razor. "I'm going to have to ask you to stop doing that… or I will get upset. You see, I came all this way to rescue him."

She had?

He tried to peel his good eye open. Blood matted his eyelashes and it was a struggle to open it, but he managed it just as the dragon released him and turned towards her, his green eyes glowing as the two fallen angels came to back him up.

"You and what army?" Zephyr grinned victoriously.

The fool thought he was going to win this fight.

"Oh, my dark lord!" The demoness standing at the mouth of the cave, clad in revealing black armour with her dark leathery wings furled against her back, clapped excitedly and bounced on her heels, sheer unadulterated joy shining in her blue eyes. "I've always wanted to say this. Wait… wait… I have to get it right. It has to be *perfect*."

She dramatically cleared her throat.

Fanned her arms to her side as if presenting something as she twisted at the waist, a charming smile plastered on her face.

"Me and this army."

Rey appeared on the ledge, his horned black helmet and obsidian armour blending with his wings and the darkness beyond him as shadows swirled around his legs. Behind him, a great blue dragon landed, beating its wings to hold itself steady, a blonde female he recognised clutched gently in his enormous paw.

Next to him, the demon king and the half-breed appeared, the male holding a broadsword as tall as she was. She twirled her smaller blade, her golden eyes bright as they narrowed on her enemies.

And in front of them stood a brunette dressed for war in tight black combat gear and a blade strapped to her back, her fiery green gaze locked on Zephyr as she raised her gun.

He had never seen a sweeter, more welcome sight.

Or heard such a unique battle cry.

Emelia squeezed the trigger and yelled.

"Die, you son of a bitch!"

CHAPTER 35

Emelia was shaking like a leaf, so she was shocked when the white-feathered dart nailed Zephyr right in the middle of his bare chest. He grunted and looked down, green eyebrows pinching hard above his narrowing eyes as they landed on the dart. He lifted his hand, paused halfway to it and shook his head, his eyes closing briefly.

Slurred, "Get them."

The two fallen angels broke past him, black armour forming over their naked bodies as they beat their black wings.

Heading straight for her.

Her heart shot into her throat and her hands trembled violently as she raced to reload the gun. She didn't know what dosage fallen angels would need, but she imagined it was more than a dragon. They were the most powerful beings in Hell, after all.

"Not… her." Zephyr shook his head again, fumbled and managed to get hold of the dart. He ripped it from his chest and growled as he crushed it in his fist.

The violet-haired male flashed fangs at her, his crimson eyes blazing as they shifted from her to someone beyond her.

Asteria chuckled low in her throat. "I think he has a hard-on for you."

Emelia could just picture Rey shrugging casually as he said, "Don't they always?"

"Got to pick the biggest guy in the room. It's all that fallen angel testosterone." She suddenly shot past Emelia, so fast strands of her hair swept forwards, pulled free from her bun.

The demoness broke left, did an impossible run up the wall, and kicked off, arching over the head of the blonde female fallen angel. The angel skidded, twisting to follow Asteria, and grinned. She launched forwards, towards an empty spot in the cave.

Where Asteria would land.

"Look out!" Emelia lunged, drawing her blade at the same time.

The demoness flashed her a wink and disappeared.

The fallen angel careened through the space where Asteria should have landed, stumbled and pivoted, skidding on the loose black dirt. The demoness popped up behind her, her grin wide and now-black eyes flashing with the fire of her elliptical golden pupils as she raked the talons of her black gauntlets down the female's wings.

The blonde screeched and arched forwards.

The violet-haired male didn't even pause to look at her. Not a flicker of concern touched his eyes as they narrowed on Rey. They collided hard and the male beat his wings, sending them shooting past Loke as he transformed into his human form.

"We'll go after them," Sable said as Emelia kept her eyes locked on Zephyr.

He was shaking the drug off already. Her dosage must have been wrong for him too.

She glanced over her shoulder, about to ask how Sable intended to fight alongside Rey and Thorne when both of them could fly.

White wings burst from Sable's back.

Emelia's jaw hit the floor.

Her friend gave an awkward shrug. "Surprise?"

Anais looked as shocked as Emelia was as she stared at the black-haired huntress.

"I was going to tell you," Sable said as she fiddled with the silver cuff on her right wrist. "Perk of being a half-breed?"

Thorne tugged her arm and grumbled, "Fight now."

She petted his hand as he grew even larger, muscles rippling and burgundy leathers creaking. He flapped his dark leathery wings, his blazing crimson eyes tracking the battle she couldn't see through the darkness. His horns curled further, curving around to resemble a ram's horns and flaring like daggers in front of his temples.

"Fight," he growled and pulled on his mate again, jerking her with him.

"Got to go." Sable pulled an awkward face and managed a small wave before she was pulled into the air by Thorne.

At the back of the cave, beyond Zephyr, Asteria was toying with the female fallen angel, practically dancing around her as she tossed barbs and taunts.

Emelia's focus locked on the dragon. She wanted to check on Wolf, but if she did, Zephyr would make his move, and she wasn't sure which it would be. Attack her, or attack Wolf to force her hand.

Her angel weakly tugged at his chains, his face a dark mask of pain as he wavered on his feet, his left wing hanging at a grotesque angle, dripping with the blood that stained it red.

She silently told him to hold on.

As soon as they were done with the dragon and the fallen angels, Rey would free him. The chains that held him wouldn't be a match for the fallen angel.

"You…" Zephyr growled and shook his head again, his green eyes rapidly clearing.

She raised her gun and fired again.

This time, she missed.

The female fallen angel shrieked and turned, scrambling to reach for something. Emelia's gaze leaped to her. Or maybe she had only missed her intended target. The dart she had fired stuck out of the fallen angel's black wing.

"Hey!" Asteria leaned to her right to see past the blonde and glared at Emelia. "I had this. Interfere again and I'll snap the dragon's neck for you. See how you like that."

"Sorry." The apology sounded weak to her ears, probably because she was confused.

The plan was they all dealt with the fallen angels and then they took down the dragon.

Did Asteria plan not to help her with Zephyr?

Her fingers shook against the hilt of her blade as it dawned on her that the demoness knew she needed closure. She knew that dealing the killing blow would give her that, allowing her to move on with her life.

But was she strong enough to take on a dragon?

"Ready?" Anais clutched her sword in front of her and Loke fell into line beside her.

She glanced at the blonde huntress and her striking turquoise-haired mate.

She wasn't alone. With their help, she could do this. She could put her past to rest, free Wolf and take her first step towards the future she wanted with him.

Loke twirled his knife, his aquamarine eyes locked on Zephyr. "I should have killed you when I had the chance."

The green-haired dragon just smiled. "Now I will be the one killing you."

He moved in a blur, so fast her eyes couldn't track him, and Loke slammed into the ground, Zephyr on top of him. Zephyr raked claws down his bare chest, snarling and flashing all-sharp teeth as golden flakes lit his eyes. Loke growled and bucked upwards, knocking the dragon off balance. He was quick to roll, dislodging Zephyr and sending him to the ground.

Emelia moved on instinct, every second of her training kicking into gear as she focused on her target, feeling Wolf's eye tracking her, sensing his concern as he continued his struggle against the chains that bound him.

She unleashed a war cry as she swept her blade towards Zephyr.

He twisted his body away from her and brought his left arm up. Her blade struck it, and she clenched her teeth and wanted to growl as green scales rippled over his skin, deflecting her strike.

It wasn't going to deter her. He couldn't defend against three of them. Anais launched into the fray, her blade swift and aim true, but meeting with the same result as scales formed over Zephyr's side.

Emelia rolled when he grabbed for her, ducking beneath his hand and coming up on the other side of him. She drew her gun again, breathing hard as she reloaded it with the final dart. Her hands shook and she backed away, watching the fight between Zephyr, Loke, and Anais closely as she looked for an opening.

The last thing she wanted to do was hit either of her friends. The drug would slow Loke, and it might kill Anais. Loke twisted with Zephyr, giving her a clear shot at his back.

She squeezed the trigger.

Zephyr tensed, grabbed Loke, and turned with him. Using him as a shield. Loke was fast to shove out of Zephyr's grip, barely dodging the dart. Zephyr dodged too, his eyes fixing on her as he shifted right and the dart flew past him, struck the wall of the cave, and clattered to the ground.

Before she could ready her blade, the dragon had his hand around her throat. He growled and shoved her back into the wall. Lightning arced down her spine, and she cried out.

"Emelia!" Wolf bellowed.

Fear crashed over her, memories pushing to the surface to steal her strength as they flickered across her eyes as she stared into Zephyr's green ones. It was all going to happen again. She had been a fool to think she was strong enough to slay the dragon. She wasn't brave. She wasn't a warrior.

She was weak.

The dragon's green eyes softened and darted over her face, his brow furrowing as he gazed down at her.

His grip loosened.

Hand rose to her face.

Thumb stroked her cheek as he looked into her eyes, conflict reigning in his.

Because he didn't want to hurt her.

Because she was his mate.

As dark and vicious as he was, as violent and cruel, his instincts still controlled him to a degree, enough that he was torn between hurting her and soothing her.

Maybe she was weak, but she still had power, and she wasn't going to waste it.

"Release the angel, and I'll be yours." She tried to keep her voice calm and her nerves in check, not wanting him to detect the lie in them.

He growled, flashing sharp fangs, and his gaze slid to his right, towards Wolf where he wrestled with the restraints, his good wing beating furiously as he shouted at her, things she blocked out because she couldn't let him sway her. This was the only way.

"Be mine, and I will release the angel," Zephyr countered.

Fuck.

If she took his blood, it would complete the bond, and she wasn't sure what happened then. She became a mindless slave? She looked at Anais, where she was slowly circling around Zephyr. Her friend was mated to Loke and it hadn't changed her.

No.

It had changed her.

It had made her immortal.

Stronger.

It was the only way.

She swallowed and nodded.

"No!" Wolf yelled and renewed his fight, his face twisting in desperation as the shackles still refused to give. She cast him an apologetic look, prayed he would forgive her for this, and turned away from him. "Emelia. No!"

Loke took a hard step towards them.

She halted him with a look, one she hoped conveyed that she had a plan and she needed him to hold back, just for a little longer. He looked to Anais, his aquamarine eyes bright with confusion. The blonde huntress shook her head, causing her ponytail to sway across the shoulders of her black T-shirt.

Zephyr grinned, raised his wrist, and bit into his vein. Emelia baulked as he offered it to her, crimson spilling over his palm. Damn, was she really going to do this?

She tried to shut out Wolf as he begged her not to do it.

She had to do it. Just not for the reason he thought she was going to do it. This wasn't about giving herself to Zephyr.

This was about taking something back from him.

Her strength.

This was about making him pay.

She would have her revenge, and the bond he had wanted to force on her would be the catalyst for it. He would damn himself with this offering of blood, and hell, she loved it.

She closed her eyes, lowered her head, and licked the blood from his palm.

He shuddered and moaned, and she frowned as heat swept through her, a strange haziness that wasn't unpleasant. It bloomed in every inch of her, sank deep into her muscles and bones, seemed to raise her up as she took more of his blood. She felt the connection as it formed.

Felt the relief that ran through him.

Felt the strength that ran through her.

"My mate," he murmured, stroking her cheek with his other hand, his tone distant.

The bond was affecting him more than she had expected.

His guard was down.

She slowly lifted her head and looked into his drowsy eyes.

"Release the angel," she husked, trying to keep him off balance, doing her damnedest to sound all compliant and lovely when really she wanted to cleave his head clean off his shoulders.

"Emelia." Wolf grunted as he yanked on the chain, gripping it in both hands and planting his feet against the wall of the cave as he arched forwards, attempting to use his body weight to free himself.

When it still wouldn't give, another white feather in his right wing turned black. And then another. And then two more. Until they were rapidly changing, more and more each time, a domino effect she had started.

"Release him!" she snapped at Zephyr, because if the dragon didn't free him soon, he wouldn't have any white feathers left, and she wasn't sure what happened then.

Zephyr had the audacity to smile. "No."

"I thought you'd say that." She didn't give him a chance to react.

She plunged her blade into his gut.

His hazy eyes instantly cleared, disbelief colouring them as he looked down at the sword protruding from his side.

"You are my mate!" he snarled.

"Not for much longer." She grunted as she gripped her blade in both hands and heaved it sideways.

He fumbled for her, claws barely missing her as she swayed to her left to dodge them and forced her sword onwards, cleaving through his stomach. He reached for her again and she couldn't dodge this time, braced herself as his hand came down towards her shoulder. It slammed into her but just rested there, and she looked up at Zephyr's face.

He coughed, blood pouring from his lips as he continued to stare at her, shock lighting his green eyes.

Because his mate had turned on him?

He was getting what he deserved for what he had done to her, and what he had done to Wolf.

She held his gaze, wanting the last thing the bastard saw to be her, to be the contempt she felt for him, and wanting him to know that even his fated one, a female who was meant to adore him and be loyal to him according to dragon lore, hated his guts.

Guts which spilled onto the black ground as she finally worked her sword free.

She retched as he went down, dry heaving as the two halves of his body separated, attached only by a small strip of flesh.

Her hand flew to her mouth and she swallowed the bile that rose up her throat as Loke calmly took the sword from Anais and brought it down, severing Zephyr's head.

The connection she had felt blooming inside her died.

But the strength remained, flowing in her veins, lifting her up.

"Incoming!" Asteria yelled.

Emelia didn't have time to react before the entire cave shook, a shock wave knocked her off her feet into Loke and red light blinded her. Liquid rained down on her, and the sound of wet slaps sounded all around her. She baulked again as something hit her, soft and squishy, and the rank odour of blood and entrails hit her nostrils.

"Oh, my dark lord." Asteria sounded as disgusted and close to vomiting as Emelia was. "Ew... get it off... get it off!"

"Well, you will fight a fallen angel in a contained space." Rey's deep baritone filled the cave. "What did you expect?"

"You could have told me she would explode!" Asteria's voice gained pitch. "Oh... ew... what is this? Is this an ear?"

Emelia really didn't want to look now, but she had to check on Wolf.

"Steady now. She is safe. Let it go." Rey.

She opened her eyes to find him standing in front of Wolf, covered from head to toe in blood, his bare hands framing Wolf's face. Wolf breathed hard, his one good eye bright gold as he stared at her.

But there was a black corona around the edges of his iris.

He gritted his teeth and snarled, the sound inhuman.

Like a fallen angel.

She was on her feet and muscling Rey out of the way in a split second, her hands replacing his on Wolf's cheeks.

"Wolf," she whispered, but he didn't look at her. He kept staring at where she had been when Zephyr had been giving her blood. When she had accepted a bond with him. "Wolf... I'm here. Listen to my voice, Wolf. You have to let it go. Please?"

He breathed harder, his bare chest heaving as the band of black surrounding his iris thickened and started to turn crimson.

"No... no... no... Wolf." She smoothed her hands over his bloody cheeks, feathered her fingers over his left eye that was swollen shut, ugly claw marks cutting over the puffy blackened flesh. "Listen to my voice, Wolf. It's me. Emelia. I'm right here. I'm right here, and I love you... so you have to listen to me. I love you, Wolf. Only you."

The darkness receded a touch, the band narrowing again and the scarlet fading.

Her eyes darted to his wings, scouring the bloodstained feathers, her heart jamming in her throat and beating there at a dizzying pace. Everywhere she looked, his feathers were black.

"He's going to fall." She looked to Rey.

Would it be such a bad thing if he did fall? Rey had retained his Echelon powers and he didn't seem evil.

Concern shone in his crimson eyes. "It is not too late. Keep talking. I am not sure what will happen to him if he falls this way."

The way he said that had her pushing onwards and refusing to give up, because he looked as if he believed it would be a very bad thing if Wolf fell.

Thorne had told her about fallen angels, about how darkness consumed and twisted them, vanquishing their softer emotions. All the ones Thorne had encountered had run slave rings and nefarious businesses, building empires on blood and death, using their power for their own gain. The way Rey kept glancing at her, silently urging her to keep trying to reach Wolf and pull him back from the edge, warned her that if Wolf fell, there was a danger the darkness she had seen in Wolf from time to time would turn him into a man she wouldn't recognise.

"I'm sorry about what I did. It was the only way. If I had known... Wolf... I wouldn't have done that to you." She squeezed his cheeks in her palms, hoping to get him to look at her. When his good eye still remained locked beyond her, her patience slipped. She shook him slightly. "Wolf, will you bloody listen to me!"

His golden eye slowly edged towards her.

Locked with hers.

Her brow furrowed as she gazed up at him and whispered.

"I love you. No matter what happens here. I will always love you."

CHAPTER 36

I love you, Wolf. Only you.

Those words pierced the dark clouds in his mind like a shaft of purest light. The shadows writhed away from it, then gathered strength and rose up to meet it, easily extinguishing it. They beckoned him when darkness fell again, promising things that had him taking a step towards them. Strength. Retribution. Freedom.

Absolute power.

Heat suffused him at just the thought of grasping hold of that. How many times had he craved the strength to crush his foes? To destroy the demons who infested this world? With such power, he could achieve that dark dream. All would quake before him.

In the black abyss, the soft voice echoed, his sensitive hearing picking up her words even as they faded from existence.

Loved him?

She had betrayed him.

Pain cleaved his chest in two, cut straight through his heart to kill it.

I'm sorry about what I did. It was the only way.

The shadows hissed at the voice, warned him not to listen to it, but his heart stitched itself back together, began to beat once again as those words swam in his mind.

Not betrayed?

If I had known… Wolf… I wouldn't have done that to you.

Truth or lie?

The shadows whispered it was a lie. She meant to deceive him now that her mate was dead.

Dead?

He frowned as a flicker of light pierced the veil of darkness again.

She had killed her mate.

Spilled his entrails across his own floor.

The black abyss shook, the assault so violent that the ground bucked beneath him and he barely managed to remain standing.

Wolf, will you bloody listen to me!

He was listening. There was no need to grow violent. He tried to sweep the shadows away, irritated by them, but they curled around his legs, and wherever they touched, his white armour blackened.

"I love you. No matter what happens here. I will always love you."

Emelia's voice rang in his ears, sang in his heart, each word a bright beam of light that penetrated the darkness. The shadows slunk away, snapping at the ground, moving to a distance as the light engulfed him. He looked at them, aware they were only waiting, biding their time until the light stuttered and died again.

"Wolf? I think all your feathers are black, and I'm scared it's my fault."

Her fault?

She had betrayed him. Of course it was her fault.

He shook his head. No. It wasn't entirely her fault. He had courted this darkness, had always failed to leash it, and had relied on it too much throughout the years, giving it a hold over him.

And she hadn't betrayed him.

He had seen the love in her eyes even as she had taken the dragon's blood, how scared she had been of what she was about to do. He had seen her strength too, had watched it flow into her as a bond between her and the dragon had formed.

She had done it to free him.

And to set herself free too.

His arms suddenly dropped, the weight of them falling taking him to his knees. The light moved with him, wrapped around him, and warmed him. He sank into it.

"All his feathers are black. What can I do? If he falls, will he be like you?"

A male voice answered. "I am not sure. Wolf has a darkness inside him the likes of which I have never seen in another angel. If he falls…"

He would become a monster.

She had said she would love him no matter what happened, but would she?

He tried to turn his head, blinked to clear his vision of the darkness. Everywhere he looked, it remained, stretching around him.

Endless darkness.

Perhaps it was too late for him after all.

He would become a monster, and she would leave him.

His eyes snagged on a bright white dot in the field of blackness.

He crawled towards it, his movements sluggish as he fought the hold of the light. Eventually, it moved with him, and he frowned as he saw what the dot was.

A single white feather.

He frowned at it and carefully gathered it into his palm. It shone in the light, blindingly bright, reflecting a thousand colours.

"Is that… oh my God." Emelia's voice echoed through the darkness as the feather disappeared from his palm.

Her relief rushed through him, flowing from the warmth touching his lips right down into his weary soul. She filled it with light until it blazed and the darkness around him finally receded.

Revealing her.

She sat before him, her hands framing his face, her lips pressed to his.

He groaned and couldn't keep from kissing her back, ached to hold her but didn't have the strength to move his arms.

"We should take him somewhere safe." Rey's voice sounded distant as Wolf kissed Emelia, lost himself in her and his thoughts, all the things he wanted to tell her.

"Not my bloody castle," a male grumbled. "No Echelon allowed."

"Will you be alright?" The half-breed. Talking to him?

Emelia answered, "Go. I'll be fine. We can take him to Rey's place and then home."

Home.

That single tiny feather danced in his mind, the shadows looming around it, kept at bay for now, but for how long?

He no longer had a home.

He was at the point of turning, had too many black feathers to be allowed entrance to his own realm again. They would hunt him down if he tried to return there. The Archangels didn't tolerate the corrupted, even when they were Echelon.

And part of him no longer thought of it as home either.

The same Archangels who would want him dead now had lied to him, covering the truth about his half-breed origins so he would loyally serve them.

No, he had no home now.

Darkness engulfed him from the outside this time, and when it receded, they were in a room. The black walls were rough, chisel marks telling him that someone had transformed a cave into a room, one that had a few items of furniture scattered around it, including a large bed.

Just beyond that bed, a natural arch led into another area of the cave. Warm air came from that direction, carrying the scent of salt and other minerals.

Rey went to set him down on the bed and then pulled a face. "You should probably wash first. There's a pool back there. The water has healing properties, a mixture of minerals, herbs and magic that combine to heal wounds quickly. Asteria got the concoction from the half-breed as a thank you present for not handing her over to the Devil or Heaven. You should rest in it for a time until you begin to heal. It does work wonders."

He looked himself over with his good eye, at the blood that covered every inch of his body, darkest on his side where Zephyr had torn at him with his claws, and then at Rey, Asteria, and Emelia. They had all fared the same. The sight of Emelia stained with blood had the darkness pushing, but he pushed back, told himself that it wasn't her blood.

Worry shone in her eyes as she looked at him.

Wolf nodded. He would bathe for her sake, to alleviate her fear, and hopefully she would bathe with him. He needed to be alone with her, to hold her and know that she was safe now. He needed to speak with her and tell her something.

"Asteria of the Second Legion," a deep voice boomed from beyond the doorway that had been hacked into the rock behind him.

"Oh, fuck," she muttered and preened her hair, puffing the tangled strands up as she flicked Rey a nervous glance. "How do I look?"

"Like a fallen angel just exploded all over you." Rey grimaced and removed a piece of skin from her hair. "Now you're perfect."

"Won't be a moment." Asteria smiled, but Wolf could see the worry in it.

The cross mark on the inside of Wolf's right wrist itched, burning low against his skin and warning him that Asteria was no longer the only demon in the vicinity.

"Put your wings away," Emelia said, a vain attempt to distract him from the fact there were now four elite demons muscling their way into the room, forcing Asteria and Rey back into it.

The largest of them took stock of him and Emelia and curled his lip at Asteria and Rey. "What happened here?"

"Well… firstly, I am terribly sorry that we killed the last team of elite our dark lord sent."

His thick black brows rose, the golden elliptical pupils in the centres of his obsidian irises glowing brighter as he stared at Asteria.

"Oooooh… you didn't know." She shrugged stiffly. "You were asking about the blood. Dead fallen angel is the chic accessory these days."

She plucked more flesh from her armour and offered it to the demon. He regarded it with a disinterested look and shifted his gaze to Rey.

"Is this about Wolf?" Rey lowered his hand to his side, claws flexing as if he was itching to call his blade.

The demon shook his head.

"It concerns his brethren. *Your* brethren." The male sneered at Rey, an edge to his eyes that said he still considered him a member of the Echelon and therefore the enemy. "Two more angels of your rank have entered Hell, and our dark lord requires your presence."

Wolf didn't like the sound of that.

Apparently, Rey didn't either.

"Why?" Rey closed ranks with Asteria.

"Our dark lord wishes to discuss the war plan with you both."

War plan? Sickness brewed in Wolf's stomach. He had left a trail of carnage in his wake, from getting Emelia pulled back into Hell to getting his realm into a war.

Not his realm.

He tried hard to make that stick, but the thought of them having to battle the forces of Hell, the image of the males he had worked closely with for centuries fighting for their lives against a superior army, ate away at him, and he couldn't deny he still felt something for that world.

He also felt sure the two Echelon commanders had come to Hell looking for him, not to start a war.

Rey looked over his shoulder at him. "The Echelon commanders could not have known that entering Hell would be considered an act of war. I will talk with the Devil and make him see that."

"I will go with you." He tried to move, but his left leg wobbled, and Emelia had to catch him.

She wrapped her arms around his waist, keeping him upright.

Rey shook his head. "Remain here. You need to rest and heal."

Heal.

He looked at his battered left wing and then his right, seeking the one feather that formed the barrier between him and becoming a fallen angel. It was as small as it had looked, a tiny downy feather near his left elbow. He wasn't sure he could heal from this.

"Come on." Emelia tugged him away from the others. "I think I saw the pool back here."

He didn't fight her as she helped him through the arch and across the uneven ground towards the sunken steaming pool, or as she stripped off his clothing. He couldn't get his mind away from what was happening, not even as he forced his wings away and stepped into the water.

It was warm, instantly soothing his tired body as he sank into it and surprising him as the expected sting of his cuts didn't come. The water certainly had magical properties just as Rey had said. He could feel it going to work, could feel the smaller wounds on his legs and stomach healing, rapidly stitching back together.

He tried to keep his mind on bathing and healing, but he couldn't stop it from wandering. He would find a way to save the two idiots who had come after him, sure they were the Second and Third Commanders. Rey would find a way to stop the war before it began, and if he couldn't, then Wolf would fight on Heaven's side in order to make amends for what he had done. He just hoped he wouldn't have to fight Rey.

He scooped up some water and grimaced as he carefully washed the left side of his face. The pain of the claw marks and his swollen eye gradually subsided, and he kept washing it, encouraging it to heal and hoping he wouldn't be left with a scar on that side.

Not because he worried that Emelia wouldn't like him with more scars.

But because he didn't want her to be constantly reminded of the dragon and what she had been through and he knew she would be if he was left with scars across his face from Zephyr's claws.

Emelia finished removing her clothes and stole his focus as she stepped into the pool, sinking beneath the water opposite him.

Sweet mercy, she was a joy to watch as she bathed, the sight of her soothing his battered heart.

For a moment, he had been sure he had lost her, that she would belong to the dragon and be stolen from his grasp forever.

But here she was, carefully washing the blood and grime away, her green eyes holding a glimmer of the relief he could feel in her. Because the dragon was dead. Slain by her own fair hand.

She had subjected herself to a bond to save him, but not in the way he had imagined. Instead of becoming the slave of the dragon, she had risen up and fought him, using the strength the bond had granted her to take him down.

His brave, cunning Emelia.

He wanted to kiss her again and hear her whisper that she loved him, wanted to tell her how much he loved her too.

He shifted towards her.

She held her hand up and glared at him.

He stilled, unsure what he had done to deserve such a killing look.

"I want a word with you... and you had better answer honestly," she snapped, the darkness in her tone feeling more dangerous to him than the shadows that had tried to pull him into the abyss.

He nodded. Might have swallowed hard.

"You know a blonde angel?"

He frowned at the fire blazing in her eyes and the anger he could sense surging through her. "I do. She is a healer."

"A healer?" she scoffed. "According to her, she's your Echelon baby maker."

His eyes widened. *"What?"*

Emelia folded her arms across her chest. "She says she was destined for you, or some shit, and you're meant for her, and that she was all over you the other day, kissing you while you were naked... before you came to me."

"Now hold on." He held his hands up beside him. "Wait."

Because he needed a moment to get this straight in his head before he said it or he was liable to mess everything up.

"She is only my healer," he said and wrestled with how to put things delicately, in a way that wouldn't make Emelia cleave him in two. She wanted honesty. The truth. He wanted to give her that, but he also didn't want to upset her. "It is... Emelia... She did kiss me."

Her green eyes went wide. "What the actual fuck?"

She shot to her feet, gloriously naked and terribly distracting. He tried to keep his focus on her face and off her body, sure she wouldn't appreciate him admiring her when she was furious with him.

"Listen to me. *She* kissed *me*. I made her leave and told her to forget it because it was not going to happen. I had no idea she had gotten it into her head that we were going to become something." And if he had known she would go after Emelia to turn her against him, he might have done a lot more than just making her leave. "I do not care about her. I love you."

She stopped advancing on him.

Stood staring down at him, so close that he could skim his fingers up her bare calf beneath the water if he was brave enough.

"You love me?" she whispered, conflict shining in her eyes.

He had told her the truth, and she still wanted to be mad at him. Females were far too complicated. It was little wonder males were always messing up.

He nodded. "I heard what you said to me, Emelia. I love you too."

"Good." Her tone hardened once more. "But if that bitch comes near you again, I'm going to rip her wings off."

He flinched, a cold shiver running down the ridges of scar tissue on his back.

Her face softened, worry lighting her eyes as she glanced at his shoulders. "Sorry... do they hurt?"

He shook his head. "Not now they are away."

Although, he could feel his left one mending, experienced it as a weird unsettled sensation in his side that he was finding hard to push to the back of his mind.

"Were you scared?" She shuffled a little closer, offering a beautiful distraction that kept the pain at bay.

"No." He tilted his head back, gazing up at her, using the luxury of time to go back over everything that had happened in the last few hours, from the moment she had stormed into that cave looking like the warrior she was. He caught her wrist and pulled her down onto his lap, wrapped his arms around her, and held her. "But I was terrified when you..."

He couldn't bring himself to say it.

She pressed her cheek to his, looped her arms around his shoulders, and sighed against his skin. "I'm sorry. It was the only way to get what I wanted."

He knew that, but the vision of her placing herself at the mercy of that male, binding herself to him, still haunted him.

"I am glad he is dead." Although he wished he had been the one to deal the killing blow, he was happy she had been the one to do it in the end.

She had found her strength and her self-belief, conquered her fear, and found the closure she had needed.

"I am too." She nuzzled his cheek and pressed a kiss to it. "And I'm glad I reached you in time. I was terrified I was going to lose you."

He was still terrified he was going to lose her, didn't want to tell her what he had learned, but he needed to be honest with her. He needed to know she could still love him knowing where he had come from.

"Will you heal?" That beautiful look of concern in her eyes warmed his soul, keeping the darkness from it.

"I am not sure. Perhaps not fully. I have never heard of an angel regaining white feathers after they had turned black." Although, he had never researched it. He only had his lessons to go by, and they had always stated that once an angel had black feathers, they always had black feathers, no matter how much good they did after gaining them. He sighed, closed his eyes and sank deeper against the edge of the pool. "There is darkness in me. Darkness I never tried to conquer and control. Now I fear that darkness has a stronger hold over me and I will not be able to shake it. I fear..."

That he would fall.

"It won't happen... and even if it did, I wouldn't go anywhere. I'll still be right here for you." Emelia gently smoothed her palms along his jaw and pressed a soft kiss to his lips, soothing the pain that had been building inside him, stealing it all away again. "We'll get through this. Somehow. We'll get through it and find a way to... not fix things... but maybe we can make it easier on you. Somehow. Reduce the risk. Maybe Rey would know something, or Asteria. We can speak with them."

She wasn't sure, sounded as uncertain as he felt as he held her, all his fears colliding inside him to drag him down into the mire of dark thoughts. He clung to what she had said, speaking of them as if they would always be together now, no matter what happened. He wanted that, but she needed to know the truth about him, because if he didn't tell her, it would eat away at him, and would eventually destroy what they had.

"Emelia, there is something else I need to tell you. Echelon... we are... according to Rey and Asteria, we are born of a union between an angel and a demon." He held his breath as he leaned back and studied her face, waiting for her to react to that news and sure it was going to be like a dagger in his heart.

She blinked. "And?"

Not quite what he had expected.

He stroked her sides, using the feel of her and the fact she hadn't pulled away to calm his nerves. "And I know after what you have been through in this realm, that it must be difficult for you to... That you must... I will understand if—"

She pressed her fingers to his lips, crushing them and cutting him off. "I'm going to make you rewind to the part where I just saved your arse and told you that I love you and that I want to be with you. I don't care where you came from, Wolf. Gaining strength so I could kill him wasn't the only reason I took Zephyr's blood. I sort of liked the sound of forever with the man I do love."

He searched her eyes. "Forever?"

Was that his voice, so breathless and filled with hope?

She nodded, skimmed her hands over his shoulders and framed his face with her palms, carefully on his left cheek as she avoided the worst of his healing claw marks. Her green eyes locked with his, overflowing with so much love and warmth that his heart filled with them too.

Her thumbs brushed his cheeks. "I figured out the answer to my problem when I looked at Loke and Anais."

"Your problem?" He wasn't following her.

"How to become immortal like you." She looked so serious, and as if she wanted to box him for being an idiot and not understanding what she was saying.

He got it now. She wanted to be immortal so she could be with him, without fear that time might separate them. He had to admit, he had been trying to figure out a way to make that happen too, because he wanted forever with her.

"You are immortal now?" He looked her over, focusing all his senses on her.

She was stronger, he could feel that, but he wouldn't be sure of her immortality until he saw she wasn't aging.

She nodded. "Anais is immortal because of her bond with Loke. I don't think the effects of that bond expire when one party dies because I still feel stronger."

So she was immortal, and she wanted to be with him forever.

Everything had felt as if it was falling apart around him, but now it felt as if everything was coming together.

He couldn't share a bond with Emelia, but they could share forever.

She stroked his cheeks, her eyes flitting over his wounds, worry creasing her brow. "Are you alright?"

Wolf nodded, pulled her flush against him, and breathed against her lips.

"I am now."

Because everything he had ever wanted was right here in his arms.

And he had just realised something.

Home was where his heart was.

With her.

The End

ABOUT THE AUTHOR

Felicity Heaton is a New York Times and USA Today best-selling author who writes passionate paranormal romance books. In her books she creates detailed worlds, twisting plots, mind-blowing action, intense emotion and heart-stopping romances with leading men that vary from dark deadly vampires to sexy shape-shifters and wicked werewolves, to sinful angels and hot demons!

If you're a fan of paranormal romance authors Lara Adrian, J R Ward, Sherrilyn Kenyon, Kresley Cole, Gena Showalter, Larissa Ione and Christine Feehan then you will enjoy her books too.

If you love your angels a little dark and wicked, her best-selling Her Angel romance series is for you. If you like strong, powerful, and dark vampires then try the Vampires Realm romance series or any of her stand alone vampire romance books. If you're looking for vampire romances that are sinful, passionate and erotic then try her London Vampires romance series. Or if you like hot-blooded alpha heroes who will let nothing stand in the way of them claiming their destined woman then try her Eternal Mates series. It's packed with sexy heroes in a world populated by elves, vampires, fae, demons, shifters, and more. If sexy Greek gods with incredible powers battling to save our world and their home in the Underworld are more your thing, then be sure to step into the world of Guardians of Hades.

If you have enjoyed this story, please take a moment to contact the author at **author@felicityheaton.com** or to post a review of the book online

Connect with Felicity:
Website – http://www.felicityheaton.com
Blog – http://www.felicityheaton.com/blog/
Twitter – http://twitter.com/felicityheaton
Facebook – http://www.facebook.com/felicityheaton
Goodreads – http://www.goodreads.com/felicityheaton
Mailing List – http://www.felicityheaton.com/newsletter.php

FIND OUT MORE ABOUT HER BOOKS AT:
http://www.felicityheaton.com

Printed in Great Britain
by Amazon